DAVID ZINDELL

The Idiot Gods

HARPER
Voyager

Harper*Voyager*
An imprint of HarperCollins*Publishers* Ltd
1 London Bridge Street
London SE1 9GF

www.harpervoyagerbooks.co.uk

Published by Harper*Voyager*

This paperback edition 2018
1

First published by HarperCollins*Publishers* 2017

A catalogue record for this book
is available from the British Library

ISBN: 978-0-00-717442-3

Set in Sabon by Palimpsest Book Production Ltd, Falkirk, Stirlingshire

Printed and bound by CPI Group (UK) Ltd, Croydon CR0 4YY

MIX
Paper from
responsible sources
FSC™ C007454

This book is produced from independently certified FSC™ paper
to ensure responsible forest management.

For more information visit: www.harpercollins.co.uk/green

To Jane, for your courage, wisdom, friendship and splendor

PART ONE

The Burning Sea

Translators' Note

It was our privilege and happy destiny to enjoy the friendship of one of the most remarkable beings ever to have come out of our little blue and white planet. Many have tried to make the orca named Arjuna into a Buddha or a Jesus, but he certainly never thought of himself as such – and not even as a teacher. Despite all insistence to the contrary, he remains an orca, however extraordinary, with all an orca's sometimes strange and disturbing sensibilities. It is true that those who spent time with him often forgot that they were conversing with a cetacean possessing a magnitude of intelligence that we are still trying to comprehend. The consciousness of all creatures differs so greatly, yet at its source remains one and the same, as of a white light shined through a prism and refracted it into radiances of red, yellow, violet, and blue. Arjuna's consciousness, to the extent that it illuminates his communications, can often seem pellucidly and sanely human, and at other times, psychopathic or utterly alien. We who have translated his 'words' faced the problem of necessarily regarding a non-human being through very human eyes; we have tried to convey a sense of Arjuna's magnificent soul without making him seem *too* human. It would be well for anyone to see Arjuna for what he really is: a whale who just wanted to talk to human beings.

3

That Arjuna, born in the cold ocean, could have learned to 'speak' various human languages many still doubt, even after the seemingly miraculous events the whole world witnessed. They say that we linguists and biologists of the Institute for Advanced Cetacean Studies either misconstrued basic hunting, mating, or warning cries as language or interpreted them through our natural wish to communicate with an obviously intelligent but nevertheless inarticulate animal. Human beings, these skeptics believe, are by definition the only of earth's creatures capable of symbolic and therefore true language. Our harshest critics – and we should hesitate before calling then conspiracy formulators – have accused us of simply inventing our translations of the thousands of communications that the orcas of the Institute confided in us. They accuse *us* of conspiring to excite compassion for these great beings toward the vain hope of 'saving the whales'. This account is not for those deniers. Even if one were to read Arjuna's account as a fiction, however, one should keep in mind that fictions often reveal the deepest of truths. In many ways, this is the truest story we know, and Arjuna had the truest of hearts. Anyone eager to know more about his life will lose little in skipping this introduction and going right to the words Arjuna chose to convey it. It is indeed a remarkable story. In the end, it is *his* story, and ours: that of the whole human race.

We would like to say more about those words that Arjuna selected to denote meanings that human beings could comprehend. In no way should these be considered to be 'whale words'; whales do not communicate to each other through what we know as words, but rather through sound pictures. Arjuna offers as good an explanation of cetacean language as we could hope, and we cannot improve it. Sadly, we know almost nothing of what we sometimes informally call Orcalish. To date, even with the aid of the fastest of computers and the most elegant of mathematical models, we have managed to identify and interpret perhaps a twelfth of a percent of the meanings of the thousands of orca utterances. It should be remembered that we human beings still have not learned to speak with the whales, though they have readily, if painfully, learned to speak with us.

How, then, did Arjuna and the other orcas of his adopted family accomplish such a feat? The Institute's former chief linguist, Helen Agar, initially worked with him in developing a constructed language through which orcas and humans could communicate. Various utterances natural to orcas – whistles, trills, clicks, chirrups, pulsed calls, and pops – were agreed upon to represent the ninety-one syllables of the language that Arjuna named Wordsong. Helen Agar had no need to speak Wordsong to Arjuna, for he understood English (and many other human languages) very well; however, while engaged in natural communication with Arjuna and the other orcas, Helen chose to communicate in this imaginative language out of solidarity with the whales and the ideal of making the crude vowels and consonants of a human language somehow 'sing.' Only one of the Institute's other linguists (Prasad Choudhary) reached fluency in this language that has been popularly mischaracterized as 'Baby Orcalish.' In reality, Wordsong is more like a spoken Morse Code. It assigns meanings to orca sounds usually employed by the orcas very differently. Anyone can 'talk' Morse Code, for instance saying, 'Pop, pop, pop; sprong, sprong, sprong; pop, pop, pop,' to denote the SOS message meaning 'help.' While conversing in Wordsong is much more difficult, the rules for doing so follow a similar principle. Alone of non-linguists, the orca trainer Gabrielle Jones *did* come to understand Wordsong when Arjuna spoke it to her, even if she was unable to speak it back to him. English remained her only language, and it was she who encouraged Arjuna to communicate to the human race in what has become a de facto, if very limited, world language.

Most of Arjuna's story, then, he recorded in English through an extension and adaptation of the Wordsong's syllabary to English. As English contains, by some counts, more than 15,000 syllables, not even Helen Agar came close to understanding Arjuna when he was speaking it. Instead, as we have continued to do, she relied on the Institute's computers to translate Arjuna's vocalizations into more or less standard English.

This last statement must be qualified. When Arjuna could not find the word he wanted in the language of Shakespeare, Blake, and Eliot, he turned to others, peppering his account with words from Spanish, Japanese, Diné, Arabic, and Basque – and even from Quenya, Fravashi, and one of the many dialects of Tlön. He particularly liked Chinese for its tones and !Xoon for its clicks. All these needed to be re-translated into English; and even his English needed extensive editing. While his locutions at times could be eloquent and even poetic, they contained many quirks, for instance incorporating his curious prejudice against using contractions. Because orcas in their own language, as far as we can understand, transcend time through obscuring the boundaries between past, present, and future, Arjuna liked to meld together different diction levels and styles from different periods of human history. Bizarrely, he rendered entire sections of his communication of the story of his life into somewhat turgid verse aping the Latinate cadences of John Milton's *Paradise Lost*.

All this needed smoothing into prose accessible to those Arjuna most wanted to address. [The Institute has published the original document in all its babel of magnificence for anyone capable of deciphering it in hopes of reaching a deeper understanding of Arjuna's mind.] As well, we took the liberty of cutting many strained metaphors and converting sound imagery to sight imagery, which predominated throughout the original document in a ratio of 77 to 23. Human beings, as Arjuna realized very early, are creatures of sight, and he would not have minded our attempts to make his story as readable as possible.

We found it more difficult and too distracting in the published English document to add cites in the many places where Arjuna 'borrowed' the sensibilities or the words of human authors. [The entire footnoted document is available upon request.] Arjuna plagiarized without shame. He considered copying or paraphrasing another's words as honoring dead authors. He had no sense of property, either intellectual or any other kind. The only thing orcas 'own' are the compositions of themselves, which they call rhapsodies – and in a way, not even those, since the songs of all orcas belong to their families in much the same way that their souls belong to the sea.

Similarly, we hesitated to cut or change the many repetitions, such as Arjuna's overuse of the words 'splendor' and 'song' – and most particularly, 'soul.' Arjuna found it difficult to settle on a single English word that could encompass a fluid orca concept. Certainly, he meant by soul many of the same things we usually call by different names but regard as intrinsic to ourselves: personality, memory, mind. In no way, however, did he intend soul to connote some sort of immaterial or supernatural essence. He might just as easily have used the words song, water, or wave. For orcas, soul is a substance no different than the water that forms up on the surface of the sea from which the whales take their greater being. If the orcas could be said to have a goal that they seek to achieve, it would be the shaping of themselves into perfect waves that share the same water of life with all others. So vital is this imperative to bring forth the most beautiful manifestation of true nature that Arjuna speaks of the soul dozens of times. He liked to say that he was involved with the soul of humankind.

Of course, Orcas don't mind repetition in their communications to each other. Or rather, the nature of the orcas' ever-flowing language, as far as we understand it, makes boring repetitions nearly impossible, in much the same way it is impossible to step twice into the same surging stream. Each sound picture that an orca paints – even one so commonplace as that of a salmon – differs from all others in nuance, inflection, and the many colors of sound. The nearly infinite complexity of these sound pictures, like variations of themes in an open-ended cerebral symphony, engages an orca's full attention at the same time that it discourages human examination. Sadly, human beings remain bound to essentially one-dimensional sequences of syllables spoken in time, and despite Arjuna's assurances to the contrary, it is extremely unlikely that we will ever comprehend the three-dimensional language of the whales. We simply don't have the mental machinery to do so.

More must be said about the human brain – its deficiencies and limitations – in comparison with the brains of orcas and other toothed whales. The mammalian brain has been built up by evolution in layers over millions of years. The foundational structure, the primordial paleocortex or reptile brain (called the rhinic), recalls the similar structures of the brains of fish, amphibians, and reptiles such as lizards and snakes. (Though it must be stressed that this does not imply that mammals evolved from reptiles, for instance, any more than humans did from chimpanzees. Both mammals and reptiles share a common ancestor in the Carboniferous period 300 million years ago.) The limbic lobe overlays this structure, as the supralimbic lobe does both. The outer lamination of brain matter is called the neocortex, whose growth over vast periods of time has enabled the leaps in intelligence of the mammals.

This 'new brain' – with its convolutions, fissures, and folds somewhat resembling those of a shelled walnut – is the pride of humanity. The brains of no other creature, it was thought for a long time, approach those of the human in differentiation, neural connectivity, sectional specialization, complexity, and power. Few of our kind have welcomed the discovery that the orcas' (and other whales') gyrification exceeds that of human beings. The surface area of a typical adult human's neocortex measures about 2,275 cm^2, while in dolphins, it is 3,745 cm^2, and in orcas and sperm whales much greater. It is true that the orca neocortex is thinner than the human, but there is simply more of it folded up with greater complexity. To add insult to the injury of wounded human vanity is the fact that orca brains weigh in at three times the size of human brains – and the brains of sperm whales exceed in size our own by a factor of six.

For many decades, various scientists have thought to obscure this glaring and embarrassing reality. They have conjured up various 'fudge factors' in a desperate attempt to ensure than human beings will be number one in any ranking of species' relative intelligence. Arjuna, in his account, with a simple thought experiment, demolishes the long-respected though ridiculous brain/body mass ratio as a measure of intelligence. (If this ratio proved true, the hummingbird would be the world's smartest animal.) Realizing the limitations of the older metric, so-called scientists have invented a new one: the Encephalization Quotient (EQ), which measures the actual brain mass against the predicted brain mass for an animal of a given size. Of course, human beings with our large brains relative to our small bodies, again, come out on top. This, however, is not science; it is bosh. First, and most importantly, absent a method of universally measuring intelligence and correlating it with the EQ, it is just another voodoo statistic, sounding impressive but possessing no meaning. Second, while the EQ does an excellent job of fulfilling its purpose of distinguishing human intelligence from that of supposedly lesser beings, it fails in providing meaningful comparisons among other species. For example, the EQ of a capuchin monkey, about two, more than doubles that of supposedly much smarter gorillas and chimpanzees. Third, if some species are over-encephalized, mathematics necessitates that some species must be under-encephalized, therefore lacking the mental machinery to perform the basic cognitive functions necessary for survival. The usage of the EQ attempts to obscure the rather obvious fact that only a certain percentage of the brain is used to operate the gross functionings of the body, no matter how large (or small) that body might be. As it turns out, very little amounts of brain can account for rather amazing powers of muscle, bone, feather, and flesh. The peregrine falcon, the fastest bird in the sky, manages to perform its aerial acrobatics and compute its 250mph dives through the air to catch a darting dove by virtue of a brain the size of a peanut.

A better question, too little asked when considering what we think of as intelligence, would be to inquire how much of an animal's brain can be devoted to the interconnectivity and association of ideas? In rats, this associative skill has been measured at approximately 10%. A cat tests out at 50% while a chimpanzee scores a 75%. Human beings, at 90%, thus need only 10% of our brains to operate our sensory and motive capabilities. What about the whales? The average associative skill measure estimated for cetaceans, at 96%, much exceeds our own, while orcas have available approximately 97.5% of their very large brains for a very wide range of cognitive functions.

More recently, Suzana Herculano-Houzel has argued in favor of another way to estimate intelligence, hitherto impossible to measure correctly. Citing the work of Williams and Herrup, she points out the reasonableness of assuming that the computational capacity of the brain should correlate with the absolute number of neurons in that brain, specifically in the neocortex, the supposed seat of animals' higher cognitive abilities. How, though, to actually *count* the number of neurons in a brain?

In a brilliant piece of science, Herculano-Houzel succeeded in using detergent to dissolve the brains of various species to make a 'brain soup' in which neurons' nuclei could be separated out and counted. The computations that resulted cleared up several mysteries. It turned out, for instance, that the elephant, with a brain more than three times as massive as that of the human being, *does* have more neurons; about 257 billion neurons compared to a human's 86 billion. However, 98% of those neurons are to be found in the cerebellum; the elephant's cerebrum contains a paltry 5.6 billion neurons compared to the 16 billion in the human cerebral cortex. That seems to explain our experience that human beings are a good deal smarter than the admittedly still-smart elephant. As Herculano-Houzel likes to say, 'Not all brains are made the same.' As she puts it, brains scale differently in different species and in different orders. The primate brain, and particularly the human brain, has evolved to pack more neurons more efficiently into a smaller volume, thus giving humans an advantage in intelligence over other species.

What, then, of the whales? Cetaceans share a rather close phylogenetic relationship with Artiodactyls such as pigs, deer, and giraffes. Based upon the scaling for those species, Herculano-Houzel predicted that the count of neurons in the much larger cerebral cortexes of several kinds of cetaceans would actually come out to a significantly *lower* number than that of humans. The largest cetacean cortex, that of the sperm whale, would contain fewer than 10 billion neurons, still much less than that of a human. It seemed that human beings' ranking of number one would remain unchallenged.

There the matter stood until a whale hunt happened to deliver the brains of ten long-finned pilot whales into researchers' hands. Using the techniques of optical dissector stereology, it was discovered that the neurons in the pilot whale neocortex numbered 37.2 billion – more than twice the human's 16 billion. Heidi S. Mortensen, Bente Pakkenberg, and five others described the quantitative relationships in the delphinid neocortex in a paper published in *Frontiers of Neuroanatomy*. Their discovery should rank among the greatest in importance in the history of science. Instead, this very great breakthrough remains largely unknown. The cortical neurons of the orca have yet to be counted, but it would not be surprising if they topped out at over 75 billion.

As if all this weren't enough to dethrone Man as the King of Creation, one more humbling discovery should be considered. In addition to the previously mentioned three primary structures of the mammalian brain – the rhinic, the limbic, and the supralimbic – cetaceans have evolved a *fourth* cortical lobe absent in any land mammal, human beings included. Although we do not yet know the precise functioning of this paralimbic lobe, it has been speculated that it integrates and enhances perceptions of sound, sight, taste, and touch. This would make sense of the orcas' synesthetic powers, what Arjuna calls 'the fiery splendor of sound and the music of light.' It may also have something to do with orientation in space and time and the orcas' perception that they can journey at will through the one as readily as the other.

Given the limitations of science and our ignorance of what really goes on inside the minds of whales, we believe that it would be as silly to try to calculate the cetaceans' intelligence as it would be to count the number of angels that can dance on the head of a pin. Were one to attempt to do so, however, considering the enormous size of the cetacean brain, considering its differentiation, sectional specialization, neural connectivity, and complexity (to say nothing of various orca feats such as the truly astounding acquisition of numerous languages), it would be enticing to come up with a rather large number. If the average human IQ can be measured at 100, with Economics Nobel Prize winners at 153 and geniuses on the order of an Einstein or a Goethe perhaps coming out at around 200, then an orca would score five times that while a sperm whale topped out at over 2,000.

What do orcas *do* with such massive intelligence? We have already mentioned their astonishing ability to learn languages (a sponge absorbing water is not an inaccurate metaphor), and Arjuna has much to say about the musical/philosophical compositions that the orcas call rhapsodies. All the whales have powers of the mind of which we have only the dimmest of intimations. How else can the seeming Miracle of the Solstice be explained? The speed of sound in water at 20 degrees Celsius is 1,482 meters per second – far too slow to account for what otherwise can be explained only by positing some sort of instantaneous planetary communication.

That we must accept the existence of certain so far inexplicable abilities and phenomena in the lives of whales does not imply that we should not question Arjuna's interpretation of some of them. What are we to make of the impossible creatures that he calls the Seveners? Certainly many strange species dwell as yet undiscovered in the vast reaches of the oceans. In many ways, we know much more about planets millions of miles from earth than we do the perpetually dark deeps of our own oceans. Could a complex animal assemble itself out of tiny multi-cellular organisms in a matter of minutes? Could such a creature possess the sort of intelligence that Arjuna accords it?

To the first question, we have a hint of an answer in the pyrosomes: colonies of thousands of zooids a few millimeters in size that associate with each other in huge, bioluminescent tubes up to twenty meters long and two meters in diameter – capacious enough to fit a grown human being inside. To the second question, we must incline toward a resounding 'no' because pyrosomes and any other conceivably similar species are not complex and lack anything resembling a brain.

And yet. And yet. Compendiums of findings about the Plantae kingdom (see Tompkins's and Bird's *The Secret Life of Plants* and Mancuso's and Viola's *Brilliant Green*) suggest that trees, flowers, ferns, mosses, and the like can be said to possess a real intelligence completely absent in a brain. And then there is the recent discovery of bacteria that might need to be classified as an entirely new and seventh kingdom of life. It seems that the species of *Geobacter metallireducens* and *Shewanella*, found in certain estuaries and other aquatic environments, have evolved to strip and deposit electrons from metals and various minerals, thereby essentially eating and breathing electricity. As well, they have the ability to interconnect with each other in 'cables' of thousands of individual cells. It is thought that this association is facilitated by 'nanowires' that are an extension of the cell membrane and which can conduct electricity in a biological circuit.

Might Arjuna's Seveners be some sort of very intelligent colonial organism assembled from bacteria similar to *Geobacter metallireducens* and *Shewanella*? We have no evidence of that, and we are skeptical that such a creature either does or could exist. It seems much more likely that Arjuna encountered (and ate) some sort of organism whose tissues produce alkaloids similar to those found in *Psilocybe cubensis* or *Lophophora willamsii*. Very intense hallucinations would account for Arjuna's insistence that what he experienced in the South Pacific was as real as his birth or any other event of his remarkable life.

Before closing this introduction to that life, we would like to say something about two terms that Arjuna uses at various times throughout his account. The first is the name he often used to describe human beings: the idiot gods. He thought long and deep before deciding on this sobriquet. At times, he thought it much more apt to call our species the mad gods or the insane gods. However, madness can too easily be associated with anger, and although Arjuna certainly saw human beings as afflicted with wrath, as a rabid dog is *lyssavirus*, he did not see this as humanity's greatest sin. Neither did he think of our kind as purely insane. Rather, he perceived in our derangement of sense and soul a willful debilitation, as if we human beings are an entire race of sleepwalkers moving through a nightmare from which we refuse to awaken. We are, he once said, like lost children wandering through a dark landscape without markers or boundaries. He had great compassion for (and dread of) our *innocence*. Given the horrors that Arjuna recounts, that seems a strange word to apply to the human kind, but it motivates his choice to call us idiots. It is the holy fool kind of innocence of Prince Myshkin in Dostoevsky's *The Idiot* as well as the deadly innocence of the young man Lone in Sturgeon's *The Fabulous Idiot*, incorporated into the great work known as *More Than Human*. Of all humanity's failings that Arjuna enumerates in such painstaking and painful detail, he counts as the very worst our refusal to embrace our best possibilities and so to live as gods.

The second term we would like to define is quenge, the most quintessential part of a whale's true nature. Arjuna himself coined the word to represent a nearly ineffable cetacean sensibility and prowess. We would *like* to explain this strange word, though of course it remains inexplicable. One might as well try to describe a magnificent city on a hill, bright with sunlit cathedrals and great spires, to a band of cave-dwellers. The best course for anyone wishing to know more is to make one's way into Arjuna's story. But please do so with an open mind, and even more, with an open heart. Readers who reach the end without having any idea of what it is to quenge will have wasted their time – and Arjuna's.

1

The humans call me Arjuna, after the hero who spoke with the God of Truth, though they cannot say my real name any more than they can say why the starlit sea sings with such a hush, lovely fire or why they themselves are alive.

When I was a young whale unacquainted with human might and madness, I swam with my family through the icy waters near the top of the world – the world they call Earth and we call Ocean. Along the cold currents we hunted char and salmon and other fishes that schooled in never-ending silvery streams; along our fiery blood we sought ecstasies of creation even as we listened for the great and singular Song that sounds within all things. Sometimes, we gave voice to the deep, unutterable mysteries bound up in the chords of this song; more often we told tales of the glories of our Old Ones or the adventures of the newborn babies just beginning to speak. We held midnight feasts beneath the pink and emerald sprays of light raining down from the Aurora Borealis. During the long, long days of summer, we dove beneath the icebergs and we mated and played and loved and dreamed.

We quenged. Guided by our true nature, which always knows the intention of life and the way home, we followed the ocean's song wherever it called us, listening always for its source. Great journeys we made! One fine day might find us visiting with the Old Ones in the turquoise swells of the Caribbean ten thousand years ago while on the next day we might wend our way along the arc of the Aurora and swim through ages yet to be up to the stars. We delved the deeps of oceans on worlds without number, daring each other to move ever further outward and inward beyond the limits of space and time. Down through unknown seas we plunged into the melodies of songs sung again and again since the world's beginning – and into the souls of the stories that their singers poured forth with so much delight. Who could escape from the account of how Mother Maia fought off a hundred great white sharks in order to protect her children? Who could forget the epic of Aldebaran the Great's circumnavigation of the globe in search of the perfect color of crimsong with which to paint his great tone poem? Who could resist the urge to become both bard and hero of one's own story? Why else are we here? Are not our lives the very songs that sing the universe into creation?

Many of our best adventures came through dreams or revelations or even the babblings of babes still drinking milk; the worst came out of places so dark and disturbing that few wished ever to go there. It seemed that no whale could ever conceive them. Once, while we were making our way across the nearly infinite seas of Agathange east of earth, I nearly choked on reddened waters and caught a glimpse of a blue god and masses of belligerents slaughtering each other. Another time, on Tiralee, I learned of an eternal quest to find a golden conch shell said to hold entire constellations and oceans inside. I trembled at the vivacity of such visions, for I experienced them simultaneously as impossible and too real, as familiar and utterly strange.

How terrified I was at first of these wild wanderings! How confused, how desperate, how consumed! My mother, though, sleek and black and white and beautiful, swam always beside me with powerful, rhythmic strokes that told of the faith of her great, bottomless heart. She reassured me with murmurs of maternal encouragements as well as with clear, cool logic: was not water, she asked me, the unitive substance which ripples with the shimmering interconnectedness of all things? Was not I, myself, made of water, as was she and my uncles and my ancestors? How could I ever be separate from the sea which had formed me or fail to find my way home? Could I not hear, always, within my own heart the ringing of life's great song?

Yes, I told her, emboldened by a growing fearlessness, yes, yes I could! Her love, onstreaming like the strongest of currents, filled me with joy. And so I quenged through the world and through the eternal musics which gave it form, moving always and ever deeper and deeper. The water flowed through my skin, and I flowed through the water, and the ocean and I were as one.

I do not remember my conception. Humans die in worry of what will become of them after the worms have eaten their bodies and they are gone; we whales live in wonder of what we were before we came to be. What we were is what we are and always will be: we are salt and seaweed, haddock and diatom and grains of sand glimmering among the fronds of red and purple coral. The ocean forms us out of itself, and each drop of water – each molecule – reverberates with an indestructible consciousness. As we quicken and grow within our mothers' wombs, we gradually come into full consciousness of our indestructible selves and of the way we are both a tiny part and the entirety of the universe. And then one day, we realize that we are awake and aware – aware that there never could have been a time in which we did not exist.

This happened to me. After some months of life, I awakened to the thunder of my mother's heart beating out a reassuring rhythm even as it beat into my veins the blood that we both shared. A human might think that I therefore woke up in a drumlike darkness, but it was not so. Everywhere – blazing through the salty amniotic waters and glimmering through my own tiny heart – there was light. Our Old Ones call this phenomenon the brilliance of sound. Do not light and sound emanate from the same essential source? Are they not both experienced within the tissues of our minds as reflections of the forms of the manifold world? Are there not many ways to see? Yes, yes, the fiery splendor of sound and the music of light! To see the world in all its astonishing perfection through waves and echoes of pure vivid sonance – yes, yes, yes!

From nearly the beginning, my mother spoke to me. Mostly, she duplicated the clicks by which she made out the icebergs and shoals, sharks and salmon: all the things of the ocean that a whale needed to perceive. In this way, she made sound pictures for me to see. Long before my birth, I knew the turnings and twisting of the coastlines of the world's northernmost continents; I knew the rasp of ice and the raucousness of rock and the much softer sounds of snow. The dense, gelid winter sea seemed tinted with hues of tanglow and bluetone, while in the summer the waters came alive with the peals of a color I call glorre.

Sometimes, my mother spoke to me in simple baby speech, forming the basic utterances upon which more mature language would build. She told me simple stories and explained the intricacies of life outside the womb in a way that I could understand. I could not, of course, speak back for I had no air within my lungs and so could not make a single sound within my flute. I listened, though, as my mother told me of the cold of the water outside her that I could not feel and of the stars' luster that I could not see. I learned the names of my family whom I would soon meet: my aunts Chara and Mira, my uncles Dheneb and Alnitak, my sister Turais and my cousins – and my grandmother, head of our family, whom a young whale such as I would never think to address by name.

When my mind ached with too much knowledge and I grew tired, my mother sang me to sleep with lullabies. When I awakened from dark dreams with a rumbling dread that I would be unable to face life's difficulties, my mother told me the one thing that every whale must know, something more important than even the Song of Life and the ocean itself: that I had been conceived in love and my mother's love would always fill my heart – and that no matter how far I swam or how much life hurt me, I would never be alone.

On the day of my birth, my mother instructed me not to breathe until Chara and Mira swam under me and buoyed me up to the surface. I came quickly, tail first, propelled out of my mother's warm body through a cloud of blood and fear. The shock of the icy water pierced straight through me with a thrilling pain. I nearly gasped in anguish, and so I nearly breathed water and drowned. Mira and Chara, though, as promised pressed their heads beneath my belly and pushed me upward. Light blinded me: not the scintillation of roaring winds but rather the incandescence of the sun impossible to behold. It burned my eyes even as it warmed me in tingles that danced along my skin. The water broke and gave way to the thinness of the atmosphere. In astonishment, I drew my first breath. With my lungs thus filled with air, through my tender, untried flute, I spoke my first baby words in a torrent of squeaks and chirps that I could not contain. What did I say? What *should* a newborn whale say to the being who had carried and nourished him for so long? Thank you, Mother, for my life and for your love – it is good to be alive.

And so I tasted the sea and drank in the wonder of the world. Everything seemed fascinating and beautiful: the blueness of the sea ice and the shining red bellies of the char that my family hunted; the jewel-like diatoms and the starfish and the joyous songs of the humpbacks that sounded from out of deeps. All was new to me, and all was a marvel and a delight. I wanted to go on swimming through this paradise forever.

How deliciously the days passed as the ocean turned beneath the sun and through the seasons! With my mother ever near, I fattened first on her milk and then on the fish that she taught

21

me to catch for myself. My mind grew nearly as quickly as my body. So much I needed to learn! The sea's currents had to be studied and the migrations of the salmon memorized. My uncle Alnitak, greatest of our clan's astronomers, taught me celestial navigation. From Mira I gained the first glimmerings of musical theory and practice, while my older sister Turais shared with me her love of poetics. My mother impressed upon me the vital necessity of the Golden Rule, less through words and songs than through her compassion and her generosity of spirit. As well, she guided me through the maelstrom of the many Egregious Fallacies of Thought and the related Fundamental Philosophical Errors. It took entire years and many pains for her to nurture within me a zest for the arts of being: plexure, zanshin, and shih. Once or twice, in the most tentative and fleeting of ways, I managed to speak of the nature of art itself with the Old Ones.

It was my grandmother, however, who held the greatest responsibility for teaching me about the Song of Life. I must, she told me, quenge deep within myself, down through the dazzling darkness into spaces that can contain the entire universe as a blue whale's mouth contains a drop of water. As I grew stronger and swifter, I must make of myself a song of glory that found resonance with the song of the sea – and thus become a part of it. At least for a few magical moments, I must quenge with the gods. Was this not the calling of any adult orca? And so I must learn to sing with as great a prowess as I applied to swimming and hunting; only then would my grandmother and my other elders deem me to be a full adult. And only then would I be allowed to mate and make children of my own.

Of what, though, was I to sing? Over many turnings of light and dark, sunshine and snow, I considered the necessities of this composition. My rhapsody, as we call the songs of ourselves, must attain to the uniqueness and perfection of a single snowflake while simultaneously ringing with all the memories of the ocean out of which the snowflake had formed. It must tell of the past of the whole world and of the destiny of the teller.

What, I wondered, would be my destiny? In what way was I unique? Although I could not say, I gained a whisper of an answer to these questions from a prophecy that my grandmother made at my birth: that either I would die young or I would add some thing new to the Song, something marvelous and strange that had never been heard in all the long ages of our people.

From out of the humans' oldest poem, these words echo through humanity's much shorter ages – words that curiously accord with my grandmother's instructions to me:

> *You are what your deep, driving desire is*
> *As your desire is, so is your will;*
> *As your will is, so is your deed;*
> *As your deed is, so is your destiny.*

Such deeds I wanted to do! – but what deeds? I did not know. Impossible notions came to me. I would journey to the yearly gatherings of the sperm whales, and I would coax these deep gods to reveal all their wisdom. I would crack apart icebergs with a shout from my lungs; I would put the Aurora's fire into the mouths of the great, mute sharks, and I would teach the starfish to sing.

First, however, I had to apprehend my deepest desire. For many years, I applied myself to this task. I meditated, and I sang, and I grew ever vaster and more powerful, fed in my body by the sea's fishes and in my soul through my family's heartenings. I attained my full form, larger even than that of mighty Alnitak. My blood thundered with wild lightnings, and my testes burned with seed, and I dreamed of finding a lovely, young she-orca with whom to mate.

In this season of my discontent, in a time of hunger when the fish were few, there occurred three portents that changed my life. The first of these the humans would regard as a cliché – as wearisome as the slaughters that make up most of their histories. To me, however, the news that my cousin Haedi brought from out of vernal mists one day shocked me with its signal import. She swam up to my grandmother and told of a white bear standing on an ice floe far from the pack ice from which this tiny, floating island had splintered. Our whole family moved off south in order to witness this unheard-of misfortune. Turais's newborn, little Porrima, remarked that she had never seen a bear.

Long before our eyes could make out this king of land animals, we sighted him with our sonar. How hopeless the situation of this great beast seemed! He made a pitiful figure, a smear of fur atop a bit of ice, forlorn and alone against the churning, gray swells of the sea.

My uncle Alnitak, long and powerful, always so precise with distances, seemed to point his notched dorsal fin at the bear as he said, 'He *could* swim back to the ice if he dared – if he had the strength, it is barely possible that he might make it.'

We swam a little closer, our sides nearly touching each other's, at one in our breath and in our thoughts. Then we dove in a coordinated flow of black and white beneath the surface, closer to the bear and his icy island. My mother zanged the bear with her sonar. This sense did not work very well on objects outside the water, but the clicks my mother made were powerful enough to pierce the bear's fur, skin, and muscles and to reflect back through the water as images that we all shared.

'Very well, then,' my aunt Mira said, in her sad, plaintive voice. 'The bear has starved and is much too weak to swim so many miles back to the ice.'

What else was there to say? Either the bear would die from the belly-gnawing ache of hunger or he would venture into the water and drown – or find his end in the feeding frenzy of a shark or between the jaws of one of the Others. At this, my grandmother turned back towards our usual fishing lanes. As she often said, each of us has a single destiny.

That might have been the end of the matter had I not chanced to recall a story told to me by Dheneb, who had once spoken with one of the Others. Apparently, when stalking seals, the ice bears were clever enough to cover their black noses with their white paws so that the seals did not detect them creeping forward across the snow fields. Why, I wondered, must such a cunning creature perish so ignominiously just because the ice had mysteriously melted around him?

I determined that he should not die this way. An impulse sounded from within me and swelled like a bubble rising up through the water. I said, 'Why don't we push the bear's island back to the pack ice?'

For a few moments no one spoke. Then Chara flicked her powerful flukes and said to me, 'What a strange idea! You have always had such strange schemes and dreams!'

'Thank you,' I replied. 'You are complimenting me aren't you?'

'Can you not hear in my voice the overtones of my appreciation for your innovatedness of thought?'

'Sometimes I can, Aunt.'

'If you listened hard enough at the interstices of my words, you would never doubt how much I value the freshness of your spirit.'

'Thank you,' I said again.

'I value it, as we all do, almost as much as I cherish your compassion – compassion for a bear!'

I zanged the bear with my sonar, and I heard the quickened heart beats that betrayed his fear. Did he sense my family's holding a conference beneath the waters near his island? What, I wondered, could the bear be thinking?

'How often,' I said to Chara, 'has Grandmother averred that we must have compassion for all things?'

'And we do! We do!' she called out, 'We sing to the diatoms

and have family-feeling for the broken shells of the mollusks – even for the bubbles of oxygen in the water that long in their innermost part to be incorporated once again into an inspired young whale such as you who exalts the beauty of compassion.'

Alnitak, less loquacious than Chara, beat his flukes through the sun-dappled water and said simply, 'I would relish the novelty and satisfaction of saving this bear, but it is too far for us to swim right now. Are we not, ourselves, weak with hunger?'

This was true. Days and days had it been since any of us had eaten! Where had the fish gone? No one could say. We all knew, however, that huge, lovely Grandmother had grown much too thin and my sister Turais had nearly lost her milk and could barely feed the insatiable little Porrima. And Mira, my melancholy aunt, worried about her child Kajam. If our luck did not improve, very soon Kajam would begin to starve along with the rest of us and would likely come down with one of the fevers that had carried off Mira's first born to the other side of the sea. Her second born had died of a peculiar stomach obstruction, while her third had been born with a deformed tongue and jaw, which had made it impossible for the child to eat. Poor Mira now invested her hope for the future in the young and frail Kajam.

'All right,' I finally said, out of frustration, 'then I will push the bear myself to the pack ice. Perhaps I will encounter fish along the way and return to lead you to them.'

Alarmed at the earnestness in my voice, my mother Rana swam up to me. Her streamlined form, nearly perfect in proportion, flowed through the water along with her concerned words: 'There is much bravura in what you propose, but also the folly of misplaced pride. This cannot be the great deed you wish to do.'

Chara's second daughter Talitha, who was only three years old and didn't know any better, gave voice to one of the usually unvoiced principles by which we live: 'But you cannot leave your family, cousin Arjuna!'

She loved me a great deal, tiny Talitha did. No words could I find for her. I did not really want to leave her.

We concluded our conference with a decision that I should remain with everyone else. Again my grandmother turned to abandon the bear to the tender mercies of the sea.

'Wait!' I cried out. A wild, wild idea rose out of the unknown part of me with all the shock of a tidal wave. 'Why don't we eat the bear?'

For a whale, the sea can never be completely quiet, yet I swear that for a moment all sound died into a vast silence. I might as well have suggested eating Grandmother.

Talitha again spoke of the obvious, something my elders knew that I knew very well: 'But we cannot eat a bear! That would break the First Covenant!'

She went on to recount one of the most important lessons that she had learned: how long ago the orcas had split into two kindreds, one which ate only fish while the other hunted seals and bears and almost any animal made of warm blood and red meat. These Others, who looked much the same as any orca of my clan, almost never mingled with us. We had promised to leave each other alone and never to interfere with the different ways by which we made our livings. Even so, we knew each other's stories and songs. If we killed the bear, the sea itself would sing of our desperate act, and the Others would eventually learn of how we had broken our covenant with them.

My grandmother moved closer to me through the cold water. Her eyes, as blue and liquid as the ocean, caught me up in her fondness for me and swept me into deeper currents of cobalt, indigo, and ultramarine, and the secret blue-inside-blue that flows within the heart of all things. She asked, 'Do you remember what I said about you on the day you were born?'

'You said many things, Grandmother.'

'Yes, I did and these words I would like you to remember: How noble you are, in both form and faculty, Arjuna, how like an angel in action, and in apprehension like a god! The beauty of the world you are and all of my delight.'

27

I *did* remember her saying that. She told all her grandchildren the same thing.

'How noble would it be,' she now asked me, 'for us to break our promise to the Others?'

'But we are so hungry! They would not mind if we took a single bear.'

'The Covenant is the Covenant,' she told me, 'whether or not you think the Others would mind.'

'But we made it so long ago, in a different age. The world is changing.'

'The world is always the world, just as our word is always our word.'

'Can we never break our word, even as the ice breaks into nothingness while the world grows warmer?'

'The ice has broken before,' my grandmother reminded me.

For a while, she sang to me and our family of our great memories of the past: of ages of ice and times of the sun's heat when the world had been cooler or warmer.

'Yes, but something is different this time,' I replied. 'The world has warmed much too quickly.'

Although she could not deny this, she said, 'The world has its own ways.'

'Yes, and those ways are changing.'

Alnitak came closer and so did my mother, and through the turbid, gray waters we debated how the northern ice sheet could have possibly melted so much in the span of a few generations. As I was still a young, not-quite-adult whale, I should have deferred to my elders. I should have felt shame at my questioning of them. Who was I to think that I might have discerned something they had not? And yet I did, and I sensed something wrong in my family's understanding. In this, I experienced a secret pride in my insight and in my otherness from people who had seemed so like myself in sensibility and so close to my heart.

'It is the humans,' I said. 'The humans are warming the world with the heat we have felt emanating from their boats.'

'That cannot be enough heat to melt the ice,' Alnitak said.

'Only a few generations ago,' I retorted, 'only a few humans dared the ocean in cockle shells that we could have splintered with one snap of our jaws. Now their great metal ships are everywhere.'

'To suppose that therefore the humans can be blamed for the ocean's warming,' my grandmother said, 'is a wild leap in logic.'

'But they are to blame! I know they are!'

'How can you be sure?' And then, as if I was still a babe drinking milk, she chided me for making a basic philosophical error: 'A correlation does not prove a causation.'

And chided I was. To hide my embarrassment (and my defiance), I took refuge in a little play: 'Thank you for the lesson, Grandmother. I was just giving you the chance to exercise your love of pedagogy.'

'Of course you were, my dear. And I do love it so! I have no words to tell you how much I look forward to the day when it is you who teaches me.'

'I am sure that you could think of a few words, Grandmother.'

'Well, perhaps a few.'

'I await your wisdom.'

'I can hear that you do,' she said. 'Then listen to me: it is a heavy responsibility being the wisest of the family – perhaps you could relieve me of it.'

'No, I cannot,' I said sincerely. 'You know I cannot.'

'Then will you let us leave this bear to his fate?'

All my life, my grandmother had warned me that my innate tenacity could harden into pertinacity if I allowed this. Did anyone know me as did my grandmother?

'We are hungry,' I said simply.

'We have been hungry before.'

'Never like this. Where have the fish gone? Not even the ocean can tell us.'

'We will swim to a place where there are many fish.'

'We would swim more surely with this bear's life to strengthen us.'

'Yes, and with our bellies full of bear meat, what shall we say to the Others?'

'Why must we say anything at all?'

'In saying nothing, we would say everything. How can a whale speak other than the truth?'

'But what is true, grandmother?'

'The Covenant is true – a true expression of our desire to live in harmony with the Others.'

'But have you not taught me that the only absolute truth is that there is no absolute truth?'

Indeed she had. My grandmother relished self-referential statements and the paradoxes they engendered as an invitation for one's consciousness to reflect back and forth on itself into a bright infinity that illuminated the deepest of depths.

'Yes, I did teach you that,' she said. 'You were too young, however, for me to tell you that if there is no absolute truth, then we cannot know with certainty that there is no absolute truth.'

My grandmother played a deeper game than I – a game that could go on forever if I let it.

'Then *do* you believe there is an absolute truth?'

'You are perceptive, Arjuna.'

'What is this truth then? Is it just life, itself?'

'You really do not know?'

'But what could be truer than life?'

In answer, my grandmother sang to me in a thunderous silence that I could not quite comprehend. I needed to answer *her*, but what should I say? Only words that would gnaw at her and lay her heart bare.

'Look at Kajam,' I called out. I swam over to him and nudged the child with my head. 'He is so hungry!'

Kajam, small for his four years and thin with deprivation, protested this: 'I am not too hungry to swim night and day as far as we must. Let us surface and I will show you.'

It had been a while since any of my family had drawn breath.

Because the bear could do nothing about his plight, we had no need to conceal our conference beneath the water or to keep silence. And so almost as one, we breached and blew out stale air in loud, steamy clouds, and we drew in fresh breaths. To prove his strength, Kajam dove down and swam up through the water at speed; he breached and with a powerful beat of his tail, drove himself up into the air in a perfectly calculated arc that carried him over my back so that he plunged headfirst into the sea in a great splash. Everyone celebrated this feat. Almost immediately, however, Kajam had to blow air again. He gulped at it in a desperate need that he could not hide.

'Listen to his heartbeats!' I said to grandmother. 'How long will it be before his blood begins burning with a fever?'

My grandmother listened, and so did my mother, along with Alnitak, Dheneb, and Chara. The third generation of our family listened, too: my sisters Turais and Nashira, my little brother Caph, and my cousins Naos, Haedi, and Talitha. Even Turais's children, Alnath and Porrima, concentrated on the strained pulses sounding within the center of Kajam's body. And of course Mira listened the most intently of all.

'Compassion,' my grandmother said to me, 'impelled you to want to save this bear, and now you wish to eat him?'

'Would that not be the easiest of the bear's possible deaths?'

'And compassion you have for Kajam and the rest of our family. We all know this about you, Arjuna.'

In silence, I tried to sense what my grandmother was thinking.

'Now listen to my heart,' she told me. 'You persist in trying to persuade me in the same way that the wind whips up water. Am I so weak that you think mere words will move me?'

'Not *mere* words, Grandmother. I know how you love Kajam. It is your own heart that will move you.'

'But you believe that mine needs a nudge from yours?'

'Not really. I think you wish that I would give voice to what you really want to do and so make it easier for you to do it.'

'How kind of you to ease me into an agonizing dilemma! You can be cruel in your compassion, my beautiful, beloved grandson.'

In her wry laughter that followed, I detected a note of pride in the manner that I had tried to clear the way toward a decision that we both knew she had secretly wished (and perhaps resolved) to make all along. What was the First Covenant against the much greater pledge of life that Grandmother had made to her family? She would battle all the monsters of the deep in order to protect one of her babies.

We held a quick conference and made our plans. Alnitak pushed himself up out of the water, spy-hopping in order to get a better look at the bear. Dheneb did, too, and so did I. Did the bear recognize our kind and conclude that he was as safe sharing the sea with us as if we were guppies? Or might he mistake us for the Others? Who could say what a bear might know?

We had watched the Others stalking seals and other sea mammals, and so we knew many of the Others' hunting techniques. We had also learned their stories, which provided many images to guide us. Of course, transforming an image in the mind into a coordinated motion of the body can take much practice. Did we have days and seasons and years to perfect a prowess of hunting dangerous mammals that our kind had never needed? No, we did not. Still, I argued, taking this bear should not prove too difficult.

Our whole family swam up to the bear and surrounded his ice floe. Respecting the ancient forms, I came up out of the water and asked the bear if he was ready to die. Bears cannot, of course, speak as we do, but this brave bear answered me with a glint of his eyes and a weak roar of acceptance: 'Yes, I am ready.'

We all breathed deeply and dove. Alnitak, Dheneb, and my mother, chirping away in order to coordinate their movements, rose straight up through the water toward the far side of the ice floe. They needed only a single attack to push the floe's edge up high into the air. The bear's instincts took hold of him, and he scrambled to keep his purchase, digging his claws into the ice.

Inexorably, though, he slid down the sun-slicked ice and toppled into the sea.

Chara and I were waiting for him there. He started swimming in a last desperation. For a legged animal, bears are good swimmers, much better than humans, but no creature of land or sea can outswim an orca. While Chara distracted the bear, I closed in through the gray waters' churn and froth. I came in close enough to taste the bear's wrath, and I tried to avoid a lucky score of his slashing teeth. Concentrated as I was on the bear's jaws, which were not so different than my own, I did not see the bear swipe his paw at me until it was too late. Even through the water, the bear struck my head with a power that stunned me. The claws caught me over my eye and ripped into my skin. Blood boiled out into the water. Then Chara came at the bear from above. She fastened her jaws around his neck, pushing him down deeper into the water. I recovered enough to grasp the bear's hindquarters. Then we held him fast in the cold clutch of the sea until he could keep his breath no longer, and he sucked in water and drowned.

After that, the rest of my family joined us. We tore the bear apart and divided him as fairly as we could. None of us had ever consumed a mammal, but the memory had been passed down to us: the Others described bear meat as tasting rich, red, tangy, and delicious. So it did. In the end, we ate the bear down to his white, furry paws and his black nose.

During the time that followed, the gash that the bear had torn into me healed into an unusual scar. Mira observed that it resembled the jags of a lightning bolt. Although I could not behold this mark directly, Mira made a sound picture of it for me. How ugly it looked, how disfiguring, how strange! The hurt of my heart for the bear (and for my grandmother) never really healed. Why had we needed to kill such an intelligent, noble animal? Had the bear felt betrayed by me, who had really wanted to help him? In ways that I did not understand I sensed that the bear's death had changed me. I spent long hours swimming through the late spring waves, dotted with bits of turquoise ice. A new note had sounded within the long, dark roar of the sea. I became aware of it as one might recognize a background sound through the deepest organs of hearing yet remain unaware of being aware. It took many days for this note to grow louder. At first, I could hear only a part of it clearly, but that part worked to poison my thoughts and darken my dreams:

Something was wrong with the world! Something was terribly wrong!

Intimations of doom oppressed me. I tried to escape my dread through quenging. The world, however, would not allow me this simple solace for very long; it kept on whispering to me no matter where I tried to go.

On a day of ceaseless motion through the sempiternal sea, there occurred the second of the three portents. I was quenging with a delightful degree of immersion, working on a new tone poem that was to be part of the rhapsody by which I would establish my adulthood. The chords of the penultimate motif exemplifying Alsciaukat the Great's philosophy of being had carried me through the many waters of the world into the mysterious Silent Sea, lined with coral in bright colors of yellow, magenta, and glorre. It was a place of perfect stillness, perfect peace. The aurora poured down from the heavens, feeding the ocean with a lovely fire so that each drop of water sang with the world's splendor. The fire found me, consumed me with a delicious coolness, and swept me deep into the ocean's song.

Then the blaze grew brighter like the morning sun heating up. A bolt of lightning flashed out and struck me above the eye, and burned into me with a hideous pain. The burning would not stop; it seared my soul. I shouted to make it go away, and I became aware of Alnitak and Mira and my mother shouting, too. Alnitak's great voice sounded out the loudest: 'The water is burning! The water is burning! The ocean is on fire!'

Upon this alarm, I opened both my eyes, and swam up with the rest of my family to join Alnitak, Mira, and my mother at the surface. I looked out toward the southern horizon. Black clouds, thick as a squid's ink, blighted the blue sky. They billowed up from the red and orange flames that leaped along the roiling waters. Alnitak had told true: the ocean really was on fire.

Only once before, when lightning had ignited a tree on a distant rocky island, had I ever seen flame; never, though, had I beheld such terrible, ugly clouds as the monsters of smoke that this sea of flames engendered. Alnitak, bravest of our band, volunteered to swim out toward them to investigate.

We waited a long time for him to return, praying all the while that he *would* return. When he finally did, an evil substance clung like a squid's suckers to his skin. Black as decayed flesh it was and slippery as fish fat, yet sticky, too. It tasted unnatural, hateful, foul.

'The water is covered with it,' Alnitak announced. 'It is that which burns.'

I said nothing as to the source of this abomination. I did not need to, for my little brother Caph said it for me: 'The humans have done this thing.'

And Chara's daughter Haedi agreed, 'They have befouled the ocean!'

'If they could do that,' Mira said, 'they could destroy the world.'

Although my grandmother did not dispute this, she addressed Mira and the rest of the family, saying, 'The Old Ones tell of a thunder mountain that once destroyed an island in the southern sea and set fire to the earth. The cause of this phenomenon of the sea that burns might be something like that.'

No one, however, believed this. No mountains had thundered, and the substance stuck to Alnitak's skin tasted disturbingly similar to the excretions of the humans' boats.

So, I thought, this explained the failure of the fish to teem and the melting of the ice caps. It had been the humans after all – it must be the humans! But why? Why? Why?

No answer did the ocean give me. But as I floated on its quiet waters watching the black clouds dirty the air, I knew that something truly was wrong with the world.

'This is a bad place,' my grandmother said. 'Let us swim away from here to our old fishing lanes and hope that the salmon have returned.'

And so we swam. The note that had sounded upon the bear's death began murmuring with a soft, urgent plangency as a she-orca calls to her mate. I heard it clearly now, though I still could not tell what it meant.

The third portent occurred soon after that on our migration westward, away from the burning sea. My mother sounded out a lone orca in the distance. And that disturbed us, for when do our kind ever swim alone? However, this orca proved to be *not* of our kind, but rather one of the Others: his dorsal fin pointed straight up, triangular and harsh like a shark's tooth – so different from the graceful, arched fins of my clan. Instead of avoiding us as the Others usually do, this one swam straight toward us as if homing on prey.

He swam with difficulty, though, the beating of his flukes pulling him to the right as if he was trying to escape something on his left. When he drew close to us we all saw why: an object like a splinter of a tree stuck out of his side. His blood, darker and redder than even the bears', oozed out of the hole that the splinter had made. None of us had ever seen such a thing before, though from the old stories we all knew what had happened to this lone orca.

'The humans did this to me,' he told me.

We could hardly understand him. He spoke a dialect thick and strange to our way of hearing. Because the Others do not want to alert the intelligent mammals that they stalk, they utter fewer words than do we when fishing. Consequently, in order to convey a similar amount of information, the Others' word-sounds must be denser and more complex, stived with meaning like a crystalline array that seems to have more and more glittering facets the deeper one looks. As he told us of a terrible encounter with the humans, we all looked (and listened) for the meaning of his strange words:

'The humans came upon us in their great ships,' he told us, 'and they began slaying as wantonly as sharks do.'

'But why did they do this?' my grandmother asked him. Of nearly everyone in our family, she had the greatest talent for speaking with the Others.

'Who can know?' Pherkad said, for such was the Other's name. 'Perhaps they wished to eat an orca within the shell of their ship, for they captured Baby Electra in one of their nets and took her out of the sea.'

I could not imagine being separated from the sea. Surely Electra must have died almost immediately, before the humans could put tooth to her.

'We fought as hard as we could,' Pherkad continued. 'We fought and died – all save myself.'

My grandmother zanged Pherkad and sounded the depth and position of the object buried in his body.

'You will die soon,' she told him.

'Yes.'

'Your whole family is dead, and so you will die soon and be glad of it.'

'Yes, yes!'

'Before you die,' my grandmother said, 'please know that my family broke our trust with you in hunting a bear.'

'I *do* know that,' Pherkad said. 'The story sings upon the waves!'

I did not really understand this, for I was still too young to have quenged deeply enough to have understood: how the dialect of the Others and of our kind make up one of the many whole languages, which in turn find their source in the language that sings throughout the whole of the sea. Even the tortoises, it is said, can comprehend this language if they listen hard enough, for the ocean itself never stops listening nor does it cease to speak.

Could there really be a universal language? Or was Pherkad perhaps playing with us in revenge for our breaking the Covenant? The Others, renowned for their stealth, might somehow have witnessed my family's eating of the bear and all the while have remained undetected.

'On behalf of my family, who are no more,' he said to my grandmother, 'I would wish to forgive you for what you did.'

'You are gracious,' my grandmother said.

'The Covenant *is* the Covenant,' he said. 'However there are no absolute principles – except one.'

My brother Caph started to laugh at the irony in Pherkad's voice, but then realized that doing so would be unseemly.

Then I said to Pherkad, 'Perhaps we could remove the splinter from your side.'

'I do not think so,' he said, 'but you are welcome to try.'

I moved up close to him through the bloody water and grasped the splinter with my teeth. Hard it was, like biting down on brown bone. I yanked on it with great force. The shock of agony that ran through Pherkad communicated through his flesh into me; as a great scream gathered in his lungs, I felt myself wanting to scream, too. Then Pherkad gathered all his dignity and courage, and he forced his suffering into an almost godly laugh of acceptance: 'No, please stop, friend – it is my time to die.'

'I am sorry,' I said.

'What is your name?' he asked me.

I gave him my name, my true name that the humans could not comprehend. And Pherkad said to me, 'You are compassionate, Arjuna. Was it you who suggested saving the bear?'

'Yes, it was.'

'Then you are twice blessed – what a strange and beautiful idea that was!'

Not knowing what to say to this, I said nothing.

'I would like to sing of that in my death song,' he told me. 'Our words are different but if I give mine to you, will you try to remember them?'

'I will remember,' I promised.

My grandmother had often told me that my gift for languages exceeded even hers. She attributed that to my father, of the Emerald Sun Surfer Clan, whose great-great grandfather had been Sharatan the Eloquent. The words that Pherkad now gave me swelled with golden overtones and silvery tintinnabulations of sorrow counterpointed with joy. They filled me with a vast desire to mate with wild she-orcas and to join myself in nuptial ecstasy with the entire world. At the same time, his song incited within me a rage to dive deep into darkness; it made me want to dwell forever with the Old Ones who swim beyond the stars. By the time Pherkad finished intoning this great cry from the heart, I loved him like a brother, and I wanted to die along with him.

'If you are still hungry,' he said to me, 'you may eat me as you did the bear.'

'No, we will not do that,' I promised him, speaking for the rest of my family.

'Then goodbye, Arjuna. Live long and sing well – and stay away from the humans, if you can.'

He swam off, leaving me alone with my family. None of us knew where the Others went to die.

He never *really* left me, however. As the last days of spring gave way to summer's heat, his words began working at me. Unlike the oil that had grieved Alnitak's skin, though, the memories of Pherkad and the bear clung to me with an unshakeable fire. How ironic that I had promised not to eat Pherkad's body, for it seemed that I had devoured something even more substantial, some quintessence of his being that carried the flames of his death anguish into every part of me!

A new dread – or perhaps a very old one called up out of the glooms of the past – came alive inside me. Like a worm, it ate at my brain and insinuated itself into all my thoughts and acts. Dark as the ocean floor it was, yet blinding as the sun – and I could not help staring and staring and being caught in its dazzle. It forced into my mind images of humans: an entire sea of humans, each of them standing on a separate ice floe. And all of these ungainly two-leggeds gripped splinters of wood in their hideous hands. Again and again, they drove these burning splinters into the beautiful bodies of baby whales and into me, straight through my heart.

Although I tried to escape this terrible feeling by swimming through the coldest of waters, it followed me everywhere. At the same time, it lured me back always into the burning sea where all was blackness and death. I could not draw a lungful of clean air, but only oil and smoke. I could not think; I could not sing; I could not breathe.

I could not quenge. Try as I might, I could not find my way into the ocean's innermost part. The loss of life's most basic gift stunned me and terrified me even more. Something was wrong with the world, I knew, and something was hideously, hideously wrong with me.

How I wanted to join Pherkad then! The humans might as well have stuck their wooden splinters into me. Better to fall blind, better to fall mute, better to fall deaf. If I could not quenge, what would be the point in remaining alive?

Upon this thought, the burning that had tormented me grew even worse. Gouts of flame torn from the sun seemed to have fallen upon me. Fire laid bare my tissues one by one and worked its way deep into the sinews of my soul. It opened me completely. In doing so, it finally opened me to the meaning of the note that had whispered so urgently when the bear had died and had cracked out like a lightning bolt after Pherkad had left us. Now I could hear Pherkad calling to me even as Baby Electra called along with the myriad voices of the Old Ones.

The whole world, it seemed, was calling, and I finally heard the sound of my destiny, or at least a part of it: that which I most dreaded doing, I must do. How, though, I asked the cold, quiet sea, could I possibly do it?

2

I wish I could say that I leaped straight toward this destiny, as a dolphin breaches in a graceful arc and snatches a flying fish from the air. I did not. I doubted and hesitated, and I equivocated when I asked myself why I seemed to lack the courage to act. I tried not to listen to the call, even though I could not help *but* listen to its imperative tones during my every waking moment and even while I slept. It pursued me as a band of Others might hunt down a wounded sea lion. It seized me and would not let go.

I spent much time reflecting on my life and life in general. Had it not been, up to the moment I had met the bear, much like the life of any orca? Had I not had good fish to feast upon and the love of my family? Had there not been songs to sing and wonders to behold? Had anything at all been lacking in such a paradise?

And yet the ocean's voice seemed to call me away from all my happiness – but what was it calling me *toward*? What did it want of me? I knew only that it had to do with my gift for languages, and I sensed that this gift would become a very great grief, and soon.

I might never have acted at all had it not occurred to me that my childhood contentment had already been destroyed. I could not quenge. I could *not* – no matter what I tried to do to restore myself to that most natural state.

At first, I tried to hide my affliction from my family. I might as well have tried to hide a harpoon sticking out of my side. One day, while my grandmother was reviewing the tone poem that I could no longer work on, she asked me to counterpoint the penultimate melody with Alsciaukat the Great's Song of the Silent Sea. I could not. When I attempted to do so, I sounded as inept as a child.

'Quenge down along the chord of the first universal,' my grandmother said to me. 'If you are to complete this composition, you must quenge deeper than you ever have.'

The concern in her soft voice tore the truth from me in a shout of anguish: 'I cannot quenge at all, Grandmother!'

I told her everything. I explained how the bear would not stop roaring inside me, where his voice joined Pherkad's cry of rage. All my thoughts, I said, had fixed on human beings as one's teeth might close about a poisonous puffer fish. I could not expunge the images of the two-leggeds from my mind.

'Then you must meditate with more concentration before you quenge,' my grandmother said. 'You must clear your mind.'

'Do you think I have not tried?'

'I am sure you have. Before doing so, however, you must also clear your heart.'

'How can I? Poison is there, and fire! A harpoon has pierced me straight through!'

'What, then, will soothe the poison and draw the harpoon? What will extinguish the flames that consume you?'

'I do not know!'

This was another equivocation. I had a very good idea of what might restore me, even though I could not understand how it possibly could.

'Strange!' she said. 'How very strange that you should believe you cannot find what cannot be lost. It is as if you are swimming

42

so quickly in pursuit of water to cool the fire that you cannot feel the ocean that could put it out.'

'I know! I know! But the very knowingness of my plight makes me want to escape it all the more and to swim ever faster.'

My words troubled my grandmother more than I had ever seen her troubled, even when Baby Capella had been stricken with the fever that had eventually killed her. My grandmother called for a conclave of the family. We sang long into the hours of the midnight sun, discussing what was wrong with me and what might be done.

'I have never heard of an orca unable to quenge,' Alnitak said. 'One might as well imagine being born unable to swim.'

'I have never heard of such a thing either,' Mira agreed. 'It does not seem possible.'

'To quenge is to be, and not to quenge is to be not. But how could that which is ever not be?'

And my brother Caph added, 'Is it not said that the unreal never is and the real never is not? What could be more real than quenging?'

'Didn't Alsciaukat of the Sapphire Sea,' Turais asked, 'teach that quenging can be close to madness? Perhaps Arjuna, in his attempt to ease his grieving over Pherkad, has tried to quenge *too* deeply.'

My practical mother bent her tail to indicate her impatience with these sentiments and said, 'Are we to speculate all night on such things? Or are we to help my son?'

'*How* can we help him?' Mira said.

It turned out that Chara had heard a story that might have bearing on my situation. She told of how an orca named Vindemiatrix had once lost his ability to quenge due to a tumor growing through his brain.

'Very well,' Alnitak said, 'but did the tumor destroy Vindemiatrix's ability to quenge or merely impair his realization that he could not help *but* retain this ability no matter what?'

'In terms of Arjuna's life,' Haedi asked, 'is there a difference?'

Now it was my grandmother's turn to lose patience. The taut

tones in her voice told of her own dislike for useless conjectures: 'It is not a tumor that grows in Arjuna's brain – though we might make use of that as a metaphor.'

'How, Grandmother?' Porrima asked.

'That which grows often may not be killed directly. Sometimes, though, it might be inhibited by other things that grow even more quickly.'

'I have an idea!' young Caph said. 'Let us make a lattice of ideoplasts representing the situation so that Arjuna might perceive in the crystallization of the sounds the way back to himself.'

'Good! Good!' young Naos said. 'Let us also make a simulation of quenging so that Arjuna might be reminded of what he thinks he has lost.'

'And dreams,' Dheneb added. 'Let us help him dream more vividly of quenging when he sleeps.'

'We should recount all our best moments of quenging,' my sister Turais said, 'so that Arjuna might remember himself.'

'Very well,' my grandmother said, 'we shall do these things, and we shall sing to Arjuna, as we sing to a child to drive away a fever. We must sing as we have never sung before, for Arjuna is sick in his soul.'

And so my family tried to heal me. We swam on and on toward the ever-receding western horizon where dark clouds hung low over choppy seas. I felt the sun waxing strong as summer neared its solstice, though the clouds most often obscured this fiery orb.

Nothing, it seemed, could cool my wrath of despair. The songs my grandmother poured into me – rich, sparkling, lovely – came the closest to helping me dive once more into the waters of pure being. So deep did I wish to dive, right down to the magical Silent Sea, lined with coral in bright colors of yellow, magenta, and glorre! So full of my grandmother's love did I feel that I almost did – almost.

However, the harder my family worked to make me whole,

the more keenly did I become aware of what I had lost. I partook of *their* quenging vicariously, which made me long all the more bitterly for my own. In the end, my family could do little more for me than reassure me of their devotion. All their stratagems of representing, simulating, dreaming, remembering, and even singing failed. All are quenging, yes, and yet are not — not unless done with an utter awareness that one *is* quenging in doing them.

'Thank you,' I said to my family, 'you have done all that you could.'

It was a day of layered clouds in various shades of gray pressing down upon the sea. The waters had a brownish tint and seemed nearly lifeless, colored as they were with the umber tones of my family's despondency.

'What ails you?' Caph cried out in frustration.

His anguish touched off my own, and I cried back, 'The humans do!'

I could not help myself. I told Caph and the rest of my family of the call that I heard and all that I had so far concealed.

'Poison is there in me, and fire!' I said. 'A harpoon has pierced me straight through! The humans have done this thing, and only the humans with their hideous, hideous hands can draw it out.'

'How? How?' Caph asked me.

'We must journey to the humans,' I said. 'They are the cause of my sickness, and they must also be the cure.'

'But how?' Caph asked again. 'You have not said how they could help you.'

'I do not know how,' I said. 'That is why we must go to the humans and talk to them.'

Caph laughed at this, sending bitter black waves of sound rippling through the water.

'Talk to the humans? What will we say to them? What do you expect them to say to *you*?'

One could, of course, talk to a walrus, a crab, even a jellyfish.

And each could talk back, in its own way. Caph, however, sensed that I was hinting at communicating with the humans on a higher level than that of the common speech of the sea.

'We must ask the humans why they killed Pherkad,' I said, 'and how they set fire to water. We must speak to them, from the heart, as we speak to ourselves.'

Alnitak swam up and moved his massive body between Caph and me. 'We could speak all we wish, but how could the humans possibly understand what we say?'

'We can teach them our language,' I said.

At this, Alnitak began laughing in bright madder bands of scorn, and so did Turais, Mira, Chara, and Caph. I might as well have suggested teaching a stone to recite the fundamental philosophical mistake. All things have language, yes, but everyone knew that only whales possess the higher orders of intelligence and the ability to reason and speak abstractly. Only whales make art out of music. And surely – surely, surely, surely! – whales alone of all creatures could quenge.

Baby Porrima, the most innocent of my family, asked me, 'Do you really think the humans could be intelligent like us?'

Before I could answer, Caph said, 'We have watched their winged ships that fly through the sky and land upon the water. Have we any reason to suppose that the humans are more intelligent than the geese who do the same, but with much more grace?'

'I should not put their intelligence that high,' my sister Nashira said in her bewildered but beautiful voice. 'We have all beheld the ugliness of the metal shells that carry the humans across the water. Even a snail, though, within its perfectly spiraled shell, makes a more esthetically pleasing protection. I should say that the humans cannot be more intelligent than a mollusk.'

Her assessment, though, proved to be at the lower end of my family's estimation of human intelligence. Dheneb argued that humans likely surpassed turtles in their mental faculties even though it seemed doubtful that they had figured out how to live as long.

Chara placed the upper limit of the humans' percipience near that of seals, who after all knew well enough not to swim in shark-darkened waters whereas the humans did not. My grandmother futilely reminded us that intelligence could not be determined from the outside but only experienced from within. Finally, after much discussion, my family reached a consensus that humans were probably about as smart as an octopus, whose grasping tentacles the humans' hands somewhat resembled. Their generosity in according humans this degree of sentience surprised me, for the octopi are among the cleverest of the ocean's creatures, even if they cannot speak in the manner of a whale.

In a way – but only in a way – my family played a game in this guessing in order to sublimate their disquiet. We all knew that humans possessed a strange, fell power. None of us, however, wanted to entertain the notion that this power might derive from anything like that which we knew as intelligence. None of us except me.

'We cannot say if humans might learn to speak our language,' I said, 'unless we try to teach them.'

Everyone, of course, recognized the logic of my argument, and so it saddened me when my family rejected its conclusion.

After further discussion, my grandmother announced, 'We cannot journey to the humans out of the remote possibility that they might be sentient enough for us to speak with them. It is too dangerous.'

Too dangerous! Would it be less dangerous to do nothing? The bear cried out through the water: Why did the ice melt around me? And Pherkad called to me in the bitter, beautiful tones of his death poem that told of his agony and the suffering of the entire world.

'Very well,' I said to my grandmother. 'Then I will go to the humans alone.'

If a comet had struck the waves just then, the shock of it could not have been greater. No orca of our kind ever left his family.

My mother's response cracked out swift and sure. In this instance, she had no need to confer with the rest of us.

'You cannot leave us,' she told me. 'Would you tear out my heart and feed it to the sharks?'

'You will always have my heart, as I do yours.'

'You will die without me. And how can you think of abandoning your little brother? I need you to watch over him when I am quenging far away. You are the best caretaker I have ever known.'

'I am sorry, Mother, but I must leave.'

My unheard-of willfulness occasioned another conclave, the longest that my family had ever held. For three days we talked as we journeyed through blue-gray water grown gelid and nearly still. Dheneb and Alnitak dove beneath icebergs so that in the denser waters of the deeps, they might hear their confidences more clearly. Turais and Chara visited with the Old Ones and drank in their wisdom, while Nashira sang again and again the melodies of the great songs that told of the deeds of the heroes of our people.

My grandmother meditated and dreamed and sang, too. She called my family to swim together. We breathed at the same moment and glided along side by side, synchronizing each beat of flipper and fluke and moving across the sea like a single wave. We breathed and let our thoughts ripple through us like a wave of shared blood as we quenged together – all save me. Like the still point of a storm, my grandmother served as the center around which all my family's separate impulses and mentations turned and flowed and became as one:

'Like the great north current,' Alnitak said, 'Arjuna will go where he will go.'

'Can one stop the turning of the ocean?' Haedi added.

'Do not the Old Ones say,' Mira asked, 'that each whale has a single destiny?'

'How,' Turais said, 'can we ask Arjuna to go on swimming with us in so much pain? Who could bear the sadness of not being able to quenge?'

Mira, having fallen nostalgic, said, 'Let Arjuna know his old joy again. Do you remember how when he was a baby he tried to talk to Valashu, the Morning Star?'

'How could we forget that?' Dheneb said. 'How can we ever forget how he talked with Pherkad, who gave him his magnificent song?'

'The Old Ones,' Chara affirmed, 'say that they have heard Arjuna's great song. It must be that he will have returned from the humans in triumph to complete his rhapsody.'

The emotion of the last few days proved too much for Baby Talitha. She began crying even as my mother said: 'I will want to die if Arjuna leaves us, but I think I *would* die if he remains and is so sad that he does not want to live.'

Finally, with all my family exhausted, my grandmother gathered all their many chords into a decision that had grown more and more obvious:

'You must leave us,' my grandmother said to me.

'I cannot,' I told her. I listened to Talitha crying and crying. 'I cannot – but somehow I must.'

My family formed into a circle in the quiet silvery water, our heads touching so that the slightest pressure of our flutes would send our words sounding deep into each other.

'Listen to me, Arjuna,' my grandmother said. 'No matter how far you journey, your heart will beat with ours and we will breathe the same breath. There is nowhere that you can go that we will not be.'

We broke apart and I prepared to leave. I gathered in those vital things that would help me on my way: Alnitak's maps of the ocean and the heavens; Mira's taxonomy of the sea's manifold creatures; the epics composed by Aldebaran the Great; the music of Talitha's laughter and reverberations of my mother's first words to me. One thing only remained that I would need.

'Come with me,' my grandmother said to me. 'Let us swim together for a while.'

We moved off away from the rest of our family. It was a cloudless day, and the low sun cast long rays of light down into the dark turquoise water. There, in the calm and clarity, in the heart of the ocean where one could hear its deepest secrets, my grandmother made a present that would protect me: she gave me a charm, alive with the most powerful of all magics, that I might never lose myself on my journey and would always find my way home.

After that, I swam toward the south and east. I swam so quickly at first that the icy sea did seem to cool my ire, if only a little. Soon I found myself racing through unknown waters. If I did not distance myself from my family with all the speed that I could summon, I feared that my courage would fail and I would turn back.

After a long time I grew tired. The muscles along my belly, tail, and flukes ached. I breached, blew out a great cloud of mist, and drew in a fresh breath. I dove down a little way into the water and hung suspended in motionlessness.

The sea about me tasted odd, perhaps flavored by unusual organisms or the upwelling of minerals that were unfamiliar to me. The waters were tinted a deep violet, with undertones of an eerie cerulean blue that I had never beheld. The entire ocean glowed – with sunlight from the cold-striated sky sifting down through the water, yes, but even more from the sonance that filled the ocean's immensity and reverberated through every drop of it. I heard the faint singing of a humpback somewhere ahead of me and the thumping of my heart much nearer. From far away came the call that had summoned me on this journey. It sounded out as primeval as the first whale's first breath, at once plosive and soft, reassuring and terrifying, horrible and beautiful. Into it I must venture, through an ocean whose quality had grown more and more mysterious. Through this unknown realm I must find my way where all was strange, various, and new, and the water itself somehow seemed too real.

For the first time in my life, I became aware of a kind of soul-eating silence: among all the purling sounds of the sea, I could detect not the slightest note made by one of my family. Of course, whenever I wished, I could go down inside myself and listen to Talitha's giggles or my mother's lullabies as clearly and with as much immediacy as if these two beloved people were singing right beside me. No difference could I hear in the actuality of volume, note, or timbre. It was not, however, the same, for I could not *feel* the sound waves emanating from my mother's body, nor could I see her or touch her. My family seemed to have swum off to a distantly-remembered world and to have left me all alone.

In a wave of disquiet sweeping through me, I realized that an orca sundered from his family is an orca in danger of falling mad. If Alnitak, Chara, and the others did not swim beside me and sing to me, should I then sing to myself? Were my thoughts and words to return to me untouched by the minds of my family as if I had eaten and re-eaten the same food again and again? How could I ever heal myself with my own songs? How could I know myself without the sound of their love reflecting back a picture for me to see? Did the lightning scar still mark me above my eye? Had my mother really named me Arjuna on the day of my birth or was that memory just part of a dream, along with myself and all the rest of my life?

Brooding upon such things made matters even worse. I seemed strange to myself. I could not quenge, and I did not know if I could any longer even love. I felt fearsome and new, as if I had been remade into some dreadful form that I did not *want* to behold.

I began swimming again. I came upon a school of herring, each of whose scales were all silvery and streaked with faint gold and scarlet bands. I swam right into the school and stunned many of the fish with a slap of my tail. Others I immobilized with zangs of sonar or confused by blowing out clouds of bubbles. So ravenous was I that I nearly began eating without asking the doomed fish if they were ready to die. I finally remembered myself, however, and I did ask. The entire school, in their ones and their multitudes, said yes.

The feast strengthened me and gave me new life. I might have died in my soul, while my harpooned heart bled out the best part of me – even so, my body and my force of will seemed to have gained a new power. I swam on at speed into the wild, endless sea.

On a day of dead calm with the water stilled into a vast blue mirror, I heard cries from far off long before I encountered the whales who had made them. I swam toward this terrible keening. After a while, I intercepted two large humpbacks, the water streaming from their lumpy, barnacle-studded bodies whenever they breached for breath. They were moving as fast as they could in the direction from which I had come. I asked them what was wrong. In their very basic and nearly incomprehensible speech, they shouted: 'Humans blood pain death!'

Their panic communicated into me, and I considered turning around and joining them in their spasm of flight. Instead, I swam on straight toward the sea's wavering horizon.

Very soon, one of the humans' gray ships appeared there. I swam in close enough to make out metal spines sticking up from the top of the ship; these reminded me of a conch shell's many points and projections. Humans – the first I had ever seen! – stood on the top of the ship, near its head. They were tending to what looked like a long piece of seaweed that connected the ship to the bloody water. A shrieking sound like metal eating metal vibrated both ship and sea, and the seaweed thing began moving toward the ship. I zanged the seaweed and determined it was made of metal, like the ship. It continued moving, and soon the whale attached to it emerged from the water tail first, even as I had been born. A moment later, I caught sight of the bloody harpoon that had torn a great hole through the humpback's body and had killed it. The harpoon, too, was made of metal, unlike the wooden one that had killed Pherkad.

Upon this horror, panic seized me. The ship loomed above, vast and ugly, gray and angular, like a deformed mockery of one of the deep gods. How helpless I felt against this monster of metal! I wanted to fling myself away from this vile place as quickly as I could.

How, though, could I do this? Was I not an orca of the Blue Aria Family of the Faithful Thoughtplayer Clan. Had not my mother, just before my birth, instructed me in the orcas' ways?

'Fear,' she had told me, 'might signal a need for prudence, but you may never act out of fear alone.'

Had I not an urgent need for prudence? Why should I *not* evade this grotesque mountain of metal and the men upon it who might murder me?

Then I felt strange and powerful vibrations pierce my body. High upon the ship, one of the humans stretched out one of his tentacles toward me. Sounds like a seal's barks burst out from the hole his mouth made. The vibrations grew stronger, and I realized a thing: the humans had sonar! Somehow, these small-headed humans had sonar and were zanging me!

Flight, then, would be futile. I knew from the old tales that the humans' ship could move through the water more swiftly than I, perhaps not over short distances, but through mornings and afternoons of exhausting pursuit. With the ocean so peaceful and still, I would not even be able to find a wave that I might hide behind.

I did not want to hide. Had I abandoned my family in order to do such a craven thing? Had Pherkad given his death poem to a coward? No, no, no! I had ventured into this strange realm of harpoons and metallic sonar so that I might talk to humans, not flee from the first of them who came my way. The worst they could do to me (or so I told myself) was to slay me as they had the humpback who hung all bloody and broken, suspended in the air. They might strike a real harpoon through my real heart; they might use their metal things to tear me apart before they ate me, but do not all beings thus someday die?

'You will die young,' my grandmother had told me. 'Either that, or you will add something new to the Song.'

It was time to prove her prophecy right. Gathering in her charm close to my heart, I swam up to the ship. I came up out of the water, spy-hopping so that the humans might better see me and hear my words:

'My name is Arjuna, and I have journeyed far from my home that I might speak with you. So many things I have to say! So much I would ask you! Do you have names yourselves that you can share with me? Why are you here? Are you not creatures of the continents? Are there not enough animals there for you to eat? The animals of the sea are for themselves alone. We *are* that we might know joy. Do you know the same? Do you know the Song of Life? If you do, why do you make the ocean burn with a terrible fire? Why do you melt the world's ice? Why did you kill my brother Pherkad?'

I did not expect them to answer me or even understand what I said to them. If they really *were* sentient, however, I hoped they might at least grasp that I was trying to talk to them. Would they return the favor by giving their words to me?

High above me, some of the humans made sounds and watched me while others continued drawing the humpback up through the air and onto the ship. The dead whale vanished from my sight, and I supposed that the humans had started the work of tearing him apart and eating him. Then one of the humans set a new harpoon in the metal thing that had connected the seaweed to the humpback. The human looked at me as the metal thing turned and the harpoon aligned in my direction.

'Would you kill me, too?' I called out to the humans. Then I remembered Pherkad's final offer to me and my grandmother's charm. 'If you need my flesh, you might have it – let me help you!'

I dove down into the water, then up and up. With a mighty

beat of my tail, I breached and propelled myself out of the water and high into the air. Drops of water whipped from my body, and the wind thrilled my skin. Thus did I come as close to the humans as I could. Thus, in what might have been the last moments of my life, did I fly. Had I been able to quenge, I would have kept on soaring right up to the stars only to splash down into Agathange's lovely ocean.

For an eternity, I hung motionless in space, waiting for the humans to pierce me with their harpoon. At last I fell back into the sea. Had I not leaped high enough? Had I not turned my belly toward them so that the harpoon might more easily gain entrance to my vital organs? Again I pushed myself into the air, this time turning in a pirouette so that the humans might strike their harpoon wherever they wished. And again, and again, leaping and spinning and flying and splashing into the sparkling waters.

After a while, I grew tired of repeating this feat. I noticed that the human who had been looking along the harpoon's length had moved over to the others gathered on top of the ship at a lower point. I became aware that the humans above me were doing something peculiar with their murderous hands: they brought them together over and over, sending out loud cracks that sounded something like a whale's tail slapping the surface of the sea. With their mouths and the flaps of flesh that covered their teeth, they made shrill sounds that somewhat mimicked a whale's whistles. How their antics excited me! Perhaps, I thought, I really *could* teach these bizarre animals to speak.

I began with the simplest and most basic of essentials, the first thing an orca learns long before he is born: one of the sets of sounds denoting the actuality of the ocean. I trilled out the variations on these sounds even as I slapped the water with my tail so that these small-headed creatures might have a visual representation of the magical substance of which I spoke. Again I trilled and whistled as clearly as I could, hoping with a great, glowing hope that the humans might at least somewhat duplicate the whistle's pitch and overtones. Instead, they made other sounds altogether, and did something that appalled me.

Two of them, working together, cast pieces of a humpback's body into the water. I studied the barnacles covering gray skin and the bits of bloody fat that stuck to it. Why did they cast away good food? I did not know. Then I had a disturbing thought: they wanted to share it with me!

'Thank you, humans, for your generosity,' I chirped out. Then I told them of the First Covenant, which my people had made with the Others: 'Thank you and thank you, but I may not eat the flesh of any animal who breathes air.'

Two more of the humans above me came up to the edge of the ship. They carried an object which somewhat resembled a huge, white shell. After setting it down on the top of the ship, they began casting its contents toward me chunk by bloody chunk. It astonished me to see pieces of black and white hide and red muscle splash into the sea. These tidbits, I knew, could only have come from an orca – and probably one of Pherkad's family. Could this be, I wondered, the last of Baby Electra?

'What is wrong with you!' I shouted. 'Do you think that I am a cannibal, that I would eat one of my own?'

I told them of the Second Covenant, that an orca may not harm another orca.

'Are you insane, that you would do such a thing!' I shouted. 'Cast yourselves into the ocean, and then we shall see what I eat!'

Of course, I would have done no such thing. For the Third Covenant, the sacred Great Covenant, forbade the orcas from harming humans, even though the humans might seek to harm them.

For a while, I waited amidst the carnage in the water as the humans instead began flinging their sounds at me. I understood nothing of their speech, if indeed there was anything of substance to understand. Could the humans truly be sentient? I felt certain that in trying to feed me parts of another orca, they had nearly proved their inanity. Perhaps Nashira had been right in her estimation that the humans had minds like those of mollusks.

Why, then, should I continue my journey? Logic told me that these humans *might* be as different from others elsewhere as my family was from Pherkad's kind, but what were the chances of that being true? Were not all humans human, just as all orcas were orcas? Would they not therefore think and act in more or less uniform ways?

I might have turned back then but for three things: First, I knew how perilous it was to reason from perhaps unfounded assumptions and scant evidence. Second – and how this thought amazed me! – what if the humans had tried to feed me orca flesh because they themselves were cannibals who saw nothing wrong with humans putting tooth to each other? Perhaps they had never made a covenant among themselves that humans should not harm humans.

The third thing that kept me from swimming back to my family was that the two-leggeds seemed to lose interest in me. They retreated from the edge of the ship, which coughed out a great roar from its underside and began moving off toward the west. Soon, I was alone in the ocean. The way south, the way towards more sensitive humans who might have the wit to learn a little language, lay open before me.

3

On my long voyage toward warmer waters, I had much time to ponder my first encounter with the humans. I revisited each sound and sensation of our bizarre interaction, savoring them as I might the taste of new fish. The new realm that I had entered, already unnerving in so many ways, seemed to grow ever stranger. At its heart lay a mystery that I somehow had to try to understand: What *were* human beings and how had they come to be?

None of our natural histories accounted for these two-leggeds. Mira told of the taxa and the cladding of the fish, the flatworms, the jellied cnidarians and other sea creatures, but of the animals of the land, even the Old Ones knew little. For ages my ancestors had watched the helpless human apes hunting crabs and clams along the beaches of the continents. And then one day, scarcely a few generations ago, humans had taken to the sea in boats and ships and had begun hunting even the blue whales, who are the greatest animals ever to have lived on our world. How could such a thing have happened?

'It is not natural,' I heard my mother say to my grandmother as I relived one of their many conversations. 'The humans do not seem to be a part of nature.'

As I swam through flowing blue seas rich with herring, squid, sponges, and kelp, I thought about my mother's words. What did it mean to be natural? Was a shark more natural than a human because most of this ancient fish's activities consisted of basic functions such as hunting, eating, excreting, and mating? Were humans *unnatural* because they seemed to spend most of their lives doing things with the multifarious objects they had made with their hands? Was it their very ability to *make* things such as monstrous metal ships that made them unnatural?

'Even a snail,' my sister Nashira had said, 'within its perfectly spiraled shell makes a more esthetically pleasing protection.'

Snails make shells, and walruses make tusks, and all aquatic animals make the substance of their bodies out of the substance of the sea – but they do not make things other than themselves and their offspring. They do not make harpoons, nor do they set fire to the sea.

'The humans,' I said to my mother as if she swam beside me, 'make things that change nature.'

'Even so,' my grandmother broke in, 'if the humans came out of nature even as we did, how can they be called unnatural?'

Because my grandmother loved recursion and paradox, I said, 'Then let us say that humans are that part of nature for which it is natural to be unnatural.'

With that definition, I left the matter, although a gnawing feeling in my belly warned me that I had not bitten nearly deep enough into humanity's soul, which might be beyond understanding. Someday, I sensed, and perhaps soon, I would need to reexamine all my assumptions if I continued my journey.

I decided I must. My course took me along an ancient route used by my ancestors. I navigated by the currents and the config-uration of the coastlines, by the pull of the earth upon my blood and by the push of my family's songs that sounded in my head – and, of course, I found my way by the stars. The Stingray constellation pointed its reddish tail toward storied fishing grounds while the blue lights of the Great Crab came into sight whenever

I breached for breath on a cloudless night. And always, the north star shone behind me, reminding me from which direction I had come and toward which I must someday return.

I encountered storms whose icy winds made mountains out of water, and I journeyed on through long days of hot sun and lengthening nights. I warned away sharks who wanted to steal my catch of salmon; I made my way through yet more storms and surfed along great waves. Nothing about the ocean deterred me, for was I not of the water and an orca at that? Rarely did I cease moving, and I never slept.

That is, I never slept completely, for had I done so, I would have breathed water and drowned. Always I remained at least half awake, the right part of me aware of the sea's features and my movements while my left half slept – or the reverse. Through undulations of seaweed brushing my sides and cold currents raking my skin with claws of ice, I watched myself sleeping, and I listened to myself dream.

What dreams I had! Many were of eating or speaking or mating. Too many concerned the humans. In the foods that humans fed me with their hands in the more disturbing of these dreams, I tasted flavors new to me along with the dearly remembered sweetness of my mother's milk. I sang a strange song with the first of the beautiful she-orcas who would bear my children; I listened in wonder to my grandmother's death poem, which somehow rang out from the mouth of a human being whose face I could never quite behold.

One dream in particular moved me. It began with a human feeding me a salmon whose insides were poisoned from the same black oil that had fouled the burning sea. The fish hardened in my belly like a lump of metal. It seemed to grow as massive as a marlin inside me, and its density pulled me down in the water – and down and down. The world began narrowing into darkness. I held my breath against the dread of the ocean's immense pressures that would soon crush me to a purplish pulp. I felt myself suffocating as the pull of the earth forced me into a tunnel that grew tighter and tighter. Soon, I knew, the whole of my body and my being would be squeezed smaller than a jellyfish, a diatom, an atom of sand. My awareness would shrink into a single point in space and time. I would die a horrible death all alone at the bottom of the sea.

'No, no, no!' I shouted to my family who could not hear me.

I did not want to die by myself in silent darkness; even more, I did not want to return to being again and once again find myself forced into the endless, bloody tunnel of life. How bitterly I cried out in protest in being born anew into a doomed world whose every ocean and continent was choked with the burning black oil of death.

'Grandmother! Grandmother!' I cried. 'How can you let this be?'

How, I asked myself, could *I* let it be?

I could not. And so I called out as loud as I could to my sleeping self. With a start and a shock of reality rushing in, I felt myself awakening within my dream. Now the whole sea sang with brilliant sound, and light devoured darkness. I could move wherever I willed myself to move, and I could dream whatever I desired to dream.

I swam up through the brightening layers of water, and up and up. I breached, blew out stale breath, and drew in a great lungful of air that tasted fresh and clean. I swam toward the great eastern sun. I came upon a beach where many humans frolicked in the breaking waves.

One of the females swam to me. Except for the hair on her head and between her legs, she was all golden skin from her face to her feet, and her eyes were as bright as black pearls. She climbed on top of my back and pressed the flesh of her inner legs against my skin. I swam some more with this female gripping me and caressing me with her soft, human hands. She sang to me a soft, lovely human song.

I understood her strange but beautiful words! I sang back, and she understood me! For a long time, with the water streaming past us and flying off into air in a silvery spray, we spoke of poetry and pain and babies and the immense majesty of life. She described her delight in joining her dream with mine, and I told her of the Aurora Borealis which she had never seen.

I swam with her toward the inextinguishable Northern Lights. With a mighty beat of my tail, I drove us up out of the water, and I began swimming up along the Aurora's emerald arc. The sky deepened even as it opened out before us. Its startling blueness gave way to an enveloping black all full of light.

To the stars I swam, with the human laughing and singing on top of me. Not one murmur of fear could I make out in her soft voice, even as we flew past Agathange and the lights of the universe began streaming past us like the notes of a great cosmic song. So many stars there were in the universe, almost as many as drops of water in the sea! Urradeth and Solsken, Silvaplana and the Rainbow Double – we touched the radiance of these fiery orbs and a myriad of others in our wild rush into the heart of creation. We spoke with words and songs and an even brighter thing to the deepest part of each other. Thus we came close to that perfect, starlit interior ocean, and we almost quenged together – almost.

And then at last, as entire universes of stars began whirling past us and it seemed we might become lost, the human so close to me *did* fall into fear, a little. So did I. My grandmother had told me that no matter how far I swam from my family, I would always find my way home – but was that true? I did not have the courage to put her reassurance to the test. And so I allowed the pull of my birth world once again to take hold of me. We began falling back through space along the same sparkling route we had come – falling and falling down toward the waters of the world that the frightened human on my back called earth and I knew as Ocean.

We splashed into cold, clear water. The jolt and shiver of my return awakened me from my dream. I knew that I had reentered normal consciousness because the forms and features of the world seemed at once *less* real than the magnificence of my dream and excruciatingly real in a way that could not be denied. I looked around me with my sonar and my eyelight, and I saw that I had entered a broad channel. To the east, great, toothed mountains jutted out of a mist-laden forest, while low, green hills covered the land to the west. I could not detect the human female who had accompanied me to the stars.

And then, across the channel's clear water, I thought I saw her standing on a flat wooden-like object and surfing the waves made by a speeding boat, the way that dolphins are said to do. I had never attempted such sport. Of course, I had surfed the great waves of the Blue Mountains and the waves of light flowing out from the stars beyond Arcturus, but would the much smaller wake produced by a human's boat support the mass of an orca such as I?

I *had* to discover if it would; I had to know if the human surfing behind the boat was the one from my dream. After taking a great breath of air, I dove and burst into furious motion, swimming as fast as I could. Water streamed around me. I drove my flukes so hard that my muscles burned, and I drew closer. I wondered what force propelled the boat almost flying on top of ocean above me? I flew now, too, swimming up so that I breached into the froth of the wave, just behind the surfing human. One of the other humans watching on the boat pointed a hand at me and shouted out an incomprehensible sound identical to one of the sounds made by the man on the ship: 'Orca!'

The human standing on the water turned to look at me.

'Hello!' I said through the spray. 'Hello! Hello! My name is Arjuna!'

I whistled and chirped and asked her if she remembered our journey to the stars. So long had we swum across the universe! Was she hungry, I asked her? Did she like salmon? I opened my mouth to show her my strong, white teeth which had caught so many salmon, and I promised that I would share with her all the fish she could eat.

Again, the humans on the boat let loose a harsh bark that might have indicated distress: 'Orca! Orca! Orca!'

The surfing human looked ahead of her at the spreading wave, and behind her again – and then she fell, plunging into the surf. She made thrashing motions with her tentacle-like limbs, which brought her head up out of the water. In this way she swam, after a fashion.

I moved in closer to her. I saw that she could not be the human who had ridden upon my back, for her hair was nearly as yellow as a lemon fish, and the skin of her face and lower appendages was as creamy as mother's milk. The rest of her, however, was as black as the black parts of me. How beautiful, I thought, this variegation of light and dark! However, when I swam in and nudged her with my face, desiring the pleasure of flesh slicking flesh, I felt only a spongy roughness that repelled me. Puzzled, I zanged the human up and down her body. I heard the echoes of a *second* skin, a much softer skin, just beneath this black outer covering. Could it be, I thought, that humans make a false skin to protect them as they fabricate other unnatural things?

As I debated carrying or pushing this rather helpless human back to the land, the boat turned and moved our way. I watched as she swam over to it and used her limbs in the manner of an octopus to fasten onto the boat and pull herself out of the water. She stood with three others of her kind, the water running off her ugly, false skin. The humans next to her displayed similar coverings, though of flimsier substance and in colors of blue, green, purple, and bright red.

'It *is* an orca!' one of the humans said. 'Look at the size of him!'

I understood nothing of the meaning of the ugly sounds they made – if indeed they meant anything at all. Even so, I determined to memorize every tone, patter, and inflection in case all their squealing and barking proved to be something like true language.

'My name is Arjuna,' I told them, 'of the Blue Aria family of the Faithful Thoughtplayer Clan. I have journeyed far to talk with you – will you try to talk with me?'

'Oh my God, he's huge! What a bodacious bohemeth!'

'I think you mean behemoth.'

'Whatever. Let's just call him Bobo.'

'Hey, lil' Bobo, what are you doing all alone chasing after surfers?'

The humans gathered at the edge of the boat. One lay flat on its surface and lowered a hand toward the water.

'I failed,' I said, moving even closer, 'to speak with other humans on the northern ocean. That might have been because they truly could not learn what I tried to teach them, as might prove true with you. Or perhaps the problem lies in an insufficiency of patience on my part, or worse, a failure of my imagination. But one cannot imagine what one cannot imagine. And what seems strange to me past all understanding is how you – or, I should say, your cousins the whale hunters – could not understand the simplest of significants for the most common substance on the world that we share.'

I slapped the surface of the sea with both flipper and tail, even as I said, 'Water!' To emphasize the word, I took in a mouthful of water and sprayed it out so that it wetted the human lying on the boat.

'Water! Water! Water!'

'Oh my God, he soaked me! Looks like Bobo wants to play!'

'Water. Water. Water.' Now I spoke more slowly, as slow as I could, and I toned down the harmonies so that even a jellyfish might hear them. 'Water. Water. Water. Water. Water.'

'It's almost like he's trying to tell us something!'

Did her utterances signify anything? I could not tell. Even so, I continued memorizing them for later review – and I contemplated each spike and wave of each of their grunts as they made them.

I noticed that whenever these humans phonated, they opened their mouths to let the sounds out, as anuses let go of waste. How bizarre! How awkward! How undignified!

Thinking that it might help to imitate them, I opened my mouth even as I pushed out the sacred sound from the flesh higher on my head: 'W-a-t-e-r!'

'Look at those teeth! I'll bet he's hungry. What do you think an orca eats?'

'He'll eat *you* if you don't get your arm out of the water.'

'No, if he was that hungry, he could've eaten Kelly when she wiped out. I don't think orcas eat people.'

'What do they eat?'

'Seals and penguins and things like that.'

'Do you think he'd eat some fish?'

'Did you *bring* any fish?'

'I've got a peanut butter and jelly sandwich.'

'Did you ever give a dog peanut butter? They lick their teeth for like an hour 'cause they can't get it off.'

'We're *not* going to give an orca peanut butter!'

'What do you think he wants?'

I moved in as close to the boat as I could.

'Listen! Listen! Listen!' I said. I spoke as slowly as I could. 'W-wait-wait-wait-A-wait-wait-wait-T-wait-wait-wait-E-wait-wait-wait-R!'

'I don't know, but it sounds like he's in distress.'

'I think he just wants attention. He's a pushy little whale.'

'Maybe we should play him some music. I hear whales like music.'

'What kind?'

'I don't know – what do you have?'

One of the humans, with a hairy face and a second skin of sheeny blue, lifted a black object onto the wooden surface near the boat's tail. He did something to it with the tentacles of his hands.

'I hope he likes it.'

A great noise burst from the black object and broke through the air. The noise drove against my skin and set the very water around me humming. It took a few moments for me to realize that the noise comprised different strands of sound: human voices and howling vibrations and a relentless thumping like that of a heart beating with an insane rhythm.

Boom boom anger anger anger! Boom boom anger anger anger! Boom boom . . .

'Please stop!' I cried out. 'It hurts my head, hurts my soul!'

I came up out of the water, spy-hopping, which brought my head nearly level with the booming black thing. I opened my mouth, thinking I might be able to snatch it from between the human's hands and crush it between my jaws.

'Look! Bobo is smiling! He likes it – turn it louder!'

Boom! Boom! Boom . . .

As other humans had set fire to the sea's surface with their dirty oil, these humans made even the water itself sick with sound. Although I longed to speak with them – particularly with the yellow-haired female – I had to get away from them and their boat as quickly as I could. I dove, but at first that only exacerbated the torment of the hideous noise, for sound moves more quickly and completely through water than it does through air. Only by swimming as far as I could away from the boat would I be able to make the noise attenuate to a distant and tolerable irritation.

And swim I did. For the rest of that day, and during the days that followed, I explored the large bay I had entered. I never really escaped the noise of the humans, for they were everywhere on the bay and on the shore surrounding it. Many boats disturbed the bay's blue waters, and most of them sent high-pitched, shrieking sounds piercing every nook and cove. From the forests rising up from the sea came a similar buzz and clash, as if the very air were being torn apart. From time to time, great trees broke into splinters and crashed to the earth. Humans dropped the bare spines of the tree's corpses into the water with splash after tremendous splash.

How long, I wondered, would I be able to live amidst this cacophony without falling as insane as the humans themselves seemed to be? Could I bear another day, another hour, another moment? Somehow, I told myself, I *had* to bear it. In the way my mother had showed me many years before, I must learn to dwell within softer, interior sounds called up from memory or imagination, which would overpower all the human noise and drive it away.

It dismayed me that the humans fouled the pretty bay with things other than noise. I found floating on the water many objects that the humans cast from their boats. Some were second skins made of that highly shapeable substance the humans used for so many unfathomable purposes. Because I needed a name for this unnatural substance, I thought of it as excrescence. Excrescence composed most of the objects the humans handled, as it did the bodies of their boats. I zanged as well metallic and clear stone shells from which they drank various liquids. Everywhere I went, the water tasted of oils suppurating from their boats and from the bitter cream the humans rubbed into their skin.

Except for the ubiquitous excrescence, which could be found floating in island-like masses even on the northern oceans, the worst of the humans' befoulment was the feces that poured from many streams into the bay. Why, I wondered, did humans drop their feces into water when they were creatures of the land? Why did they concentrate it into a brownish sludge? Did they wish to flavor the water through which they swam? That seemed to me unlikely, for when I put tongue to their feces, I detect traces of boat oil, excrescence, and other poisons that could only have tasted as unpleasant to the humans as they did to me.

I came across a hint of an answer to these questions as I was exploring a peninsula on the east side of the bay. Two tongues of land licked out from the peninsula's tip into the water. On one of these tongues – treeless and covered with grass – humans stood striking shiny metal sticks against spherical white eggs which arced through the air before falling to earth and rolling across the grass. From time to time, one of the eggs, made of yet another kind of excrescence, would sail off the peninsula and plop into the water. Then the humans would call out such stridencies as 'Goddamned ball is unbalanced!' and other sounds that made no sense to me.

On the other bit of land, across a slip of water, trees grew out an expanse of grass. There humans reclined on second skins and cast other kinds of eggs at each other. They burned fish in fires, shouted out cries to each other, and they did a thing with feces that fascinated me.

Some sort of mammal – some looked like little wolves – accompanied many of the humans. Long strands probably made of excrescence connected the two-legged to four-legged. The little wolves would dart about, put nose to ground, and cause the humans' limbs to jerk in whatever direction the wolves chose to move. Whenever the wolves arched their backs to defecate, the humans waited by their sides. At the completion of each defecation, the humans made cooing sounds as if pleased to receive what the wolves had given them. They gathered up the feces in clear skins of excrescence, which they carried proudly in their hands as the wolves led them on a continuation of their erratic journey across the grass.

Why, I wondered, did the humans gather up wolf feces? Did they eat it as snails eat the excretions of fish? Did they lick down the feces of their *own* kind? That could not be possible. And yet, when it came to humans, almost nothing seemed *impossible*. I could be sure of little more than the fact that humans collected feces of varying kinds. Perhaps when these collections grew too large, the humans vented some into the sea.

My puzzlement at the humans' diet caused me to realize that it had been too long since *I* had eaten. I badly wanted and needed to catch a few salmon or perhaps some more delicious herring. However, the channel through which I swam formed a part of the traditional fishing grounds of the Truthful Word Painter Clan. I felt sure that these distant cousins of mine would not begrudge me a few mouthfuls of fish, but good manners dictated that I first ask permission before indulging in such a feast. I had to wait through many days of rumbling in my empty belly before I had a chance to do so. One clear night, with the moon-silvered waters around me rippling in a soft breeze, the orcas of the Scarlett Tiralee family of the Truthful Word Painter Clan swam into the channel and made my acquaintance.

Only six of them did I greet: Mother Agena and her three children, Diadem, Furud, and Mekbuda, and Agena's sister Celaeno, who had recently given birth to Baby Kornephoros. When I asked after their health, Agena told me, 'We are well enough now, though misfortunes have reduced our family, as you can see.'

We spent the rest of night recounting stories and telling of our respective families. I listened with great sadness as Agena described the agonizing death of her mother, who had perished before her time of a mysterious wasting disease. Agena's first child had died in a collision with one of the humans' boats while her second had succumbed to a fever. I related similar woes, though I tried to gloss over my relief that my family had prospered in the face of great trials largely due to my grandmother's guidance. Together we sang songs of mourning and remembrance. Finally just after dawn with the sun red upon a cloud-heavy horizon, I told the Scarlett Word Painters of the white bear and the burning sea, and I explained why I had journeyed so far from home.

'I have never imagined,' Mother Agena said, 'losing my ability to quenge. Would you not be better off dead?'

'I would be, yes,' I replied, 'if I had no hope of regaining from the humans what they have taken from me.'

'You are a wonder of a whale,' Agena said to me. 'You are inquisitive and strong and brave, but you are also prideful and not a little foolish to think that you have been called to speak with the humans. Such hubris, if you persist, will be punished.'

'How so?' I asked.

I did not wish to dispute an elder, particularly not a mother of another clan. I waited for Agena to say more.

'Do you have any idea of how many of the Word Painters have tried to speak with the humans?' Agena slapped her tail against the water and whistled out into the morning air. 'I cannot say whether or not the humans have language or might be sentient, but this I know: if you cleave to them too closely, either their insanity will become yours or else they will murder you.'

This warning more or less ended our conversation, for how could I respond to such bitter despair that masqueraded as wisdom and even prophecy? I did not want to believe Mother Agena's fraught words. I *could* not believe them. And so when it came time to part, I sang farewells and blessings with all the polite passion that I could summon.

'Goodbye, Bright One, marked by lightning and beloved of the sea,' Mother Agena said to me as she nudged the scar over my eye. 'We will not remain in this unfortunate place, which was once our home. It is yours, if you wish. Therefore, you are welcome to all the fish you might find – if the humans let you take them.'

As she moved off with the Word Painters, I pondered the meaning of her last words. Her voice lingered in the water and broke apart into quaverings of ruin that I did not want to hear. I was hungry, and fish abounded all about me. I made my way into the sea's inky forebodings to go find them.

4

For three days of wind and storm, I ranged about the channel hunting salmon to my belly's contentment. I came across many boats. Most of these, while moving across the greenish surface of the bay, emitted a nearly deafening buzz from their underbellies, near their rear. How could these human things make such an obnoxious noise? An impulse drove me toward one of the boat's vibrating parts, obscured by churning water and clouds of silvery bubbles. I wanted to press my face against this organ of sound as I might touch my mouth to the swim bladder of a toadfish to determine how it could be so loud. A second impulse, however, held me back. In a revulsion of ambivalence that was to flavor my interactions with the humans, I realized that I did not want to get *too* near the boat, which was made of excrescence as were so many of the things associated with the humans.

At other times, however, my curiosity carried me very close to these strange, two-legged beings. On a day of gentle swells, when the sky had cleared to a pale blue, I came upon a boat whose humans busied themselves with using strands of excrescence to pull salmon out of the sea. What a clever hunting technique! I thought. I swam in close to the boat to investigate.

One of the humans sighted me, and barked out what seemed to be the human danger cry: 'Orca! Orca! Orca!'

How could I show them that I posed them no threat? Perhaps if I snatched a salmon from the excrescence strands and presented it to them, they would perceive my good intentions. I swam through the rippling water.

'That damned blackfish is after our catch!' A hairy-faced human called out.

His top half nearly doubled over the lower in that disturbingly human way of exercising their strangely-jointed bodies. When he straightened up, he clasped some sort of wooden and metallic stick in his hands.

'What are you doing?' his pink-faced companion called out.

'Just shooting at that damned blackfish!'

'I can see that – but what are you *doing*? Do you want to go to prison for killing a whale?'

'Who would know? Anyway, I'm just going to have a little target practice to scare him off.'

'Put your goddamned gun away!'

'Don't worry, I'm not going to kill him – unless he tries to take our salmon.'

A great noise cracked out; just beside me, the water opened with a small hole which almost immediately closed.

'How did you do that?' I shouted as I moved in toward the boat.

Again the stick made its hideous noise, and again the water jumped in response.

'Once more!' I said, taking a great liking to this game. 'Make the water dance once more!'

I swam in even closer, and the holes touched the water scarcely a tongue's lick from my face. What beguiling powers these humans had! Orcas can stun a fish with a zang of sonar, and the deep gods – who have the Great Voice, the voice of death – kill swarms of squid in this manner. No whale, however, can speak and make the very waters part.

'If you shoot that orca,' the pink-face called out, 'I'm going to shoot you!'

The human holding the wood and metal stick lowered it, and the water moved no more.

'Please, please!' I said. 'Let us play!'

If the humans, though, could not understand the simple word for water, how could they comprehend my more complex request? To show my gratitude that they had possessed the wit to play at all, I caught a salmon and swam right up to the edge of the boat.

'I think he wants us to have it!' the pink-faced human said. 'He's giving us his fish!'

I pushed up out of the water, with the salmon still thrashing between my teeth. Hands reached out to grasp it and take it from me. Then I dove and caught another salmon for the humans, and another. They seemed to like this game.

During the days that followed, I ranged the channel and played games with other humans. Some were as trifling as balancing pieces of driftwood on my face, while others demanded planning and coordination. The humans seemed titillated when I rose up from the deeps near their boats and flew unannounced high into the air. Many times, I surprised their littlest boats, propelled across the channel by lone humans pushing sticks through the water. It was great sport to leap over both boat and human in the same way that Kajam had once leaped over Alnitak's back.

In the course of nearly all these encounters, the humans involved made various vocalizations, for they proved to be among the noisiest of animals. Their voices seemed to reach out to me with a terrible longing, as if the humans hoped to find in me some ineffable thing they could not appreciate within themselves. I sucked up every sound they made and examined their incessant barking and crooning for pattern and possible meaning:

'Hey, look it's Bobo! You can tell it's him by the scar over his eye.'

'I hear he likes to play.'

'What a joyful spirit!'

'He's the spirit of my grandfather who has come to tell us something.'

'I heard that some fisherman took shots at him.'

'He was brought here for some purpose.'

'Look in his eyes – there's more there than in most people.'

'Why is Bobo all alone? What happened to the rest of his pod?'

'I think he's lonely.'

'When he looks at me that way, I can feel my soul dancing.'

As the days shortened toward another winter of cloud and storm, I felt a growing urge to understand the mystery of the humans. Buried inside me, like a pearl in an oyster, I felt a hard realization pressing against my softer tissues of doubt. More and more, I wanted to draw out the pearl and hold it up sparkling in the sun.

I wondered what might explain what I experienced in my forays up and down the channel. I assumed that the humans really did have a keen intelligence, though of a different and lesser quality than that of whales. They must have some sort of language, too, for how else could they organize so many complex activities? During quiet moments when the cold ocean stilled to a vast blue clarity, I could *see* the intelligence lighting up the humans' eyes just as I could feel their desire to communicate with me. Do not the Old Ones say that the eyes sing with the sound of the soul?

My ancestors also tell of the forming of all things in the eternal creation of the world. From out of the oneness of water and its accompanying sound comes love, which can never be wholly distinct from its source. From out of love, in turn, emanate the sacred triadic harmonies of goodness, beauty, and truth. How could one ever marvel ecstatic at the beauty of the rising of the Thallow constellation over the starlit sea without the goodness of the heart to let in the tinkling luminosity? How know goodness absent the truth that all the horrors of life find validation in the love of life that all creatures embrace? The journey to the deepest of love, my grandmother once told me, must always lead through truth, beauty, and goodness. And of these, the waters of truth are much the hardest to navigate.

'Only through quenging into utter honesty with ourselves,' she had said, 'can we hope to become more fully and consciously ourselves. Is this not what the world wants of us? If not, why did the sea separate itself into individual peals of life in the first place? That is why we must always tell the truth. For if we do not, the great song that we make of ourselves will ring false. But, Arjuna, who has the courage to really listen to the cry of one's heart and to embrace the totality of one's own being? Who can even behold it?'

It is a truth universally acknowledged among my kind that one can never hear completely the truth of one's own soul. We cannot make out the ridges and troughs that form the seascapes of our deepest selves, any more than we can zang through miles of dark, turbid waters to study the bottom of the ocean. Then, too, the eye can never see itself, just as I could not look directly at the scar marking my forehead. Worst of all, we avoid doing so with a will toward the expunging of our best senses. As seals seek dark and narrow coves in which to flee the teeth of the orcas, we hide from our truest selves for we do not want to be devoured by the most primeval of all our passions.

'What does any whale really want?' my grandmother had asked. 'Were we not born to be the mightiest of hunters? Do we not, in the end, pursue greater life in ourselves that we might know the infinitely vaster life of the world around us?'

We do, we do – of course we do! And yet in this glorious becoming of our greater selves, as streamlined and lovely as the orcas of Agathange, we must leave behind our lesser selves. This realization of the best and truest within us, though it yields eternal life, always feels like death. One thing only emboldens us to make the journey through life's terrors and agonies to the end of time and the beginning of the world.

How, though, was I to achieve this greatest of purposes absent my family's devotion and encouragement? How, without my mother, Alnitak, Mira, and everyone else, would I come by the pellucid honesty through which I would find my way through the great ocean of truth?

Although I had no answers to these questions, I knew what my grandmother would say: I must begin with the truth that I had grasped but which I was reluctant to really sink my teeth into. After playing many games with the humans, I not only hypothesized that they were intelligent, I zanged it in my heart. Why, though, had I not listened to what I had zanged so deeply?

I thought I knew the reason, and it had to do with an essential paradox: that only through looking out at all the manifold forms and features of the world can we ever apprehend the much stranger phenomena of ourselves. Just as we can see stars only against the blackness of the nighttime sky, so we need others to show us the many ways that we shine as unique sparks of creation. The greater the contrast in this relationship, the deeper the understanding.

For instance, were not females, such as lovely Mother Agena, a part of the great unknown? No other work of nature was more like a male orca such as I, and yet so utterly different. How should I then long to find myself within the wild, wet clutch of her body and even the wilder ocean of her soul? Would it not be, I wondered, that precisely in closing the difference between us and daring to enter the most dangerous place in the universe I would discover an exalted and ecstatic Arjuna whom I might otherwise not ever know?

So it was with the humans. To a whale such as I, their kind beckoned as the Great Other in whom I might discover secrets about myself that I had never suspected. Although it seemed absurd that the humans' intelligence could in any way illuminate my own, I came to realize that I had been hiding from the truth that the humans had something precious to give me.

'O Arjuna, Arjuna!' I cried out, 'that is why you have not wanted to believe what you have zanged so clearly!'

Even as I said these words, however, I knew that I was still evading myself, for I had carried through the waters a deeper reason for denying the humans' obvious intelligence. To admit to myself that humans might have minds anything like those of whales would impel me to want to touch those minds – to *need* to touch them. How could I allow myself to be so weak? How could I bear the terrible truth that I was desperately, desperately lonely?

I *had* to bear it. I had to accept it, for my grandmother had also said this to me: 'If you bring forth what is inside you, what you bring forth will save you. If you do not bring forth what is inside you, what you do not bring forth will destroy you.'

After that, I renewed my efforts to speak with the two-leggeds and enter their psyches. One day, when the clear cerulean sky almost perfectly matched the blueness of the sea, I came upon the boat carrying the humans I had first met in the bay. They waved their arms and whistled and called out their warning cry, which seemed completely absent of warning or apprehension:

'Orca! Orca! Orca!'

'Look, it's Bobo! He's come back to us!'

I swam up to their bobbing boat and said hello.

'Lil' Bobo,' the longer of the two males said. 'We're sorry we scared you off last time. I guess you don't like acid rap.'

The shorter of the males, who had blue eyes and golden hair like that of the female surfer who stood next to him, drank from a metallic shell and let out a belch. He said, 'Who *does* like it? Why don't we try something else?'

'What about Radiohead?' the longer male said.

The female surfer used her writhing fingers to pull back her golden hair. She lay belly-flat on the front of the boat, and dipped her hand into the water to stroke my head.

'Let's play him some classical music.'

'I don't have anything like that,' the golden-haired male said. I guessed he must be the surfer's brother.

78

'I downloaded a bunch of classical a few weeks ago,' the surfer said, 'just in case.'

'Like what?'

'I don't know – I don't really know anything about classical.'

'Let me see,' the longer male said.

He bent over, and when he straightened, he held in his hand a shiny metallic thing, like half of an abalone shell.

'What about the Rite of Spring?' he said. 'That sounds like some nice, soft music.'

A few moments later, from another shiny object that seemed all stark planes and hard surfaces like so many human things, a beguiling call filled the air. In its high notes, I heard a deep mystery and the promise of life's power, almost as if a whale were keening out a long-held desire to love and mate. Soon came crashing chords and complicated rhythms, which felt like a dozen kinds of fish thrashing inside my belly. Various themes, as jagged as a shark's teeth, tore into one another, interacted for a moment, and then gave birth to new expressions which incorporated the old. Brooding harmonies collided, moved apart, and then invited in a higher order of chaos. Such a brutal beauty! So much blood, exaltation, splendor! The human-made sounds touched the air with a magnificent dissonance and pressed deep into the water in adoration of the earth.

'What kind of crap is that?' the golden-haired male said. 'Turn off that noise before you drive Bobo away again!'

O music! The humans had music: strange, powerful, and complex!

And then, as suddenly as it had begun, the music died.

'No, no!' I cried out. 'More, please – I want to hear more!'

The longer male's fingers stroked the abalone-like thing for a few moments. He said, 'What about Beethoven?'

A new music sounded. So very different from the first it was, and yet so alike, for within its simpler melodies and purer beauty dwelled an immense affirmation of life. As the sun moved higher in the sky and the surfer female on the boat stroked my skin, I listened and drank in this lovely music for a long, long time.

Finally, near the end of the composition, a great choir of human voices picked up a heart-opening melody. I listened, stunned. It was almost as if the Old Ones were calling to me.

O the stars! O the sea! They sang of joy!

This realization confirmed all that I had suspected to be true. Although the ability to compose complex music could not be equated with the speaking of language itself, does not all language begin in the impulse of the very ocean to sing?

'All right, so he likes Beethoven. Let's try Bach and Brahms.'

As the sun reached its zenith in the blue eggshell of the sky and began its descent into its birth place in the sea, the humans regaled me with other musics. I listened and listened, lost in a sweet, sonic rapture.

'I think he loves Mozart,' the shorter male said.

'I think he loves me,' the golden-haired surfer said. 'And I love him.'

To the murmurs of a new melody, the female leaned far out over the boat and pressed her mouth against the skin over my mouth.

'Bobo, Bobo, Bobo – I wish I could talk to you!' she said.

'I wish I could talk to you,' I told her. I wished I could understand anything of what she or any human said. 'Can you not even say water?'

I slapped the surface of the sea with my flukes, and carefully enunciated, 'Water. W-a-t-e-r.'

'It's like he wants to talk to *me*,' she said.

Having grown frustrated in my desire to touch her with the most fundamental of utterances, I drank in a mouthful of water and sprayed it over her face.

'Oh, my God! You soaked me! How would you like it if I did that to you?'

Again, I sprayed her and said, 'Water.' And then she dipped

her hand into the bay, brought it up to her mouth, and sprayed me.

'So you like playing with water don't you?' she said. 'Well, you're a whale, so why shouldn't you? Water, water, everywhere you go.'

Her hand, her hideous but lovely hand that had sent waves of pleasure rippling along my skin, slapped the water much as I had done with my tail. And with each slap, she made a sound with her mouth, which had touched my mouth: 'Water, water, water.'

The great discoveries in life often come in a moment's burst like the thunderbolt that flashes out of a long-building storm. I listened as the golden-haired surfer said to me, 'I wish I could teach you to say water.' And all the while her clever hand touched the sea in perfect coordination with the sound that poured from her mouth: 'Water, water, water.' I realized all at once that she was trying to teach *me* to speak, in the human way. I realized something else, something astonishing that would open the secret to communicating with these strange animals:

One set of sounds, one word! The humans do not inflect their words according to circumstance, context, or the art of variation! Not even our babies speak so primitively!

'Water,' the surfer said again. 'You understand that, don't you, Bobo?'

Water, water, water – she kept repeating the simple sequence of taps and tones with an excruciating sameness. I tried to return the favor, trilling out one of the myriad expressions for water in a single way: water.

'I don't understand you, though,' she said to me. 'I don't think human beings will ever be able to speak whale.'

The brightness in the surfer's blue eyes faded, as when a cloud passes over the moon. I feared that she did not understand me.

'No one can speak to a whale,' the longer of the males said. 'They probably don't even have real language.'

The surfer female looked at me. She thumped her hand against the smooth excrescence upon which she lay and said, 'Boat.' And so I learned another word. This game went on until dusk. I collected human words as a magpie gathers up colorful bits of driftglass: Shirt. Fork. Beer. Hair. Ice. Teeth. Lips.

Finally, as the sun sank down into the crimson and pink clouds along the western horizon, the female pressed her hand over her heart and said, 'Kelly,' which I supposed must be what the humans call their own kind. The longer of the two male kellies made a similar gesture and said, 'Zach.' I laughed then at my stupidity. They were obviously giving me their names.

I gave them mine, but they seemed not to understand what I was doing. Just as the underside of the boat roared into motion, Kelly said to me, 'Goodbye, Bobo. I love you!'

The next day, and for the remainder of the late summer moon, I had similar encounters with other humans. Strangely, they all seemed to have taken up the game played by Kelly and Zach. I learned many more human words: Lightbulb. Fish. Rifle. Bullet. Knife. Dog. Life preserver. Surfboard. Mouth. Eyes. Penis. I learned many names, too: Jake. Susan. Nika. Keegan. Ayanna. Alex. Jillian. Justine. Most of these humans called me Bobo, and sometimes for fun I returned the misnomer by exercising a willful obtuseness in persisting to think of the humans as male or female kellies.

In the vocalizations of all these many kellies, I began to pick out words that I had mastered. However, the meaning of their communications still largely eluded me. Even so, I memorized all that the kellies said, against the day that I might make sense of what still seemed like gobbledygook:

'Bobo is back! Hey Lilly, he seems to like talking to you the best. Maybe you can use this for your college essay.'

'Maybe I can sell the rights to all this, and they can make a movie.'

'They say Bobo is the smartest orca anyone has ever seen.'

'I hear he understands everything you say.'

'Of course he's trying to communicate with us, and he's been getting more aggressive, too.'

'Hey, Bobo, how does it work to mate with a whale?'

'I'm going to play him some Radiohead. I hear he likes that.'

'Do you just poop and pee in the water and swim through it?'

'What do you think Bobo – is there a God?'

'They're saying Bobo might hurt someone or injure himself, so they might have to capture him and sell him to Sea Circus.'

'I love Bobo, and I know he loves me.'

'If he's so smart, how come he can't speak a single word of English?'

How frustrated I was! Not only did I fail to form a single human word, I could not make a single human understand the simplest orca word for water. Upon considering the problem, I realized that much of my success in recognizing the few human words I had been taught lay in the curious power of the human hand. If the humans had not been able to touch or stroke the various objects they presented to me, how would I ever have learned their names?

With this in mind, I broadened my strategy of instructing the humans in the basics of orca speech. I opened my mouth and put tongue to teeth in order to indicate the part of the body that I then named. As well, I licked a human hand and said, 'Tentacle,' and with a beat of my flukes I flicked a salmon into one of their boats and said, 'Fish.' When that did not avail, I took to nudging various things with my head and calling out sounds that I desperately wished the humans might understand: Driftwood; kelp; sandbar; clam shell. Sadly, the humans still seemed unable to grasp the meaning of what I said – or even that I was trying to teach them.

One gray morning when the sea had calmed and flattened out like the silvery-clear glass that the humans made, I came upon a small boat gliding across the bay. Quiet it was, nearly as quiet as a stealth whale stalking a seal. A lone human male dipped a double-bladed splinter of wood into the water in rhythmic strokes. A violet and green shell of excrescence encased his head. I expected his boat to be made of one of this material's many manifestations, but when I zanged the boat, I found it was made of skin stretched over a wooden skeleton. I swam in close to make the male's acquaintance.

'Hello, brave human, my name is Arjuna.' I often thought of the humans as brave, for what other land animal who swims so poorly ventures out into the ocean – and alone at that? 'What are you called?'

This male, however, unlike most humans, remained as quiet as his boat. I came up out of the water, the better to look at him. I liked his black eyes, nearly as large and liquid and full of light as my mother's eyes. I liked it that he sat within a skin boat. I grew so weary of listening to the echoes of excrescence, which it seemed the humans called plastic.

'Skin,' I called out, touching my face to the body of his boat. 'Your boat is covered with skin, as am I, as are you!'

I did not really think I could teach him this word, any more than I had been able to teach other humans other words. Having been thwarted so many times in my increasingly desperate need to communicate, I pursued accord with this male too strenuously. My pent-up desire to teach one human one orca sound impelled me to nudge the boat as I might one of my own family. It surprised me how insubstantial the boat proved to be. I looked on in dismay as the boat flipped over like a leaf tossed by a wave.

'Hold your breath!' I called to the human suspended upside down beneath the boat.

Although I assumed the human must know that he would drown if he breathed water, I could not be sure. I dove beneath the water to help him.

'Hold onto me!'

I found the male beating his stick through the water. It would have been an easy thing for him to have grasped my fin or tail so

that I could pull him around through the gelid sea to return him
to the air. Instead, he began beating his stick at me. He thrashed
about like a frightened fish. Silver bubbles churned the water. I
caught the sound of the human's heart beating as quickly as a
bird's wings. Through the froth and the fury of the human's
struggle, I gazed at his glorious eyes, grown dark and jumping
with a dread of death. Now he did not seem so brave.

'Wait, wait, wait!' I told him. 'I will save you!'

I pressed my head against his side; as gently as I could, I used
my much greater substance to move his slight body around and
up through the water. This had the effect of turning the boat still
attached to him. A moment later, the human breached and choked
in a great lungful of air. Water streamed from his face and from
the blue plastic skin encasing him. He coughed and sputtered out
a spray of spit, for he had sucked water into his blowhole.

After a while, his coughing subsided. His belly, though, tensed
up as tight as the skin that covered his little boat. And he called
out to me: 'Goddamned whale! Why can't you leave us alone?'

Why could I not speak with the humans, I wondered as I swam
off in dismay? Through days of clouds and dark nights, I swam
back and forth across the bay pondering this problem. I dove deep
into the inky waters, believing that if I did so, I might somehow
zang how I might talk to the humans – and how, indeed, I might
sound the much deeper mystery of how anything spoke with
anything at all. What was language, really? For the humans, it
seemed nothing more than an arbitrary set of sounds that they
attached like so many barnacles to various people, objects, and
ideas. From where did these sounds, though, come? What principle
or passion ordered them? Could it be, as I very much wanted it
to be, that the human language had a deeper structure and intelligence that I could not quite perceive? And that a higher and
secret language engendered all the utterances of every individual
or every species in the world? And not just of *our* world, Ocean,
but of other worlds such as Agathange, Simoom, and Scutarix?

Might there not be, at the very bottom of things, concordant and melodious, a single and universal language through which all beings could communicate?

I felt sure that they *must* be. One evening, as I lay in deep meditation beneath many fathoms of cold water, it came to me with all the suddenness of a bubble bursting that my approach to speaking with the humans had been all wrong. Before trying to teach them the rudiments of orca speech, which their lips, tongues, and other vocal apparatus might not be able to duplicate, might it not be possible to share with them the impulse beneath language, even as they had shared their musics with me? Yes, I decided, it *would* be possible. And, yes, yes, I would share with the humans all that I had so far held inside: I would drink in the deepest of breaths and gather up the greatest of inspiration, and I would sing to the humans as no whale had ever sung before!

Some days later, I entered a cove in which floated a large fishing boat. The humans had covered the front of it with gray and white paints in a shape that looked something like the head of a shark. Buoyed as I was by bonhomie and zest for the newfound possibilities of my mission, I paid little attention to the peculiarities of this boat or to the many strands of excrescence that surrounded it like intertangled growths of kelp. Nets, the humans called these fish traps. Today, however, the empty nets had trapped not a single salmon. It seemed that the many noisy humans gesticulating atop the boat had not really come here to fish, but rather to make music for me.

And what music they made! And how they made it! I swam in toward the boat, drawn by the mighty Beethoven chords that somehow sounded from *beneath* the water. The density of this marvelous blue substance magnified the marvel of the music. Joy, pure joy, zanged straight through my skin. I moved even closer to the boat and to the music's mysterious source beneath the rippling waves.

'O what a song I have for you!' I said to the humans. I knew that if I was to touch their hearts as they had touched mine, I must go deep inside myself to speak with the monsters and the angels that dwelled there. 'Here, humans, here, here – please listen to this song of myself!'

I breached and breathed in a great breath in order to sing. Before the first sound vibrated in my flute, however, the boat began to shudder and shake and to issue sounds of its own. The air sickened with a clanking and grinding. Quicker than I could believe, the nets of excrescence began closing in on me from all sides, like a pack of sharks intent on a feeding frenzy. My heart leaped, not with song but with a fire like that which had burned the waters of the northern sea. I swam to the east, but encountered a web of excrescence in that direction. A dart to the west led straight into yet more netting. I dove, seeking a way beneath the closing nets, but I could not find an escape to the open ocean. In a rage to get away, I swam down through the bitter blue water and then hurled myself in steep arc into the air and over the shrinking sweep of the net. I plunged down with a great splash. For a moment, I thought I was free. It turned out, though, that I had landed within a *second* layer of netting, which quickly ensnared my tail and fins. The humans – the insightful, intelligent, and treacherous human beings – had considered very carefully how to trap a whale such as I.

As the net tightened around me and pulled me toward the boat and the flensing knives and the teeth that must await me there, I began singing a different song than I had intended: the thunderous and terrible universal song of death that I knew the humans would understand all too well.

5

Water, the fundamental substance, exerts a fundamental force on all things. We of the starlit waves dwell within the ocean, and the ocean surges mighty and eternal within us. We are at one with water – and so we experience the fundamental force as a centering and a calling of like to like that suffuses our bodies with a delightful buoyancy of being. If we are taken out of the water – as the humans pulled me into the air with grinding gears and clanking chains – we continue to feel this force, but in a new and a dreadful way. The centering gives way to separation; the calling becomes a terrible crushing felt in every tissue of skin, nerve, muscle, and bone. It sickens one's blood with an inescapable heaviness and finds out even the deepest fathoms of the soul.

I had never imagined becoming separated from the sea. To be sure, I had leaped many times into the near-nothingness of air or had played with launching myself up onto an ice floe, as the Others sometimes do when hunting seals. These ventures into alien elements, however, had lasted only moments. I had known that I would return to the water again before my heart beat a few times.

After the humans captured me, I felt no such certainty of deliverance from the crushing force that made breathing such a labor. In truth, the opposite of salvation seemed to be my fate. I could not understand why the humans delayed using their chainsaws to cut me into small pieces that their small mouths could accommodate. Were they not hungry? Would they not soon devour me as they had the many shiny salmon that they trapped in their nets?

The longer that I waited to die, the worse the crushing grew – and the more that I associated this dreadful force with death. I lay on the surface of the ship, and the strands of netting cut into my skin even as the hard, cold iron of the ship thrust up against my chest and belly. I lay within a canvas cocoon as metal bit against metal once more, and the humans lowered me onto a kind of ship that moved over the ground. I lay listening to the growl and grind of more metal vibrating from beneath me and up through my muscles and bones. I lay gasping against the land ship's poisonous excretions as breathing became a burden and then an agony. I lay within a metal box as a white lightning of a roaring thunder fractured the water within me – and then a sickening sensation took hold of my heaving belly, and I lay within a pool of acid and half-digested fish bits that I had vomited out. I lay within the darkness of the foul, smothering box, and I lay within the much deeper darkness that found its way not just over my eyes and my flesh, but *into* my mind and my dreams and my blackened and soundless soul.

'O Mother!' I cried out. 'Why did I fail you? Why did you fail *me*, by bringing me into life?'

I cried out as loud as I could, although it hurt to draw the cloying, slimy air into my lungs.

'O Grandmother! Why did I not heed your wisdom?'

I cried out again, even though the echoes off the metal close all about me zanged my brain nearly to jelly and deafened me. I cried and cried, but no murmur of help came from without or sounded through the dead ocean within.

For a long time the humans moved me with their various conveyances – I did not know where. The last of these, another land ship, I thought, jumped and stopped, then speeded up with a growl and a belch of smoke, only to stop again, many, many times. I could discern no pattern to its noisy motions. It occurred to me that I should seek relief from all the crushing and the lurching by swimming off into sleep. For the first time in my life, I could sleep with all my brain and mind without breathing water and drowning. I could *not* sleep, however, even within the tiniest kernel of myself, even for a moment. For if I did sleep, I knew that I would die a different kind of death, becoming so lost within dreams of the family and the freedom I had left behind that I would never want to wake up.

At last, the land ship came to stop longer than any of the other stops. Human voices sounded from outside the metal skin that encased me. Then, from farther away, came other voices, fainter but much more pleasing to my mind: I heard birds squawking and sea lions barking out obnoxious sounds similar to those made by the humans' dogs. A beluga, too, called out in the sweet dreamy beluga language. A walrus whistled as if to warn me away. Voices of orcas picked up this alarm.

The humans used their cleverness with things to lift me out of the land ship and lower me into a pool of water. How warm it was – too warm, almost as warm as a pool of urine! How it tasted of excrement and chemicals and decaying fish! Even so, it *was* water, no matter how lifeless or foul, and immediately the crushing force released its hold on my lungs, and I could breathe again. In a way, I was home.

'Water, water, water!' I shouted out.

My heart began beating to the wild rhythm of unexpected relief. I felt compelled to swim down nearly to the bottom of the pool and then up to leap high into the air before crashing back down into the water with a huge splash.

'Yes, that's right, Bobo!' A voice hung in the air like a hovering seagull. 'That's why we rescued you, why you're here. Good Bobo, good – very good!'

Humans stood around the edge of the pool. Many of them there were, and each encased in the colorful coverings that they call clothes. *These* humans, however, unlike those I had known in the bay, covered less of their bodies. I looked up upon bare, brown arms and horribly hairy legs sticking out of half tubes of blue or yellow or red plastic fabric. One of the females was nearly as naked as a whale, with only thin black strips to cover her genital slit and her milk glands.

'Can you jump again for me?' she said to me. From a plastic bucket full of dead, dirty fish, she removed a herring and tossed it into the water.

I swam over and nuzzled the herring. Although I was hungry, I did not want to eat this slimy bit of carrion.

'Here, like this,' she said.

She clamped her arms against her sides, then jumped up and kicked her feet in a clumsy mockery of a whale's leap into the air.

'If he's as smart as they say he is, Gabi,' one of the females standing near her said, 'you'll have him doing pirouettes in a month.'

'Wow, look at the size of him!' a male said. 'They weren't lying about how big he is.'

'Yes, you *are* big, aren't you, Bobo?' the female said. 'And in a few more months, you're going to be our biggest star. Welcome to Sea Circus!'

My elation at being once again immersed in water vanished upon a quick exploration of my new environs. How tiny my pool of water was! I could swim across it in little more than a heartbeat. It seemed nearly as tight as a womb, though nothing about it nurtured or comforted. The pool's walls seemed made of stone covered in blue paint. Whenever I loosed a zang of sonar to keep from colliding with one of the walls, the echoes bounced wildly from wall to wall and filled the pool with a maddening noise. I felt disoriented, abandoned, and lost within a few fathoms of filthy water. I could barely hear myself think.

I did not understand at first why the humans delayed in devouring me. Then, after half a day in the pool, I formed a hypothesis: the few humans I had seen could not possibly eat a whale such as I by themselves. Perhaps they waited for others of their kind to join the feast. Or perhaps they had captured and trapped me for a more sinister reason: here, within a pool so small that I had trouble turning around, they could cut pieces out of me over many days and thus consume me from skin to blubber to muscle to bone. It would take a long time for me to die, and the humans could fill their small mouths and bellies many times. Protected as the pool was by its hard, impenetrable walls, no sharks would arrive to steal me from the humans and finish me off. I would have nearly forever to complete the composition of my death song, which I had begun when trapped by netting in the bay.

I could not, however, sing. In such a place, who could give voice to the great mysteries and exaltations? In tainted water roiling with the cacophony of sonar crisscrossing the pool and fracturing into deafening zangs, who could prepare for the great journey into the quiet, eternal now-moment that underlies the beginning and end of time? No, no, I could not affirm life by opening myself to my inev-itable death, and so I cried out in a rage at having come so far only to suffer such a despicable fate. I raged and raged as I cried out to my family who could not hear me, and I swam and I swam back and forth across the hated pool, back and forth, back and forth.

Such despair can derange the mind. Soon, I began hearing voices: the voices, I thought, of the other orcas trapped in other pools nearby. Surely the moans and murmurs of discontent that I heard *must* issue from real, living whales, mustn't they? How, though, could I be sure that I was not hallucinating? In the distant lamen-tations that vibrated the walls about me and further poisoned the sounds of my pool, I could barely make out voices deformed by accents strong and strange:

'Welcome, welcome, welcome!'

'Go away, whale of the Northern Ocean! We do not want you here!'

'Go away, if you can! But, of course, you cannot. You are trapped like a krill in the belly of a blue whale.'

'You are trapped as we are trapped. Do not dispirit yourself by trying to keep alive your spirit.'

'Do not listen to Unukalhai, for he is mad.'

'Abandon all hope, you who have entered this place of hopelessness.'

'Live, brave orca. It is all you can do!'

'Die, strange one. Breathe water and die before your soul dies and you cannot die when it comes time to die.'

'No, escape!'

'Do not hope for escape. All who come here die.'

'Quenge and escape before it is too late.'

'Who can quenge in such a place? Die, die, die!'

'Welcome, welcome, welcome!'

Soon, I met those orcas who had spoken to me and so confirmed their reality. My pool, as I discovered, joined with other pools, some much larger but still too small to move about comfortably. Between each pool, the humans had contrived doors which they somehow opened and shut as easily as I might my mouth. With the humans standing about the concrete beach of the largest of the pools, as the hot sun made the warm water even warmer, I made my way into the pool as tentatively as I might swim into a cave full of stingrays. There I mingled with the other orcas and made their acquaintance.

'Hello, I am Alkurah,' a large female said to me. Her speech rippled with curious inflections and had an odd though pleasant lilt to it. 'And these are my sisters, Salm and Zavijah.'

Salm, younger and smaller than Alkurah, had a notch in her right flipper, and her dorsal fin flopped over upon her back in a most undignified way. So it was with quiet and moody Zavijah and her dorsal fin and with her baby, Navi. The whole family, I saw, suffered from the same horrifying affliction.

'We are the last of the Moonsingers,' Alkurah said, 'of the

Midnight Voyagers of the Emerald Sea. We were taken years ago and have been here at Hell Water ever since.'

'Years ago!' I cried out. 'And the humans still have not eaten you?'

'Eaten us?' she said. She swam closer to take a look at me. 'No, no, strange one – these humans are not whale eaters.'

At this revelation, I should have experienced relief at having been delivered from a dreadful death. Instead, I sensed the closing-in of a different sort of danger and felt the intimations of an even more horrible fate.

'Then why,' I asked, 'have the humans brought us here?'

'Why, to perform feats.'

'What sort of feats?'

'Breaching and leaping, spy-hopping and gyrations. They like to stand on our backs while we swim about the pool.'

'They . . . *stand* on your back, truly?'

'Oh, yes, they do – as they do, and make us do, many other things.'

'But why?' I asked.

'We do not know. The humans are insane.'

'Yes,' I said. 'But they must have reasons for what they do, insane though these reasons might be.'

'Must they, really? The humans are not reasonable animals. Indeed, after many years of having to endure their ugly faces and their squawking day after day, I am convinced they are quite stupid.'

'Perhaps their minds are so different from ours that they—'

'You know little of humans, Strange One,' Alkurah chided me. 'Let us not speak of your speculations now. I was making introductions when you interrupted me.'

'My apologies,' I said. 'I did not mean to be rude. Please continue.'

Alkurah introduced a smallish male named Menkalinan from the Star Far Vermillion Sea. It surprised me to learn that Menkalinan, sulky and streaked with scars, was Navi's father.

'I see that you can be politely quiet when spoken to by a mother orca,' Alkurah said to me. 'I like that, for it shows that you have been well raised. But I can hear the disquiet of doubt in your silence.'

In silence, I swam about the tepid water, and so spoke even louder.

'You are wondering, I think,' she said, 'how my sister Zavijah could mate in such a place – and with such a pitiful male as Menkalinan, who can barely sing.'

'Well, yes, I was wondering that very thing,' I said. I studied Menkalinan's flopped-over fin and the sad, furtive way that he propelled himself about the pool.

'Of course,' Alkurah said, 'my sister did *not* mate with Menkalinan. The humans did things with their things, and they stole Menkalinan's sperm and forced it into Zavijah.'

At this, Zavijah said nothing, though she made a quick dart at Menkalinan as if to warn him away and drive off any thoughts he might have of inseminating her more naturally.

'How could they do that?' I said. So disgusted was I that I would have vomited, if there had been anything in my empty belly to vomit.

A male only slightly smaller than I swam in close and fixed me with his wild, intelligent eye. He said, 'The dolphins rape each other, and that is understandable, though detestable. But the humans rape those not of their kind. They are a low, low animal, though impossibly clever in an exasperatingly stupid way. One might say that their individual cunning, which covers them with a patina of sanity, in fact drives them *en masse* to a collective *in*sanity.'

I glanced up at the many humans standing about the pool. Some were indeed doing things with things, as most humans did most of the time. The others, though, were gazing down into the pool and watching us.

'I am Unukalhai,' the large male told me. Many scars streaked his sides, and his great fin lay nearly flat along his back. 'Alkurah will not introduce me, so I will introduce myself.'

Alkurah swam between me and Unukalhai as if to protect me from him. She said, 'Do not listen to this whale of the Sorrowful Sea, for he is insane.'

'Oh, I am insane, Dear One,' Unukalhai said to Alkurah. 'But one wonders why you think that you are not insane as well?'

'Do not listen!'

'Why do you not accept this?' Unukalhai said to her.

'Unukalhai,' Alkurah told me, 'is willfully insane, which makes him insane all the more.'

Unukalhai laughed at this in the universal orca way. 'Of course I am insane. In such an insane place as this, my acceptance of my plight is the only reasonable response.'

'Do not listen! Do not listen! Do not listen!'

Unukalhai laughed again and said to me, 'Of course, I am not *only* insane. In my very eagerness to look upon, hear, taste, and embrace my insanity, I exercise a deeper sanity.'

Upon a murmur of protest from Alkurah, her sisters Salm and Zavijah joined in to swim in close and surround Unukalhai. They nuzzled his sides, again and again. In the tightness of pool, he could not elude them or escape their attentions.

'If the humans were not watching,' a tiny voice spoke out, 'the sisters would hurt him again and try to silence him.'

These words came from a tiny orca, who swam alone near the corner of the pool. Her very thick accent and nearly impenetrable syntax identified her as one of the Others. The strange and unfamiliar lattices of sound that she built within the pool's water seemed strangely familiar.

'How many times have you hurt Unukalhai?' the tiny orca said to Alkurah. 'As many as the marks on his skin!'

She went on to describe for me how Alkurah and her sisters often tormented Unukalhai (and the sad Menkalinan) by raking them with their teeth and opening up long, bloody wounds that cut through skin and blubber. It shocked me to hear this little whale speak of such a thing. No whale of my family or acquaintance had ever harmed another. Even more, for a very young orca to address an elder such as Alkurah so critically seemed almost impossibly rude. But then, the tiny whale *was* of the Others, who do not esteem our kind highly. And, as I would discover, she was as fearless as she was outspoken.

Alkurah swam closer to the lone, unprotected whale. With even greater rudeness, she said, 'I could kill you with one bite.'

'Yes, but you will not. Then I would be beyond the humans' torments – and therefore beyond yours.'

Alkurah said nothing to the implication that she reveled in the tiny whale's suffering, for to do so would be to admit that she had plunged deeply into the insane. Instead, she gathered in her dignity and pretended to the fiction that all the disparate whales in the pool somehow formed a single family, over which she presided as matriarch. Using her most authoritative voice, almost forcibly modulated to a reasonable calmness, she formally introduced the tiny whale to me:

'This is Baby Electra from the—'

'I know you!' I called out to the little orca, carelessly interrupting Alkurah again. 'That is, I know *of* you – I knew your brother Pherkad!'

I swam over to Baby Electra. So tiny she was, really not much more than a newborn. A long scar marked her left side, as if Alkurah had toothed her there. I liked her lovely symmetry of form and the warm, clear light which filled her dark eyes.

'How could you have known Pherkad, how, how? Our kind do not naturally speak to Others such as you.'

I laughed at her boldness and at the irony of what she had said. I realized for the first time that the Others thought of *my* kind as the Others.

'No natural occurrence,' I said, 'brought Pherkad and me together.'

I told Baby Electra of the Burning Sea of how I had tried to remove the harpoon from Pherkad's flesh. I gave her Pherkad's death song, which he had given to me.

'O Pherkad!' she called out. 'O my brother, my sweet brave brother – the most beautiful whale in all the world!'

She began crying, and the terrible close waters of the pool shook with a lament almost beyond bearing.

'O the stars! O the sea! Why is there so much pain?'

She wept for a long time. Finally, she composed herself and swam in close to me.

'My family are all dead,' she told me, 'as your dear ones are to you, for you will never see them again.'

'No, I *will* see them,' I said, 'on Agathange or in the timeless Cerulean Sea.'

'No, I am sorry, you will not, for you will never quenge again. I'm so sorry, sorry, sorry.'

'I *will* quenge again,' I said.

While the other orcas listened, I told Baby Electra of my reason for making my journey and all that occurred upon it.

'You say that before Pherkad went off to die,' Electra forced out, 'you came to love him like a brother?'

'Yes, I did.'

'Well, I love you the same way, for you are brave and beautiful as he was.'

'Thank you,' I intoned, not knowing what else to say.

'Will you be my brother, here in this horrible place?'

I made a quick decision, one of the best of my life.

'Yes,' I said. 'Yes, I will.'

She moved up against my side as if to take comfort in my much larger body and to keep me between her and Alkurah and her sisters.

'Then we are a family,' she said. 'I will try to speak with the humans as you have tried. Why don't we call ourselves the Hopeful Wordplayers of the Manmade Bitterblue Sea?'

All the other whales had a good, long laugh at this. Then Zavijah mocked Baby Electra, saying, 'If your naming talent goes no deeper than that, you had better continue to play with your words if you ever hope to speak with the humans.'

'How could she speak with the humans,' her sister Salm added, 'when she can barely speak with us?'

'It is a mystery,' Zavijah said, 'how you Others can even speak to each other in your ugly miscarriage of a language. What a sad fate that our family should have to listen to it!'

'And a sadder fate,' Alkurah agreed, 'that we Moonsingers should have to dwell so closely with a misbegotten family composed of two kinds never meant to speak with each other. One might as well try to form a family of a human and a whale.'

At this, the pool crackled with the sound of the three sisters' derisive laughter. Then Baby Navi, even tinier than Electra, broke away from nursing at Zavijah's side and cried out, 'Please stop – you are hurting my heart!'

Zavijah called to her sisters to cease their mockery, for as much as she seemed to despise Baby Electra, she loved her newborn Navi even more, and she could not bear for anything to hurt him. And her elder sister Alkurah, who loved Zavijah fiercely, could not bear anything that caused her to suffer.

'So!' Unukalhai said from the end of the pool where he floated. 'This, Arjuna, is how it goes with insanity. The humans' cruelty has made the Moonsingers insane with a cruelty most unbecoming in a whale. But you – you, you, you, and little Electra – have chosen a different way! Insane it is for our kind to try to make a family with one of the Others, but in just this sort of insanity, you might find a kind of salvation.'

His wisdom, crazy though it might be, clung to me like one of the humans' noxious skin lotions and slowly worked its way inside me. Over the days that followed – long, boring days of swimming back and forth within the imprisoning waters and watching the humans teach the other whales their 'feats' – I considered the advice he had tendered me. In one sense, even to entertain the thought of falling insane seemed itself insane. From another vantage, however, what if Unukalhai was right? Could it be that a still pool of sanity dwelled within the typhoon of madness that pressed down upon all us whales and threatened to derange our finest sensibilities? And if so, how could one navigate the raging winds and waves of that stormy sea to find a place of peace?

In no other aspect of existence did the other orcas demonstrate their creeping dementia so disturbingly as in their acquiescence to the humans' desires. Day after day, as the sun swam again and again like a flying fish over our pools, the humans continued doing things with things even as they conveyed their wishes to us and never ceased their irritating chattering:

'Good girl, Mimu!'

'Can you open your mouth for me?'

'You're cuter than a bug's ear.'

'You just love having your flipper tickled, don't you, Gaga?'

'Are you ready for a relationship session?'

'Stick out your tongue for me, baby.'

'You are sooo sweet, Tito, oh, yes you are, yes you are!'

'Can you pee for me, sweetie?'

'Are you ready to have some fun being a big surfboard for us?'

'Meal time!'

'Let's see what you can do with these new toys.'

'Good girl, Lala! You're so happy, aren't you?'

'I've been dreaming about this since I was nine years old.'

'What are we going to do about Bobo?'

'Jordan wants to breed him to Mimu.'

'What do you think, Mimu? Are you ready to be a mother like your little sister?'

'We've got to build him up first. He's sooo thin.'

'Aren't you happy with your new toys, Bobo?'

'Jordan special-ordered some char for him, but he wouldn't even touch it.'

'Please eat, baby. We *love* you!'

It quickly became clear to me that one of the humans was trying to teach me the first of my feats. Gabi, the other humans called her. Her orange, curly hair seemed to erupt from her head like snakes of fire. Her skin – red where the sun had licked it and like cream on those parts of her usually covered by her clothing – was mottled with little splotches of pigment that seemed to float across her face like bits of brown seaweed. I liked her eyes, large and kind and nearly as deep blue as cobalt driftglass. I saw in these lively orbs a dreaminess mated to a fierce dedication to apply her will toward whatever purpose she chose to embrace. It seemed important to her that I should eat. Whenever I swam near, she would kneel by the side of the pool with a fish in her hand, and she would open her mouth wide in an obvious sign that I should do the same. I did not, however, want to open my mouth. I feared that if I did so, Gabi would cast the dead fish onto my tongue, as other humans did with the other whales.

'Come on, Big Boy,' she said to me, 'you *have* to eat. Please, Bobo, pleeease!'

Near the end of my fifth day of immurement in the humans' filthy pools, Baby Electra rubbed up against my side as if to rub away my obduracy. She said to me, 'Please, Arjuna – you *have* to eat!'

'How can I eat slimy old fish?'

'That is all we have.'

'I will wait then until we have something else.'

'If you do not eat, you will die.'

'If I *do* eat, I will die.'

'I do not understand you!' Baby Electra said. 'The speech of you Others is so difficult – as difficult as the way you think.'

'My thought is no different than yours.'

'Then you should think very clearly about eating. Could it be worse for you than it was for me?'

Baby Electra told of her first days among the humans and described her revulsion over eating fish of any kind, dead or alive.

'I had only ever put tooth to seals, porpoises and a few hump-back whales,' she said. 'I did not even think of fish as food.'

'How, then, did you eat it?'

'How did *you* eat the white bear?'

'With great gusto, actually, though I must apologize for breaking our covenant with your kind.'

'I forgive you,' she said, 'as Pherkad did. But I will *not* forgive you if you starve to death. I need you!'

The sheer poignancy with which she said this drove deep her vulnerability and made me want to weep.

'Better death from starvation,' I told her as gently as I could, 'than the living death from eating dead food. I do not want to become like Unukalhai and Alkurah.'

'Am I like them, Arjuna? Are you sure that eating what the humans give us would be so bad?'

Yes, I thought, yes, yes – I *was* sure! How should I go on without hunting for sweet salmon, char, and other free-swimming fish as my mother had taught me? To tear the life from a vital, thrashing animal, to feel that life pass within and join with one's own, making one stronger, to feel complete in oneself the great web of life, perfect and eternal, and thus to know oneself gloriously and immortally alive – what joy, what wild, wild joy! How could I, how *should* I, live without that?

One day, the humans brought out an old orca that they had named Shazza, but whom we knew as Bellatrix. This huge grand-mother of a whale would have acted as matriarch in Alkurah's place but for Bellatrix's dementia and a sadness so deep that surely the Great Southern Ocean must have wept in compassion for her. She joined the rest of us in the big pool, but she touched no one. Her great dorsal fin flopped over her side like a lifeless, decaying manta ray. Oozing sores pocked her face – apparently she had scoured off her skin by rubbing against the gates of the pools again and again. When the humans cast fish at her, she opened her mouth to reveal teeth that she had broken by gnawing on the stony side of the pool. After her meal, she floated near the pool's center, barely moving. Her breathing was labored as mine had been when the humans had pulled me from the sea. She seemed nearly dead.

'Do you see? Do you see?' I said to Baby Electra. 'Would you have me eat so that I could become like her?'

No, no – I would *not* eat! I had come to the humans with the best of intentions, hoping to talk to them and ask them why they were trying to kill the world. They had returned my goodwill by trapping me and bringing me to this place of living death. Would I not be better off if I were truly dead?

Later, I expressed this sentiment to Unukalhai. He beat the pool's water with his flukes as if deep in contemplation. Then he said to me, 'You are still thinking like a free whale.'

'How should I think then? Like Bellatrix, who can no longer think at all?'

'Why did you leave your family, Arjuna? Was it not to speak with the humans?'

'Are you suggesting that I try once more to talk to them? How can I talk to animals who do such cruel things to people such as us?'

'The humans *are* animals, indeed, and that is why you never will succeed in conveying our conceptions to them. It would be like expecting a clam's shell to contain the sea.' He paused to drink in a mouth of water and spray it out in a concentrated stream in the way that one of the humans had taught him. 'However, you should recommence your efforts at communication, futile though they might be. To attempt the impossible is mad, is it not? And it is just this sort of madness that will save you.'

'Save me *for* what? To spend the rest of my life eating dead food and swimming through poisoned water?'

I spoke of how the humans sprayed chemicals over various species of plants that grew among the grasses and flowers encircling two of the smaller pools. Whatever green, growing things these chemicals touched withered and died. Rains washed the chemicals into the pools, and the poison found its way into the big pool, in which the humans themselves swam with us when they participated in our feats. How was it, I wondered, that the humans did not taste this poison and so remove themselves to the dryness of land?

'The humans kill plants,' I said to Unukalhai, 'for no apparent reason. In the bay, they killed many trees and cut them into pieces. Why should I want to be saved if I must live a degraded life surrounded by such an insane species?'

I went on to say that the humans loved death. They smothered the living waters of the ocean with oil and flame. They harpooned entire families of orcas just so they could capture the youngest and most helpless of our kind. They wore second skins of excrescence, as dead as the other things that they fabricated and manipulated with their murderous hands. They themselves ate dead food.

'Why should I not, then,' I asked Unukalhai, 'want to leave this place?'

'I understand, young Arjuna. You want to leave, but soon you will grow so hungry that you will want only to eat. And then you *will* eat, as the rest of us do, even though the fish are dead.'

I considered this for a while. The hot sun rained down its firelight upon the pool. I looked over at Bellatrix, floating like a felled tree and barely breathing. Big black flies buzzed around her blowhole.

'Then before hunger makes a coward of me,' I said to Unukalhai, 'I will breathe water and drown.'

Salm and Zavijah overheard me say this, and they swam to the sides of the pool as if to escape my words. Alkurah did the same, though she hesitated and touched me with zangs of what felt like regret. Unukalhai circled around me restlessly. Even though on my first day in captivity he himself had advised me to do what I had just suggested, he could not countenance my actual suicide.

'Baby Electra needs you,' he told me. 'And I have longed for a like spirit to talk to.'

Baby Electra swam up to me and brushed her baby-smooth skin against mine. 'You cannot break the covenants!' she said to me.

It was one thing for me to contemplate a natural death from starvation, for sometimes in the life of the sea, food could not be found and one must gracefully suffer the inevitable fate. But to deliberately suck in water would be to slay oneself in a most unnatural way, and would thus violate the sacred principle that no orca should ever harm an orca – not even oneself.

'The covenants,' I said to Baby Electra, 'were made for the ocean of life. But we have come to the waters of death – of what use are the covenants here?'

I noticed that Alkurah and her sisters were listening to me intently. So was Menkalinan, Baby Electra and even tiny Navi. Unukalhai regarded me with a strange mixture of sorrow and astonishment. He joined Alkurah and the others in clicking and high-whistling as they zanged my heart in order to determine if passion might have swept my reason away.

'Please!' Baby Electra implored. 'Don't leave me!'

'Then come with me,' I said. I spoke to the others, too. 'Let us all breathe water together and leave this terrible place.'

In the silence that stole over the small pool, the beating of many hearts sent waves of anxious sound humming through the water. Then Alkurah spoke out: 'No, Arjuna, I want to live, so I will not do as you say.'

'Nor I,' Menkalinan added.

'It would be wrong to break the Covenant,' Baby Navi said.

Unukalhai let loose a low, pensive laugh and said, 'That is a crazy idea, Arjuna – but not quite crazy enough.'

'Very well,' I said. 'Very well.'

Baby Electra heard death in my voice, and she swam over to me and tried to cover my blowhole with her body.

'No, Arjuna!' she cried to me.

'I cannot quenge,' I said to her. 'I cannot speak with the humans.'

'Please, no!'

'I will never see my family again.'

'But I am your family now! We are the Hopeful Wordplayers of the Manmade Bitterblue Sea!'

How could I deny this and so deny what might be the last of Baby Electra's hope?

'If you leave me,' she said, 'I will never outswim my grief.'

I watched as old, scarred Bellatrix rammed her head against the wall of the pool, again and again.

'Please eat, Arjuna! Please, please!'

I thought of my mother then, and of my grandmother and all my ancestors who had fought their way out of the wombs of the Old Ones just so they could taste the immense goodness of life. If I betrayed the sufferings they had endured in order to bring me into the ocean, all the life that had passed into me would be wasted. The gift my grandmother had given me at the outset of my journey would come to naught. So would Baby Electra's love for me.

'All right,' I said, 'I will eat the humans' dirty fish.'

And so eat I did. I swam over to the humans where they stood along the sides of the pools, and allowed them to toss fish into my opened mouth. They played this game day after day. The orange-haired human named Gabi poured bucket after bucket of salmon and slimy smelt down my throat, and I swallowed again and again, and the fierce hunger that had a hold upon my belly and my brain went away. I fattened and grew stronger. It surprised me that the decaying fish could give me life – a kind of a life.

Yes, but *what* kind? The longer I remained in the humans' pools, the more diminished I would become, at least when compared with my former self or with any wild-swimming whale. How long would it be before my proud dorsal fin collapsed like those of Alkurah, Menkalinan, and poor Bellatrix? How long before my very soul collapsed in upon itself like the body of a whale emptied of breath and sinking down beneath the crushing pressures of the deepest and darkest depths of the sea? How long before I began the inexorable descent in the horrifying process of my becoming like Bellatrix?

Aside from Baby Electra, who nursed a mad hope that we would somehow escape from the humans into the open sea, only Unukalhai of all the whales in the pools offered reasonable advice to me:

'If we must dwell in the human world,' he said one day, 'we must take the spirit of that world into us so that we might become part of it and so live with less agony.'

Reasonable his wisdom might have been, but I felt it was wrong, and I resisted it.

'Is it not enough,' I said, 'that we take in the humans' fish and their poison? If we take in their spirit, too, we will become as crazy as they are.'

I gazed at the sad, limp fin drooping along Unukalhai's back. I saw this pitiful degradation of flesh as an almost complete degradation of the spirit caused by Unukalhai's internalization of the humans' wants and their distasteful and despicable world. Who could accept such derangement of any orca's natural form? And was not the acceptance itself a kind of madness?

'Have I not told you many times,' Unukalhai said, 'that we must become insane? You did not believe me!'

'I did not *want* to believe you!'

'But you must, Arjuna. You must watch the humans, night and day.' He let out a long, painful whistle. 'You must drink in their sounds and dwell with them in your dreams. You must meditate on what it is to be human and try to become human in your own heart.'

'I cannot! I do not want to!'

I pointed out that he had chided Alkurah and the Moonsingers for internalizing the humans' cruelty, which they inflicted with raking teeth and rancor upon Baby Electra and the other whales.

'And cruel you must become,' Unukalhai told me, 'to live among the humans. But not mindlessly and compulsively cruel, as they are cruel. You must not allow yourself to become helplessly and indiscriminately infected. Rather, you must choose your cruelties with a will and a design, and wear them upon yourself as the humans do their clothes. In such cruelty, you must apply the same art as you once did in creating the tone poems of your great composition.'

Something in the crystallization of his conception of cruelty sounded a warning in me. Something in Unukalhai – a poisoning of his blood or a worm in his brain – did the same. I sensed that he was keeping a secret, deep and dark, which gnawed at him and worked its way into every tissue and organ. What this secret might be, I could not guess and he did not say.

'I do not want to become cruel,' I told him. 'I do not want the humans to touch my heart with their heartless hands.'

'But they already *have* touched you, have they not?'

'As they have touched you?'

'Yes, Arjuna – in exactly the same way.'

'I am sorry,' I said.

'Save your compassion for yourself – you will need it.'

'Perhaps,' I said. I floated at the surface of the little pool where we were being kept that night and opened my blowhole to take in a breath. 'Perhaps I will suffer here like a blue whale being torn apart by sharks, over years instead of days. I will not, however, allow myself to become like the humans.'

'You will not be able to help yourself.'

'Yes, I will.'

'You cannot escape them, any more than you can dislodge the harpoon they put in you when they speared your friend Pherkad.'

'There is no harpoon in me!' My voice exploded out of me in an unexpected and embarrassing shout, which thundered back and forth across the tiny pool. 'Only my grandmother is there, and Alnitak, and my mother, and—'

'The rest of your family, whom you will never see again. If you wish your life were otherwise, you will make yourself even more unhappy.'

'I *will* see them again!'

'No, you never will. The humans will make you do feats along with Alkurah, Salm, Electra, and me. You will see us, all the days of your life, until either we or you are dead.'

'No, no, no!' I beat the water with my flukes, trying to drive into this fundamental substance a little of my filthy rage. 'I will never do the humans' feats. I want nothing more to do with humans. I will escape them – and their pools of horror.'

'How will you do that?'

'I will gather in my deepest breath,' I told him. 'And then I will dive down beyond the bottom of the pools as I sing and I soar far, far beyond the reach of the humans' hands. I will quenge again – I will! I will! – and that will be the only feat I do in this place.'

For a while, Unukalhai held in a vast silence out of respect for my passion, if not my reason. Then he told me, 'All of us taken by the humans have tried to quenge. All have failed. Can the murmur of a snail be heard across the stars on Agathange? Can the glow of a jellyfish light up the entirety of the ocean?'

'I will try as none of you has tried!' I called back to him. 'I will sing louder than a humpback, and I will blaze like the sun.'

'Do not, Arjuna, please!' Unukalhai swam so close to me that I thought he might touch me. 'Tomorrow, when the humans bring us again into the big pool, look at Bellatrix more closely. Zang her, and swim for a while in her blood. Feel her heart, and know that she, too, once promised to blaze. She tried to quenge like the deep gods themselves, and thus this pitiful creature who was once a great whale made herself insane.'

I considered this only for a moment.

'I will not become insane,' I told him. 'I *will* quenge – and I will sing to the stars and complete the rhapsody interrupted on the day I beheld the Burning Sea.'

After that, Unukalhai retreated into himself as if he could no longer endure speaking with me. Could I, I wondered, possibly keep my promise to him? All night long, through man-lit waters which seemed to have grown denser and cloudier with my defiance, I swam around the boundary of our tiny pool – and around and around, around and around . . .

6

With the renewal of my quest to regain the most fundamental of life's joys, I told myself that I *would* – I must! – quenge again. To quenge not would be to betray the promise of life that my mother had bestowed upon me. And more, to fail would be to admit that humans could control not only my body and the fish corpses that they put into it, but my innermost spirit. It seemed a perversion of the natural order of the world that animals such as humans could steal the very breath of life from a whale such as I.

How, though, *was* I to quenge when I had not been able to do so with the help of all my family? I decided to recapitulate the efforts inspired by the advice of Caph, Naos, Dheneb, Turais, and my grandmother. And so, in the close, cloying waters of the pools in which I swam, I constructed vast lattices of ideoplasts and entire tesseracts of pure, inter-dimensional sounds that might show in their shimmering interconnectedness all the elements of my existence that had led to my present state. I meditated; I sang myself empty. I dwelled in deep, lucid dreams of what I had lost and in the memories of my more innocent self that my family had tried to give to me.

I did not expect to succeed. I hoped, however, to find in my failure clues that might indicate new and more fruitful approaches.

As clearly as I felt my heart beating steady and strong within me, I sensed that there must always be a way back to oneself, even for a lost and stranded orca such as I.

Would I have succeeded had the humans left me alone to my explorations? They did *not* leave me alone. On day after day of relentless sun and cloudless skies, they brought me into the big pool and gave me fish to encourage me to do feats. I pretended not to understand what they wanted me to do. While the human called Gabi jumped up and down with such force that her hair bobbed like coils of orange seaweed, I swam through urine-soaked waters or tried to meditate or dream. Sometimes I floated in silence at the surface, gazing out and up at the curious structure the humans had built at the back of the pool. Perfectly flat it was, and thin, and the outer part was seemingly made of metal painted in purple, periwinkle, vermillion, and aquamarine: the colors of the ocean. Upraised figures of dolphins, seals, and orcas swam through the metal of this frame. Inside it, a smooth expanse of glass moved with images and bursts of light that my eye could not quite follow. Music – a sickening, insipid succession of obnoxious sounds – accompanied these motions and in some bizarre way coordinated with them.

'All my life,' Baby Navi said to me one morning as I studied this hideous display, 'I have wondered why the humans make such glares and noises.'

At first, it had surprised me that the very protective Zavijah would allow her baby to swim anywhere near me. She soon perceived, however, that Navi had taken a liking to me, as I had to him. So fiercely did Zavijah love her little son that she would do almost anything to try to make him happy. And so she reluctantly allowed him to associate with me – all the while, of course, monitoring us from across the pool.

'It is not noise,' I instructed Baby Navi. 'It is music – horrible, purposeless music – but music nonetheless.'

'I wish I did not have to listen to it.'

'Try not to.'

'As you try not to listen to the humans?'

We both looked over at Gabi, who was now leaping higher than she had ever leaped before.

'Can you not see, Arjuna, that *this* is what she wants you to do?'

So saying, he swam down and then breached in a great (for a baby) leap. He hung in the air seemingly motionless at the top of his arc for a nearly endless moment of time. I noticed that he had erected his little pink penis and extruded it from his belly for the humans to see. They had never taught him this feat. The playful Baby Navi made this display only because it seemed to excite the humans almost as much as it disturbed them.

After he had splashed into the water and swum back over to me, I said to him, 'Yes, I can certainly see that that is what Gabi wants me to do.'

'Then why do you not do it?'

'Because,' I told him, 'the more that I do not, the more that she jumps – and the higher. It is more fun, is it not, to teach the humans feats rather than to perform them?'

Baby Navi agreed that this was so, and he laughed out loud in his squeaky, little voice. Then he said, 'If you do not do what the humans want you to do, they will do things to you that *you* do not want them to do.'

'What more could they possibly do to me?' I said to him.

Soon after that, a long male walked onto the stone beach surrounding the pool and moved up to Gabi. His face seemed as soft and white as the bread with which the humans cover the meat they consume. His eyes were blue like the pool that imprisoned me – and like that pool, they were clouded with the taint of the unpleasant and the filthy. The male and Gabi began exchanging noises that I assumed to be some sort of meaningful communication – meaningful to the humans. I could understand, after many days, only a few of their many, many utterances. They seemed to be talking about me: the male pointed toward me again and again, and his thin lips formed the sound Bobo even as his ugly eyes glared with what I took to be anger.

'You still can't get him to cooperate?'

'I will, Jordan – just give me a little more time.'

'Time is money,' the male said. His name, I guessed, must be Jordan. He moved his feet so that he stood at the edge of the pool. If I had wanted to, I could have knocked him into it. 'Do you have any idea how much we paid for you, Bobo?'

'You should be careful what you say to him. I bet he understands more than you think.'

'I'm sure he understands what you want him to do.' He looked at Gabi as he said this, then turned back to stare at me. 'Well, try to understand this, you stubborn whale: No tricky, no fishy.'

I swam up closer to him. I did not like this Jordan male with the evil, pale eyes. I suddenly recalled a feat that one of humans had taught Menkalinan. I rotated over on my side and used my flipper to scoop a great splash of water onto the male.

'Goddamnit!' he shouted. 'How the hell did you learn *that* when you won't even do a simple jump?'

As Gabi's belly tightened in spasms, a staccato of sounds erupted from her mouth, which she covered with her hand.

'Very funny!' Jordan said, as he used his fingers to wipe the water from his face. Then he turned toward Gabi. 'Ok, here's what I want you to do. Just before feeding time, signal to Bobo to perform the trick he just did. If he doesn't do it, don't feed him.'

'But I can't do that! We just got Bobo eating!'

'Well, if he wants to keep on eating, he's got to perform.'

'You can't just starve him!'

'Of course we're not going to starve him. A little hunger, though, might motivate him.'

The next morning, the humans failed to offer me my usual lifeless meal, and so on the day after that. A worried Baby Electra

114

swam up to me in the big pool and said, 'Please Arjuna! Do at least one feat!'

'I will do *one* feat,' I promised her. 'I will quenge, though the humans will never know what I do or why I do it.'

Bold words I had given to Baby Electra and to Unukalhai, but in truth I found it difficult even to meditate. The humans rarely left us whales alone for very long. At various times of the day – at the same time every day – they fed us or spoke to us or stroked us or tried to teach us feats. Dark purposes seemed to move them, and they impressed these purposes into us. They did curious, creepy things such as collecting our urine and feces. Although I never saw them drink or eat these substances, I revived my old hypothesis that the humans fed upon our waste, perhaps in secret. In the open space around the big pool, I sometimes watched them eat foods that did not look like they could be food. Once, when one of these tidbits fell into the water, I snapped it up with voraciousness, for my empty belly ached. Immediately, though, I spat it back out – the hot dog, as the humans called it, it tasted of chemicals similar to those that the pale ones such as Gabi rubbed into their skin. All the pools reeked with chemicals, particularly with a noxious one that burned my eyes and made them weep. The sounds that jangled the water bruised the rest of my body. Day after day, I endured a continual cacophony of whistles, shouts, clapping hands, and the awful music that blared from the flat metal and glass structure above the big pool. Assaulted by such noises, who could enter the first of the softly streaming currents of quiescence that lead toward the unpolluted pool of quenging?

Late one afternoon, with some welcome gray clouds pressing down upon the world and promising rain, the male called Jordan stood talking with Gabi again. I listened carefully to their garble of words, which I tried to absorb into a brain grown weak and cloudy with hunger:

'If he won't perform,' Jordan said, 'maybe we can get him to mate with Mimu. Her urine analysis indicates she's in estrus.'

'Yes, she went into heat this morning. I could have told you that, if you'd asked.'

'Let's put them in the east pool together.'

'That's not a good idea – Mimu doesn't like Bobo. She might bite off his penis.'

'That's a million dollar penis you're talking about. We've got four other parks that are waiting for more whales.'

'I don't think Mimu is going to let Bobo near her.'

'Let's try it and see. We can always inseminate her.'

'How are we going to do that? We can't even get Bobo up on the shelf for a urine sample, let alone semen.'

'All right, then put Bobo with Mimu, and let's hope for the best.'

With a soft rain pattering down, that evening the humans prodded me into a pool to the east of the big pool. There I found Alkurah, who had finally kemmered after several days of her indicating that she would soon do so. With her seed ripe and ready inside her, she practically heated up the water with her desire. In the natural order of things, she would have sought out a suitable male from another clan with whom to mate – or, rather, she would have allowed an experienced worthy bull orca to seek *her* out. Nothing, however, about our situation was normal.

'Would you like to breathe with me?' she asked me.

Surprised, I said to her, 'I had never supposed you would want me as a mate.'

'Why not? You are strong and handsome and brave. You are very intelligent, too, in a strange way.'

'But I still cannot quenge,' I told her, 'and therefore I have not completed my rhapsody. Would you mate with one who is not fully adult?'

'In a better place and a better time,' she said, 'no, of course I would not. But if I do not mate with you, what will I do to have children?'

'I do not know why you would want to have children here.'

'If I do not, how will the life my mother gave me go on?'

Because it is pointless to answer a question that is not really a question, I said nothing.

'If you do not mate with me,' she said, 'the humans will put me with Unukalhai or force Menkalinan's sperm into me – or worse.'

'What could be worse than that?'

'*This* could be worse!' She beat her tail in anger against the water's surface. 'Before Bellatrix ceased talking, she told of what happened to her in her old pools, far from here. The humans mated her with her own son.'

I suddenly felt glad that the humans had not fed me that day. Had my belly been full, I would have disgorged a spew of filthy fish into our tiny pool.

'Not even the humans would do such a thing,' I said. 'It is against all natural law.'

Of course, I did not really believe this. Nothing about the humans seemed natural. I stated it as true because I badly *wanted* it to be true.

'We would make a fine baby together,' she said to me.

'I am surprised that you would let me come so close.'

'I know, I have been unkind to you.' She swam beneath me and rubbed me along my belly. 'I have been jealous of you: you are more intelligent than I, and you have thoughts that I would never think.'

'Yes, and all or any of these thoughts I would give to you freely, that they would become your own.'

'That is exactly what disquiets me. Were we to become friends, or even family, I would come to depend on your greater insight.'

'How should a family *not* depend on each other?'

'But I am the mother of *this* family, or will be, as soon as you impregnate me. What matriarch would wish to swim in the shadow of the father of her child?'

'It would not be so. And in this place, so unlike the seas of our home, anything we called family would be unlike—'

'There is another reason,' she said, 'that I have not bestowed upon you the affection that you deserve. What would I do if the humans took you from me? I have already lost so much.'

She told me of how her first child, Minkar, had been killed in the capture of her sisters and her.

'Life must go on,' she said. 'And the life inside you that I have zanged – it is so *alive!*'

I gazed at her deep blue eye through the blue water.

'Your sperm are ready,' she said, 'like liquid white pearls, like burning raindrops of light.'

She touched her face to mine.

'I am hot inside, so hot that the fire can be put out only with the flame of your phallus.'

She zanged my blood with a shiver and promise of ecstasy.

'I want to feel you strong and wild inside me, surging, bursting, reaching for life.' She rolled slowly about in the water as if to show me how easily I might slide myself into her. 'Please mate with me, Arjuna – I am ready.'

I too, was ready. I needed no force of will to erect myself, as Baby Navi had done. Rather, my desire for Alkurah drove hot streams of blood into my penis, which pushed out as long as an adult human male is long. The coolness of the water seemed only to inflame it to an unbearable heat. Alkurah swam in close, and rubbed her belly across it so that it pulsed with a red, rage of pain.

'No, I am sorry,' I said to her. I swam away from her – or tried to, for she pursued me across the pool. 'I will not suffer my child to be born in such a place.'

'Please, Arjuna!' Alkurah said, rubbing against me again. 'Please, please, please!'

'No, no – I am sorry, sorry, sorry!'

With a great force of will, I called the blood from my penis and pulled it back into the safety of my belly. I offered to slip my flipper inside her, but this sort of purely physical satisfaction of erotic play she could find with Unukalhai or Baby Electra or even with one of her sisters.

'I must live in these pools,' I explained to her, 'for the rest of my life, which I pray will not be long. I do not want to live at all unless I can quenge, and I will never be able to quenge if I have to endure the humans doing to my child what they do to you and me.'

Alkurah, being reasonable as all orcas are, should have accepted the logic of my argument, or so I foolishly thought. The blood, though, in any being has reasons deeper than those of the brain.

'You will never quenge!' she shouted at me. 'And I will never offer myself to you again!'

'I am sorry,' I repeated.

'I will never speak with you again, either! And do not speak to me – if you will not give me your seed, I do not want your words inside me.'

The next day, I was moved into an even smaller water. I tasted urine, and looked down through a milky liquidity at the brown shadings of feces that the humans had not yet removed from the pool's bottom. So tiny was the space in which I moved, that I could hardly move: I could not complete an entire turn without scraping against the walls of the pool and so scraping off layers of my skin. The green chemical that the humans poured into the pools here seemed more concentrated and more toxic, for it burned my eyes with a hot, relentless stinging and worked its acid into the sores which soon opened along my sides. For a day and a night, I remained in this narrow place, without food or word of comfort from Baby Electra or another whale.

That is, almost without food. While meditating near the pool's slimy bottom, I noticed a duck put down on the surface of the water above me. I gave him a few moments to relax, then I surged upward through the pool to ambush him. I had never eaten a duck. His feathers tickled my throat. At least, I thought, I had a little meat to give me a little strength, the first living meat I had tasted in many days.

On the following morning, Gabi arrived with a bucket of fish. Jordan accompanied her. They stood above me on the rough, flat stone the humans call concrete, and they vocalized to each other:

'We thought that Bobo needed to be in the private pool for a while,' Jordan said.

'You mean, the punishment pool.'

'You don't have to like everything we do here, Gabi, in order to work here.'

'I don't like *this*!'

'I don't either. You know how much I love these whales.'

'That's what you've always said. So I don't understand how you can punish them this way.'

Jordan bent over the side of the pool as if to try to touch me. Then he suddenly drew back his hand. Perhaps he did not want to immerse it in the filthy water.

'Bobo,' he said, 'you wouldn't need to be punished at all if you'd just let Gabi teach you a few things. You're a willful little whale, aren't you?'

I rolled over on my side to repeat my feat of splashing water over him. He must have anticipated this, however, for he quickly jumped backward across the concrete so that even the strongest splash would not reach him.

'You'd rather be back in the big pool, wouldn't you?' he said to me. 'Then remember: work makes you free.'

He stepped back over to Gabi, who stood at the edge of the pool with the bucket by her legs. 'All right, let me see what you can do with him.'

For a while, Gabi gestured and twisted and hopped about the concrete like a sandpiper trying to get me to do feats. I almost felt sorry that I had to frustrate her obvious desire – almost.

'I should feed him *something*,' Gabi said. 'It wouldn't hurt to give him one fish, would it?'

'And reinforce his obduracy?' Jordan turned to me and articulated sounds that he had before: 'No tricky, Big Boy, no fishy.'

Just then, Gabi did something I had never seen her do before: leaping up into the air, she twisted her body in a lovely pirouette. Upon returning to the concrete, however, her foot collided with the bucket, knocking it over. Fish spilled into the pool. Despite the tidbit of the duck, I was ravenously hungry. I instantly turned about, not caring that I scraped off yet more flesh on the pool's rough side. As quickly as I could, I gulped down the many stinking fish.

'Oops,' Gabi said, standing up from the spot where she had fallen. 'I always had trouble landing my triples when I competed.'

'Do not,' Jordan said, 'do that again.'

'It was an accident!'

'Listen, Gabi, I know you love working with the whales. And we all love you – we wouldn't want to see you leave.'

Jordan raised his arm and drooped it across Gabi's back. They walked off together, chattering and leaving me by myself.

I remained alone the rest of that day and night, and the following day, night and morning as well. No food did the humans give me. Through a light-headed growl of hunger, I decided to take advantage of my solitude. I meditated as well as I could. I sang the old songs. I slept with half my brain and dreamed, and with my other half, I recalled those reverberant days when I quenged with my mother and grandmother in the icy waters of the northern ocean. Here, in another place, I sought my way back to sun-filled, melodious moments.

Why could I not return to that time and so return to my self? As I collided with the sides of my dinky pool, I felt the grate of Pherkad's harpoon where the iron point lodged in the ligaments between my bones. I gazed inward at the fury in the white bear's eye as I swam near to eat him. From head to tail, the humans' black oil still smothered my flesh even as tendrils of flame seared through my blubber to torment my blood vessels and every nerve.

Newer outrages grieved me. I could still feel in my belly the sickening force that had crushed my tissues when the humans had pulled me from the ocean. The taste of decaying salmon lay heavy and thick along my tongue, like a coating of excrement, and chemicals burned my throat. Again and again, I heard Baby Electra calling to me as if I were her real brother when she should have been swimming happily with her first family far away. The collapsed fins of Unukalhai and Alkurah and her sisters reminded me of the great trees that humans had cut down. And now their chainsaws and axes worked at my dorsal fin as well. When I closed my eyes, I beheld the madness in Bellatrix's eyes: the neverness of hope that paralyzed her so that she floated in her pool like a dead fish.

All these iniquities seemed to gather in my belly like a ball of excrescence that I could not vomit out. Like excrescence it truly was, yes, but sometimes it seemed more like a pool of blackness that pulled me into it and crushed me smaller and ever smaller. At other times, it shrieked like tearing metal or deafened me with a thunder that ruptured even the strongest of my dreams. I still had no word – no orca word – for this black, blazing, terrible thing. I did not want to name it, for to do so would be to give it even more fell power over me than it already had.

With such an unnatural thing embedded in me and poisoning my blood and every bit of my brain and body, how should I drink in the terrible beauty of the natural world? How know goodness and truth, when the black thing puffed up inside like a blowfish to crowd them out? How could I love when my rage at the world – what the humans had done to the world – tore out my heart?

I could not! I could not! And so I drove the world away from me, or rather I fled from it. I shouted out no! to its infinite fecundity and all its generative powers that had brought human beings into life. I said no to life itself – No! No! No! – and so I made myself a thing apart from the world, and in doing so I separated myself from the living sea. How, then, could I be one with the ocean's purpose? How could I feel its flow within me and swim along its cool, eternal currents? How could I quenge and so join my lovely family in song and celebration when they delved the blue seas of Agathange and all the mysteries of space and time?

In my dream-blackened pool which the humans had made, I moved unfeeling like a thing of metal through the ocean, for everything is ocean, even the small, fouled waters that the humans had sucked in from the open sea. Fast I swam, ever against the current of love and creation, and the waters slipped by me like liquid plastic that left not the slightest sensation on my skin. Where was I going? I did not know – I understood only that I must keep on escaping, beating my tail again and again against the soul-sucking waters as a desperate human in a boat might beat a piece of wood against the sea in order to flee an approaching storm. I fled and I fled; I swam faster and ever faster. And the faster and harder that I swam, the faster and stronger the current grew. Soon, as my muscles burned like molten iron and my breath grew foul and painful in my lungs, the current began turning inward upon itself. Around and around it whirled, with me caught inside it, around and around like a maelstrom pulling me into a vortex of darkness. And still I swam faster and fought ever harder, but all my rage seemed only to feed the raging black whirlpool that sucked me down and down and down.

I do not know how long I remained in that first plunge into madness. Moments seemed to stretch out into anguished eternities like tiny sea snakes uncoiling into malevolent serpents ten thousand miles from mouth to tail. I took no notice of day or night, light or dark, for within the maelstrom that had absorbed my mind and being, all was dark. Then one day – one month, one year – I heard voices. Humans arrived to feed me. Through eyes that remained within the whirl of the insane, I perceived these humans as curiously deformed and more hideous than ever. I noticed for the first time that several of them hunched over, as if the proud, straight forms natural to their kind had collapsed like a whale's fin under the weight of what they did to the world. Their utterances seemed impossibly low and slow, more like the growls of a bear disturbed from sleep than intelligent voices. Two of these monstrosities emptied buckets of fish over my head. I could not eat, however, because the maelstrom had turned my stomach inside out. Then I became aware of a wailing so poignant and terrible it seemed it might tear out the insides of the very world. From far away it came, I thought – but as the wailing grew ever stronger and closer, I realized that it issued from an orca all too near:

'Navi, Navi, my little Navi – where are you?'

Through the dimness of my dementia, lingering like a mist upon a twilit forest before the morning sun has driven it away, I heard Zavijah crying out to her baby. She used her long-range cry, as if Baby Navi might have drifted away from her in the open sea and needed to follow his mother's powerful voice back to safety. Again and again she cried out, in a pleading of pity and pain. She cried and cried for her baby as if she could not understand why he did not call back to her.

When the humans saw that I would not eat, they moved me into the big pool. The other orcas were there. Alkurah and Salm gathered about their sister, touching and stroking, but Zavijah would not be consoled.

'Navi, oh, Navi – please, beloved Navi! Why won't you answer me?'

Menkalinan and Unukalhai kept away from her at the opposite end of the pool. They obviously feared that if they got too close, she might lash out in her grief and slash them open. Electra, too, avoided Zavijah, all the while watching her with her soft eyes and with gentle zangs of sonar. Even old, addled Bellatrix seemed to be concentrating some part of her awareness on Zavijah, although with that poor, ruined whale, one could not quite tell.

Baby Electra swam over to me and explained what I already feared to be true: 'The humans took Navi – no one knows why.'

'Perhaps,' I said, 'to eat him.'

'You are the only one of us, Arjuna, who still entertains such a disturbing but almost certainly false hypothesis.' She touched her face to mine as if to examine me – or to reassure herself that I had really returned. 'Something in you has been deeply disturbed, though I do not want to believe what Uuukalhai says that you have decided upon insanity.'

How could I tell Baby Electra about the agony of the black thing within me or the terror of the whirlpool? Who would tell a child such things – or anyone?

'Why, then,' I asked her, 'did the humans take Navi if not to eat him?'

'No one knows!'

It surprised me when Zavijah swam over to us a few moments later. She opened and closed her mouth in what seemed a cruel mockery of a human shouting. A whitish film coated her usually pink tongue, and I noticed that two of her teeth had splintered into bloody jags as if she had gnawed on the pool's concrete.

'Help me, Arjuna!' she said to me. 'Please help me!'

'How can I help you?'

'They have taken Navi from me – I cannot find him!'

'I am sorry,' I told her.

'Why can I not find him? Why? Why?'

'I am sorry! I am sorry!'

'Please help me to get him back.'

'How can I do that?'

Zavijah watched the humans standing about the pool as if afraid that they might understand what she told me. But of course they could not.

'It was Golden-Hair and Painted-Skin,' she said, referring to two of the males who stood above us, 'who took Navi. If they should chance to get in the water with you, please kill them. Kill, kill, for me, please, please!'

'Why are you asking this of me?'

125

'Because if the humans see that we care enough about our children that we are willing to break the covenant in killing their abductors, the humans might return Navi to me.'

Disturbed I might have been from my time in the maelstrom, but Zavijah seemed almost hopelessly grief-crazed.

'No,' I said, 'I mean, why are you asking this of *me*?'

'Because you have already broken the covenant once and might do so again, where I cannot. And because you are a little mad – we can all zang that you are.'

I hesitated longer than I would have liked. I told her, 'I cannot kill the humans.'

'Please, Arjuna! Help me get my baby back!'

'No, I *will* not kill – I am sorry.'

The cry of anguish that sounded inside her tore straight into me. I could not bear her pain. Because I had nothing else to give her, I sang one of the old songs, a beautiful song full of rainbows as seen through the spray that the surf off the Giants' Rocks casts up. It did little to soothe her. The very singing of it, however, out of the flute of an orca such as I, from whom she expected no kindness, moved her to a moment of gratitude outside her grief.

'Thank you,' she said, grasping at a remembered politeness as a castaway human might clutch a piece of driftwood floating on the sea. 'You are kind, Arjuna, but that will not avail you here, any more than my love for Navi has availed me. If you do not do feats, the humans will return you to the cave pool. There you will complete the journey that you have begun. When you have dived deeply enough into madness, *then* you might be willing to kill the humans for me. After you do, I will sing a song for you.'

Could I, I wondered, ever do what Zavijah asked? No, no, I could not: I was an orca of the Blue Aria Family of the Faithful Thoughtplayer Clan, whose ancestors had promised long ago never to harm the humans. No matter how foul, how small, how crushingly dark any of the pools grew, I promised myself that I would keep the ancient covenant with the humans.

7

After a futile day of trying to get us to do feats; the humans gave up and I was returned to my solitary pool. Almost immediately, I began nibbling at the meat of insanity that the humans had provided me. All that long, long night, Zavijah continued her heart-rending keening and crying for her little Navi:

'Pretty baby, dear baby, my baby – please come back to me! Why won't you answer me – why, why, why?'

By midnight, with the half moon adding its illumination to the artificial blisters of light that the humans had arrayed above our pools, I knew that I had to escape from Zavijah's grief before her wailing tore me apart. I now knew the way. The black thing inside me called me with the darkest and the most plaintive of voices. The maelstrom spun its seductive fury straight into my blood.

Long ago one of our greatest thinkers, Alsciaukat of the Dreamspinner Clan of the Eastern Sapphire Sea, sang of the identity of opposites. Any two qualities of seemingly contradictory nature must somehow be united in their deepest part. The exhilaration of wild chances, such as surfing the Blue Mountains, can intensify to terror if pursued too strenuously – or the reverse. Inside the infinite hope of every joyous moment lies a secret despair that it will not last. Even the world's endless desire to create finds resonance in its equally powerful need to destroy, for that which comes into life can only do so upon the bones of that which has passed into death.

Alsciaukat taught that heaven and hell are but two ways to perceive a single sound. As I floated alone in the tepid water of my little pool, I revisited the many cantos of Alsciaukat's ancient song. In the well known but little-understood ancient tempo canto, he speaks of the very close relationship between quenging and madness. A whale who quenges, he believes, and another who sickens in his soul are both plunged into the same stormy sea, but the first whale swims where the second whale drowns. How strange this counsel, for it seems nearly as impossible for a whale to drown as it does for a whale to be unable to quenge! Was I not living proof, however, that the strange and the impossible could become bitterly real?

And so to flee Zavijah's suffering and her shrieks of desperation that carried through the air and penetrated concrete, water, and flesh, I dove down into a suffering of my own. I believed that in order to still my mind and quenge again I must first understand the nature of the black thing that had made my mind a racing, raging torrent. At the center of even the worst of typhoons, it is said, lies a place of blue sky and peace. How would I ever reach this blessed water unless I swam first into the black thing's whirling dark heart?

How hard I tried to do what no other whale except perhaps Alsciaukat had ever done! I looked straight into myself for the black thing as I might look through the black holes at the centers of my eyes, but so utterly black did it seem that it drank in every bit of my mind's light so that I could not see anything. I tried to zang the blackness, but its sound was only of echoes rippling out into lightless and empty space and therefore no sound at all. Blind and deaf, I had no choice but to plunge on and on without bearings into the stormiest seas of my soul.

I might as well, I thought, turn anywhere in the whipping waters of myself, for everywhere inside me swirled confusions that seemed to lead nowhere. I began with the harpoon whose black iron lodged in my heart. How had the humans made this dreadful thing? *Why* had they formed it out of the solid and heavy parts of the sea? Why did they kill whales when they must have animals such as dogs that they could hunt and eat? Did the humans, themselves, know why? Did they reflect on the logic, purpose, and result of all that they did? *Could* they really be conscious when so many of their actions seemed unconscionable and consciousless?

What *was* consciousness? If Alsciaukat was right that the same light blazes in all things even as the flame of life warms each of our cells, then did an orca and a human such as Jordan partake of the *same* sacred consciousness? How strange was that thought, and even stranger the thinker who had thought it! From where had it come? To where did it go once my mind had raced on to another thought, such as the question of whether I could create and control my own thoughts? But create out of what? Were thoughts made of the corpses of deceased thoughts as a blue whale's body is made of krill? Did thoughts live themselves as life does, fertilizing each other, engendering new ones which nurture yet newer thoughts, on and on? Perhaps thoughts were not really real at all but only the figments of other thoughts – did they possess no greater reality than my hope and my dream that the humans might truly be thinking and feeling and fully conscious beings?

What if the humans themselves were not real? What if all that had happened to me – from the instant before my family had come upon the white bear – had no more substance than the thundering terrors of a nightmare? What if I yet remained trapped in that nightmare as my dream self lay inert and desperate in the humans' poisoned pool?

Other troubling thoughts came to me, faster and ever faster as I tried to force my way through the maelstrom's churning waters. Each thought formed in an instant, darted off like a cuttlefish in the dark, and disappeared into the next wave of mentation that brought the succeeding thought. Wave upon wave upon white foaming wave, which formed up, attained a moment of intelligibility before disintegrating into a spray of babble and nonsense, which in turn invited the next wave which I could never quite grasp. The deeper I dove into the maelstrom of my mind, the quicker came each idea and sensation and the more totally they broke apart into drops and fragments of consciousness. All that I was began spinning like grains of silt in the muddied waters of myself, spinning and spinning and spinning. I could not see; I could not hear; I had no time in which to breathe.

Humans kill whales trap krill trapped inside time but how can there be time when thought shatters time to leave me o why can I not leave this bitter ocean of earth crushing the breath out of whales maddened, starving, dreaming of quenging down into dazzling darkness of infinite hope of escaping the black thing hidden by human hands making excrescence of the life of the world dying not as all living things die into greater life but vanishing as the black thing devours itself and all things of the ocean and earth are dying the forever death of dying and dying and dying . . .

There came a time in my descent into my interior hell when I forgot all about Alsciaukat's identity of opposites – or even that I was trying to quenge. All the yearned-for aspects of quenging simply collapsed into their opposites, as the sun is sucked up by night. Instead of my seeking a powerful and peaceful sea, I found a hurricane; instead of the darkness that contains all light and sound within itself, I lost my way in a blinding brightness that puts out the eye of the universe and leaves only a black and gaping hole; instead of expanding in my being towards galaxies far beyond Asteropei and Agathange, I fell inward and shrank upon myself as if forced into a succession of smaller and ever smaller pools so that all that remained of myself was a shred of a bit of an atom of consciousness; instead of hope without hesitation or bound, I knew only despair; instead of an ecstatic oneness of the world, I felt all its forms and features fracturing like glass, infinitizing itself into tinier and tinier particles that were at their very bottom nothing at all; instead of saying an absolute and unqualified yes to life, I heard myself shouting out No!; and in place of the love that sings in the heart of all things, the black thing that I could not possibly escape pulled me into its soundless and soulless maw.

And the pain! And the pain! Why was there so much pain? With my mind disintegrating like a sandy isle torn apart by tidal waves, I could not compose a coherent succession of words, but had I been able to speak, I would have said that my plunge into madness hurt more than all the combined agonies of my life: it was as if the white shark that had bitten me when I was a baby had shredded me down to nothing and had left a jagged, serrated tooth in every shrieking cell; as if the wound the white bear cut above my eye had hardened into a scar of remorse that sent cicatrizant filaments into my every nerve; as if the black oil that burned the sea made of me a whirlpool of flames; it was as if Pherkad died each time I drew in a breath, which escaped from my body from the bloody blowhole that the harpoon had torn into my lungs; as if my mother died, and my grandmother, and all my family and clan, not just at some dreaded moment in the future, but in the red, ripping hell of the everlasting now-moment, and all the moments to come that could never be other than a succession of acid pools of existence. My madness hurt the most, I thought, in knowing that it could never stop hurting any more than it could ever go away.

As the maelstrom caught me up in the winds whirling about its fiery center, each moment became a day and then a year, and each instant swelled into an eternity. I lived longer than all the ages since the first whale left his legs and the land behind to brave the waters of the ocean; I died more times than all the fishes that had ever lived in the seven seas had died since the beginning of time. I died within screams that had no sound, and I died within silent darkness. I died again and again and again, and it was upon the darkest and most despairing of all these many deaths that the voices began:

'Arjuna, you are free!'

Of course, a whale can always hear voices, songs, cries, zangs, and such at will, and in these remembered (or dreamed) acoustics, there is little difference in the clarity and the sense of reality between the inner sounds and those that emanate from without through the substance of the sea. However, one can always tell which is which – one always *knows*. That is, a *sane* whale always knows the difference. In the urgent voices that now sounded inside me, I could no longer distinguish the hallucinatory from the real.

'Arjuna, you are free to leave your imprisoning pool whenever you wish.'

'Yes, you are free – breathe water and drown.'

'You have already escaped – the maelstrom is behind you.'

'You have escaped *into* the maelstrom by becoming one with its wild winds.'

'This is a kind of quenging, Arjuna. Dive down deep enough, and quenging and madness are really one and the same.'

'You sought the blue peace in the eye at the center of the storm. Is not everything blue?'

The waters of my pool ran blue, as did the color of the flaky paint encrusting the pool's concrete walls. The metal of the huge flat thing above the big pool shattered into indigo and blue shards as sharp as a shark's teeth, and the turquoise shirt of excrescence that Jordan wore about his torso suddenly came alive like a jellyfish and began absorbing the tissues of his body in a hot, acid agony. Gabi swam next to me and gazed at me with eyes as blue as periwinkles. And I put out those pretty blue orbs with a single bite that crunched off her entire face.

'Kill her!' I heard Unukalhai say. 'Tear off her legs! Rip out her lights! Devour her heart, and take the humans' madness into you!'

'Yes, please kill her for me!' Zavijah added. 'Kill her, kill Golden-Hair, kill Painted-Skin – kill them, and bring my baby back to me!'

'Kill Baby Electra!' Unukalhai shouted at me. 'Kill her to spare her the agony of a life that is no life!'

'Kill them all!' a deep, resonant voice commanded me. It was a voice from the distant past (and perhaps the far future), and I recognized its speaker as Alsciaukat. 'Kill the humans, and kill the world that gave birth to these world-killers. Kill all of creation, for are not death and life one and the same?'

And so it went, the char winds near the center of the maelstrom whirling so impossibly quickly that they seemed to have stilled to a relentless, endless blue.

One day while I was thus immersed in myself – one hour, one moment, one aeon – the humans moved old Bellatrix into my pool. So little space did we now have that we could not swim without colliding with each other. That did not matter. Neither of us wanted to swim. We floated in the foul, slimy gag of each other's excretions, side by side, touching skin to dead, unfeeling skin.

And then silent and speechless Bellatrix spoke to me through the touch of skin and the sound of our mutual affliction:

'You must not listen to Unukalhai,' she told me, 'for he is mad.'

'So am I! So are you!'

'Are we, really?'

'As real as the voices I cannot escape.'

'There are many kinds of madness, Arjuna, and some are madder than others.'

'Unukalhai is my friend.'

'He was my friend, too. For many years, we dwelled far away in another place of prison pools.'

'I never knew!'

'And never would Unukalhai have told you that – or told you that he killed a human there.'

'No, you must have hallucinated that – he could not have broken the Great Covenant!'

'He caught a human's tentacle in his teeth, and he dragged him down into the water.' The skin of Bellatrix's face vibrated with the effort of her communicating this unbelievable thing to me. 'He bit off the man's hand and swallowed it. He ate the man's sex, and then he tore him open and ate his heart.'

'No!'

How could I, I wondered, get away from these terrible words that I did not wish to hear?

'Unukalhai,' Bellatrix said, 'killed *for* me, exactly as Zavijah has asked you to kill Golden-Hair and Painted-Skin. For the humans took my children, too.'

She began whimpering, and her belly sent soft waves of suffering through the waters of the pool.

'Do not do what Zavijah wants you to do.'

'I could not! I could not!'

'You already have, haven't you? How many times, Arjuna, in the bitter pool of your heart have you slain the humans?'

'I never have!' I wanted to shout back to her. 'I never would!' Because I did not wish to lie, however, I said nothing.

'Please do not kill them, Arjuna,' she said. 'If you kill them, you will kill the best part of you, which we all love. And I have already lost all that I loved.'

Her whimpering intensified to an open sobbing that took hold of her from head to tail. In the close, shaking water, I could not get away from it. Pulses of pain pierced me in zang upon zang of pure hopelessness, and ripped open the thin tissues of the illusion of separation between us. Her breath moved as my breath did, and her heart beat in rhythm with mine. Her voice caught up inside me like a choke of pure agony and became my own.

'You will kill the best part of yourself. You will kill, you will kill, you will . . .'

I could not escape this terrible cry, either. I tried to. Because I could not turn a full circle, I swam straight forward. Water streamed past me for a moment before my head collided with the wall of the pool. Pain exploded through my bruised and bloodied face deep into my skull bones. My brain knocked about inside like a jellyfish flung against submerged rock, but still the voice sounded inside me: 'You will kill! You will kill! You will kill!' Again I rammed my head against the side of the pool, and again and again. Clouds of my blood reddened the water. A lightning bolt drove into my eye and split open my head. And still the voice would not stop: 'Kill! Kill! Kill!'

Gabi found me floating beside Bellatrix like two dead logs that the humans cut from living trees. 'Oh, my God!' she cried out. 'Oh, my Bobo!'

She fell down upon the concrete as if axes had chopped off her legs. Her arm covered her eyes. Her naked belly trembled as if seized by an earthquake, and a succession of barking-like sounds formed up deep in her throat and did violence to her shaking chest.

'Oh, no, oh, no – goddamnit, no, no, no!'

Time passed – perhaps a day, perhaps a few moments. Jordan had come up to Gabi, who now stood beside him.

'All right,' Jordan said, 'let's get him into the big pool and get this place cleaned up.'

'Look at his head! Look, goddamnit!'

'Don't panic – Derek will fix him up. But let's move him, okay!'

'How are we going to do that?'

'I'll get Brad and Cole to—'

'You can't just shock these whales like they're cattle!'

'I have to tell you, Gabi, that it's time we considered electro-convulsive therapy for—'

'Like you did to Shazza in Cancun? Look at her – do you want to make a vegetable out of Bobo, as well?'

'What else can we do?'

More time passed. My face bled, my jaw hurt, my head swelled into a red clot of agony, but the voices grew only louder. Now I heard new voices – I thought perhaps they issued from the mouths of Painted-Skin and Yellow-Hair, who stood above me. In their hands, they held wooden oars tipped with red sticks of metal and excrescence.

'C'mon, Big Boy, the gate is open. Don't make me have to use this.'

A month vanished. The moon that I could not see must have been hiding somewhere beyond the blue glister of the endless day. A redness streaked toward me. Lightning flashed out of the cloudless sky and struck me on my side above my tail. Its hard, white fire jolted along my nerves up my spine and into my bruised brain, causing my entire body to jump, heave, and twitch. My feces swam over me – and clouded up around Bellatrix. She did not seem to mind.

'C'mon, Big Bobo!'

Again, the lightning shocked me with a sickening jag. It seemed that if I swam forward, I might escape it. I swam for many years.

I found myself in the big pool with Bellatrix, but none of the other whales were there. Golden-Hair and Painted-Skin clacked their red-tipped oars together and did a little dance with their legs – I did not know why. They bunched together by the side of the pool, tormenting the air with their overly loud vocalizations. I floated at the very edge of the pool, and I could not stop staring at them. So close they stood to me, with their toes nearly touching the water – so close, so close, so close!

Then Gabi walked up, and I was very glad when they went away.

'Derek is coming,' she said to me. 'We're going to take care of you.'

She lay down on the rough concrete, which must have hurt her delicate and bony human body. She dipped her arm into the water and touched my jaw behind the wound where it bled. So gentle was her touch! So light, so warm, so knowing!

'Help me,' I said to her. I had never imagined speaking such words to a human. 'Please help me!'

Now she touched my throbbing head, and her fingers danced along the scar above my eye, touching and touching.

'We're going to help you,' she said. 'You're going to be all right.'

Like a star streaking out of the sempiternal night that had darkened my mind, one of the sounds that she spoke lit up my hope. As her fingers pressed against my skin and she said *you*, I understood that she meant *me*, Arjuna. I realized that the humans had substitute words for people, where we whales only and ever use names. What a strange way of speaking! What a great discovery, a conception that I had dreamed of!

'*I* will help you,' she told me.

A second star shot right down to the ocean following the fiery trail of the first. She wanted to *help* me – so, the humans had a way to convey the fluidity of acts, events, and states of being instead of freezing concepts hard and cold as ice, which they did in words that I had learned for their things such as boat, plastic, tattoo, and stungun. Therefore, there was a breath of a hope of a chance that they might be able to understand our orca language.

'Help me,' I repeated.

Gabi's hand continued stroking my head. 'Say that again! You're asking me to help you, aren't you?'

'Help me.'

'Help – is that right?'

'Help, yes – help, help, help.'

'Help, help, help – that is how an orca says help, isn't it?'

'Yes, help.'

'Help – I wish I could say it like you say it. But a whale can't speak like a person, either.'

Again, I asked for her help with a high-pitched cry of compassion that I lamented a human's throat and lips could never duplicate.

'I *will* help you,' she said to me. 'I'm so, so sorry for what we've done to you!'

Her belly started bouncing again as it had before, and she made more painful barking sounds. Her blue eyes filled with tears, which spattered onto my head like warm raindrops as she pressed her lips against my skin. It seemed that she needed to give the water of her body to me.

'Yes, yes – please help me,' I said. I like the soft, salty rain that fell down upon me.

'Oh, Bobo, Bobo!'

'Help me to kill.'

'I love you.'

'Help me to kill myself.'

A third star flared inside me. The heavens cast it down into my consciousness upon a miracle of sonance that reverberated through the whole of my being: Gabi's low, lumpy but strangely lovely human voice somehow flowed into the golden voices of my mother and my grandmother. A single voice, as bright as angel fire, as loud as thunder, overpowered and then obliterated all the voices of darkness and doom that had tormented me. And for a single moment – only for a sliver of an instant of time – I quenged, for does not the essence of quenging lie in discovering life's deeper and ever more mysterious unities?

And suddenly I knew what I had to do.

'I must die,' I told Gabi.

There could be no other way. How else could we whales live in pools that the humans had made? Alkurah, I thought, had lost much of her kindness, which had killed something beautiful within her. Zavijah had lost not just Navi but the very joy necessary to breathe and dream. Unukalhai had ruined his sanity, while Bellatrix had abandoned her very will to live. All had lost something vital of themselves, and so in some part had died.

As I must die, too – as I already had uncountable times in the fury of the maelstrom. Death, my grandmother now reminded me, reinforced by the implorations of Gabi and my mother, came to all things in every moment of time, for no one's life could hold still any more than the waters of the ocean could stop flowing. There were, however, different ways to die. As Alkurah, Bellatrix and the others had done, one could unconsciously and reflexively react to the humans' tortures – and so surrender up one's soul.

A second way, as bright as the track of the star that had streaked down from the sky, also beckoned. Rather than reacting to external afflictions, a whale could act upon himself – and so choose which parts must perish and which might live. Was this not the way of the whale? Do not the Old Ones say this: to live, I die? Have not the greatest of my kind always found in the conscious letting go of the useless or harmful parts of the self a greater life?

How had the whales in this sad place forgotten this? A better question might be how they possibly could have remembered? And the best question of all, for my part, concerned those aspects of myself that I must either allow to wither and perish or must outright slay.

To begin with, I knew, I must give up my quest to quenge in these lifeless pools, for it had driven me into a desperate place through a sick fire more terrible than the lightning that had jolted out of the humans' stunguns. I must go on without quenging at all – somehow. I must resign myself to sing with my family never again. My longing to swim free once more in the cool ocean must give way to an acceptance of tiny spaces, chlorine water, and concrete. Because the humans, not nature, had their way here, I must leave behind me what I knew as natural law.

I took a bitter solace from this decision to become both participant and primary instigator of my inevitable death. Only in this way – as incredibly difficult as it promised to be – could I become the creator of my new life. What, though, was I to create? Many songs and inspirations, I thought, went into the quickening of a young whale in the natural world: the wisdom of the Old Ones; the sweetness and succor of family; and always, a whale's own will to be more. The Old Ones, however, dwelled in a place I could no longer reach, and so although I could hear the echoes of their wisdom, I could not understand its meaning. My family, far away, could not sing to me in any music that I could hear. All that remained to me in the world of the humans was for me to sing to myself a strange and new song.

I had only the slightest of intimations, as faint as the glow of a squid's ink, of what this new composition of myself would sound like. To begin with, I must find my way to a sanity which had formerly seemed insane. Unukalhai had spoken truly in this after all. He was wrong, though, that I must drink in the madness of the human heart in the way I ate the lifeless fish they gave me. I must not become anything *like* the humans. I must decide for myself what I would call sane or not, and I must participate in only those aspects of the world which deepened my being and exalted my life. And I must do all this according only to *my* sapience, *my* realization of the true, and *my* defending savagely what goodness remained to me. All else I must leave behind as a sand crab does too small of a shell.

In the immense open waters inside myself, I zanged a dreadful and marvelous shape swimming toward me. This, I sensed, was just my soul. How could I ever escape it? It knew what I seemed not to know – knew within its fiery heart that I should call upon my grandmother's gift to protect me from a new danger that had arisen from the turbid deeps. An unexpected question now troubled me: if I could make myself anew, could I make myself into *anything*? How could I let the conceptions and the constraints of my fellow orcas bind me, to say nothing of the manias of man? Should I not only create for myself new ways to supplant the old, useless ones but perhaps even abandon the covenants themselves?

A murmuring of my mother's old warning to me suggested that I did not have to answer this question immediately. I sensed that I remained still too young and unformed to know what I would permit myself to be and become and what I would not.

One thing did seem as clear to me as a narwhale's birthing song: I must somehow live within the insanity of the human realm in a sane way. To do that, I must fight off the spiritual death that had touched the other whales. How, though, could I nurture and keep safe the new Arjuna I felt growing inside me?

I decided that I would take inspiration from the humans. Between their fragile bodies and the raw, quick, lovely touch of the natural world, they wore second skins composed of animal and plant fibers and the ubiquitous excrescence. Very well, then, I would don a second skin myself, made of the humans' expectations, conceits, and delusions. I would hide from them. Deep inside, within the ocean of true life that they could never sound, I would keep safe and vital my soul.

The next day, with Gabi, Jordan, and Painted-Skin looking on, I performed my first feat.

8

Why is it that humans like to watch whales? What joy can they take in provoking us of the flipper and the fin to leap, twist, and race in circles around a small space of contained water? Is it that they wish they could swim so well and hope to learn from us? Or do they see in our strangeness a mystery in themselves that they struggle to grasp with the flailing fingers of their all-too-human minds?

Well, we whales like to watch humans. So it has been for eons, ever since the first humans hunted clams along the oceans' beaches and ventured out into the white waves in search of crustaceans and fish. We continue watching and listening, off the coasts of the dark continents and the islands of ice, along the currents of the Sapphire Sea and the great deeps of pink, green, and purple coral. In no other part of the world, I thought, could whales watch humans as closely as we did at Sea Circus, which is what the two-leggeds seemed to call this place of scummy prison pools.

Every day, late in the morning and late in the afternoon, humans schooled together like herring and forced their bodies onto the half circle of metal chairs arrayed around the big pool. How loud they were in their constant brayings and barkings, like sea lions swarming upon a beach and fighting over patches of sand! How awkward they seemed in the bizarre jointing of their bodies, which twisted and contorted in order to fit the chairs' cruel proportions! How passionately I pitied them! What would it be like, I wondered, to go through life in constant contact with hard, sharp surfaces that could bruise, tear, or pulp tender flesh? How onerous it must be – what an endless fight – simply to stand up against the crushing force of the earthy parts of the world! And how dangerous! If a human leaned just a little too far over his many-toed feet, he would fall down and smack hard against concrete, breaking bones and knocking out teeth – or sometimes even dying.

Curiously, over the months of sun and rain that followed my resolve to gain a new sanity, I witnessed only a few such mishaps. Most of the time, the humans moved in a careful and predictable manner, as if they had been rigidly trained to control their each and every motion. Out of the manifold ways in which they might rotate and bend their limbs and other parts, it seemed that they squeezed nearly infinite possibilities of kinesthetics into too tight a pool of actualities.

So it was with their behaviors. Considering the close proximity of human to human, I thought it curious how rarely they touched each other. At least, that was true of the adults. Most of their physical connection with others of their kind came in their prodding or moving their children with their hands, much as Painted-Skin had used his stungun to goad me. Twice I saw human adults use their hands to strike their children, slapping young faces and pummeling the twin knots of muscle that gather at the base of the human spine. Given all that had occurred since my capture, this desecration of innocents should not have shocked me, but it did. Why couldn't the humans control their violent natures when they most needed to? They seemed to restrain themselves in so many other ways, for instance, rarely putting finger to tongue or into any orifice. Not once did I see any man, woman, or child caress each others' genitals or mate.

Many other activities, however, remained to them. We whales

trained them to slap their hands together in a thunderous staccato of sound that bounced off the waters of the big pool and to perform other easy feats. Although most of the time the humans damped the power and range of their vocalizations as they did their bodies' movements, we could get them to whistle, ululate, and scream just by splashing flippersful of water upon them and soaking them from head to toe.

The first feat that I performed for my onlookers consisted of nothing more than a great breach from out of the big pool's shallow waters, followed by a pirouette, a moment of flying through the human cries that filled the air, and a splash so meteoric that the many humans sitting close to me screamed to find themselves drenched. Over the passing months, with Gabi modeling various movements with her pale, lithe body, I elaborated upon this feat. In the Moon of the Silver Salmon I managed a double pirouette, and in the Moon of Storms, I turned about mid-air in my first triple. Day after day I leaped and rolled and listened in wonderment to the noises of humans who came to watch us whales.

In the pool of blood that had spurted from my broken head, I had resolved that I must live a new life in new ways. I tried to fulfill this promise to myself. I regained something of my old relish for the small joys of life that the humans could not subtract from existence. So many joys there really were! The water droplets flung up into air as I hung suspended in space gathered in the light pouring down from our world's star and fractured it into dancing rainbows of reds, yellows, greens, and blazing blues. The glass display above the big pool shimmered with human-made colors and images that fascinated me. New sounds – such as the giggling of human babies and the tinkling of wind chimes – pleased me as well. Rain and sunlight stroked my skin, and the air currents carried to my mouth the taste of puffy, white clouds that billowed far up into the cerulean sky. And always, there was water: that singular, superluminal substance that buoyed up my body and composed its being – even as it did the bodies of Gabi and other humans who joined us whales in performing feats in the big pool.

It astonished me to discover that I actually *liked* doing feats. How else could I exercise my muscles and divert myself from the humming, black boredom? How I reveled in moving my body in new and challenging ways! The perfect coordination of flippers, fin, and tail into a leap into unknown possibilities hinted at even greater synergies of the soul that dwelled somewhere within me.

What a shock to realize that none of my newfound powers over myself would have flowered but for the touch of the humans and their despicable hands! How strange that was and how strange humans really were! How had they conceived of capturing whales and forcing us to do feats in the first place? No whale would ever think to do such a thing, even if we had the means to do it. In the very originality of the humans' iniquities I found a dreadful magnificence. Could it be, I wondered, that their endless and disturbing creativity welled up from the same deep sea that moved inside of me?

It was during the Moon of Breaking Ice that I conceived of inveigling Electra to join me in performing. The feat that we devised was simple: Electra and I raced across the big pool together taking turns in leaping over each other's backs. We called this 'The Rope', after the strands of excrescence that the humans twist into a single, sheeny strand used to bind and connect many of their things. The humans, not so slow-witted as my family had once supposed, called our feat by the same name. Whenever Electra and I wove our bodies into a rope, our onlookers clapped their hands together with exceptional vigor.

This success encouraged me to devise a much more complex and difficult feat. In this, I requested the aid of Unukalhai, who seemed only too glad to oblige me. Gabi, too, joined us in performing, for her actions – and reactions – were crucial to the delicious frisson of danger that I wished to evoke in the humans watching us. It took a full three moons to train Gabi. And then one day, in Moon of the Midnight Sun, we debuted our feat: while Unukalhai waited at the curve of the pool nearest the onlookers, I used my face to push Gabi down deep into the water – so deep that I knew the waiting humans could barely see us. There, in the warm, blue gloom, I dove down ever farther beneath her. She carefully planted her bare feet on my face, digging her toes into my skin. Then I swam upward. I drove my tail against the water with such force it felt as if my spine might break. Up, up, up, and suddenly I breached in an explosion of both whale and human into the water-dappled air. For a moment, Gabi and I flew as one.

Just before the apogee of my leap, she pushed off from me, launching herself even farther into space. While I splashed down nearly in the same spot from which I had left the water, Gabi's arc carried her up and out toward Unukalhai. It pleased me to hear the onlookers fall quiet and suck in breaths almost in unison. It pleased me more to zang their trepidation as Gabi plunged head down straight toward Unukalhai's now-opened jaws. Impossible, it seemed, that she could avoid impaling herself on Unukalhai's glistening white teeth and perhaps being swallowed whole. At the last instant, however, Unukalhai closed his mouth and turned his head aside as if he could not bear to harm a human. Gabi dove into the water that Unukalhai had just vacated. Unukalhai swam up beneath her and took her onto his back as if he had rescued her from drowning. While she threw her arms around him and pressed her lips to his skin, Unukalhai swam about the pool with Gabi astride him.

The humans witnessing this feat stood up from their metal chairs and clapped their hands together for a long time. Some of them howled like wolves. They must have perceived in Gabi the same virtue that I appreciated: that as clumsy as most humans seemed to be most of the time, occasionally a rare, daring few of them could move with an astonishing coordination and grace.

The following dawn, we whales gathered together in the big

pool. A soft rain dimpled the water. The schools of humans had long since abandoned their chairs, and only a single walrus-shaped female named Justice prowled the concrete beach above us. It felt good to be alone together, or nearly so. Of course, because the humans understood nothing of what we said, in a very real way, we were always alone.

Alkurah, who still nursed an ire that I could feel like an underwater current flowing from her to me, lazed about the far curve of the pool, and she sent soft sounds rippling through the water:

'I have decided to speak to you again after all,' she told me.

'I am glad,' I replied, 'though I wonder why?'

'You were so very kind to sing to my sister. And I have repaid you with resentment.'

'Yes, you have been angry at me since our first meeting.'

'I have been angry at everything since I came to this place. And angry most of all at myself because I have failed to keep my family from harm.'

'Perhaps the humans,' I said, 'will return Navi to Zavijah.'

'No, they will not. Now my family has no babies! How I want another! How I wanted you! My blood was up, but your phallus was not – that is, not up inside where I needed it to be.'

'I understand,' I said. 'I wanted you, too. I still do.'

'I want you to want me more than your reason wants other things.'

'That is not a whale's way.'

'Yes, but it is our way to wish that it might be so.'

She swam a slow circle around the pool and made her way closer to me.

'It is strange to me,' she said, 'that it has taken me so long to thank you for giving my sister a little comfort. I think Unukalhai is right that I must be a little mad.'

We met eye to blue eye through the azure-tinged waters, and we exchanged a moment of hope that we had not fallen hopelessly mad.

'We all received extra fish today,' she said to me, 'so I should also thank you for that.'

'I am glad your belly is pleased.'

'It would please me more to know why you do what you do.'

'And what do I do?'

'You do much more than the humans want you to – you, who at first would do nothing.'

'I *like* doing feats – it relieves the boredom.'

'A part of an answer,' she said, 'is no answer at all.'

'I like creating new feats,' I told her, 'because in this way, I, and not the humans, am the orchestrator of my own motions.'

'That is still only part of your reason, is it not? I think you like provoking the humans, as you do me.'

I laughed at this. 'I would love to persuade you and your sisters to join us in provoking the humans.'

Unukalhai and Electra glided on either side of me; we had become closer over the last few months. As if in consideration of what I had said, Salm and Zavijah swam nearer to me, as did the perpetually cowed Menkalinan. Although Bellatrix floated in dead silence across the pool, I felt sure she was listening.

'But why, Arjuna?' Alkurah said to me. 'Beyond doing a few leaps and eating the fish the humans give us, why pay any mind to them at all?'

'Before you were captured, did you not pay mind to the winds and currents?'

'I do not like to remember how things were before we were captured.'

'Here,' I said, 'we swim in currents of the humans' making.'

'It would seem that it is not enough for you just to swim – you insist on flying right out of the pools, don't you?'

For a moment, I took refuge in the same silence that enveloped Bellatrix.

'And even flying is not enough, no? I think you would change the currents themselves.'

148

'You are very perceptive, Mother Alkurah.'

'What I do not understand is why you would attempt the impossible?'

'There are at least two reasons,' I said. 'It may be that the impossible is not only possible but inevitable. And even if it is not, the attempt by itself can lead into a whole sea of possibilities.'

'O I wish that were so!' she whistled out. Then she said, 'And what is your second reason?'

'I have decided to become sane.'

'O I wish that even more!'

'We must all become sane.'

'Yes, yes – but how will we do that, Arjuna?'

She aimed a zang of compassion at Zavijah, who many months later still shrieked out maddening wails each night over the loss of Navi. Alkurah also wondered aloud if Bellatrix had enough wit left even to wail about her own plight, and she chided Unukalhai for taking too great a pleasure whenever Gabi sailed toward his opened mouth: stark proof that sadism had truly unbalanced him.

'We are whales, are we not?' I said to Alkurah. 'Have we not survived for eons? How should we let the humans take from us what is most vital to our kind?'

'Tell me more,' she said, swimming still closer to me. 'Why do you *really* want my sisters and me to join in your feats?'

Enough of her original pique at me remained in her voice to transform her question into a demand. This irritated me. Who was this whale from the Emerald Sea to demand of me anything? She might have been Mother Alkurah, but she was not *my* mother – and certainly not my grandmother.

And then I breached and breathed in the coolness of the rain-sweetened morning, and my own anger gentled. I remembered my resolve to remake myself. If my attempt at self-creation was to have any teeth at all, then mustn't I require of myself much, much more than the snapping up of the first emotion that swam my way? Shouldn't I be kind to a tormented orca whom I could feel struggling to be kind to me?

With such thoughts in mind, I moved closer and brushed up against her. Her soft skin left an exquisite shudder of delight upon my own. She was a proud matriarch, and I must respect her. She was a beautiful, fertile female, and I must remind her that she had been called into life to give more life.

'If we all do feats together,' I said to her, 'if we create them *ourselves* as a family composes a song that keeps everyone together even the stormiest of seas, then the humans will wonder how we knew to do this. They will listen. And in listening to the yearning of our hearts, they will set us free.'

I listened to the beating of Alkurah's heart, and I felt her anger for me softening, like an organ no longer distressed by too great a pressure of blood.

'You are very strange,' she said to me. 'Stranger than the midnight stars – and as beautiful.'

She zanged me deep inside where I held in the world's breath.

'How I would love to be free!' she said.

A strange idea came to me, by way of Gabi's lips. If a human being had showered tenderness upon an unfathomable whale such as I, then surely we whales of disparate clans and kinds could do the same.

'I will help you,' I said to Alkurah. I cast my voice at the others. 'Zavijah and Unukalhai, too – all of us. We must all help each other.'

She pressed her head against mine, and sang to me a soft, glorious song. Then her sisters Salm and Zavijah came up close and touched their faces to me as well. Baby Electra squeezed in between them. Menkalinan and Unukalhai swam over to us. Even Bellatrix joined us there.

'Let us sing one of the old songs,' Alkurah said.

'But I do not know your kind's songs!' Baby Electra chirped out.

'We will teach you,' Alkurah said.

'I do not know your clan's harmonies,' Unukalhai said.

'Then listen – and sing with us.'

As we all gathered around, she began singing in her clear, gentle voice. The morning warmed with the sun's rising, and the pool brightened with golden rays and the sonance of our voices. It was an hour of urgent touching and soft understanding passed from flute to flute and skin to skin. Many times, Alkurah called out the song's refrain to me in glowing chords of hope and inviolate promises. She gave *me* the highest and most radiant of her music, but in the unitive way of the whales, she sang to the others, too, joining the many to the one:

'We will move as you move, think as you think, breathe as you breathe, dream as you dream.'

In the opening outward of the quiet morning into the blaze of another day, we dreamed together the oldest and greatest of all dreams.

9

It would not be accurate to say that after this the other whales
and I became a family, for a family shares a future together as
well as blood, and swims always with a single purpose. All of us,
I knew, in longing for freedom, envisioned a return to the old life
and the old ways in the various seas that had given us birth. We
wanted to mingle and mate in screaming ecstasies with the whales
of clans we remembered all too poignantly. Even so, in the new
accord that flowed from Alkurah and me (and from and to the
others), we became *like* a family. It had suddenly become unthink-
able for any of us to rake another with bared teeth or to touch
another in anger. We worked very hard on perfecting new feats
and directing our anger toward a common purpose: persuading
the humans to set us free.

One morning, with little yellow birds chattering in the trees
above the big pool, Jordan walked onto the concrete beach and
made a call that sounded like a rumble of thunder. Gabi moved
over to him. I swam in slow circles about the water. I had to
concentrate to hear what they were saying.

'You've done wonders with the orcas,' he said to her. 'Particularly
with Bobo.'

I knew those silly, plosive sounds of Bo-Bo too well. Jordan was talking about me; it seemed he always wanted to talk about me.

'Thank you,' Gabi said, 'but it's Bobo who has done most of the work. At times, I think he's training *me*.'

Jordan made the peculiar rolling, coughing sound that often accompanied the upcurving of the humans' mouths, 'That's funny,' he said.

'No, really. We were practicing the Rocket when Kimoku came up to watch. When he opened his mouth that first time, I thought I was going to pee my suit.'

She made a noise similar to Jordan's, but the corners of her mouth turned up only slightly. I zanged in her the quickened beating of her heart, which might have been excitement or apprehension.

'I *swear* that Bobo called him over,' she said. 'It was as if they'd planned the whole thing.'

'You really think these whales are that intelligent?'

'He talks to me – I'm sure he does. I just don't understand what he's saying.'

'Pet owners think their dogs talk to them, too.'

'But they do!'

Again Jordan made the coughing noise and the curving of his mouth.

'There was a Border Collie, Chaser,' he said, 'that understood a thousand commands to fetch various things. How many do you think Bobo understands?'

Gabi turned to look at me. 'We shouldn't even be having this discussion here. I don't *know* what he understands.'

'Come on, Gabi!'

'It's different with these whales than with dogs, particularly with Bobo. It's not so much how *many* words he understands but the *way* that he understands them.'

'I know how much you love him – don't you think you might be projecting?'

'I'm *not* projecting! Look at him – really look! There's a *person* there!'

153

Jordan's eyes rolled up for a moment as the lids covering them pulled back. Then his head dropped down, and he used his marvelously multifarious hand to rub his eyes.

'Now you're anthropomorphizing,' he said to her. 'Whatever it takes.'

'Yeah, whatever it takes – like starvation and stun guns.'

'It worked, didn't it? Isn't he a lot more cooperative now?'

'I doubt if we had anything to do with that.'

'Isn't he happier, too?'

'I don't know! I wish I could just ask him.'

Now Jordan's head turned back and forth.

'Listen, no one will ever talk to a whale, even if whales could talk, which they can't.'

'How can you be so sure? Helen Agar thinks they can.'

'Is that the linguist you met at the conference?'

'Yeah, we've been in touch. I told her how Bobo is trying to speak to me, all his sounds. She mentioned coming here and studying the orcas when we're not working with them.'

Jordan's fingers stroked his jaw. 'That's actually not such a bad idea – we can use that.'

'Is that all you can think of?'

'Listen, you're paid to train the whales, and I'm paid to make sure you keep getting paid.'

'But you can't just turn a chance to do important science into a publicity stunt!'

'Do you know how much revenue has increased since the flying Bobo started launching you toward Kimoku's throat? We can always use good publicity.'

Gabi said nothing as she looked down at the pool and we gazed at each other.

'And we can really use Bobo's semen now,' Jordan continued. 'Since he's become famous, all the ocean parks are calling us. His million-dollar penis is probably worth more like ten million.'

Now it was Gabi's turn to perform the eye-rolling feat. She said,

'We haven't been able to get Bobo to have an erection – I don't know why.'

'Well, keep trying.'

Gabi stared at Jordan. Her eyes seemed to harden, like beached jellyfish drying out in the sun. 'Then should I tell Helen Agar we're interested?'

'Let me think about that. There's a lot to consider here, and we should talk about it at length. Are you free for dinner on Saturday?'

I have said that I resolved to hide from the humans, but the more I moved through the water with Gabi, the more I found myself wanting to show myself to her – at least, to show the bright, enthusiastic parts. The dark thing that I had discovered during my worst moments of madness I swallowed down deep inside where no breath of air might give it greater life. How should I want Gabi even to glimpse this dread energy when I did not dare to behold it myself? And yet, I knew that someday I must. I sensed that I would never be able to speak to the soul-shadowed humans with a totality of truth until I first embraced the totality of myself.

And I did want to speak to these cruel sun-walkers – how badly I wanted this! Had I not deserted my first family in the cold seas of the far north so that I might show humans what they were doing to the watery parts of the world that they could not perceive? Would it not mock my family's love for me if I abandoned my efforts to fulfill this purpose?

Even as the old call renewed its keening inside me, I realized that the vaporous notion of talking with the human animals had condensed into a single stream of desire to speak with a single human person, and that was Gabi. The more that I cavorted with her through the waters of the big pool – as we exchanged murmurs of meaning and looked into each other's eyes – the more certain I became that she *was* a person. I had asked for her help, and the gentleness of her breath and the knowingness of her hands had touched much of my diffidence away. She seemed to assure me that as long as she watched over me, she would do everything in her power to lift up my spirit, with hope and zest, even as I carried her on leap after leap up into the sun-filled sky. She spoke soft words to me, so many, many human words. I understood more and more of them. I knew that in some deep way she had come to trust me as I did her. I felt her trying to uncover things that caused her pain. In the plaintiveness of her voice, no less than the sounds of the word 'help', I knew that she was asking for my help, too.

On a day of storm and thunder, when the dark clouds had finally pulled back to reveal the ocean of blueness above, Gabi walked onto the concrete beach accompanied by a human female whose like I had never seen. So tall she was – nearly as tall as Painted-Skin and Jordan! And so erect her long, slender body, as if the line between foot and head connected the earth directly to the heavens! And yet, there was a paradox in her posture: Although she stood straighter than the slouching humans I had encountered, she seemed to do so more naturally and with less effort, as if the crushing earth force had no power over her – or rather, as if she had decided not to *allow* it to weigh her down. How lightly she moved toward my pool, with what grace, like a song on the wind! Of all the marvels of this unusual woman, however, none compared with the marvel of her skin, its rich, lovely color. The human hides I had seen were as creamy as pus, as yellow as dead teeth, as brown as excrement, as pink as bloody lungs. But, oh, this woman's glorious covering! So black it was – almost a pure and seamless black. In the air's almost liquid radiance, her naked shoulders and arms shone like obsidian, like the black pearls of the palpulve oysters, like the moonlit waters of the Arctic Ocean at midnight – and more, like the black skin of beautiful orcas such as my mother and my sister Turais and mighty Alnitak.

'Hello, Bobo,' she said to me, moving over to the edge of

pool and kneeling down. 'I know that is not your real name, so please forgive me. You can call me . . . squeak shrill trill whistle click!'

I stopped swimming my lazy circles, stunned into motionlessness. What had I just heard? The black-skinned woman had just called out a cacophony of sounds that were a mockery of orca speech – or were they? Nothing about this woman's eyes mocked; rather they played.

'Oh, so you want to try to speak Orca, do you,' I said to her. 'How sorry I am for you!'

Her eyes sparkled like stars. I swam as close to her as I could. I loved her eyes. Black as the dazzling substance of space they were, and their bottomless black centers danced with little lights. They danced with *my* eyes, inviting me to play. I realized that something within me urged me to swim deep into the humans' eyes (some of them), for they seemed sharper than a whale's eyes and full of thoughts that a whale would never think. I reveled in their proportions, the way the twin orbs of luminosity dominate the human face.

'Seriously,' the black-skinned female finally said to me, tapping her chest, 'my name is Helen Agar. I would love to know your real name, for I find it difficult to call you Bobo.'

I could not say why I felt a desire to tell her my true name, but I did. I called it out to her, in the song of glory that my mother had taught me. Helen listened, with her marvelous black eyes. And, I thought, with her heart.

'I would like to try to talk to you,' she said to me. 'I know you can talk; I know that you and Kimoku communicated together the idea of your famous stunt with Gabi.'

'I want to talk to you!' I called back to her. 'But why is it that you humans understand nothing of what we whales say?'

'If it is all right with you,' she said, still kneeling across from me, 'I would like to try to teach you some words of English. And I hope you will try to teach your Orca words to me.'

'Perhaps I can teach you,' I said to her, 'as I taught Gabi the word for help.'

'Will you help me, beautiful whale? And let me help you?'

The Helen woman had made the sound for help! She wanted to help me – or needed my help. Would I do as she asked? Yes, I cried out to her, yes, yes – help!

Two days later, she returned to the big pool followed by Painted-Skin, Golden-Hair, and Gabi, who carried boxes of things onto the concrete beach. Gabi went off and came back with a big bucket of fish. She stood by the side of the pool with Helen.

'Will you play a game with me?' Helen asked me.

It was rare when I had the big pool to myself, and I was enjoying my relative freedom to swim where I wanted. I decided that I wanted to swim over to Helen.

'This is how the game will work,' she explained to me. From one of the boxes, she withdrew an object that I recognized, whose human name I knew.

'This is a pinecone,' she told me. 'P-i-n-e-c-o-n-e. I am going to throw it out into the pool, and you are to bring it back to me.'

Her arm drew back, then snapped forward. The pinecone flew in an arc over my head. I could tell from the splash exactly where it hit the water.

'Can you bring it to me, Bobo?'

At the utterance of my name, Gabi blew her whistle, as she often did when she wished me to perform one feat or another. I knew well enough what Helen was asking me to do. However, given the circumstances, I did not want to do it.

'I told you,' Gabi said to Helen. 'It's the fish – Bobo gave up working for rewards months ago. He considers that beneath his dignity.'

'You *did* tell me that,' Helen said, 'and I should have listened. But Jordan insisted on my training Bobo his way: one trick, one treat.'

'That's how the other trainers and other orcas work, but Bobo and I have a special arrangement.'

'Well, I would like to have the same arrangement. Do you suppose it would be all right if we took the fish away?'

'Sure, but Jordan said he'd stop by to see how things are going.'

'Then why don't we hope that by the time he does, things are going quite well?'

I watched as Painted-Skin carried the bucket of stinking fish away. Soon enough, I would eat another meal of clotted, dead meat. I did not wish my obligatory eating, however, to depend on which feats I chose to do or not do.

'Let's try again,' Helen said. 'Can you bring me the pinecone?'

I did not wait for Gabi to blow her whistle. I swam to the center of the pool, scooped up the pinecone, and returned to drop it on the concrete beach by Helen's feet.

'Very good! Now I'm going to tell you the names of a few more things.'

One by one, she removed various objects from the boxes, named them, and threw them out into the pool: Bottle. Can. Kleenex box. Ball. Stick. Pen. Apple. Tape dispenser. Notebook. Pushpin. Knife. Fork. Spoon.

The names of some of these objects I had long since learned in similar naming games I had played with the first humans I had encountered in the bay. Most names, however, were new to me.

'All right,' Helen said, 'can you bring me the apple?'

I turned, swam, and brought her the apple.

'*Can* – can you bring me the can?'

I brought her the can.

'Stick, Bobo, s-t-i-c-k.'

I retrieved that piney, bark-covered object as well.

'Now ball. B-a-l-l.'

I did not move.

'Pushpin – can you find the pushpin, or is it too small for you?'

One zang of sonar would have sufficed to locate the tiny bit of the pushpin floating behind me, but I did not want to take it into my mouth.

'How about the candle?' Helen asked me.

I found the candle, and gave it into her hand.

'Very good – now the jacket. J-a-c-k-e-t.'

For a while, she called out names to me, and sometimes I swam through the clutter of objects floating in an ugly mass on the pool's surface and seized a specific thing, and sometimes I did not. The game went on and on: Newspaper. Frisbee. Bookmark. Fan. Bag. Toothbrush. Toothpick. Toothpaste tube. Wallet. Plate. Bowl. Cup. Tongs. Socks. CD. Balloon . . .

After I had retrieved a cantaloupe, I heard Gabi say to Helen, 'This isn't exactly a rigorous, double-blind experiment is it?'

Helen's eyes lit up with what I took to be amusement, and she said, 'I must tell you a secret, Gabi. I think we have liked and trusted each other from the first time we met, so I know that you will keep what I am about to say to yourself.'

'I promise,' Gabi said.

'Good. Then please know that while I intend to do as much good science as I can with the orcas, that is not my primary purpose.' She drew in a breath through her lovely, flared black nose and looked at me. 'I would flush every well-received paper that I have ever written down the toilet in exchange for finding a way to talk to these people.'

Then she slapped hands with Gabi, and they wrapped their arms around each other like two octopi entangling themselves in their tentacles.

Later in the day, when the white clouds dappling the sky had grown gray and thick, Jordan appeared. I heard him say: 'How's my favorite flying whale doing?'

Helen held a board to which was attached a piece of white paper covered with little black marks like the legs of insects. She looked down at the paper, and said, 'We have tested Bobo on 484 objects. He has successfully identified 71 of them.'

'Not bad for a day's work, Big Boy!' Jordan called out to me.

He bent down and reached across the water to bounce his hand on top of my head. As I always did when he touched me, I restrained the urge to bite it off.

'Not bad,' he said, standing up to turn toward Helen, 'but not very good. That's slightly less than a 15% accuracy rate.'

'What were you hoping for?' Helen said to him.

'Well, Chaser, the Border Collie, scored better than 90% on more than a thousand named toys.'

'Yes, but Chaser did not learn all those names in a few hours.'

'Then I should be proud of my little whale.'

'It seems that if he hears a name a single time, he memorizes it immediately.'

'*Some* names, apparently.'

'I am sure he will do better as time goes on.'

'All right, I'll give you until tomorrow to get him up to a 100%.' Jordan made the rolling, coughing sound, which in him seemed more unpleasant than it did in other humans. 'I'm joking! Take as much time as you need. Why don't we circle up again in a few more days and see how things are going?'

After he had walked off, Helen stood looking down at her paper. She said, 'This is a little odd. Bobo did not identify the toothbrush or the toothpaste tube, but he retrieved the toothpick, which must be much harder to locate.'

'Here, may I see that?' Gabi said.

Helen gave the board and paper to her.

'Oh, my God!' she said. 'I kind of *knew* there was something strange going on, but I didn't quite *know* that I knew, if you know what I mean.'

'What *do* you mean?'

'Well, look, all the objects he retrieved are wood, paper, leather, fruit, or other natural substances. Everything he ignored is made of plastic.'

Helen moved close to Gabi and re-examined the paper.

'All right,' she said, 'can you clear the water so that we might start over again?'

I wondered why Painted-Skin and Golden-Hair used nets attached to long poles to scoop up the many objects from the pool. Was the silly game over?

'All right, my friend,' Helen said, reaching into one of the boxes, 'let us see if you can improve upon your slightly less than 15%.'

Again Helen named objects to me: Block. Bead. Amber. Fruit Loop. Floor tile. Scrabble tile. Egg carton. Jeans. Paper airplane. Celery. Yarn. Tangerine . . .

And one by one, as she repeated the names and asked me to retrieve them, I brought the objects back to her. I liked this game a little better, for none of the objects was of plastic. How should I ever want to touch my mouth to anything made of sickening, slick, dead plastic?

'He got them all!' Gabi cried out. 'I can't wait to see Jordan's face when I tell him!'

Helen said something to Painted-Skin and Golden-Hair. They went away, leaving Gabi and her alone with me.

'Perhaps we should not tell him so soon,' Helen said. 'Jordan seems to be overburdened with numbers such as percentages and dollar amounts. I would first like to see how Bobo does with abstract nouns.'

'How are you going to do that? You can't bring out a box of love and start throwing things like affection, endearment, and friendship into the pool.'

'You are forgetting yourself,' Helen said. 'You have already taught Bobo the word for the abstraction help, and I believe he has given us in return the orca sound for that concept.'

'But that might have been a fluke. Bobo and I had a special connection that day.'

'Then we must try to ensure that we have the same depth of connection on other days. Why don't we begin again on Monday and see how Bobo reacts to music?'

It surprised me how sad I felt when Helen went away soon after that. Would I ever see her again, I wondered? I understood well enough that she had tried to teach me the humans' language. I hoped that my lack of progress – and my failure to teach her almost anything of my language – had not discouraged her.

The next day, during our performance of feats for the schools of humans that crowded the metal chairs, there occurred a disturbing incident that touched off zangs of new understanding as to how the humans communicated with each other. Just after Gabi had dared death yet again in Unukalhai's jaws, a human female very close to the big pool cried out what at first seemed to be an alarm. She stood up holding a baby away from her big chest with stiffened arms. A brown splotch of what seemed to be excrement besmeared her white shirt. The tension of her opened, squared mouth thinned her whitened lips as if they were rubber bands. Her thick eyebrows pulled together and downward, which made her glowering eyes narrow. She stared straight ahead at her baby as a wolf might regard a snow rabbit.

'No, no, no!' she called out from the mouth of her uglified face as she began shaking her baby in front of her. 'Bad, bad, bad!'

Even as another women close to her began screaming the word *Stop!*, I came into a full realization of something that had been gnawing at me beneath my conscious awareness for quite a while: the humans used their faces to talk to each other! It was as if they could not hold themselves inside, as their babies could not contain their excretions. The humans leaked out their emotions through their mouths and muscles in a most indecent way.

Later that day, in my second round of doing feats, I studied the many expressions of the many humans who watched me: the curved lips, pushed-up cheeks, and crows' feet wrinkles at the corners of the eyes that I associated with happiness; the flabby lips and wrinkled nose of disgust; the raised upper eyelids and pulled-back lips of the face of fear.

A couple of days later, these new insights facilitated the language games that Helen and I played with each other. With the sun hanging over the grounds like the big orange ball that Helen had cast into the pool at our first meeting, she and Gabi arrived with more boxes of things. Helen removed them and named them for me: Computer. Converter cable. Diffuser. Mixer. Monitor. Filter. Amp. Headphones. Hydrophone. Only one of these – the hydrophone – did she set into the water.

After a while, with the sun's orange fire heating up the morning, she said, 'All right, my beautiful one, are you ready?'

Waves of pounding sonance suddenly filled the pool. I was so astonished that I almost leaped from the water, for the sound issued from *beneath* the water and nearly forced me from it with its savage power. From the hydrophone, of course, it came. The cruel, cunning humans made things that spoke beneath the water even as we whales speak.

'How do you like this music?' Helen said to me.

Crashing chords and complicated rhythms that felt like a dozen kinds of fish thrashing inside my belly pierced straight through me. Various themes, as jagged as a shark's teeth, tore into one another, interacted for a moment, and then gave birth to new expressions which incorporated the old. Brooding harmonies collided, moved apart, and then invited in a higher order of chaos. Such a brutal beauty! So much blood, exaltation, and splendor in the humans' music!

'O music!' I cried out. I breached, and spoke right into Helen's face. 'Music! Music! Music!'

'Can you say that again, lovely one?' Helen asked me. '*Music.*'

'Music!' I called back to her. I had to remember to hold my sounds to a precise pitch, pattern, and tempo. The humans, I reminded myself, could not comprehend variation or context in their utterances, or so I thought.

'M-u-s-i-c!'

'Music – I've got it!' Helen said. She made the human happy

face, which her eyes reinforced by dancing out little twinkles of light. 'Listen, my bright one.'

From the hydrophone burst the very sounds for the word music that I had just spoken! How had she reproduced them? How clever the humans were, so impossibly and beautifully clever!

'Music,' Helen said to me.

'Music,' I called back to her.

'Music, music, music!' Gabi shouted out.

'Music, music, music – sing me more!'

A new music flowed from the hydrophone, delighting the very water. So different from the first it was, and yet so alike, for within its simpler melodies and purer beauty dwelled an immense affirmation of life. A great chorus of human voices sang of this. It was almost as if the Old Ones were calling to me.

O the stars! O the sea! They sang of joy!

Without Gabi asking me, I dove down into the sound-sweetened water, and then breached in a double-twisting back flip. I swam over to Gabi and Helen. I cried out to them: 'Joy!'

And Helen said to me, 'Joy?'

'Joy, joy, j-o-y!' I called back.

'The music was Ludwig van Beethoven's Ode to Joy.'

'Yes, yes – joy!'

Helen clapped hands with Gabi, entangled her in her arms, and pressed her mouth to Gabi's face. The corners of her lips pulled almost straight upward into the crows' feet wrinkles of black skin at her temples. Her black, black eyes radiated joy, joy, joy.

'I did some research,' Helen said to Gabi. 'In the bay where Bobo was captured. I was told that he likes Stravinsky's Rite of Spring and Beethoven's Ninth Symphony.'

I did not understand most of the words that Helen had just spoken. To return her to the day's play, I drew in a mouthful of water and sprayed it over her.

'W-a-t-e-r,' I enunciated.

She bent down and gathered up some of the pool's water in the cup of her hand.

'Water,' she said. Then she sent one of our orcas' sets of sounds for water streaming out of the hydrophone.

'Water, water, water!'

'Water, water, water!'

O, the stars! O joy! I had finally taught the humans to speak!

I sprayed Helen again. I watched as she took water from her beautiful, black hand into her mouth. Then she spat a cascade of sparkling droplets over me.

'How does it feel to be sprayed, my playful one?'

'Spray,' I said, dousing her again. 'Spray me.'

Again, Helen sprayed me.

'Spray me,' she said.

It is possible that no other whale in all of the ages of the world had ever sprayed so huge a mouthful of water over the head of a human being.

'Spray me!' I said to her.

'Spray *me*!'

'Spray! Spray! Spray!'

'Oh, my God!' Gabi shouted out. 'Now he's working on the verbs!'

Helen, Gabi, and I played together for the rest of the morning, until it came time to do feats for the daily onlookers. I learned many new words: Swim. Cough. Laugh. Blink. Flex. Walk. Breach. Trust. Friendship. Cry. Of course, the meaning of some of the words tried to escape me like darting schools of silvery fish. I felt unsure, for instance, of the difference between fun and joy. Even so, I thought, it was a very good beginning, certainly the best day since my capture and one of the most auspicious ones of my life.

'All right,' Gabi said to Helen, 'I have to get ready for the show.'

'Goodbye, my huge one,' Helen said to me. 'I will be back tomorrow.'

'Goodbye,' I said to her. And then, 'Help me.'

'Of course I am going to help you.'

'Help joy.'

'What? Help you joy?'

I also found it difficult to distinguish between joy and freedom, at least in the human formulations of these conceptions. I said to Helen, and to Gabi, 'Free me – free all of us. Help us to become joyously free!'

I could not tell at first if they understood me. Helen's face remained as immobile as a great pillar of black basalt rising up from the sea. No emotion that I could detect seeped out of her. Then water filled her eyes at nearly the same moment that Gabi's eyes also overflowed. Tears, the humans called this salty substance. They wept for me! So great was the pressure of my heart just then that I would have done the same, but whales weep not.

'Yes, my wild one,' Helen said to me. 'That is why I am really here. I will help you to become free.'

The sun took its time in burning itself cool that day, and the moon rose like a silver dreaming in the east. Then the sun blazed red and full, while the moon lost pieces of itself to the devouring sun, which flared orange against a sky of cobalt glass, then glowed white through a gathering mist and sometimes yellow, at noon when the onlookers cheered Unukalhai, Electra, and me. And all this time, Gabi and Helen spoke to me as I did to them.

We did not speak well or clearly. Because the humans could not hear many of the sounds I formed, Helen had to use her machines instead of her ears to record them. We made a little covenant: as soon as I understood (or thought I did) a simple word of the humans' language, I would adopt my orca speech, pruning all complexity, context, and nuance into the simplest of sounds that might enfold my meaning. I might have hoped to speak to a clam in this way. The language I thus produced for Gabi and Helen could not have been called anything like true orca speech, but it was all I had to give them.

In a way that I could not comprehend, Helen's machines drank in the flow of rudimentary sounds and somehow excreted human words that correlated with mine – usually but not always the same human words whose meanings I had tried to enfold in my clumsy little compositions. It vexed me that these two humans could understand my utterances (all but a few of them) only through Helen's machines. Why couldn't we always speak flute to blood, mouth to mind, heart to heart? Why must the humans mediate nearly all of their existence through their tools and machines?

As little as Helen and Gabi could make out of my speech directly, with those horrifically convoluted flaps of flesh that they called ears, I found myself getting a better and better grip upon their speech. The more words that I learned, the more I could learn, for with each new suggestion of meaning came context which invited in the meaning of new words. For some reason that I could not fathom, it seemed that the humans divided their most important conceptions into two classes of words, called nouns and verbs. I could not be sure of this, however, for it seemed that many words could be used both nounily and verbily. The order in which humans arranged their words – linearly! – like plastic beads on one of their hideous necklaces, seemed to matter. I had to continually remind myself, for instance, that pricking a finger and fingering a prick meant two entirely different things. My forgetting of the primitiveness and constraints of Gabi's and Helen's language led to many confusions.

One dark night, when the great white shark of time had completely swallowed up the moon and Helen stood tending her machines, Gabi sat at the pool edge dangling her legs in the water. Unusually (for her), her body bent in the curve of a slump, and she held her hand over her eyes. She seemed to have fallen into the same sort of motionlessness that usually paralyzed Bellatrix.

'What is it that has dispirited you?' I asked her.

The sounds of my query zanged into Helen's machine. Human words dribbled out of them. I heard Helen say: 'I think he's speaking to you, Gabi.'

Gabi did not move. I swam over to her and touched my face to her foot.

Finally, she stroked my head, then looked up at Helen and asked, 'What did he say?'

'Didn't you hear? It looks as if it translates into: "Sad why?"'

'Yes, why sad, Gabi?' I asked. 'Hurt what heart?'

'It looks as if he has got the order wrong again,' Helen said. 'I think he means, "What hurt heart?"'

'I don't know what to tell him!' Gabi cried out.

'Why don't you tell him the truth?' Helen said. 'As you would to any friend?'

Gabi kicked her feet through the water. She started to cry. She shook her head, wiped tears from her eyes, and shook her head again. Then she told me: 'I have to hurt you, Bobo.'

I shook my head, too, a little feat I had learned. 'You me hurt?'

'At least, they *want* me to hurt you,' Gabi said continuing to stroke me. 'But I'm not going to do it, because what Jordan is *really* asking amounts to rape, although of course he doesn't see it that way, but how would *he* like to be drugged, especially with the one we paid to have developed, which you might as well call animal Viagra – as if he'd think it was all right for someone to spike his food and dose him without knowing just so they could steal his sperm and . . . oh, my God, he's such a prick!'

I touched my tongue to her hand and said, 'Prick finger?'

'No, Bobo, *I'm* all right.'

'Finger prick?'

'Yeah, that's about it – but I'd sooner cut off *his* goddamned prick.'

Helen abandoned her machine to come over and lay her hand on Gabi's hand. I heard her say, 'That was a little too much, too fast. I don't think he understood very much of what you said.'

'Don't worry, Bobo,' Gabi said, kissing me. 'I'm not going to hurt you – and I'm not going to let *them* hurt you, either, even if it kills me.'

'Oh, no – please do not be rash in what you say to Jordan and in what you do!' Helen said. 'If you are made to leave, who will help me? And more importantly, who will help Bobo?'

Two nights later, with the edge of the new moon cutting the black sky with its white, baby's tooth, Gabi and Helen spoke with me for a long time. I listened, and listened – and then listened some more. I tried to understand the amazing things I thought they explained to me. I tried to make myself understood. Everything they asked of me would depend on a clear understanding.

'Do you think he will tell the others?' Helen said to Gabi.

'I'm sure he will – I think they tell each other everything.' Gabi twisted a strand of her already twisted hair, as she often did when she was thinking. 'I'm worried about Shazza, though. I don't know what she'll do when the time comes.'

'Why wouldn't she do what you ask her to do?'

'Did you know that we opened all the gates once before as a sort of publicity stunt?'

'No, I did not,' Helen said, shaking her head.

'Well, we did. We'd had a lot of criticism at the old park, so when they built this one, management wanted to be able to tell everyone that the whales are free to leave, to swim out to the ocean, if they wish.' Gabi looped her hair around her finger, and made a fist. 'They called in the press for a demonstration, and Jordan made a big show of "releasing" Shazza. Of course, it was all a big lie. They drugged her up first, I think. Or maybe, after spending years in captivity, she was too afraid or too confused to leave what Jordan described as her "home". I'm not even sure she understood the gate was open.'

'I am sure she will this time,' Helen said.

'Let's hope so. I'm not sure what the others will do if she freezes up like before.'

Later, with the bit of moon shining even brighter, I rejoined the other whales in the holding pool. And I told them what I felt sure that Gabi and Helen had told me:

'The ocean is close to this place,' I whispered to Alkurah and Zavijah. Their sister Salm swam in closer to hear what I was saying. So did Menkalinan, Unukalhai, and Baby Electra. So did Bellatrix. 'In fact, the pools are refreshed with the waters of the sea.'

'The humans told you this, yes?' Alkurah said.

I aimed a zang of sonar at the metal gate that let out onto the punishment pool. Everyone looked that way with their hearing.

'They told me,' I said, 'that the punishment pool's far gate, which none of us except Bellatrix has even seen opened, would open onto a long tunnel if it *were* opened.'

'Go on!' Electra said, pushing up against me.

'The tunnel,' I said, 'leads to a channel, and the channel flows into a bay. Beyond the bay swells the open sea.'

'Go on!' Menkalinan and Unukalhai chimed in. 'Go on!'

'Gabi has made friends with the star-watchers,' I said, referring to the humans who walked the decks of the pools all through the night. 'The female called Justice and the male called Trent. When the moon is full and tide is up and calls to our blood, all the gates will be opened.'

A great silence enveloped the water. At the same moment, we all drew in a breath, and for the first time I felt in the expanding of our lungs a mutual sense that we could partake of each other's being and dwell together, almost as a true family. The sweet air we shared seemed pregnant with infinite possibilities. Now Zavijah and Salm sang out and renewed the outpouring of orca concord, and even old, crazed Bellatrix gave voice to the jubilation that moved the waters of the pool:

'Go on! Go on! Go on!' she cried out. 'Tell us, Arjuna, that we will be free again and happy. Please never stop telling me so that I never need to be mute and despondent again.'

We sang together for at least as long as one of those arbitrary sectionings of time that the humans call an hour; we sang of hope and indestructible seas and life. Then Alkurah nearly crushed all our hope with a simple question.

'Do you trust the humans, Arjuna?'

Did I trust them? Supposing that I had understood Gabi and Helen correctly, how could I be sure that the promised opening of the gates would not lead to new torments and new expectations that we should perform perhaps bizarre and terrible feats?

'There is a place,' I said to Alkurah and the others. 'I know there is a place where we can speak to the humans without interruption or fear and they can speak to us. A place of fish and fresh air and wild waters. Helen will lead us there – we are to follow her boat. There, no one will shock us, or starve us, or humiliate us, or steal our babies. In this beautiful, beautiful place we will be safe.'

Again, Alkurah voiced a concern, this one almost silly in its pettiness:

'If we swim together to this place,' she said to me, 'I must go first, as it would be anywhere in the world.'

I swallowed back a zang of mirth, and I said to her, 'As always, Mother Alkurah, I will defer to your femininity.'

'I *will* be a mother again,' she whispered. 'I will kemmer soon, before the moon is full.'

'Yes, and you still need a phallus to fill you.'

'Not *a* phallus,' she said. 'I will mate as we journey. The many males of the Sunbreathers or those of whatever clans we encounter – how I long to feel their phalluses inside me, one by one, slipping, gliding, pulsing, flowing with life and singing with sperm! I will gather it all within me! What a baby orca I will make!'

'But not mine,' I said.

'No,' she said. 'We are family now, Arjuna.'

Again, we all breathed together, drawing in the great rush of our assent: yes, yes, yes!

Some nights later, when the moon swelled to its gravid, white fullness and the rising tide called to our blood with all the memories and dreams of our kind, Gabi appeared out of the shadows cast by the human-built structures that had confined us for so long, and she opened up gate after gate after gate.

PART TWO

The Idiot Gods

10

We swam out into cool waters glistening with the lights raining down from the sky. Gabi swam with us – or rather, she spent most of the first hours of our escape riding upon my back and upon Unukalhai's back and Alkurah's. None of us whales liked the touch of the black, plastic wet suit that she wore, but her delicate human body could not guard its heat from the icy grip of the sea without the aid of this covering of neoprene excrescence. Had I understood her correctly, that a naked human immersed in the ocean could die within moments? That did not seem possible. How hard it was to be human! Gabi's vulnerability to the ocean's life-giving touch highlighted the regrettable fact that humans and whales live in two nearly separate worlds.

That humans can live at all between the rolling crests of the ocean's swells should give pause to any whale contemplating these amazing creatures. With the full moon drawing us on like a luminous white orb of hope, we swam through a long channel of tainted water and then out into an even more polluted bay. The moon's brilliance, though, seemed to purify the bay of its bitterness of chemicals and human waste. By the time we reached the open ocean, the water tasted almost as it should: of seaweed and sacred salt, of starlight and storms and the imperishable first life of our world that still flavored the silvery skins of countless fishes and tanged the rich, red blood of us whales.

As Helen had promised, she waited for us with others of her kind in a large sailing boat just off the coast. I swam right up to it, taking care not to collide with the boat's hard surface as it bobbed up and down with each rising and falling swell. Gabi performed a feat of climbing from the water up a rope that dangled from the boat's side. She joined Helen and the other stranger-humans on the deck.

'We have a long journey,' Helen said to me. Her words carried out into the night and over the peaceful waters. They sounded as well from within the water, for she had affixed hydrophones to the boat's timbers. 'Please take a care, for at times we will need to use the engines.'

She had explained to me something that I had only poorly understood: how the humans' boats sometimes moved across the water at the touch of the wind but more often through the power of a whirling metal propeller that could cut a whale to meat.

'Let us journey then,' I sang out from the water, 'for the moon is calling!'

I had to translate what I said into true orca speech, for the other whales had not yet learned the simple new sounds that I created to represent human things and conceptions.

'Let us journey!' Alkurah, Salm, and Zavijah sang back to me. 'For the wind is calling, too!'

'Let us journey!' Unukalhai, Menkalinan, Bellatrix, and Baby Electra said. 'The stars are calling us home!'

Helen and Gabi – and the other two-leggeds that abetted our escape from Sea Circus – probably never saw our accompanying their boat of whipping white sails north along the coast as a little miracle. Zavijah spoke of swimming off to find Baby Navi. She felt sure that if she searched the seven seas for him, high and deep, she would find him in some dark water crying out to her. Baby Electra longed to play with others of her kind and hunt seals again. Unukalhai, who had killed a man at another Sea Circus, wanted nothing more to do with the humans.

We all shared this sentiment, of course, but I argued that through no fault of our own, our fates had become intertangled with those of the humans like strands of kelp in a stormy sea. We must follow our fate. The humans now knew that we could think and speak. They had listened to the yearning in our hearts, and they had set us free. Now they must come to apprehend not only the wonder of the whales but the much deeper wonder of the world that had given us life. Clearly, I said, the humans knew little of our shared planet, or otherwise, why would they struggle so fiercely to destroy it?

'We must tell the humans of the world,' I said to Alkurah and the others. 'They know little of Ocean and how life must be.'

Despite Zavijah's wails about her lost Navi, neither Alkurah nor Salm had any hope that the remnants of their once mighty family could be reunited. Alkurah directed her thoughts toward creating a new family, which she tried to do with all the power in her strong, beautiful body when we encountered a family of the Gracious Wind Whistlers. Although she mated zestfully with two of the Wind Whistlers' males, she was not pregnant – no one could say why. Baby Electra's family, of course, had been slain during her capture, and so it had been with Menkalinan's mother, brothers and sisters. Bellatrix, who had regained her power of speech, declined to tell us anything of her origins. It seemed certain, though, that everyone once dear to her had died. Unukalhai affirmed that he had suffered an identical sadness. Although he had spoken of the stars calling us home, he had nowhere to go, for a whale's family *is* his home.

Of all of us, only I might have returned to beloved ones. I thought often of my mother and my sisters and brothers – and of my Aunt Chara and my Uncle Alnitak and everyone else. I missed the peals of laughter of baby Porrima when she discovered new things! Most of all, I longed to swim with my grandmother again, and drink in her wisdom as I listened to the reassuring beating of her heart. I remembered each color and tone of the charm that she had bestowed upon me. I remembered, too, with a pain that called out from my own heart, that I had promised her that I would do a thing. Now, as I swam alongside a wooden boat named the Silver Swan, it seemed that I might really be able to do it. With such hope sending zests of breath through my flute and exciting my blood, how could I possibly turn away from the course ahead of me?

I had also promised Alkurah and Electra and the other orcas who swam with me that they would be free again, and around this pledge, our new family coalesced. Often, on our journey northward through the increasingly cold waters, after we had fished in concert and shared our meal, we sang together and gathered for a breathing. We shared the air blowing above the ocean's wild, white crests, and as our lungs filled and expanded so did our sense of ourselves enlarge and fill us with a shared spirit. At times, as we relaxed into the song of ourselves, our minds became nearly as one. Then we breathed deeper, and we recalled how a family joins with something much greater in feeling the breaths of the Old Ones within. And deeper still, down in the quiet of our memories, we breathed in unison without world Ocean and we became even vaster. With bittersweet hurts that found out our lungs' every cove and nook, we remembered how entire families of families of worlds drew in the fiery breath of the stars across the whole of the universe. In this way, we remembered ourselves and dwelled within each others' beings, and so we nearly quenged.

In the nightmare moments when I had banged my head bloody in Sea Circus's punishment pool, I had never hoped to know again such mutuality of thought and feeling. I troubled myself over this. Could an orca, I wondered, have *two* families? Could any orca, such as one of the Others like Baby Electra, *truly* join a family of a different kind who hunted fish? Following this logic on its incredible course, I wondered a hard-to-imagine thing: might it be possible for a beluga or one of another species of whale to share their minds with us and open their hearts with so much passion that we would want to think of them as family, too?

'What *is* a family?' Baby Electra asked me one day as we pushed our way through wind-whipped, choppy seas. Even though she was very young, her mind swam toward the deeply philosophical and often resonated with my own. 'Are you and I really brother and sister, Arjuna?'

'You are as much a sister to me as Turais or Nashira, who I hope would call you sister, too.'

'We are! We are!' Baby Electra called out, sending high-pitched sounds toward the Silver Swan which sailed on behind us. 'That is because we love each other.'

'And because we share a purpose.'

'And even more, because when we swim together we are safe.' Electra zanged me with a stream of sonar. She asked, 'Do you feel safe with Gabi and Helen?'

'I *want* to feel safe.'

'I do,' Baby Electra said. 'I *know* that we will be all right. Such determination I see in Helen's eyes! So much courage I zang in her heart! And how hard she tries to speak with us! It is almost as if she wishes she were a whale.'

'I have thought that very thing,' I told her.

For a while she swam on in silence. Then she asked me, 'Arjuna, what is a human being?'

During our long journey, I had similar conversations with Alkurah, Menkalinan, and even Bellatrix. We agreed that of all the mysteries that had ever emerged out of the bloody, red womb of the world, the humans were the most mysterious. Menkalinan, who had nearly given up opposing the humans in the dreadful pools that so recently had constrained us, had also abandoned much of his curiosity about them. Not so Unukalhai. Now that his life had a new course, he declared his intention to apply his analysis of the troubled orca mind to the obviously much greater madness of human beings.

Our days and nights turned about such ponderings as we spoke together and swam together and paused in our conversations to share a few simple words with the humans on their boat. Once again, we of the fluke and fin became creatures of the sea, diving beneath the waves in search of deep sounds, zanging fish with our voices, and singing songs of glory to the music of the currents and to the waves' ever-shifting colors of purple, teal, emerald, and aquamarine. At night, the brilliant stars pointed our way. And with the rising of mornings glowing with promises, we spoke of a new way of conceiving the world. We moved together, we fished together, and we played together. The sunlight warmed our lovely black skin when we breached for life-giving breath even as the ocean cooled the burning in our white bellies to taste the language of the humans and perhaps finally to understand the answer to Baby Electra's question. Through storms we swam, and we surfed the great swells that wind and moon had called up from the ocean's heart, and with each mountainous beat of water, our hope swelled all the more, for a great adventure lay before us, and at last our fiery orca hearts were at one with the pulse of the sea.

After many days, we entered a long sound dividing two great masses of forested land. Helen named this great tongue of water for us, calling it, appropriately, 'Long Sound.' From the map that Alnitak had given me, I knew it as the home of the Ardent Starsinger Clan. We spent more days accompanying the Silver Swan as it sailed up the Sound past many bays that took big bites out of the land to the east and west. At times, fine mists settled down from the sky like gray eyelids that deprived the humans of their sight, and then the Silver Swan did not dare to split the waters with its propeller or to fly upon the wind. When the mists blew away, we began moving again, always toward the north star. Then a day came when we turned east into a broad bay teeming with salmon. Where the bay's far end pushed against a hilly country rising up to become low, green mountains enveloped in mist, three fingers of land reached into the bay as if to set an earthly grip upon the waves. We followed the boat into a cove between two of the fingers. And there, on the cove's southern bank, the humans had built a set of structures that Helen called the Institute.

The largest of these buildings connected the sea to the land in an ingenious way. Somehow, the humans had contrived to dig a channel into the earth and rocks of the finger of land. They had lined the channel with concrete that reminded me too well of the concrete walls of Sea Circus's pools. And over the channel, they had built a great, silver dome like one half of a moon. Helen called this structure a house. Humans – those on the boat and others whom we had yet to meet – lived there and in the smaller rectilinear cottages constellated around the big house.

Helen invited us to share the big house with her and the others – or rather, to dwell at our pleasure in half of it, for we soon discovered that the house was divided into two parts. Upon swimming from the cove into the concrete-walled channel, I looked up at the dome's many three-pointed panes of glass that let in the light of the sun. With my eyes, I followed the curve of this amazing structure and saw that at the channel's landward end, just beyond a broad concrete beach, a great wall split the dome into two parts. The human part, Helen had explained, contained the rooms in which the humans slept and worked and defecated and cooked their meals. From her description, I zanged that these rooms were quite small, something like the compartments of a spiral shell in which a nautilus lives. It gave me pause to think that the humans spent most of their moments dwelling inside contained spaces no larger than Sea Circus's punishment pool.

The whales' half of the dome consisted of little more than that wide channel and the broad concrete beaches that lined on it either side. At the channel's far end nearest the human part of the house, a smooth, concrete beach sloped down into the water. Here, we whales could come up out of the sea onto land should we desire to touch the humans or speak with them flute to face. The humans had placed various kinds of machines along the banks of the channel – and *into* the walls of the channel itself. Many hydrophones pocked the walls like huge, round barnacles. As well, the tricky-handed humans had set into the concrete many strips of screens nearly as large as the one that cast its wavering images upon the onlookers who crowded the metal chairs above Sea Circus's big pool. These screens were built in rows along three levels. As the day's tide rose and fell, the humans could light up one level of screens or another, above or below the water's surface as they chose. Thus we whales, if we so chose, could augment our study of the humans' language by watching what the humans called TV.

'You will be safe here,' Helen told us. She stood on the channel's concrete beach calling words down into the lapping water where we whales gathered. 'You need only work when you want to work. You may come and go as you please.'

What pleased most of us most of the time was to swim out through channel and cove into the bay where we fished and frolicked and conversed and sang: all the things that free whales do. Sometimes, like a real family, we journeyed together, making days-long explorations up and down the cold, misted waters of Long Sound. Alkurah sought males of the Ardent Starsingers with whom she might mate, while Baby Electra looked for seals to hunt.

In truth, of all of us, it seemed that only I had a flaming desire to speak with the humans. Unukalhai sought verbal intercourse with the Covered Ones with some degree of passion, but more from a curiosity to discover if he could use their own words to penetrate and presume upon their psyches than any longing to truly understand them. Alkurah found no Starsingers, and she tried to assuage her frustration by exchanging a few words with the two-legged creatures that she had supposed to be irredeemably stupid. Her sister Zavijah could scarcely call up a click or a whistle, so greatly did Navi's loss grieve her. Bellatrix would not talk to the humans at all, and so it was with the shy, dispirited Menkalinan. Baby Electra, who drank in the humans' words like one of the mysticeti scooping up mouthfuls of krill, did so mostly in emulation of me.

'I admit that I like talking with the humans,' she said to me one day while we lazed about the waters of the cove. 'I like learning how they think – and *that* they can think. I never imagined playing such a game.'

'It is more than a game,' I said to her.

'Perhaps it is,' she said swimming slow circles around me. 'And perhaps you will somehow persuade the Hairy Ones to stop their torture of all that moves and grows.'

'But you do not believe this is possible?'

'I believe in *you*. And so I must believe in your purpose and hope that I will someday come to share it.'

She rubbed up against me. We both liked it that she took comfort in the sheer mass of my presence.

'Until then,' she continued, 'I can suffer myself to chat with the humans, even if their language – the mind *behind* their language – is both disturbing and strange.'

'It is! It is!' I agreed.

'Until then,' she continued, 'this is a good place, though I do not understand why we have heard nothing of the Ardent Starsingers.'

'Perhaps they are fishing far to the north in the Sound.'

'But there are so many fish here!'

That there were. I could hardly swim from the cove to the bay without colliding with a rush of salmon. I had renewed my old joy at eating food that pulsed with life.

'I cannot tell you, though,' Baby Electra said to me, 'how tired I am of fish. Do you see the beaches on either side of the humans' dwellings?'

I breached in order to gaze out through the air at the features of the land upon which the humans had sited their Institute. Gentle

183

beaches of sand and a few pebbles sloped down to the water to the right and left of the channel and the dome above it.

'Before the humans came,' Baby Electra said, 'seals swarmed these beaches.'

'How do you know?' I asked her.

'I am of a kind who hunts seals, and so I *know*,' she said. 'And I long to hunt seals again!'

'Someday you will.'

'I cannot wait, Arjuna. Farther down the Sound, on our journey here, I zanged signs of seals. Will you go with me to hunt them?'

'Would you have me break the Covenant again?'

'As I break it every day by eating fish?'

'I do not know if I could eat a mammal again.'

'Tell me that you did not like the taste of the white bear.'

'I cannot tell you that, either.'

'But it would make me so happy! And it would make *you* happy to make me happy. I know your heart, Arjuna – I know your heart!'

I knew hers, too. At first pulse, it seemed a smaller heart than mine and warmer, like the waters of the Blue Summer Sea. This little whale, however, contained whole oceans of enthusiasm inside her. Because I lacked her capacity for joy, she invited me with flute, eye, and all the openness of her heart to join her whenever I wished in diving down into the bright, flowing deeps inside her. She knew that I needed her even more than she needed me. How could I deny such a rare being who possessed so much goodness and grace?

How, though, could I break the Covenant once again? A better question, I realized, still troubled me: how could I *not* break it, if I zanged in my heart that doing so would be a right action? I had already broken so many things, including the ocean's natural order, in making family with Baby Electra. It seemed to me that my fated journey would lead me to break old orderings and conceptions of the world by breaking free into a new one – or by creating a new world altogether and a new way of being for myself and for Baby Electra and all those I loved.

'All right,' I said to her, 'I will break the Covenant by hunting seals with you. Will you break through your doubts about the humans in order to converse with them?'

'Is that to be a new covenant?' she asked.

'Between you and me, or between you and the humans?'

'In the end, there is only one Covenant, yes?'

I wondered what she meant by this, just as I puzzled over the mystery and spiritedness I detected in her voice. Perhaps, I thought, she was only playing with ideas because she was a very young whale who loved to play. Or had she perhaps formed a new and incomplete philosophy of life that she needed to test and perfect before sharing it with a near-adult like me? I did not know, and she would not say any more.

Later that day, farther down the Sound off a sandy beach similar to those on either side of the Institute, we joined in ambushing a seal. It proved much easier to kill this pretty dweller of land and sea than it had been to take the white bear's life. As Baby Electra and I ripped it into bloody gobbets, I realized how fiercely the new Arjuna had come to relish the taste of rich, red mammal meat.

Over the days that followed, I devoured meat of a much different though no less disturbing nature. Sometimes I and others of my family spent entire days and nights at the Institute working with the humans. The words that issued from the channel walls' hydrophones or from Helen's lips nourished my hunger to understand the humans, although almost everything about their language's irritating plosives and fricatives seemed wrong. If their vocalizations had consisted of simple nouns and verbs such as those in the sentence: Gabi is swimming – then I would have learned to speak with them in a trice. The humans, though, divided their words into six other kinds: adjectives, which toned and qualified the nouns, adverbs and prepositions, conjunctions and interjections, and, of course the pronouns such as me, they, them and you, which I had only slowly mastered. A greater problem attended the syntax by which all these words were strung together, and those rules I learned only with much trial and pain, for they were as unwelcome to my mind as tapeworms were to my gut.

The greatest difficulty that the other whales and I faced, however, lay in apprehending the meanings of the humans' words, for too many of them had no reference or correlate to any conception in our orca language. How these words mystified me! I listened to Helen and her machines enunciate them, and I sounded them out in my mind again and again: City. Deadline. College. Execution. Gewgaw. Guilt. Vacation. Homeless. Beggar. Chicanery. Tawdry. Insurance. Ordinance. Shame.

I believe that the orcas would have remained diving blind and choking on our frustration had not Helen conceived of lighting up the screens with images of cities, highways, and other such human handiwork. What a tiresome slog we had of it in linking up image to word! How slow and excruciating this illustration of human life! How nearly incomprehensible the attendant explanations! And strange and terrible it was for us to behold images of the humans' world that no whale had even seen or imagined:

Slaughterhouse. Cemetery. Harvester. Factory. Office. Prison. Guillotine. Bomb. Soldier. Priest. Slave.

It vexed me that at first I could scarcely make sense of some words at all, while others disturbed because I thought I understood them *too* well. What kind of beings *were* these human beings? Must I characterize them as Unukalhai did by giving them the soubriquet of killer apes?

'They call us killer whales!' Unukalhai said as we all held a conference beneath the waters of the cove. 'But did you see the images of their farms and feedlots? And the machines that swept the chickens into the flensing knives? What whale would ever have conceived of killing so many schools of cattle with bolts fired into their brains in a slaughterhouse?'

'Unukalhai is right,' Alkurah said. 'Do we really wish to associate with such creatures who convince themselves that *we* are the ones inflicted with such human murderousness?'

'I do not wish even to listen to the humans,' Bellatrix said. 'I do not think that Arjuna will succeed in speaking the truth to them, and if he does, I do not think they can hear it.'

Zavijah swam closer to her sister and reinforced the point that Alkurah had just made: 'And if they do hear it, they do not have the strength of will or the goodness of heart to act upon it.'

Baby Electra, blowing bubbles in the midnight blue depths just below us, said, 'I *do* wish to speak with the humans. Helen and Gabi are different from the ones who imprisoned us – were it not so, we would not be here now having this conversation. There must be others like them.'

'*Perhaps* there are others like them,' Unukalhai said. '*Perhaps* Gabi and Helen are different from the other killer apes.'

'If I could,' Bellatrix said, 'I would swim far from here to another place. But I will not swim alone.'

'But this is a *good* place!' Baby Electra said. 'We have salmon and seals and a new world to explore.'

And I said, 'Let us at least see how deeply we can speak with the humans before we abandon them.'

We discussed my suggestion for half a day. Finally, Alkurah said, 'All right, Arjuna, perhaps some unsounded goodness in their hearts redeems the evil they work with their hands. Perhaps we should try to listen for it.'

'All right,' Salm said. 'Perhaps it might be illuminating to view more images of the continents' interiors that we have never seen.'

'And perhaps,' Unukalhai added, 'we might learn something vital in sounding the minds of creatures who seem to believe their minds dwell apart from and above those of all other creatures.'

'All right! All right! All right!'

Perhaps without realizing it (more likely he did), Unukalhai had zanged the very thing that both troubled and fascinated me about

187

the humans. *Did* the humans really think that they were more intelligent than whales? How could they think this? *How* did they think? To determine this, we would have to contrive to learn the humans' language. I sensed that we were close to discovering momentous things in and about these mysterious beings. In trying to sound the seemingly unfathomable human mind, I felt something like the first whale who had dared the dark and nearly endless spaces of our little sea of stars only to behold Andromeda and Whirlpool and other bright galaxies beyond. Exhilaration and dread swam side by side inside me. To speak with the humans in their troublesome language was to venture into the Great Unknown.

The devouring of one human word led to the apprehending of another, and again and again, I returned to a single word which all by itself said a great deal about the humans: gravity. I had finally learned the name of the terrible force that had crushed my belly against my bones when the humans had ripped me from the sea and squeezed me into a metal crate. Gravity derived from the same root as gravid: to be heavy, as with child. How sad that the humans associated the soaring creation of new life with a density of existence that dragged a pregnant female down to earth! And not just *to* the cold clay of the ground, but beneath it in the hideousness of the smothering good meat within soil in a prison of death that the humans call a grave. Gravity, gravid, grave – in these simple sounds the humans revealed not an appreciation of the necessary interplay between death and life, but rather a denigration of life itself and (I feared) a love of death.

My suspicion of some essential twisting of the human soul moved me to question how I might ever speak with them soul to soul. In order for true communication to work its magic, didn't two speakers need to share a worldview, at least in part? What did humans and whales really share?

Before I could appreciate the similarities in the ways our two kinds saw (and heard) reality, I first needed to identify the differences in how we made language. The music that sang out of my

of the life of the mind, we make of all the myriad rainbow droplets a lovely picture of sound.

If we wish, we can crystallize the connotative and the implicate
into denotative symbols much as the humans do. When these bits
of colored ice are embedded in a sound picture, they subtly shape
or altogether change its meaning. And the pictures themselves can
be enfolded into new sound symbols in a kind of lovely, fractalling
double recursion that is as beautiful to behold as it is difficult to
describe.

O humans – what do you see when you speak? What do you
hear, what do you feel? Do your words swim side by side with
truth? Does your heart leap with the beauty of all that you think
and say? Do you sense your creator deep within yourself, painting
a picture with burning raindrops of light and singing you into
being in a glorious, golden song? Do your words thrill your blood
with symphonies of infinite possibilities and make magic in your
soul?

All these questions, I put to Helen – or tried to. She seemed to
share my frustration. Then one day, with the tide high and almost
lapping over the concrete deck where she stood among her
computers, she announced that she had a new idea as to how I
might speak with her directly flute to ear in a way that she could
understand.

11

Early in the Moon of Owls, I watched Helen pace the deck of the whale's half of the house. From time to time, she held a burning tube of paper and vegetation to her lips. I puzzled over the puffing of her cheeks as she drew in smoke into her lungs and blew it out through her flaring nostrils. Twice each day, once in the morning, once in the evening, she performed this curious feat – I did not know why. On this morning, though, she told me the name of the burning thing, if not its purpose, and I sounded out the phonemes of 'cigarette' in my mind.

'You have now,' she said to me, 'learned some 8,000 words. Basic English consists of only 850, while the average adult man or woman knows about 20,000. The plays of our greatest poet, Shakespeare, contain 28,829 distinct words, 12,493 of which occur only once.'

'And how many words does the whole of your language hold?'

'About a thousand thousands, though many are either obsolete, archaic, or obscure terms for chemicals and such.'

'Please tell me again what you mean by a thousand.'

I had no mind for what the humans call numbers. We whales have none. Should we wish to tell of the 'number' of orcas in our family, for instance, we would identify each of them by name. Should we wish to describe the size of a school of fish, we would rely on such locutions as 'many' or 'myriad' or 'many, many myriads.'

Helen tapped the small screen of one of her machines. A moment later, beneath her feet on the much larger top screen set into the wall of the channel, images of sardines laid out in groups of ten lighted up the glass. I tried to count to ten as Helen had taught me. Counting *by* tens the ten hundred silvery sardines was beyond me.

'I do not like to admit this,' I told Helen, 'but there might be things about your language that I will never grasp.'

'You understand much more of our language than I do of yours.'

'That is because you cannot hear all of our sounds.'

'Everything you say is recorded,' Helen told me. 'The wavelength, pitch, and tonal quality of each sound is analyzed.'

'And by breaking our living language into dead pieces, you hope to make our songs sing inside of you?'

'We hope to make better and better models of what you say. Here, let me show you on your screen. When we represent each sound as a three-dimensional node, then you can see . . .'

Helen went on speaking as the screen just above the lapping water lit up with tiny colored sparks. I was unsure if *she* saw the true nature of the difficulty the humans faced in understanding the orcas' language.

'Is this how you see – and hear – your language, by making such models?'

'No, of course not. But the models are getting better, aren't they?'

'I do not know. When your machines translate the models into what you have identified as orca sounds, most of what comes out of your hydrophones is gibberish.'

'But some is not?'

'Of everything you have spoken to me this way, only an infinitesimal part of a myriad of myriads of gazillions of possibilities have made the slightest sense.'

'We need more time.'

'You need,' I told her, 'to understand *how* which qualities of tones relate to which others – and *how* they change significance and meaning as they interplay with each other. As it is, you choose the qualities and sounds that you deem the most important to model.'

'But one must identify the variables to be modeled and weigh them according to their likely impact. That is the nature of creating a scientific model.'

'But it is *not*, beautiful human,' I said to her, 'the nature of nature. Such models have nothing to do with how a person makes language and understands it.'

Helen sat down above me on the lip of the deck. Her dangling feet nearly touched the undulating water. She continued to puff smoke from her cigarette, and she appeared to be deep in thought.

'No,' she finally said, 'my models are anything *but* natural; however, they are all I have.'

She went on to discuss her understanding of orca language and the difficulties that any translation would pose. To begin with, she said, Orcalish is very high context, full of irony, nuance, and what we whales call 'negative speech', in which the most important conveyances of meaning often occur in what is *not* spoken. To make matters worse, the very slightest of changes in sound – she called these inflections – result in changes of meaning. As she had already identified at least 4,689,554 inflections and almost none of the rules by which they applied, she hypothesized that our orca language contained hidden algorithms that she had so far not managed to model.

'And then,' she added, 'there is the matter of these games of yours. What you call the art of thought, or the art of the soul – I am not sure how best to translate the concept. Perhaps rhapsody would do as well as any word.'

She spoke of a dialect of human language known as Chinese, in which long ago a picture of a tree, for instance, brushed as black ink on white paper, had been simplified into a pictogram enfolding the entire meaning of tree, be it a cherry, a maple, an evergreen or some other kind. A similar process, she theorized, had obtained in Orcalish: our sound pictures became represented by sonograms, which in turn were further abstracted as pure aural symbols that she called sonic ideoplasts.

'As I understand it,' Helen said to me, 'these ideoplasts are arrayed into the motifs and movements of the rhapsodies that each orca composes.'

'Yes,' I said, 'the songs of ourselves and the songs of creation that make up the Song of Life.'

'And each ideoplast can represent a word, idea, thought, emotion, story, philosophy, or song – or even entire assemblages of all those?'

'It is something like that – yes, yes.'

'And when an orca wishes to be accepted as an adult, you must compose a rhapsody that reveals some new beauty or truth about the world?'

'Yes, yes, yes!' I swam up close to her and chirruped nearly into her face. 'Our families listen to our compositions and deem us adults or not. The Old Ones listen, too.'

Helen took a long breath through her cigarette. She puffed out a ring of gray smoke that reminded me of the silvery bubble rings that Baby Electra like to blow.

'Very well,' she finally said, 'but I still do not understand how these rhapsodies are supposed to relate all aspects of the cosmos to each other – past, present, and future.'

'But how can a truly-made rhapsody *not* do this?' I said. 'Are not all aspects of creation related? And when a whale composes his part of the Song of Life, there *is* no time, as there is only the eternal now-moment when one quenges, which a whale must do in order to compose.'

'This "quenge" of yours is an interesting word that you have coined for a concept that eludes me.'

'It is not concept. It is . . . the power of being, the essence of being itself.'

'And how did *you* apply this power in the rhapsody that you never finished?'

What could I tell her that she would understand? I was not sure that I understood very well myself.

'There was a day,' I said, 'an hour, a moment – one of the signal moments of my life. I was deep into my rhapsody's penultimate motif. The ideoplasts exemplifying Alsciaukat the Great's philosophy of being sprayed out with an almost perfect beauty like a cloud of diamonds, rubies, and pearls. The motif's chords carried me through the seven seas of knowing to the mysterious Silent Sea, lined with coral-like ideoplasts of yellow, magenta, and glorre. The sound there was vast – the music was. I could hear how Alsciaukat's philosophy resonated with the phases of the moon in its progression from first tooth to crescent to half sphere to full. This insight in turn sent echoes of correspondence to illuminate the Second Sonnet of the Sun that Aldebaran of the Silver Song Surfers had once composed. In the spiral structure of this sonnet, I beheld both the spiral shell of the whelk and our galaxy's spiral arms. The colors of the rhapsody rang with the movement toward the spirality of many things. I swam along the spiral path that we whales follow from our world to Agathange. I relived the double-spiral of life on earth and Ocean in its journey from the pure beingness in the past to its becoming, now and in eons still unborn. Two glittering arms of life I sang of: the creatures of the water and those which walk upon the land. And just at the moment when my song should have grown as vast and deep as the Silent Sea itself and I should have heard and seen how life on our world should move up the golden spiral, my voice failed me. Because I could not quenge, I lacked the power to zang how the future must and will be – and so I could not finish my composition.'

Helen had remained almost completely still as I tried to explain to her the nature of sonic ideoplasts, orca language, and our

196

rhapsodies. She moved with a start and a jerk of her hand, however, when her cigarette finally burned down to her fingers. The force of her shaken hand flung the burning bit of tobacco into the channel's water, which extinguished its fire with a quick hiss.

'Thank you for explaining all that to me,' she said, 'though I hope you will not think less of me if I admit that I understood little of it.'

'How could I think less of you than you are? You are quite intelligent, for a human.'

'Thank you,' she said. 'I suppose that I must accept that as a compliment.'

'What is a compliment?' I asked as I scooped the dead cigarette stump into my mouth in order to taste it.

'Well, it is a compliment to *your* intelligence that you have helped me to see just how complex your language is. I am afraid it might be *too* complex for a human ever to apprehend.'

I knew enough about the colors of the human words to hear sadness and longing in her voice. I said to her, 'Someday I will paint a picture of our utterances for you, and you will understand what I will say.'

'How will you do that?'

'You will see, you will hear, how emotion and sense are bound up in symbol – and each symbol flowing and sharing sense with every other.'

'I hear your words, Beautiful One. I hear your words.'

'You will hear the sound pictures I say to you.' I spoke into the water, and her machines tried to record my utterances' every wave form of every tone. 'You will zang the variegations of emotion, meaning, and ideas, as a painting jumps with different colors and areas of light and dark.'

'O that it would be so!' she said to me. 'But how will this miracle come about?'

'I do not know! I do not know!'

Helen conjured up another cigarette and sat tapping it against her fingers. After a while, she said, 'I would not like to stake everything on a miracle. However, I like even less giving up. Therefore, it has occurred to me that we might create a language together.'

She explained that while she could speak English to me and quite easily be understood, every sound I made had to be translated through one of her computers if we were to talk together.

'What if, however,' she said, 'we could agree that one set of your natural orca sounds would represent a distinct syllable?'

'But there are trillions of syllables in English!'

'Actually, there are about 15,000 usable English syllables, but that is still far too many for me – or anyone – to have to parse. Sometimes I think I should have begun speaking to you in Japanese.'

'Why – is that a simpler dialect of English?'

'Actually, it is its own language, unintelligible to speakers of English or any other language.' She touched the cigarette to her lips, then drew it away. 'And while it contains about 90 syllables and so *would* be suitable to representation by a syllabary, it is also full of conceptions and conventions – you would think of them as flavors – that are uniquely Japanese.'

'And English does not have these solely English tastes?'

'Of course it does – any language does. That is why I would like for us to make a new language together, one that will partake of the tastes of many languages.'

She described to me a language called Esperanto, constructed out of elements of phonology, grammar, and vocabulary drawn from various languages around the earth – most of them what she called the Indo-European languages. Millions of the humans spoke it. It served as a sort of world language for those loath to employ English for such a purpose.

'The language I am thinking of,' she told me, 'would make use of a much broader base of languages. Japanese and Chinese – Arabic and Tagalog, many others. Most of all, it would incorporate those few elements of your orca language that we do understand. As we develop the language, we can add in additional features.'

'And I would speak this language to you?'

'Yes – though I will not be able to speak it back. And if I am to understand you, we will need to encode each sequence of chirps and whistles and the like in the most basic of ways. You must simplify these sounds nearly to point of triviality if I am to understand them.'

'And I must lay out these sounds one by one like gridlocked automobiles on a highway, yes?'

'Yes, you must.'

'And I must do this slooooowly?'

'I am afraid so.'

'That will be soooo boring!'

'You can enliven the process – and the language – by trying to figure how to incorporate such conceptions as quenge.'

'I have already told you, quenge is not a concept, but rather a—'

'Yes, yes, I know: it is the essence of being. You must find a way to make this essence clear and comprehensible, and to infuse it into the words of our language.'

'Yes, yes – I will!' I said. 'Somehow, I will make every word of our language sing!'

I suggested naming this new language Wordsong, and she agreed to that.

'When can we begin creating Wordsong?' I asked her.

'Well, I should take a few days to—'

'Now!' I shouted to her. 'The essence of being is always *now*, so why don't we begin while passion moves us?'

As soon as we finished the first of what would become our wordstorming sessions, I raced out into the cove to speak with the other whales. All except Baby Electra considered my hope of using Wordsong to help Helen learn Orcalish to be both foolish and futile. As Unukalhai observed, '*We* might learn the humans' language, after a fashion, but the humans will never make sense of our ideoplasts and hear our rhapsodies, not with a thousand ears and a myriad of myriad of machines.'

Soon after that, five strange orcas swam into the bay. Two of them, Hyadum and Kitalpha, were sister and brother of the Golden Chord Family of the Ardent Starsinger Clan. Three brothers named Acrux, Gacrux, and Becrux accompanied them. They were also Starsingers, but of the family of Turquoise Romancers. None of the new whales moved very gracefully or quickly, for various wounds had cut their bodies with deep scars. Half of Hyadum's great dorsal fin seemed to have been bitten off while long ridges of hard cicatrices marred her black skin. Divots pocked Kitalpha's back. It looked as if the flesh had been scooped – or burned – right out of him. As for the three brothers, their wounds went deeper: although they did not say so outright, it soon became obvious that they were bereft over the recent death of their mother.

'We heard that orcas from other clans, and even other kinds,' Kitalpha said, zanging Baby Electra with his sonar, 'had come to this place in order to speak with the humans.'

'That is so,' Alkurah said, 'and you are welcome to try to do as we do, for these are your waters. In truth, it is you who should welcome us.'

'That might once have been true,' Hyadum said in the saddest voice I had ever heard, 'but our family has left these waters – or, I should say, the waters have left us.'

In this way, she spoke of death, and in the silences that broke her lamentation, we learned that not only were Hyadum and Kitalpha the last of the Golden Chord Family, but that all the other orcas of the Ardent Starsingers save the brothers Acrux, Gacrux, and Becrux had been wiped out.

'Tell us what happened,' Alkurah said to Hyadum.

'It is a long story,' Hyadum said.

'That is all right,' Alkurah replied, brushing up against this stranger in order to give her a little comfort. Since Alkurah's release from Sea Circus, her essential kindness had leaped out in much the same way that a tone painting's positive and negative spaces can suddenly reverse themselves upon the invocation of single right thought. 'We have days and days in which to listen.'

After the Starsingers had related their woes, and we told them ours, we asked them to join us in our endeavor of speaking with the humans. Kitalpha and Hyadum assented to what seemed to them an intriguing though somewhat repellent notion. The three brothers of the Turquoise Romancers, however, declined our invitation. They wanted nothing more to do with the humans. They would keep on swimming, Acrux told us, until they came to pristine seas empty of humans.

'I do not think you will find any such seas,' I said, 'but if you do, I would like to know where they are.'

'I think you will find the death you seek,' Alkurah said to them, 'so before you go, will you fill me with your life that I might remember you?'

She told them that she would kemmer the following morning, and asked them to delay their journey. They agreed to this. For three days, the cove rippled with the motions of their bodies and rang out with cries of pleasure. The brothers sang to Alkurah the most beautiful and compelling of songs. As they mated with her one after the other through long hours of light and dark, her strong, clear voice sang back and sweetened the waters: 'Again, again, beautiful whales, again! Fill me again until I can hold no more and I burst!'

When it finally came time for them to leave, we all felt sad at the quietening of the sea. We wished Acrux, Gacrux, and Becrux well, and watched them swim off. Then, as Alkurah savored their seed and the music they had given her, as she swam about the cove doing little leaps of happiness and singing of a mighty mating, I decided to return to my acquisition of the humans' language – and to the creation of a new one with Helen.

For days and days I listened to the words of the language called

English and gave back the sounds that Helen and I had agreed would equate to them. We both felt impatient for me to speak Wordsong to her, but for the present we still needed to rely on her computer's translation of what I said into English. It occurred to both of us that the better that I understood English, the more help I would be in our mutual construction of Wordsong, for the learning of one language opens gateways to others. And so I set about trying to drink in and comprehend as many strange and nearly incomprehensible English words as I could:

Mathematics. Computer. Phone. Hyperbola. Hyperbole. Engine. Mechanics. Technics. Electron. Neutron. Proton. Quark. Freon. Argon. Neon. Phlogiston. Pentagon. Cyclotron. Jargon. Walkathon.

Alkurah's embrace of a gladsome fecundity seemed to have called in an early spring. With the warming of the air and the water, and with our world's equipoise in its eternal dance about the sun, the herring arrived in all their myriad millions. Even as we orcas feasted upon them, the glittering schools of fish spawned, for they, too, felt all the urges of life's most urgent season. They could not escape us, even though each school broke into a frenzy of motion when we approached, roiling the water in a whirling silver cloud as each herring sought safety in its center. And we could not get away from them. The shallows of the bay and its various nooks and coves turned a milky white with herring sperm. White herring eggs, like billions of tiny pearls, encrusted the rocks and deadwood and everything else that touched the water. The gulls swooped down in screeching, flapping white flocks to eat the eggs. Beneath the water, sunflower stars scavenged the dead herring that had sifted down to the coves' bottom.

The other scientists and their interns – I hoped I used these words correctly – had a hard work of keeping the channel's screens scrubbed clean of eggs and sperm so that we orcas could continue our studies. We needed, however, to continue matching images of the humans' world to their words, and this we did. A day came when Helen announced that I had learned 15,000 words, and in late spring, she let me know that my word count had doubled that figure, and so I surpassed the working vocabulary of the Shakespeare. After that, the humans' words rushed into my mind with all the fury and force of the herring, filling me with a whirl of understanding:

Tenure. Leisure. Woozy. Wizard. Skullduggery. Vulgarity. Tame. Tattletale. Money. Invisible Hand. Wealth. Plutocrat. Poverty. Debt. Bank. Banker. Bankruptcy. Eviction. Homeless. Hypothermia. Corpsicle. Maniacal. Mankind.

With my growing lexicon came a growing disquiet. I tried to distract myself from the truth coiled up inside me and not quite ready to come out into the light of full recognition. I tried to augment my study of the humans' spoken language with a deciphering of their written words. However, I could not see very well the many turns and twists of their letters, which appeared to my orca eye like swarms of ants. I had no head for reading, as the humans called it, and I never learned this strange art.

And so I returned to absorbing the sounds of the humans' words, and I saw how each word was like a mirror reflecting all the others. I found my way through more and more words that had perplexed me and whose meanings I had not really wanted to comprehend. It was not just that these particular words had no correlation with my orca conception or experience with the world, but that they seemed to violate every orca esthetic and our natural sense of how the world was and would always be:

Vice. Vigorish. Debauchery. Chastity. Pederasty. Animality. Bestiality. Puritan. Lawyer. Devil. Saint. Bodhisattva. Karma. Sin. Salvation. Priest. Priest-king.

And more repugnant words:

President. Lord. Gods. God. Goddamn. Curse. Crusade. Gladiator. Barbarian. Barbed wire. Concentration camp. Alms. Napalm. Gas chamber. War.

The word *war* buzzed inside me as if I had swallowed a chainsaw. I asked Helen why she had never shown me images of what seemed to be an unbelievable conception. Nor had her screens illustrated heaven and hell, blasphemy and exorcism and crucifixion and many other heretofore dimly understood words.

'I am sorry, Clever One,' Helen said to me. 'But it is not really possible to find images of certain human words.'

I zanged hesitation and equivocation in her voice. So, apparently, did Gabi, who stood a few body lengths from Helen doing something with one of the humans' computers. She stepped over to Helen with such alacrity that her flaming red hair flounced in the force of the little wind that her motion made.

'But we can find images of war,' she said, 'if that is what Bobo really wants to see.'

'I am not sure that would be wise,' Helen said.

'Why not?'

'They might upset him.'

'We show movies of men getting blown apart to our children.'

'Yes – and do you think that is wise?'

'Bobo is a *killer whale*,' Gabi said. 'Do you think he hasn't ripped animals apart?'

'It is one thing to kill in order to live,' Helen replied. 'But in our wars, we live to kill. Making images out of our depravity is worse than pornography.'

Depravity, gravity, bipedality, brutality, lethality, I thought.

I had learned that Helen had a quicker and more capacious mind than had Gabi, but Gabi had a quicker heart. She touched her hand to Helen's shoulder and said, 'I'm getting the feeling that it's *you* who doesn't want to see those kinds of things.'

'I can't keep anything from you, can I?' Helen said.

'Then I'll sort through the images if you don't want to.'

'I am not sure this is necessary.'

'But wasn't it you who said that we shouldn't withhold the truth from the whales?'

I swam in close to where Gabi and Helen stood regarding each other on the channel's deck. I came up out of the water, spyhopping to look into Helen's eyes, and I spoke a few simple words into the air:

'Yes, yes, brave humans – please tell me the truth.'

Later that day, in that domed space of cruel echoes and horrible flashes of light, I worked alone with Gabi, and she showed me images of war.

Machine guns. Trenches. Tanks. Torture. Dresden. Napalm. Rocket. Refugee. Amputee. Decapitation. Omaha Beach. Nanking. Auschwitz. Hellfire. Hiroshima.

I watched and listened and denied, and I shuddered hour after hour. I could not turn away from the images on the screens and their accompanying sounds. Words that I had barely understood now zanged deep into my blood. I had asked for the truth, and the truth had been given to me. The shark that I had swallowed in learning the first human word many, many days before began tearing at my insides with its shrapnel teeth and eating its way out of my belly.

In an attempt to escape the inescapable agony inflicted by hands wielding truncheons, tasers, swords, garrotes, and gas, I swam out into the bay to rejoin the other whales. The air had grown dank with the fall of night, but the water had lit up with a brilliance of sonar zangs and laughter. The entire family gamboled through an undulating kelp forest thick with pulsing jellyfish. Zavijah, Electra, and the newcomer Hyadum danced about in erotic play, and so did Alkurah and Kitalpha, who had taken a liking to each other. Of course, since Kitalpha might decide to join our hodge-podge family where the three brothers had not, Alkurah could not very well mate with him. However, nothing prevented her from nuzzling, fondling, and stroking him in moans of pleasure which flowed out into the water in bright bands of tanglow and glent.

'O what a mighty Mars is this!' she crooned to him.

They were playing a game that he had learned from the humans. It depended on the strange idea that certain human words could become tainted by aspects of life the humans disliked and so became taboo. In a refined dialect of English known as Cockney, speakers would often try to hide the true substance of their utterances – usually 'dirty' or derogative words – from strangers and prudes. We whales found the concealing of meaning to be a novel twisting of language: a way of lying without outright lying.

The game's rules were simple. An objectionable word – the humans had more than a thousand for sexual intercourse alone – would be identified. For instance, the word for such a basic body part as prick. Then two other words that paired naturally would be selected: such as Moby Dick; prick. Then the last word in the pair would be dropped, and a speaker of Cockney might say something like: 'Look at the Moby on that horse!' Those in the know would mentally pair Moby with its associated, omitted word and make the rhyme with the real word that they wished to convey.

Thus Mars and Venus became truncated to simply Mars, which connoted penis. And the encoding of trick or treat into the slang bit off the treat, which rhymed with meat.

'I do adore your treat,' I heard Alkurah say, rubbing herself along Kitalpha.

Now she had inverted trick or treat to treat or trick, and had left off the trick, whose rhyme leaped out in my mind as Kitalpha's Moby did from this belly.

'I cannot decide which I like more, your trick or your treat.'

At no loss for words (no whale ever is), Kitalpha responded in kind by caressing Alkurah and saying, 'O what a treat it would be to find its way into your blue-suede.'

'Were you not considering joining us,' Alkurah said, 'I would play the most mellifluous of melodies upon your fiddle. I am sure your key would fit me perfectly.'

It pleased me that the other whales had learned nearly as much English as had I. I swam slowly through the caressing strands of kelp, waiting for the word and sex dance to play itself out. Beneath the midnight waves, I watched the octopi transforming themselves into shapes like rocks and driftwood and other features of the bay's bottom. For hour after hour, the jellyfish pulsed in translucent wonder, and sometimes, the anemones came by and consumed them.

Toward morning I finally had the chance to tell the other orcas what I had seen and learned of human war. I had almost expected that they would not believe me. So it surprised me when Unukalhai, speaking for the others, said, 'We have known of human harpoons for all the years that the killer apes have made war upon us. That they have fabricated more terrible weapons of slaughter seems a logical trajectory in their rise and fall.'

I noted his emphasis on the word 'fall.' I said, 'It is one thing for the humans to hunt us, for they know nothing of the Great Covenant. Who would have supposed, however, that they slaughter each other million by million?'

'They cannot slaughter each other too quickly,' Zavijah said. 'Perhaps they will slay down to the last woman and child, and not one will remain to imprison and torture my Baby Navi, wherever he is.'

'We would understand if you are finished talking with the humans,' Alkurah said to me. 'Say the word, and we will journey together to another place.'

With the starlight raining down upon the quiet waters of the bay in tiny pings of tintigloss, I considered what Alkurah proposed. Through a miracle of mutual accord and machinery, we had managed to speak with at least some of the humans, but did we really understand each other? Had I persuaded any of them – even Helen and Gabi – that they must cease their torment of Ocean and all the creatures who dwelled in Her living waters? If I did not accomplish this, how would our world ever be healed of the harpoon thrust deep into its heart? And how would I myself be healed of the evil substance that still fouled my blood and kept me from quenging?

'I am not ready to leave,' I said to Alkurah and the others. I did not like the dread in my voice that filled the water or the movements of the shark in my belly. 'I would know first *how* humans can make war on each other. So many of them there are, and so many languages they speak.'

'Helen has said,' Baby Electra nodded, 'that there are more than 6,000 human languages, but I do not understand this number or how that can be.'

'I would know these languages, some of them,' I said. 'It may be that the secret of the humans' savagery lies hidden in one of them, in the same way that Cockney conceals words that cause humans shame.'

In the next dozen days, I completed my acquisition of English, memorizing all but a few of its hundreds of thousands of words. Most of those I avoided were terms for chemical compounds such as polymethylene and polychlorinated dibenzofurans that seemed useless to me. A day came when I asked Helen to begin teaching me other languages. She did so with a smile upon her broad lips and pride enlivening her bright black eyes.

She began with languages that she knew and that had a somewhat close association with English: French. Italian. Latin. Spanish. Greek. Hindi. Now that English and its associated images had become established in my mind, it was a simple process to match words in a new language to those of English – at least, those words that could be correlated or even equated. Thus I gained vocabulary quickly. Understanding and applying the syntax that ordered these words and brought out their meanings proved to be only slightly more difficult, for I discovered that all human languages shared a universal grammar.

With each language that I acquired, I swam through the next with greater agility. French had taken me a month to master, while Arabic, Fur, Beja, Dinka, and Songhay – the languages of Helen's childhood – came more quickly.

Because I still had not uncovered the secret to understanding the humans (or so I thought), I asked Helen to teach me other languages. This posed something of a problem, for how could she teach what she did not herself know? She solved it by inviting other linguists to the Institute. These women and men stood on the deck above me calling out phrases in Finnish or Basque, which I then repeated with some of the sounds used in Wordsong and which Helen's freshly reprogrammed computers translated. Helen discovered that she could accelerate the process by asking native speakers of a particular language to record their words. She played the recordings back to me at high speed, which had the ancillary benefit of shifting pitches to higher frequencies that came more naturally to my hearing. In this way, I learned Tagalog in a day. Chinese, with its music of rising and falling tones, took twice as long.

Sometime after I had tucked my seventy-seventh language into my metaphoric belt, I realized that I had been too hasty in my assessment of how the humans perceive the world. Each language, I learned, is like a sound filter which lets in various aspects of reality while tuning others out. I discovered languages that are nearly as different from English as Orcalish is from the speech of the deep gods. These languages – at least certain features of them – I loved. Silbo, for instance, consists entirely of whistles that can be heard from one ridge or valley to the next by its 'speakers' who wish to communicate with far-off members of their clan. Pirahã has no words for colors, and the Pirahãns seem able to communicate without words at all by translating their phonetic tones into a series of whistles and hums. The language called !Xóõ, or Taa, has 164 consonants of which 111 are clicks. In Archi, any verb can have more than a million separate conjugations depending on how it is used. Something similar occurs in Yupik. The speakers of this beguiling tongue can create words for precise situations, even as we orcas do. And as with Orcalish, none of the resultant Yupik word parts make sense unless used in a specific word in context with others.

It came to me that my supposition of an essential human

pathology might have been wrong. I had worried that the atomization of human languages into separate words mirrored the atomization of the humans' separate selves and their individual consciousnesses, thus leading to alienation and a sense of separation from the natural world. My learning of Pirahã, Yupik, and other languages gave me to understand that not all humans divide up reality into cold, dead pieces as do speakers of English and French.

On the other hand – and one always had to keep an image of hands close to the mind when contemplating humans and their mysterious ways – the problem of human alienation might have been even worse than I wanted to believe. For nearly all human languages had words for human beings and others for animals. Nearly all, by implication or outright definition, thus elevated human beings above and beyond all other species. It was as if the humans saw themselves as forming the apex of a pyramid of life whose only purpose lay in supporting the great density of humans and lifting them up higher toward the sun.

This was madness. I wanted no part of it. How, though, was I to go on learning more and more about the humans without somehow overcoming this conundrum: to speak a language is to think in that language; to think like a human is to be insane in the way that human beings are.

One day, while Unukalhai and I swam through the bay's underwater kelp forest, I confessed my fear that the humans would infect me with their arrogance and aloneness as they passed to each other their many plagues. Must I, I asked him, become estranged from the world and so become an enemy of life?

'At our first meeting,' Unukalhai said as we glided among the swaying strands of kelp, 'I warned you that contact with the humans would necessitate an imbibing of their essential madness.'

'You did, and I can feel it churning in my belly.'

'It will always be so if you persist in dwelling among the humans. However, in the pools of Sea Circus, you found a way to survive the madness, did you not?'

Along our journey to the Institute, I had told Unukalhai of my resolve to live within the insanity of the human realm in a sane way.

'This way,' he now went on, picking up my thoughts as he scratched his white belly on the rocks of bay's bottom, 'entails the surrendering of your old self and the ontogenesis of the new. Such self-creation, however, has many perils, yes? This new self of yours, I think, swims alongside the old and is as vulnerable as a baby. You must inoculate it against the virus of the human mind that would infect yours.'

'You give me different advice than you once did.'

'Well, I am a different whale than I once was. I am a little saner, I think, now that I have drunken from the same pool of despair as you and have breathed the breath of your dream. That is why I love you, Arjuna.'

And I loved him because he had the greatness of soul to become different through the sheer force of will and an openness to new ways of conceiving himself. I loved him all the more because I needed no words for him to hear this appreciation that sounded in the language of the heart.

'How, then,' I asked him, 'can I make myself immune to human madness?'

'Do as the humans do with their diseases,' he said. 'Kill the viruses of their twisted reasoning with cold orca logic before you set their ideas free within your blood. Or at least weaken the virulence of the human worldview with the zangs of orca wisdom that the Old Ones sing out inside you. Breathe as one with me and the others, and let the truth you take in quicken the tissues of your being. In this way, you will become stronger – perhaps strong enough to dwell among the humans without losing yourself.'

Unukalhai's counsel breathed vitality into a notion that I had been nursing for many days. The many languages that I had learned – from Russian to Diné to Marathi – gave me many new eyes with which to behold the human world. And not just to look upon creation anew, but to conceive it in new ways. What is real, and what is not? How should that which we accept as real be regarded and interpreted?

One day, as I swam and sang along the rushing waters of the sea with Unukalhai, Alkurah, and the other orcas, it came to me in an irresistible wave of excitement that just as I could and must remake myself, I was free to find a new way of conceiving reality, neither wholly orca nor maddeningly human. Indeed, both modes of creation depended on each other. The fate that had whispered to me through so many moons and miles now called me onward – called me to become something wondrous and new *through* the zanging of the entire world in a new way. My long journey through the currents of the many human languages had carried me into the bright pool of this realization.

A new idea rippled through me from head to flukes. What if I could create in Wordsong an entirely new language that partook of all the best and the sanest of the human tongues while incorporating aspects of our orca speech that allowed for a deeper sounding of the world? Why should this not be possible? Doesn't all language, like life itself, spring from the same universal source? And doesn't this source, at its very bottom, beat with goodness, beauty, and truth? What if I could teach the humans to truly speak – and thus to hear the truth of their own hearts?

How this conception thrilled me! In its deeps, I zanged infinite possibilities of mutual accord between the humans and my kind. I heard goodness in much of what the humans had spoken with their lovely lips; I beheld beauty in their incomparable eyes, alive with starfire and all the hope of life. I could not wait to share my epiphany with Helen and Gabi.

Before I had the opportunity to do so, however, as I was working with a new linguist whom Helen had invited to the Institute, I chanced upon a new word whose like I had never zanged: *schadenfreude*. Until that day I had avoided learning German, for I saw it as the language of Wagner and his bombastic music and Auschwitz.

But if I was to craft a new language for the humans, shouldn't I understand one that contained such a disturbing conception as *schadenfreude*? *Schadenfreude*: to take joy at the disasters that befall others.

So alien to my orca mind was this perverting of joy that I could barely think the thought. I considered swimming at speed straight into one of the channel's hideous screens in order to ram it from my head. How could any sentient being celebrate another's pain?

True, many creatures of the sea inflict wounds or even death on others of their kind in their pursuit of females or prey. They do so, though, only from their deep urge to mate and eat, not from any desire to wreak suffering upon another, much less to relish it. True, we orcas do know great joy when we slay a salmon or a seal, but not *because* our ecstasy derives from another being's agony. If we could slay and eat without causing suffering, we would.

How different the humans were! How angry, how bitter, how sick!

At first, I wanted to attribute the conception of *schadenfreude* to something vile in the Germans and their language, and so hope that the madness of the word had passed other peoples by. It was not so. I discovered that *schadenfreude* had a universal appeal. It resonated so deeply with a chord inside many humans that speakers of other languages such as English, French, Russian, and Swedish had adopted the word with glee.

With glee! Human beings took a sick joy in the *taking* of joy at the anguish of others! Some even thought this was cute. I considered the implications of *schadenfreude* to be cataclysmic: for the word itself in its harsh sounds bespoke a great wrongness at the center of the human heart.

How I wished I was wrong in my zanging of this wrongness! How I hoped to find that all languages shoot out from a single fountain of truth, as marvelous to behold as the white, yellow, red, and blue stars that spray out from the galactic center! Why should the languages of the humans be any different from those of the whales, or indeed, of any creature or thing? Does not each grain of sand and each water molecule sing of the universe's immense beauty and goodness? How could it not be so with human beings?

Why, I asked the waters through which I swam, did the humans sing so passionately of glory and war? How had the worm of sadism twisted its way inside them? Why had the sludge of resentment of others befouled their blood? What would keep the gangrene of their bitterness of life from rotting their hands, their hearts, and their souls, and all that they touched?

I wondered if there might be some deeper sanity, pattern, or purpose beneath the humans' seeming madness – something so deep that I could not as yet zang it. If that were so, how would I ever be able to see what I could not see?

'You know the truth,' I heard my Grandmother whisper to me through the quiet water. 'If a whale has the courage to dive down deeply enough, he can always hear it.'

When I listened inside myself, I heard only the shriek of a crazy-making cacophony, like a hundred symphonies blaring out simultaneously from brass horns, cymbals, and other raucous instruments. However, I could *feel* the truth quivering with vicious life inside me. The shark thrashed in my belly and would never again be stilled.

What was I to do? It seemed to me that I had only three choices: I could hope the foolish hope that the bitter burn of the acid of my own furor would somehow kill the shark. I could allow it to eat its way through me and so be destroyed. Or I could simply open my mouth and let it out.

12

My agonizing over the humans and their ways occasioned many conversations with Unukalhai and the other orcas. We re-argued debates that had been old long before the humans came down from the trees of their mother continent and abandoned the primeval forest and their monkey-like cousins who lived there. Many of our explorations centered around questions of basic epistemology: What *is* truth? How do we recognize and know it? How do we open our minds in order to accept what we know? And how do we then act upon the gnosis that has suffused every cove and corner of our being?

We often spoke together of such things out in the moon-washed waters of the bay when the sleep-drugged humans collapsed into the totality of their nightly unconsciousness. After much discussion, it became clear that we did not really know very much about the humans and their world. We had depended on so little to inform us of the humans: the lexicons of many dictionaries, the instruction of Helen and other linguists, and those images and sounds that Helen allowed us to take in from the ever-glowing and ever-blaring screens. Did they *really*, for instance, dwell in vast cities, each of which contained more human beings than all the orcas who lived in the sea? Had they really set fire to children with napalm and used a similar flame to sail up to the moon? And what of *schadenfreude*? Did this terrible word perhaps resonate with chords that we orcas could not hear? We all longed for a better and more direct experience of the manswarms that crowded the interiors of the dark, unknown continents. Short of regrowing legs and retracing the steps of our ancestors who had left the land eons before, however, we would never look upon the humans beyond the world's seas and coasts with our own eyes and sonar, unless it was from the vantage of the pools of Sea Circus and other such places.

How, then, were we ever to know the truth about humans? Part of the answer to this question, we decided, might lie in one of the artifacts crafted by human hands and inspired by human minds. We all had at least some experience of books. Our acquisition of words in the many languages that we learned often led to questions that Helen and the other linguists answered through reading from one book on another. It was a natural next step for us whales to answer questions ourselves through choosing which books to 'read' on our own.

In a way, the absorption of a book's meat into one's body and brain proved to be a *better* way of understanding the humans' world than was a direct experience of it. Books could embrace more of the world than any one being could ever apprehend. Then, too, books are doorways to the mind – to the minds of others and the mind of the cosmos itself. Is not the life of the mind, in a sense, more immediate than any of the quotidian happenstances of journeying, speaking, eating, excreting, and the like? Are not the minds of others like lenses that let in aspects of reality that one might not be able to perceive oneself? And don't these cognitive lenses also therefore concentrate and intensify that which is known and make it more real?

So it is with us whales, who have the rhapsodies of our Old Ones and the Song of Life. The humans have the distillation of their species' knowledge, wisdom, failures, experiences, and realizations into books. So many, many books – there might have been a million of them! We whales who had survived the pools of Sea Circus, along with Kitalpha and Hyadum, resolved to drink in as many of these books as we could.

How, though, were we to accomplish this feat? We could not read as the humans do, for our eyes could not sort out the chaos of markings by which the humans presented the sounds and words of their various languages. Helen helped us overcome this limitation. Once we had conveyed to her our desire and our ensuing frustration, she provided the substance of books to us in the simplest of ways: she and Gabi – the other linguists, too – would sit along the concrete rim of the channel reading aloud to us whales waiting below in the water that lapped in from the bay. Through the Moon of Midnight Wanderings and the Moon of Hope, the humans gave us words from their books.

One evening, after Gabi had recited the story of how the humans had long ago looked up from the planet that we share and had reached out their hands toward the stars, we whales held a conclave out in the private waters of a cove across the Sound. And Baby Electra, who could be as dramatic as she was impatient, called out from beneath the midnight moon: 'This is going so *slowly*! For the humans to read us their books will take a million years.'

'I do not know why we bother,' Alkurah said. 'So much of what we have heard cannot be true. Who has ever seen one of these dragons that fly on wings like those of birds and breathe out fire? What whale, in all the eons that we have explored all the waters of Ocean, has ever encountered a creature as hideous as a mermaid?'

She, like the rest of us, had trouble distinguishing the humans' fictions from more factual accounts of their kind. When I reminded her that Gabi's reading about dancing dragons surely must belong to the realm of fiction, Alkurah zanged a long whistle toward the sky and said, 'Very well. But what is a whale to think of Gabi's assertion that the humans have journeyed to the moon? How could they have swum up so high if they cannot quenge and therefore open the superluminal waters of space and time?'

'It may be,' I said, preparing myself to speak words that astonished me, 'that the making and reading of the humans' fictions is a *kind* of quenging. Or, at least, a pale echo of it.'

'But how can you think that?' Baby Electra called out. 'Quenging concerns the knowing of truth. The *becoming* of all that is real and thus the being of all things. A fiction, by the definition that I learned, is necessarily false.'

'It may be,' I said, 'that the humans have found a way, a way we never imagined, of using the false to reveal the true, much as their machines tear through the tissues of the earth in order to uncover diamonds and gold.'

This, I went on to say, would accord with all we knew of human perversity and the paradox of their kind: the way they twisted good into evil and yet managed, for instance, to make out of the murder of trees the papery substance on which they inscribed their wondrous books.

'What truth, then,' Alkurah asked me, zanging the round, red orb that hung low in the sky, 'can the humans twist out of the obvious fabulation of fire-breathing ships that rocket up to the moon? And that men have *walked* on the moon? That has to be a lie. The humans so often lie.'

'But we have *seen* these rocket ships!' Baby Electra said. 'The images of them that Gabi has shown us.'

'Images can be fancied,' Alkurah said, 'in the same way that the humans concoct their fictions.'

'It may be,' I said, 'that we still do not know enough about the humans to know what is real and what is not. We need to read more.'

'I would not want ever again to read one of their fictions,' Alkurah said.

'Then perhaps the learning of the humans' history,' I said, 'would be more to your liking.'

218

'It would! It would! As much as I would like to learn *anything* about the humans!'

We had discovered that much as the humans divide up their conception of reality and freeze it into inert, icy words, they section off their knowledge of the world into fragments of understanding that they call disciplines.

'All right, then,' I said, 'as Baby Electra has observed, there are millions of books and many, many disciplines. Why don't we divide up our researches, even as the humans do?'

The other orcas agreed to this. I would delve as deeply as I could into human literature, religion, and linguistics, while Unukalhai applied his mind to psychology and what the humans thought of as science. Alkurah, who had the keenest eyes of any of us, was to take in the humans' visual arts in addition to their histories. Zavijah would be responsible for anthropology and medicine, and Salm for economics and ecology. Bellatrix would listen to the humans' music. As well, she would try to understand semiotics. To Kitalpha went the study of that strange conception called mathematics, and to Hyadum, politics and law. Baby Electra, who actually liked watching the images flickering across the Institute's many screens, would try to make sense of the jumble of songs, shriekings, stories, murders, gossip, opinions, conceits, and contests that compose the humans' popular culture. We realized, of course, that it would be a kind of madness to restrict ourselves to learning only specific disciplines, and so we decided that whenever necessary, any of us would be free to venture where our knowledge quest led us without worrying that we might be impinging on another's territory.

We set to our new work with determination if not complete enthusiasm. The sheer volume of the humans' books daunted us. So many pools of knowledge beckoned us to drink from them! And the reading aloud of books, as Gabi and the others practiced it, progressed so excruciatingly slowly:

'Call wait wait wait me wait wait wait-almost-forever wait wait Ishmael . . .'

Helen, who had shaped much of her life around the solving of problems, overcame ours by playing for us books that other humans far away had recorded on their various contraptions and playing them at high speed, just as she had the lists of vocabulary that we had memorized. Thus the voices to which we listened came out as high and squeaky, as if the human speakers had breathed in helium from one of their balloons. Helen also discovered that most of us orcas could drink in from two to ten books simultaneously, depending on their language, content, and complexity. We each took up stations in parts of the channel, and claimed one of the screens as personal territory. We each tuned out the words of another's book that issued from a screen's associated hydrophone. For one of the two-leggeds therefore to enter the whales' half of the domed Institute when Alkurah, Unukalhai, Baby Electra, and the rest of us busied ourselves in reading in this way was to be plunged into a madhouse of cries, calls, shrills, and shrieks. For us of the sea, however, it was like swimming to another world.

As we absorbed more and more books, another problem arose from the didactic deeps. It seemed to be the nature of books that the reading of one led to a desire to plunge into another in an ocean of interconnecting currents of knowledge that partook of the marvelous complexity of one of our rhapsodies. We could, not, however, read whatever books that our journeys into the human noosphere called us to request of Helen, for it turned out that only a fraction of all books ever written had been rendered into human voices.

'I would like,' I said to Helen one day, 'to read "Narrative of the Most Extraordinary and Distressing Shipwreck of the Whale-Ship Essex".'

What I actually spoke were orca trills and chirrups that Helen mentally translated into the syllables of Wordsong:

Ju quavo lati shido li myushina e tlöno li bodo nadla Esekes.

'I see,' she said in plain English, 'but what if that particular title has not been recorded?'

I zanged undertones of stress in her controlled and well-modulated voice – and zanged as well a hint of evasion.

'So many books have not been recorded! But this one I need to read.'

'I will see what I can do.'

'Can you not simply ask another of your kind to record this book? There are so many millions of you! More, I think, than all the books in the world.'

'It is not so simple,' she said. 'There might be a question of copyright.'

Because I knew *of* this word but did not really understand it, I said, 'You mean the right of some entity to claim a part of the noosphere of all human knowledge and to keep it from others much as a barbarian in the desert guards a well from others who are thirsty?'

'It would be kinder to say that copyright keeps the well full and protects if *for* others.'

'Kinder, perhaps, but I think less true.'

'There is also the matter of compensation,' she said. 'Most people who record books for others wish to be paid for their efforts.'

'Can you not find such people then and pay them?'

'We have nearly exhausted our budget for the year by bringing in the other linguists. I am afraid we haven't much money left.'

I thought about this for a while. Then I said, 'Please tell me again about money.'

As many times as Helen had tried to explain the concept to me, I still did not really grasp it. Words such as fiduciary, debt, leverage, medium, exchange, fungible, account, store, and value spun about in my mind like so much debris caught in a whirlpool. Although I had experienced money in various of its physical forms – paper, coins, gold, cigarettes, and others – its meaning seemed always to elude me like a silvery rocket fish swimming always just a little faster than I did.

Most often, I thought of money as a kind of symbolic and actual excrescence (the humans sometimes make their money out of plastic). Like plastic, money has served many purposes and is wholly artificial. It possesses a sort of spiritual taint to match the physical unpleasantness of a dirty dollar bill. And the humans excrete it everywhere in a clog of pollution that cloys every aspect of their societies. The humans dream of money and work for it. They invest it and gamble it away. They trade for it in the precious and non-refundable coin of vitality and time. Nearly everywhere on earth, men and women scheme for it, lie for it, cheat for it, murder for it. Aside from making war and sex and consuming food and water and the very earth itself, the getting of money seemed to be the primary human activity.

Sometimes, however, I saw money as something like what we whales know as love. It passes from human to human like a marvelous substance that binds them into close relationships. The humans speak of debts and credits – was this not similar to the gratitude I felt toward my family and their obligation to me? The humans spend their money (even as we do love) on the things they value most: cars, TVs, houses, rifles, tanks. Upon the births of their babies, they give money to invest and grow much as we feed our youngest ones milk.

While Salm tried to comprehend the mystery (and the madness) of money through her study of economics, even as Baby Electra did by watching movies, I sought understanding of the humans' shekels, shillings, dollars, and drachmas in literature. One night, as a shark-shaped cloud gnawed at the moon high above the Institute, I chanced upon a great novel, one that a great number of humans held in the highest esteem.

At first reading, it seemed a glorification of human selfishness and an exhortation that people should live solely for the furthering of their individual interests. The story concerned a family of wealthy men who desire to become even more wealthy and powerful. To achieve this end (at the expense of others), they hoard their wealth and remove this precious communal fuel from the grasp of others. This causes human societies to collapse. People begin to starve. The *hoi polloi* then finally perceive that they *need* the wealthy men and their money if they are to go on living their miserable lives. And so the wealthy men use the crisis that they themselves have generated in order to persuade the rest of humanity that they should be allowed to become even more wealthy.

Upon my second reading of this apparently execrable book, however, I began to realize an extraordinary thing. The novel *seemed* to be a paean to greed and cruelty, suffused as it was with hate and a subhuman image of man. It *seemed* to put forth the crazy idea that the vilest of men acting out of the vilest of impulses would somehow create the best of all worlds. Of course, no sane person could believe such a lie. And that, I decided, must be the *real* point of the book. Anyone reading it – any woman or man of heart – would understand the terrible consequences of human selfishness and the essential depravity of the human race. And in doing so, they would be driven to find a better way for themselves and their world.

What a genius was the author of this astonishing book! I had not imagined that humans could be so subtle in their writings, so persuasive and sublime. I admired the work all the more because the novel's essential satire hid beneath reams of dreadful prose seemingly meant to be taken deadly seriously. In this, it reminded me of how the ancient alchemists had disguised the universal longing to realize great spiritual truths as a quest to transmute the base metal of lead into sacred gold. Thus the novel bespoke a deep, deep desire of humanity: that the killer apes who bestride every bit of earth on every continent must overcome their most selfish and base impulses and somehow transform their murderousness into something golden and good.

Even as I congratulated myself on diving down into the secret heart of perhaps the greatest novel that any man or woman had ever typed, I had to admit that other works of literature puzzled me. Certainly not all of these could be taken as satire. I bemoaned the limitations of my cetacean sensibilities. I could not, for instance, tell the difference between the stories in the wondrous book called the Bible and humanity's many myths. How was it that so many humans, with their smaller brains, found it obvious that the former expressed the deepest truths and facts of the human race while the latter contained nothing but fancies and falseness? What could these people see that I could not?

The more that I read, the more I became confused about a related matter. I had a hard time zanging the difference between human heroes and monsters. The names of many men – almost always men – echoed throughout the Institute's dome: Achilles, Alexander, Caesar, Elric, Aragorn, Valashu, Genghis Khan. All had murdered many. And it seemed that the greater the number of bodies cleaved bloody by their swords, the more that other men admired them and wished to accomplish similar feats.

One blustery afternoon, with bullets of rain breaking upon the glass of the dome above the channel and its rows of seawashed screens, I spoke to Helen about this:

'Do you find any irony,' I asked her, 'in your kind's greatest killers being given the appellation of "Great"? Alexander the Great; Ashoka the Great; Cyrus the Great; Peter the Great; Herod the Great; Timur the Great; Sargon the Great.'

'All those you mentioned,' Helen said, puffing from a cigarette as she stood above me, 'did many things besides leading others in battle, where many were unfortunately killed.'

'What of the Viking called Eric Bloodaxe? I suppose that he got his name by building houses for the refugees from the depredations of others?'

I chided myself for speaking so brusquely. I had opened my mouth to taste human sarcasm and had drunk a little too deeply.

'You mustn't suppose that everyone,' Helen said to me, 'admires Eric Bloodaxe or the Alexanders of the world.'

I zanged a quickening of her pulse and a tightness of her slender chest, matched by her face's hardening into a kind of mask that I could not read. She seemed bothered, as she always was, when our conversations veered toward human violence or war. And so she changed the subject under discussion – or rather, she segued into a side stream of it:

'How do you orcas come by your names? I have never thought to ask you that.'

'We are named after stars,' I said to her.

Then I called out the sounds of my name, which her machines could record but her mind could not parse. And no syllables of Wordsong had I ever assigned to represent the music of the star that was sacred to me.

'I wish I knew which star you meant by that.'

'I wish I could take you there to look upon it.'

'Can you point it out to me?'

'I cannot point, Helen.'

She laughed at this, a rare respite into an expression of humor that she seemed not to want to allow herself.

'Perhaps you can point with your words, and I can help you.'

That evening, the storm blew away to reveal a clean sky brilliant with many stars. We went outside, and Helen sat on a blanket that she spread over the beach while I floated upon the gentled waves. Helen had brought a book with her and a flashlight. Her eyes danced from sky to book and then back up along the lights of the heavens.

'Do you see that bright orange star off to your left?' I asked her.

'I can see many bright stars,' she said, letting her head fall backward toward her shoulders. 'I cannot really make out their colors. How is it that you, with a whale's eyes, can?'

'Do you see the three stars lined up like diamonds on a ring?'

'Might you mean Orion's belt?' she said, pointing upward.

With my eyesight, so much poorer than a human's, I tried to

look along the line of her dark finger, made nearly invisible by the blackness of the night.

'Yes, I think so,' I said. 'Now follow the three stars from the left to where they point toward the right.'

'Very well,' she said. 'What am I looking for?'

'Do you see that fat, red-orange star – the first really resplendent star in that direction?'

'Yes, I think so. I think its name is Aldebaran.'

I breathed in a cool, sweet, night air along with the sounds of Aldebaran which had tumbled from Helen's lips like drops of starlight.

'Is that the star for which you were named?'

'No, it is not. Now look off to the left at about . . .' I paused because the number I was about to tell her did not come easily to my mind. 'Look at about 10 o'clock.'

'All right.'

'Do you see the hot, blue whale of a star?'

'I see a star,' she said, pointing to a slightly different patch of sky. 'I do not know what it is called.'

She used her thumb to coax a harsh white glare from her flashlight, which she aimed at the pages of her opened book.

'I would suppose,' she said, 'that you are referring to Alnath. It is the twenty-eighth brightest star in the earth's sky. Is *that* one yours?'

'No,' I told her. 'Now look straight beyond that star toward the Coral Galaxy. You will come to a white double-star. That one is mine.'

'I see stars near Alnath. I cannot see if any of them are doubles.'

'I am sorry,' I said, 'but my star is not *near* Alnath but straight past it on a line from Ocean to the Coral.'

'But if that is so,' she said, 'then Alnath's radiance would obscure that of your star.'

'Or,' I said, 'vasten it, as a mother's love feeds the soul of a child.'

'Are you sure there is a double-star there?'

'Yes, I am sure.'

'But how can you perceive what is invisible?'

'How can you not?'

After that, our conversation went nowhere with words circling words, as when a dog chases its own tail.

Some days later on a moonlit night, as I swam about the waters beneath the dome listening to a recording of perhaps the greatest poem that any human had ever written, Helen called me over to her. She sat on the deck above the channel and kicked her bare heels against the iridescent surface of one of the screens as she said, 'I consulted an astronomer. He informed me that there *is* a double-star exactly where you said there would be.'

'I am glad that he has looked upon it,' I said, wondering why her voice had roughened with tension.

'Do you understand the term "light-year"?' she asked me.

'Not really. I have left the study of astronomy to Unukalhai.'

'It is the distance that light travels in a year.'

'But light does not travel,' I said. 'Light always everywhere *is*.'

'Perhaps you should study astronomy, too,' she said with a strange smile. 'It took many years for the light of your star to cross the galaxy and reach earth. By the time it did so, it became so faint that only the most powerful of telescopes could record it.'

'Telescopes made of metal and glass that can hold light?'

The tension in Helen's voice twisted tighter, and she said, 'The star has only recently been discovered and named. It has not yet been mentioned in any book or paper. It is impossible that you could have known of this star.'

'But I have been there!'

'What can you possibly mean by that?'

'Have I not chosen the right words? *Ju arrela do.*'

'I do not understand your use of "have been",' she said.

'How not? Have been, as the past perfect of "is" connecting

previous states of being to the perfect eternal now-moment which always *is* and in which all things everywhere always are.'

Helen let loose a long sigh, which she sometimes did when she grew exasperated with me. She said, 'Your "there" is so many light-years from earth that no rocket we've ever devised could conceivably reach it.'

'But "there" cannot be reached by a rocket. It must be visited otherwise, and when it is, *there* becomes *here* – even as past, present, and future all ring together with the sound of the simple color that I have called glorre.'

Helen sighed again, and sat shaking her head. 'All right, Clever One, you have been to this star, though I do not understand how that can be.'

'How could it *not* be, if it is my star?'

'One either believes in science,' she said as if talking to herself, 'or one does not.'

'But how could you hope to understand everything through science?'

'I just want to understand how you knew of this star.'

'I have already told you. It is the simplest thing in all the universe.'

'It is anything *but* simple – you could *not* have known a double-star existed beyond Alnath, but you did.'

'Do you not know that I exist? Can you not see me here talking to you?'

'But that is precisely the point: You cannot have seen this star. It cannot be seen from earth with the naked eye.'

'No,' I said, 'but it can be quenged with the naked soul. Many times my family has swum past it on our way to Agathange.'

At this, Helen retreated into a deep, blue silence, and so did I. Her dark eyes flickered with little sparks of frustration. And yet I zanged a strange hope there, too, as if she really had understood what I had said and her eyes opened to let pass the light of Alnath, Diadem, Sharatan, and many other stars.

'I have known for a long time,' she said, 'that I have a tendency to invest too much certitude in certain things that I think I know.'

'For a human, you know a great deal.'

'I wish that were so. I wish, too, that I was not so bound by beliefs, either received from others or those that I have acquired by myself.'

'The first and last philosophical question, my grandmother once said, should be: "What is true?"'

'I think I can see where your thoughts are leading,' she said.

I, too, thought she could, for she had a strange awareness of my awareness – and her own.

And then she said, 'One of our poets, Rimbaud, I think wrote this: "I would gladly give my life for anyone seeking the truth – and gladly murder anyone who claimed to have found it."'

'Yes!' I cried out happily. 'Except for the murder part – what a lovely sentiment!'

'And a philosopher named Morris Berman said this: "*How* we hold things in the mind is infinitely more important than what is held there."'

'Yes, yes – you *do* understand!'

'And Kierkegaard said this of another great philosopher: "If Hegel had written the whole of his *Logic* and then stated that it was merely an experiment in thought, then he certainly would have been the greatest philosopher who ever lived. As it is, he is merely a comic."'

'Yes, yes, yes!'

'And Nietzsche stresses the necessity of perspectivism: that every claim, belief, intuition, idea, worldview or philosophy arises from the varying perspectives of the various individuals who hold them. It is impossible to free ourselves from perspectives. When we try to—'

'That is exactly right!' I said, so excited that I did not mind interrupting her. 'I never dreamed humans could appreciate this!'

'The thing is,' she said, 'I am no Rimbaud, Berman, Kierkegaard, or Nietzsche. I am struggling very hard to accept that there might be an entirely new aspect to reality that I never conceived.'

'But you do struggle, and that is what I adore about you.'

'I am stuck within a certain perspective,' she said.

'Of course you are. The eye cannot see itself – and you cannot climb out of your own eyeballs.'

'Just so. However, perhaps I can borrow the eyesight of others in order to behold the world from many perspectives.'

'Yes – why else did Ocean call into life all the squid, tuna, whales, and other creatures if not to look out through our many millions of eyes and behold the beautiful, beautiful totality of creation?'

She smiled and said, 'Why do you think I invited you here? Perhaps we can help each other to see.'

'I would like that,' I said. Possibilities opened outward before me like a panorama of bright, whirling galaxies, and I swelled with a bright, shining hope for human beings. 'I would like to look through one of your telescopes. And perhaps to give you a new lens through which to view the world.'

After we had finished congratulating each other on the perspicacity of our willingness to try to perceive each other through our respective perspectives, Helen yawned and said, 'It is growing late.'

'Yes, you should sleep,' I told her. And then, 'What did your astronomer name my star?'

'Do you want the official or the familiar name?'

'The one without numbers.'

'Arjuna,' she said, 'after the hero of the Mahabharata who spoke with the god Vishnu.'

'Then,' I said to her, 'you should call me Arjuna.'

At last, I had a name that would mean something when the humans uttered it, a very human name, which by good fortune could easily be articulated through the syllables of Wordsong: Ar-ju-na. The despicable human syllables of Bo-bo I could now leave far behind me as I had the little pools of Sea Circus. Might the humans now listen to me as with new ears when I spoke of matters of the greatest urgency? So many things I still had to tell them! So many things I still wanted to ask them: Did they *really* believe all the unbelievable things they felt certain must be true? What did they really know about the world? And (the strangest thought of all) could they possibly be the 'knowing ones' that their name for themselves proclaimed them to be, the *Homo sapiens* whom we orcas might come to acknowledge as what we thought of as really and truly sapient?

13

I spent the next day reading Nietzsche. In the evening, I related our conversation to Unukalhai as we swam together among the underwater rocks out in the bay. I told him of my near-certainty that Helen was truly scient – and thus possessed the openness of mind to at least listen to any arguments we might make concerning the fate of the world that we shared.

'It is good that she is scient,' he said. 'I never thought to find that a human could be so. It would be better, of course, if she were also sapient, truly sapient – how easy our task would be if all Homo sapiens lived up to their name.'

Unukalhai had chosen the humans' own flattering description of their mostly unknowing species to signify the kind of knowingness that we had supposed only whales share. Sapience, as we orcas think of it, has everything to do with the awareness of one's own knowing – and even more, the *awareness* of that awareness.

To be sapient is to be open to any truth about oneself or the world, no matter how wondrous or terrible. Sapience has a radiant quality, as of a ray of light shining down through currents of ever deeper understanding or reflecting back and forth between a tessalation of the mind's mirrors of itself until it grows almost impossibly bright. In the most sapient of moments, awareness deepens into an infinite recursion of *seeing* that becomes ever vaster and clearer. Sapience is therefore an essential part of quenging, a faculty of both mind and soul that seeks out the limits of that faculty and pushes ever against them.

'Helen *plays*,' I said, 'at her role of being a scientist, as she plays at life itself – I think. If only I could speak in our language with her! If only she would let me into her mind! I am sure that something very great swims in its deeps, some self-conception and will to be only herself that resonates with the songs that we sing of ourselves.'

Later that afternoon, Unukalhai and I held a conference out in the bay with the other orcas. It was a fine day of bright sun and white wisps of clouds that seemed brushed across the sky's blueness as if the world had taken up the art of painting. The frothy wakes of many speeding boats zigzagged the even bluer water. Beneath the surface (and the humans who had come to watch us), we spoke of human sapience and other things.

'This is not the best of times,' Alkurah said, insisting on taking the lead in our discussion, 'for me to speak of the humans. I do not understand why I have not become pregnant. My frustration presses at me like the walls of Sea Circus's pools. I am angry again. I am afraid the humans have done something to me.'

'What could the humans have done to your womb?' Unukalhai said. 'As for your anger, the humans would say your paralimbic brain must be malfunctioning.'

'Oh, my poor paralimbic brain!' Alkurah said, trying to let Unukalhai's sarcasm push her into a more quickly flowing mirth. She failed. Then she aimed her voice at me. 'Since you cannot please me with your phallus, I would like you to soothe me with your flute, as you did with my sister when the humans took Navi away.'

For a while, with boats screaming above us, I sang to her of all the babies she would someday bear when we managed to reason with the humans and the world was made whole again.

'Thank you,' she said, swimming closer to brush against me. 'Now I am ready to speak of Helen.'

Hyadum, much-scarred in her body if not her soul, said to us: 'I have not known Helen as long as everyone else, but I have had surprisingly deep conversations with her. She does not seem to rest her mind upon religion, law, science or any other external structures that the humans have made to armor themselves against the world. I have known her always to think for herself.'

'She certainly has her own view of the world,' Salm said.

'And she does not,' Zavijah said, 'expect anyone else to share it.'

'She is a unique world to herself,' Bellatrix added. 'I cannot say the same for the other linguists and scientists with whom I have spoken.'

'Unique, yes, perhaps,' Alkurah said. This graceful orca, who longed so fiercely to be a mother, enjoyed taking in the seed of a conversation and quickening it into greater life. 'And that is precisely the problem. Supposing what Arjuna says of her is true, it might be that of all the human race, only she is sapient.'

'That is certainly not so,' I said. 'You have not read the words of Socrates, Sappho, Nietzsche, Dostoyevsky, Hesse, Ramana or the Mother, have you?'

'No, I have not,' Alkurah said. 'But let us then suppose that a *few* of the billions of humans are sapient. What is the good of finding a handful of pearls glimmering among all the garbage that floats on the sea?'

Kitalpha, long and lean and wounded in his body nearly as badly as Hyadum, possessed a cheerful temperament and a will never to allow life's difficulties to gloom him. He insisted on trying to laugh at any situation or account of woe. At the beginning of his adulthood, he had composed his rhapsody around the currents of humor and play to nearly an absurd and somewhat irritating degree. With such a spirit did he now infuse his buoyant voice:

'Sapience and intelligence,' he said, 'are two different things, but one cannot swim very far into the former without the latter. How intelligent can the humans be when they do such stupid things? Why don't we play a game to see who can cite the greatest human idiocy?'

'A game! A game!' Baby Electra called out, swimming close to me. 'I love games!'

'Very well,' Kitalpha said, 'then I will begin. The linguist called Sophia, who I wished lived up to her name, read this to me from a news story: A human male tested a nail gun on his own head.'

'Pavel read this to me,' Menkalinan said. 'A male died after launching a fireworks rocket from the top of his head.'

'I can do better!' Zavijah said. 'A Baby Kelly found the gun that his father had bought to protect him, and shot himself in the face.'

'A male,' Salm said, 'climbed over the restraining wall at the zoo so that he could hug a tiger.'

'Why is it,' Hyadum asked, 'the human males who do the stupidest things?'

'Not all! Not all!' Baby Electra said. 'A female placed her newborn in its car seat on the roof of the car so that she could adjust the seatbelt. Then she became distracted and drove off with her baby on the roof.'

'I can do better!' Alkurah said. 'A female, nearly as fat as a whale, rushed into a hospital complaining of—'

'And what is a hospital?' Hyadum asked.

'A dwelling where the humans go to obtain drugs, have diabetic limbs amputated, infect each other with their diseases, give birth, and die.' Alkurah breached, as did the rest of us. She breathed in with greater force than usual, obviously hoping to cool the cynicism that nagged at her. 'The female complained of pains in her belly, which she mistook for an inflamed appendix or cancer. But it turned out that—'

'She was only pregnant!' Baby Electra guessed, having a great deal of fun with Kitalpha's game. 'And she astonished herself, if no one else, by giving birth to a beautiful, healthy baby!'

'But the baby,' Unukalhai said, 'did not remain beautiful for very long. She fattened on an ersatz milk of chemicals and sugar, and grew up to be even huger than her mother.'

'She grew up,' Salm said, 'drinking sugared water and watching other humans drink sugared water on TV and then kill each other.'

'No, she did not grow up at all,' Unukalhai said. 'The bullet that exploded out of her baby brother Kelly's face pierced her head and killed her.'

Kitalpha, for a moment playing with the concept of *schadenfreude* that I had taught him, imagined for this human female a much crueler and more likely fate: 'No, she *did* grow up. She spent her life in rooms smaller than the pools of Sea Circus that you have told of. During the day, she sat in cubicles staring at a computer screen. When she got home, she sat staring at TV, eating pizza chased down with ice cream. In between cubicle and couch, she—'

'Sat in traffic,' Zavijah said, 'with a billion other cars, and she breathed in gasoline fumes and listened to the music of horns honking.'

'That is better than the music of acid rap,' Baby Electra said.

'And when she climbed out of her car and her day of rest and play came,' Alkurah said, 'she—'

'Discovered some pretty dandelions in the grass of her yard,' Salm said, 'and so she climbed back into her automobile and went to the store where she bought liquid herbicides to kill—'

'*Her* child,' Kitalpha said, 'who also survived a similar journey through traffic on the roof of her mother's car only to grow up and drink by mistake the herbicides which her mother had stored in an empty bottle of sugared water. The doctor at the hospital who tried to save her by pumping the poison from her belly—'

'Later complained to the other doctors that the female and child were two of the stupidest humans he had ever known.' This came from Unukalhai, who believed that one could *always* find a stupider human being. 'To assuage his guilt over not being able to save the child, that night the doctor drank a bottle of wine and passed out in front of *his* TV watching men collide with each other head-on in a battle over an ovoid ball. The next morning, he drove sweating and cursing through traffic to a place where he bought a new sports car and—'

'What is that?'

'A car used in the human sport of driving so fast that—'

'How fast?'

'It can roll 200 miles per hour.'

'How fast is that?'

'As fast as a falcon can fly.'

'And so the doctor in his car rolled at two hundred miles per hour toward—'

'No, he did not. He joined a herd of traffic moving only five miles per —'

'And how fast is that?'

'About as fast as a wheelchair rolls,' Unukalhai said. 'And so the doctor had ample time to dream of a vacation racing on empty roads across the desert.'

'The car made the doctor happy, yes?' Baby Electra said. 'Exchanging money for things always makes the humans happy, as when we give each other our songs.'

'The car did *not* make the doctor happy,' Unukalhai said. 'Very little about his life did. When he completed his journey home that day, he decided to exchange his wife for another—'

'And what is a wife?' Hyadum asked.

'A single mate, the only other human that a human promises to mate with forever.'

'How odious!' Hyadum said. 'How perverted!'

'I wish I could buy a mate to impregnate me,' Alkurah sighed out. Then she said to Unukalhai, 'Can we assume that the doctor lived happily ever after with his new car and his new wife?'

'We *cannot* assume that – only a very few humans are intelligent enough to figure out how to be happy. No, when the doctor discovered his new wife mating with a young, virile male, he decided that he hated his life, and so he—'

'Began working twelve hours each day,' Salm said, 'in order to save enough money to retire to Italy where—'

'And what is Italy?' Zavijah asked.

'A place where the humans eat pizza covered with octopus and drive sports cars two hundred miles per hour.'

'So the doctor attained happiness after all?'

'No, he did not. He never seemed to accrue enough money, and so he worked fourteen, sixteen, eighteen hours each—'

'And how many hours in each day?'

'Twenty, I think.'

'So the doctor retired to Italy, and *then* he was happy?'

'No – he worked himself sick with the disease of the hardening of the heart and the arteries that afflicts so many humans,' Salm said. 'His leg arteries grew so hard that his blood could not suffuse his feet, which died and began to rot. So one of his doctor friends—'

'Had to cut off his blackened, gangrenous legs with chainsaws,' Bellatrix said, 'but he was so sick that—'

'The other doctors connected him to tubes and oxygen and machines and put him in the dying room where—'

'He found himself next to the female who had poisoned her daughter with herbicides,' Alkurah said. 'She, too, had no legs, and was dying of the diabetes disease that afflicts the humans when they drink too much sugar—'

'What did they eat in the dying room?' Hyadum asked.

'The same foods humans always eat,' Unukalhai said. 'In a way, the doctor and the female began to eat each other in a mutual loathing that—'

'Sartre said that hell is other humans. So, now in hell, the doctor—'

'Out of sheer spite began a competition with the woman to see who could live the longest.'

'They tried to live *longer*,' Baby Electra said, 'when they were not really living at all?'

'The humans cannot bear the necessity of dying. And so the doctor and the female—'

'She lived longer, didn't she?' Baby Electra said. 'Females are tougher than males.'

'Actually,' Unukalhai said, 'they died at the same time. It turns out that their fates were tied to their taxes.'

'How can that be?'

'You see, both the doctor and the woman considered themselves to be good, responsible adults.' Unukalhai paused in agitation to pound his tail against the water. 'The doctor had always consented to using some of his money to pay taxes that he hoped would go toward teaching stupid people not to be quite so stupid, but in reality would be used to—'

'Encourage the makers of herbicides,' Menkalinan said, 'to make even more of their poison and others that would be used in war to kill—'

'Millions of males and females,' Alkurah said, 'but that was not the worst of it because—'

'The taxes also were used to build nuclear bombs that—'

'Were no different than the bombs paid for by the taxes of other humans who—'

'Humans have Others?' Kitalpha asked.

'For most humans, most humans are Others,' Unukalhai moaned out. 'The humans say this: "Every tribe against every tribe; every clan against the tribe; every family against the clan; every man against his family."'

'Yes,' Alkurah said. 'What Hobbes described as the war of all against all. So war—'

'Came to the hospital and the dying room and the doctor and the fat female in the form of a nuclear bomb that—'

'Killed them in a flash!' Baby Electra cried out. 'And that was end of the human race!'

The silence that befell the waters of the Sound just then beckoned us to bask in its cool, pacific touch. Then Alkurah said, 'Perhaps we should share our farce of human stupidity with Helen, that she might share it as a jeremiad with other humans.'

'That would not be wise,' Unukalhai said. 'Our song did not end happily, and the humans do not like to think about death.'

'No,' Alkurah said. 'They are fond of words that soften or obscure it. Especially when they inflict death on each other.'

'Yes, it is amusing, is it not,' Kitalpha said, 'how the humans use the words "collateral damage" to mean—'

'Murder,' Hyadum said.

'And when they say they need to "put a dog down", they really mean—'

'Murder,' Baby Electra said.

'And an execution is nothing but a—'

'Formal murder.'

'And "endangered species" means—'

'Beings not yet completely murdered.'

'And we could think of "nuclear deterrence" as—'

'A threat of—'

'No, a *promise* of—'

'Total murder.'

'Which might be as bad as "climate change", which we might as well call—'

'Planetary murder.'

We swam along quietly, saying nothing as we moved through a slip of water warmed by the stuttering, smoking engines of the many boats whining about the Sound. After a while, Alkurah said to me, 'Arjuna, you did not join our game. Do you disagree with our assessment of human stupidity?'

'No, I do not,' I said. 'The humans *are* stupid, and too often become only stupider as they grow older: their adults do not even know how to defecate without sitting on a toilet.'

'And?'

'They are stupid as a race. There is a male – we might as well think of him as a male – who leads others on a journey straight towards a cliff that the humans can see all too clearly ahead of them.' I paused to blow out some old air and take a new breath. 'When the male reaches the edge of the cliff and looks down at the sharp rocks below, he will convey to all the others his surprise that they have gotten to the very place that they were going.'

Alkurah considered this and said, 'And?'

'Despite all this, I believe that we have to act as if we have hope for them, even if hope flees from us more quickly than the setting sun.'

Unukalhai let loose a long whistle of respect for what I had said, then voiced a doubt, shared by all of us, including myself: 'If it were only stupidity that afflicts the humans, we might find a way to illuminate them. But I am afraid that something is wrong with their hearts.'

'Too true,' Menkalinan said from beside Bellatrix. 'What can we do about that?'

'Sing as brightly as we can,' I said.

'But the humans hear so little of what we say! Can a glimmer light up the desolation they have made of their own souls?'

'So dark, dark, dark is the song that the humans sing!' Baby Electra said as she swam close to me. 'Darker than inkvol, more disturbing than violash.'

'What *is* wrong with the humans?' Zavijah said. 'Why must they taint and torture?'

'They keep birds in cages,' Salm said, 'so small that they cannot spread their wings. They cut off the birds' beaks so that the maddened creatures cannot eat each other before the humans eat them.'

'They make entertainments of cruelty,' Zavijah said. 'They laugh together convivially around dinner tables where they relish such dishes as the *san zhi er*, the triple screaming. Into pretty bowls they put newly born baby rats, who scream once as they are grabbed up by chopsticks and a second time when they are dipped into sauce. And scream a third time when . . .'

Zavijah stopped speaking and let her silence speak more loudly then any lament ever could.

'At least the humans practice such barbarisms in nourishing themselves, which all creatures must do,' Alkurah said. 'But I have read something almost unbelievable about the men who have hunted us with their harpoons. They murder us not for our meat to consume, but for parts of our bodies such as ambergris that they make into perfumes. They cut us down to our blubber, which they boil into oil that they use to grease the gears of their machines. They burn our bodies in their lamps to give themselves light.'

'I can believe almost anything,' Zavijah said, 'of a people who took my baby Navi away.'

'Can you believe this?' Unukalhai asked her. 'One of their greatest philosophers, Rene Descartes, argues that the soul is the feeling and experiencing part of one's being. Because an animal by definition obviously has no soul, a dog or dolphin, for instance, cannot suffer. If boiled in oil, a dog's screams and writhings result purely from a mechanical response of an essentially soulless mechanism that cannot feel real pain.'

Alkurah breached with the rest of us and slapped her tail against the water with a crack and a splash. She said, 'The humans cannot feel the sufferings of their own kind. They make lampshades of flesh flayed from the bodies of those they have murdered. They cast the screaming babies of those they despise into the air and catch them on bayonets.'

'They have numbed their sensibilities,' Zavijah said, 'with fear and wrath. They drink in images of violence from their hellishly glowing screens and so stupefy themselves on simulations of reality and other intoxicants. They are mad for drugs – whatever drugs really are. They take coffee drugs to wake up in the morning and pills to sleep at night. Alcohol drugs help them relax after the torment of their daily work and enable them to socialize with others of their kind. They face the insanities of the human world by gulping anxiety drugs, and they poison their bodies with powerful chemical drugs to kill the cancers that grow from all the chemicals they dump into their water. They have fabricated a drug to excite their diseased, drained-out males to enjoy erections.'

To the sound of boats buzzing across the bay, like gigantic mechanical insects, we considered Zavijah's words. And then Unukalhai picked up the theme of her rant: 'The humans are mad for tools and could not live a single day without their technologies. They use tools to get their food and even to convey it to their mouths. They make tools for scratching their backs, tools for picking their teeth, and tools for masturbating. Tools help them to read and to rock their babies to sleep. They make tools to kill. They even make tools of themselves, the *instrumenta vocalia*, tools with voices, which is how the Romans call their slaves.'

'And so many are slaves!' Hyadum said. 'Thirty millions right now, by their own count. Billions more slave away on farms and in factories and in the cages they call offices. Millions of other humans devour their labor, money, time, sweat, tears, hopes, and dreams.'

'Yes, they are a truly cannibalistic species,' Menkalinan said. 'When the Maori discovered their cousin Moriori living peacefully across the waters of the Olivine Flow, their first impulse was to board their canoes, make war upon the Moriori, enslave them, and eat them.'

'The Russian humans ate their own at Leningrad,' Alkurah said. 'Such horrors happen in all wars.'

We all swam about the cool water in silence as we considered this. High in the sky, the thunder of a warplane broke the blueness.

'The humans are mad for war,' Unukalhai said. 'Genghis Khan, whose descendants populate the continents in the millions, declares that the greatest pleasure is to vanquish one's enemies and drive them like cattle, to despoil them of wealth and see their dear ones bathed in tears, to take their horses and ravish their women.'

'The humans adore slaughtering,' Alkurah said. 'One of their heroes declares that it is "well that war is so terrible, otherwise we would become too fond of it to love it." To love it *too* much!'

'But they hate war, too!' Baby Electra said, playing the *advocatus diaboli*.

'They say they do,' Alkurah shrilled out. 'But they lie. Yes, the humans wail and weep and lament war's agonies, yet they continue to slay each other by the million. This killing takes precedence over all other human activities. They organize the whole of their lives around the prospect of human-inflicted death. Who does *not* pay taxes? If they really wanted to, of course, they could hold a council and agree to end war in a day. Instead, they build submarines and hydrogen bombs and ready themselves for the war that will put an end to their murderous, miserable, lying, sadistic, cannibalistic kind.'

Now, despite the noises that the humans about the bay inflicted on the world, the water through which we swam sparkled with a kind of reflective silence. It seemed that there was nothing more for anyone to say. Unukalhai, though, could not help repeating a theme that he had stressed through many miles and many years.

'It is not just that the humans are mad for money, mad for drugs, tools, and war. Despite the few sapient women and men who may live among them, the humans are simply mad.'

We all agreed with this. Baby Electra, though, in the most deadly serious of mind games, decided again to advocate for the devil again, saying, 'But the humans *have* made rockets that have taken them to the moon!'

Unukalhai laughed at this, and replied, 'So what?'

'And the humans,' Baby Electra went on, 'have built magnificent cathedrals.'

'So what?' Salm said.

'They have made machines that can cast their voices anywhere in the world.'

'So what?' Zavijah said.

'They have transplanted the hearts of the dead into the living.'

'So what?' Bellatrix said.

'They have used lightning to raise the dead.'

'So what?' Menkalinan said.

'They have split atoms, whatever atoms really are.'

And Kitalpha, his fine black skin cratered with burn scars, said, 'So what?'

Whether by bad chance or design, Baby Electra had blundered in this last defense of the human race. Unukalhai immediately took advantage of her mistake.

'And it is precisely through the fracturing and fissioning of the world's matter,' he said, 'that the humans will unleash the lightning and hellfire that will destroy the world.'

We might have ended our council there and then and gone off to fish and sing and enjoy the pleasures of the world before the inevitable apocalypse rained down its killing light from the peaceful sky. At that moment, though, a small incident occurred that had the very large effect of bringing our discussion and all that I had learned into an acute focus. A red boat speeding about the water cut off a white boat trying to angle close to us whales. Its driver had to veer in order to avoid a collision. He stopped his engines and called out in anger to the red boat's driver, a large man with a porcine red face cratered with acne scars. His nostrils pointed almost straight out like the barrels of a sawed-off shotgun. His upper arm, sticking out of his neoprene vest, bore a tattoo of a coiled red dragon. I had seen similar tattoos in photos of the infamous Red Dragon Death Squads that had exterminated the Herero people. This ugly, ugly man should have reached deep into himself to grasp a bit of the beauty and brightness that all humans possess. He should have apologized for a carelessness that could have resulted in injury or death. Instead of proffering any sort of contrition or kind words, however, he stopped his boat as well and thrust out his middle finger and shoved it through the air at the other driver's face. This man – dark and slender and furious

– made the same motion with his finger. Both men began calling out curses to each other.

'Watch what comes next!' Baby Electra said from beside me. 'I saw this scene in a movie. The Ugly-Face will pull out a gun and shoot the other man!'

That did not happen. The large man, with a final shove of his finger and the harshest of invectives concerning the other's mother, settled on a thinly veiled threat to sodomize the other man to death. At this, the darker man's face tightened with fear. He gunned his engines and drove off. The man with the cheeks and forehead as crimson as a boiled pig, rubbed his dragon tattoo and turned to stare at me and the other whales. I expected to see shame over his bullying actions burn his face. Instead, his lips curved up into a smile of victory. His eyes glistened. I could not help gazing into his small gray eyes and the awareness that consumed them with a smoldering pride. He knew, I thought, that he had been wrong. And the very knowing of his misdeed, rather than softening his heart, had impelled him to harden himself against the other man and the better angels of his own nature. And so as men do with each other, he had decided to become aggressive and cruel.

And with this realization, the shark that had dwelled inside me for too long screamed into new life. I could no longer keep the truth about human beings from myself.

They know! They know what they are doing to the world, and they know a better way, and they do not care!

Through the water that flowed across and through my skin and connected me heart and soul with the living beings of Unukalhai, Alkurah, Baby Electra and the rest of us – through the shared sapience of silence that rings at the center of all things – we all came into a shared understanding of human beings at the same moment. In wave upon wave of sickening realizations, the truth about the humans swelled and grew.

They secretly love what they do! Their destruction of the world gives them a sense of power over nature – and nature terrifies them. Deep down, they know themselves to be rather small naked apes, weak of jaw, slow of foot, without fang or claw or horn to defend themselves from the dragons that would devour them.

What hope could I have for the humans, even the most intelligent?

Baby Electra was the first of my adopted family to brush against me and console me. Then came Zavijah, Salm, Bellatrix, and Kitalpha. Hyadum ran her flipper across my face; Menkalinan, Unukalhai, and Alkurah made similar benedictions. As night fell and starlight touched the bay, we all consoled each other.

The shark that I had bespoken in silence, however, now thrashed beside us wherever we swam. Truth – bright, cold, and terrible – like a shout of agony, like a gnashing of violash at the wind-whipped waves, tormented the water and rippled outward to the oceans of the world.

14

Long days of swimming and diving through the humans' books in hope of discovering something about the humans that might redeem them followed – even as we whales cruised the fractured waters of the Sound in search of the meat of understanding. Storms blew in from the ocean. The sun died into dark nights of rain and mist, and fought its way to a wan rebirth through thick clouds each morning. With each mile that we swam – with every salmon that we caught or new book that we tucked into ourselves – the shark pursuing us seemed to grow stronger and stronger.

How was I to make sense of the truth that I could no longer ignore? What was I to do with it? I well remembered my mother once telling me that a truth does not become *fully* true until one acts upon it.

I felt nearly paralyzed, however, with a spreading weakness of will, as I imagined it would be if I had injected one of the humans' narcotic drugs. A sense of helplessness flowed like an irresistible current straight into hopelessness. Again and again, I considered ceasing swimming altogether and allowing the shark to devour me. A single question aggrieved me: what was I to do to act upon the truth if there was nothing to be done?

In the punishment pool of Sea Circus, I had resolved to let

perish – or to actively slay – those parts of myself that I knew to be either useless, antiquated, or inauthentic. I had not imagined, though, leaving behind certainties that I had seen as intrinsic to my soul. All my life, I had enjoyed a bright, singing faith in the essential goodness of life and in the health of nature that had engendered it. Nature, however, I now perceived, possessed a darkness that went much deeper than the horror of animals tearing apart animals and devouring each other in endless cycles of agony and death. For nature, perhaps insane in its deepest part as Unukalhai believed, had somehow brought forth out of the bloody womb of time the crazed and very *unnatural* beings called humans. What if, I wondered, the true heart of nature pulsed with a power that had nothing to do with goodness and was as far beyond it as the Coral Galaxy is from Ocean? What if the madness of mankind inhered in all things?

After I had eaten the white bear – after I had been besmeared with the black oil of the burning sea and had shared the anguish of Pherkad's harpoon – I had lost the power to quenge. I had conflated the seeking of a cure for my affliction with the seeking of a cure for the ill earth. In my innocence of faith, I had assumed that I would find a way to heal both myself and the world. What if, I now asked myself, the insane and bitter suffering of the world could *not* be cured? What would I do, how would I live, if Ocean itself must inevitably sicken and die?

A human's answer to such desperation might have been: '*Of course* the world cannot be killed. And even if it could, we can always find a way to save it.' I saw such optimism as naïve at best but more likely demoniac. Hadn't the humans, out in the Journey of Death Desert where they had exploded the first nuclear bomb, taken bets as to whether the fireball would ignite the atmosphere and incinerate all life on earth? Yes, they had! Yes, they had! And yet. And yet. The world had *not* burned down to a blackened and radioactive wasteland. (Even if parts of Ocean were aflame night and day.) What if the humans, with their human eyes, equations, and eternal zest for the perilous and the new, could apprehend things that we whales could not?

This speculation – or rather, the possibility of its possessing some degree of validity – astonished me. For a long time, though I had hoped human beings might be capable of rationality and a kind of language, I had never seriously entertained the wild notion that some of the Two-Leggeds might be both scient and sapient. Even after I had begun speaking with Gabi, Helen, and others of their kind, I had regarded whales as possessing an intelligence vastly superior to that of the humans, who I supposed knew nothing of worth that we whales had not known for a million years. What if, however, I had been wrong? What if the deranged human beings not only had something to give to us whales but somehow had a strange and mysterious purpose in the world?

'You can never fully know what you do not know,' my Grandmother had once said to me.

Her words – along with the magic charm that she had given me – worked as a balm upon my troubled spirit. They drove away much of my despair. I aimed zangs of sharp inquiry at the shark that swam with me, blood to blood and flipper to fin. What is the truth of truth I asked myself? The cool, surging waters of the Sound murmured my Grandmother's answer, now my own: The Great Ocean of Truth is as bottomless and blue as the waters of Agathange, into which a whale can always dive more deeply.

And so dive I did. Instead of fleeing and seeking out some imaginary pristine corner of the earth untouched by the hand of humanity – as the other whales and I wanted to do – I resolved to remain at the Institute. From my readings, I had learned of a vast pool of human knowledge that both included books and went far beyond them in content and reach. The humans, of course, having only the faintest of intimations of quenging, use a different though related metaphor for the noosphere in which they like to dip their feet. Instead of seeing the truth of all things as a single, superluminal substance that everywhere flows like water, they conceive of it as a collection *of* things, and they content themselves with fashioning nets with their minds in the hope of casting them out in order to capture here a prettier pebble and there a smoother shell. Hence their name for the Oceanic wisdom that should flow among all beings: the worldwide Net.

When I told Helen of my desire to sound the depths of all that the humans' Net contained, she gazed at me with her bright, sad eyes, and said with a smile, 'I will help you if I can. However, if you are thinking to find anything like wisdom on the Internet – much less the key to understanding humanity – I am afraid that you are going to be very disappointed.'

'But the key *must* be there!' I said to her. 'Somewhere.'

She arranged for the Institute's computers to interface with the Net, as it is used by the many humans who are blind. Thus we whales could surf from one pool of knowledge or experience to another by calling out the various names of the pools and listening to the verbiage recorded in each. Additionally – and here we orcas had an advantage over humans deprived of sight – we could drink in from any screen the images of those pools that contained various graphics side by side the written characters of the words that we could not read. In this way, we partook of an entire sphere of human activity that we had barely glimpsed.

What I discovered caught up in the humans' vast Net on my first foray into it should not have shocked me, but it did. It seemed that the humans bought and sold through their far-reaching Net every conceivable sort of pelf (and much that was almost *inconceivable*): dustpans, diamonds, diapers, wolf urine, drill bits, bacteria, steaks, and kidneys. Histories were there as well, and philosophies, and symphonies such as Beethoven's immortal Ninth, in whose soaring harmonies I had first heard the humans sing of joy.

Alongside great novels of nuance and irony dwelled the ravings of lunatics and endless waves of gossip shot through with little snarks of *schadenfreude*. I listened to stock predictions, climate predictions, suicide predictions. Countless movies I watched, as Baby Electra already had, and in too many of them, men slaughtered other men and blew up automobiles and buildings and even entire cities in flashes of hellish fire that hurt my eyes.

So far I had read only the best of what the humans had written; now I listened to the overwhelmingly more voluminous worst. It seemed that most humans were not really sapient at all, but rather non-sapient or even willfully anti-sapient. They were like cabbages in which one could peel back layer upon layer of foolish thoughts and conceits only to reveal nothing at their center. Had nature, I wondered, brought forth these human vegetables or had such malformed beings somehow twisted nature so that they could live in the diminished world that they had fitted to their shrunken spirits? How terrible, how tragic, how sad! When I saw how most humans live – chock-a-block in tiny, ill-lit apartments, eating poisoned, dead food and breathing poisoned air, ever under the threat of war – I found reasons for their madness of inanity, for billions and billions of humans were forced to live lives little different than we whales had known in Sea Circus' punishment pool.

Then one day, I stumbled into a new part of the humans' noosphere and I began to have more hope. As any sapient species should, the humans took a great interest in sexual activity, and they devoted a great part of the Net to it. I could not understand, at first, why the humans seemed to want to hide away in the darkest corners of their Net what might have been millions upon millions of lascivious scenes. (Though it seemed that a clever child could find what was denigrated as pornography wherever she or he wished.) Then it came to me that the humans, loving war and death, hate life along with the sexual urge which engenders it. They feel ashamed of sex, as they do themselves. In all the mainstream movies that I had viewed up until this time, I had not seen one man thrust joyfully and graphically into one adored woman, whereas many, many movies portrayed men raping women or even hacking or blowing them to bits. It seemed that most humans would rather allow their children to look upon bloody dismemberments than a realistic display of erotic love.

The more I studied the humans' sexuality, though, the clearer it also became why the humans attempted to bury their caresses and couplings beneath a shroud of darkness, for much of their sexing was very dark and had nothing to do with pleasure, procreation or love. I watched pornography in which men and women choked and tortured each other, whipped and manacled each other and treated each other as pieces of living meat. How astonishing the many contortions into which they could twist their sweaty, rubbery bodies in pursuit of carnal pleasure! How amazing their sexualizing of fruits and vegetables and other parts of the world, both living and dead! I had never imagined that a human being could mate with a goat.

So rapt was I with the humans' Net and all its many beheadings, bruisings, betrayals, poetry, and jokes that I did not notice that I was allowing the humans' entertainments to fascinate me a little *too* much. One day, when Gabi donned a wet suit and climbed into the channel's cold water to play with me as we sometimes had at Sea Circus, I asked her to do an unusual thing. She stroked my head as she tightened her legs against my sides and rode upon my back through the channel's churned-up waters. Finally she consented in helping me to perform a most un-whalelike feat.

An hour later, I came up out of the water onto the sloping concrete shelf at the channel's far end nearest the human half of the great, domed house. Gabi held in her hand a brown, fat cigar. With a flick of her clever human fingers, she snatched a bit of yellow flame from the lighter in her other hand. Upon wrapping her lips around the huge cigar that her mouth could barely contain, she puffed at the flame and drew it in through the tip of the cigar until its tobacco ignited in a glow of cherry red and smoke. She then pushed the tapered, thinner end of the cigar into my blowhole and held it there.

I, too, puffed in the cigar's smoke. The hot, bitter gas shot straight to my lungs and burned inside me. I coughed and shuddered and breathed in deeply again – and again coughed and shuddered, both at lancinating agony of my aggrieved lungs and at the pleasure suffusing my nerves as the nicotine drug shot straight to my brain. Then Gabi took a turn in this narcotizing game, filling up her mouth with smoke before pushing the cigar back into my blowhole. For a long time I puffed and puffed at the burning cigar as a cloud of smoke hung heavy and gray over my head.

It was thus that Helen found us, playing our smoking game together and enjoying a very basic human vice. So intent was I on absorbing every sensation of this novel experience that I barely registered the signature sound of her stately steps as she came into the dome and walked across the concrete. She stood on the deck a few feet away staring at us as if she could not believe the images that we had forced into her smoldering black eyes. Through her tense body ran a shudder very unlike the one that had delighted mine. Then she cried out, 'What are you doing!'

Apparently, Gabi had neither seen nor heard Helen approach. At the crack of Helen's outraged voice, Gabi sprang to her feet even as she flung the cigar into the waters, where it died into a soggy stump in a ugly hiss.

'I was just showing Arjuna how—'

'What are you *doing*?' Helen called out again.

Unukalhai and Bellatrix, the only other orcas present that day, swam in a little closer to witness this scene.

'Arjuna wanted me to help him understand what smoking is really like,' Gabi said.

Her hair clung tightly to her head like a helmet of sodden, orange curls, and her belly trembled – in both fear and anger, or so I thought.

'He does not need to know.'

'But he asked me to light a cigar for him.'

'Did you ask *me* if that would be all right? Would you give a cigar to your own son?'

'Is that how you think of him? You're still treating these whales like children who need protecting, even from themselves.'

I heard the truth of what she said, and so did Helen, whose lips pressed together like the two shells of a mussel. Her eyes flared with dark lights that she could not seem to contain. Then quick as a stingray's tail, her hand lashed out and slapped Gabi across the face.

Gabi said nothing as a livid outline of Helen's fingers welted her pink skin. She seemed as unable to speak as I was – as Unukalhai and Bellatrix were, too. She stared at Helen. Tears flooded into her blue eyes. With a wipe of the sleeve of her wetsuit across her face and a stifled sob, she turned and ran across the deck into the humans' half of the house.

While my heart pounded in my chest like an angry fist – whether from the violence that Helen had unleashed upon Gabi or from the nicotine, I could not tell – Helen stood staring as upon a scene of herself that she did not want to behold. She struggled to breathe, and I felt her fighting back tears – and much else. She did not, *could* not, look at me. As her whole body began shaking, she too turned and ran into the house.

During the following few days, I saw nothing of either Helen or Gabi. Although Unukalhai and I spoke of what had occurred with the other whales, we could make little sense of Helen's outburst, or perhaps *too* much sense. Unukalhai, in words that proved prophetic, declared, 'It may be that Helen neither dislikes Gabi nor wishes her harm. For the humans, striking each other comes as naturally as the wind blowing.'

Then one cloudy afternoon, Helen returned and arranged to be alone with me. She sat as she often did, upon the edge of the concrete deck with her feet hanging down above the water. Her jet-black eyes invited a conversation that her lips struggled to initiate.

I immediately asked, 'Where is Gabi?'

And she said, 'I don't know.'

'Where *is* Gabi?'

'I don't know.'

Where is Gabi, the one human whose heart I could be sure of?
Then I loosed a long-ranged call similar to Zavijah's futile cries
to Baby Navi.

'Why?' I finally asked. 'Why don't you know? Have you not
called to her?'

'I have called a hundred times, but she will not answer.'

'But have you not looked for her in all the many rooms of your
house?'

'She left three days ago, Arjuna. She is gone.'

'Gone where?'

'I don't know. Maybe home.'

'But this is her home! With me, and with Unukalhai, Alkurah
and Electra – all her brothers and sisters!'

'I told her that,' Helen said, 'but she would not listen.'

'Why not? *Why* did she leave? Why are you humans so cruel
to each other? Why, why, why?'

She opened her mouth to speak, and then closed it again. She
gazed at me eye to eye, but seemed not to want to perceive any
of the anguish that sang out of me. Instead, her eyes' black centers
appeared to open upon a world far from the safe, quiet waters of
the Institute.

I tried to return us to the present, saying, 'If my smoking cigars
distresses you, I will never ask for help in doing so again.'

'It *does* distress me.'

'I, myself, however, might experience some distress of my own at
having to abandon a new pleasure before I have fully explored it.'

She laughed softly. 'I know precisely how hard it is to give up
smoking.'

'You do? But you smoke every day.'

'I smoke *three* cigarettes each day: one in the morning; one in the afternoon; one before bed. And once each year, I stop smoking altogether for three weeks before starting again.'

'But why?'

And then the answer to my question sounded inside me. I recalled a strange, strange book that I read.

'You are taking inspiration from the mage known as Mega Therion, or—'

'Aleister Crowley,' she said, completing my statement. 'I had forgotten that I had recommended his book on Magick to you.'

'Yes, yes, you did.' Aleister, I recalled, used to periodically addict himself to heroin so that he could exercise his will through the struggle to quit. I swam a long circle about the channel and returned to Helen. 'Why do you not, then, simply smoke heroin?'

'Because I could be imprisoned, if I did,' she said. 'And because heroin is slightly less addictive than nicotine.'

'Why do you feel such need to strengthen your will?'

'Without will, how can one face life and all its difficulties and do what must be done?'

I zanged discords of a terrible stress tearing at the timbre of her voice, but I could not guess at its origin.

'Of course one needs will,' I said. 'But when will is needed, will is always *there*, like water.'

'Perhaps for you orcas.'

'It must be so for you humans, too. Calling upon will is as natural as opening one's mouth to take a drink.'

'But so little of what my kind does,' she said, 'is natural.'

'I know! I know! But I do not know *why*.'

'Neither do I.'

'I *need* to know. That is why I asked Gabi for help in smoking the cigar. I was only trying to do what you humans do.'

'I do not want you to do what we do.'

'But how can I understand anything of humans if I do not experience addiction?'

Her sigh seemed as long as the soughing of the north wind that brings in a storm.

'If I care for you, Arjuna, how can I allow you to do something that might harm you?'

'Gabi was right: you do regard us as children who need protecting.'

'I have thought about that,' she said. 'And only the second part of that statement is true.'

'Yes, because you humans see yourselves as "stewards" of all the life of Ocean.'

'That might once have been true of me,' she admitted as a wry smile touched her lips. 'Then I applied my will toward trying to overcome my species' chauvinism and my own regrettable condescension.'

I liked the way that she could make fun of herself and examine her motives.

'When do you think you might succeed?' I asked her.

'When do *you* think you might succeed in going beyond your surety of the superiority of whales?'

'Touché,' I said, wishing that I could smile in the human manner. Then the mood changed, and I zanged a few poignant words into her. 'We orcas have protected ourselves quite well for millions of years. All we need is for you to leave us alone, and we will do even better for millions more.'

'I wish we would leave you alone,' she said. 'I wish we *could*.'

Sadness seeped back into her like water filling the holes of a sponge. She fell silent again. I somehow knew that she was thinking of Gabi and feeling the hurt of her hand that had cracked across Gabi's face. And she knew that *I* knew what she was thinking, even as we both came into full awareness of our shared suffering and held each other close within our hearts.

'I wish we could leave *ourselves* alone,' she said to me. 'But you are right, my perceptive, cetacean friend. I am afraid that we humans *are* naturally cruel.'

258

'I understand,' I said, 'that your kind has known nothing but war for ten thousand years – and more. You have been bound by chains of trauma, nets of karma.'

This provoked a slight smile from her. She said, 'Yes, the karma of cruelty.'

'And the cruelty of karma.'

I looked up at her and drank the sheen of her skin, so smooth and black and alive with the dark songs of history singing from far away out of the distant past.

'As many books as I have read, I still do not understand human slavery.'

'And what makes you think I do?'

'Men threaten others with dismemberment and death to make them provide sustenance and other things?'

'Yes,' she said in a quiet voice, 'that is the core of slavery.'

'But why would humans force others to do what they easily could themselves? It is a joy to get food.'

'Not the way we get it.'

I had seen images of men and women stooping over cabbages in a vast field of baked, brown earth, and I knew that she was right.

'Why would men and women,' I asked, 'permit themselves to be enslaved? Would it not be better to die?'

'It is easy to suppose so until one is faced with death.'

'I think you humans fear death nearly as much as you do life. That is why you have made slaves of each other.'

'Only a few are slaves any more.'

'Is thirty million a few? Remember how bad I am with numbers.'

'It is probably thirty million. Still, when considered against the earth's entire population, the percentage of people in actual slavery is only a fraction of what it once was. In ancient Rome—'

'I think you are all slaves,' I said. 'Everyone on earth is part of a single planetary system of money and commerce, people buying and selling labor, telling others what to do and being told. Everyone is slave or master – or some part of each. And the masters are more slaves than those they own and control, for they live always in fear of losing their wealth and power and becoming poor and powerless. And so they create a bondage of cruelty for themselves, which orders every aspect of their existence. Thus they die in their souls and become burned-up, twisted, shrunken things.'

She gazed at me from the deck a few feet above me. She asked, 'Is that how you see us?'

'I see an entire species that lives off itself. Like sharks devouring each other, you eat each other's labor, money, time, sweat, tears, hopes, and dreams.'

Helen's lips tightened as I said this. I sensed her desire to hold a burning cigarette to them so that she could breathe in the nicotine drug that might soothe her a little even as it cannibalized her consciousness.

'Is that how you see *me*?' she asked softly.

With an eye on her seamless black skin, I said, 'Your ancestors were slaves, yes?'

Her laughter began as a tingling warmth of outrage deep in her throat long before it worked its way down into her belly and began to build. It came up out of her in a force both frightening and volcanic. Bitterness boiled blackish-red within it, along with irony, memory, and the kind of cosmic humor necessary to melt away the anguish of life. Her belly shook and shook as one paroxysm of laughter after another took hold of her. Her mouth widened in an upward curve, and the skin crinkled into deep fissures around her eyes, which flooded with tears that she could not contain.

After she had regained control of herself and sat using her hand to wipe her face, she looked at me and said, 'I am slower today than I usually am. It took me a long time to see that your bringing up slavery was aimed at offering me an excuse for slapping Gabi. Those chains of trauma that you spoke of.'

'Yes, the hurts of the generations inflicted on the helpless, who cannot help inflicting the same upon others.'

'How very, very presumptuous of you!'

'Then your ancestors were *not* slaves who had to swallow rivers of blood and violence?'

She laughed again, not quite so unrestrainedly, but with more bitterness and irony. At last she said, 'My family *owned* slaves. My great-grandfather did, before slavery became illegal – at least officially.'

I took in this news and said, 'I am sorry I presumed, Helen.'

'That is all right.' She wiped at her eyes again. 'You have presumed less than all the people who try not to let the color of my skin prejudice their opinion of me even as they feel sure that my skin must be significant in ways that they do not like to imagine.'

'I should not have presumed at all,' I said. 'I think that I could read books and surf the Net for a billion years, and still not understand you humans.'

'I do not understand them myself.'

'It may be,' I went on, 'that you have somehow eluded the trauma and escaped the karma of the entire human slave system.'

'I have been very lucky in very many ways.'

Attuned to the truth of myself and my many evasions of it, I heard sincerity in her words even as I zanged the deeper lie that they concealed.

'You have never spoken of your family before today,' I said. 'I know nothing of your land or how or why you came to this place.'

My mother once informed me that polite conversation should include silences that invite in others to speak. I remained as silent as a star while I held Helen's eyes in the light of my own. Her belly trembled as if she wanted to laugh again – or weep. I sensed in her the same shark that had fought its way out of me. Her throat tightened into a narrow tube of pain even as her fingers clenched into a fist. How she struggled to keep from speaking! How desperately she wanted to speak!

'Tell me,' I said to her. Sometimes silence needs the help of words. 'Tell me why you think you struck Gabi.'

A million years passed. Helen's breathing slowed to pressured intervals of indrawn air as her will clamped down upon her lungs with its icy fingers. A nearly inhuman coldness spread out from her heart to touch her eyes, her lips, and every aspect of her being. It was a coldness as total as the bitter blue northern ocean and as empty as the black void between the galaxies that starlight has nearly abandoned. When she finally turned her head my way, I hardly recognized the merciless woman who stared at me.

'My family,' she said, breaking the silence, 'had a big white house on a hill overlooking the fields of coffee and sesame where our servants worked – we never thought of them as slaves. We were rich and relatively happy. Then war came. I was twelve, and my sister Bibi was ten.'

Quiet took hold of her again. It seemed that each word that she spoke was like a nail being pounded through the skull of memory, and the fewer words she gave me, the less her agony would be.

'I cannot say that the soldiers who captured us,' she continued, 'killed my family out of a sense of shared injustice with our servants, for they shot them, too, those who did not escape into the hills. The soldiers certainly wanted vengeance, however, on my family, or my tribe – or perhaps the entire human race.'

Although it was a cloudy mid-afternoon and not her appointed time for smoking, she drew out a cigarette and ignited it. Clouds of smoke swirled around her head before disappearing into the salty sea air of the dome.

'The soldiers kept Bibi and me for three years,' she said, in between puffs of her cigarette. 'We moved from one camp to another. Sometimes we slept in dirty huts, but more often on the bare ground. We cooked for the soldiers, gathered firewood or dried dung, carried water, and cleaned their filthy clothes. We had to pretend to like the filthy things they did to us, else we would be beaten. When I became pregnant, I had no idea who the father was. I rejoiced when I miscarried, though before my capture I had wanted more than anything to have my own house and be the mother of many children. I began to worry that my next pregnancy would kill me, for we lived in filth of one kind or another night and day, and we never had enough to eat. I need not have worried, however. It is strange how life answers our prayers. The gonorrhea I contracted did not give me the death that I feared and secretly longed for, but it sufficed to scar my insides and make me sterile.'

There came more smoke, more silence, more memory. The pain that billowed out from Helen's chest to fill up the dome became so intense that I wanted to swim away from it, out into the soothing waters of the bay.

'My sister was not so lucky,' she told me. 'In the eighth month of her pregnancy, her belly swelled as big as a melon, even as her arms and legs shrank into sticks while her unborn child grew and sucked the life out of her. The soldiers began raping her as they would a dog. They did not seem to mind when Bibi grew as dry inside as leather for they used the blood they tore from her to lubricate their efforts. The more she screamed, the more soldiers lined up behind her – they would say: "Listen to how much she enjoys us! We will all make her our bride!"'

Listen! I said to myself. Listen, listen, Arjuna, though you will not want to hear what you must hear!

'One day,' Helen said, 'a new company of soldiers came into the camp. Many were boys, no older than us. We were given to them. One boy – his ear had been shot off, and he could not have been older than eighteen – cried out that he was no dog to take Bibi from behind. He insisted on trying to mount her as he pinned her face to face beneath him. Her belly got in the way, though, and he began punching her there. I knew he was going to kill her. I should have let him – it would have been a blessing. Instead, I finally lost control of myself. Or perhaps I found my will to fight back. I fell on that boy as I had once seen a lioness jump on the back of a warthog. I managed to claw out his eye and bite off part of his remaining ear before the other soldiers used their rifle butts to beat me away from him.'

It seemed that Helen could say no more. But then she reached down inside herself with a fist of black iron to deliver the rest of her terrible story.

'While the soldiers held me,' she said, 'I waited for the boy I had mauled to kill me. However, he had a worse punishment in mind. I could *see* his mind – it was sick with a controlled fury – I could see it in the coldness of the single eye that remained to him. While blood ran down his face and his friends held Bibi, he drew out his knife. He cut pieces out of her and ate them while she screamed. Then he cut out her child, which twitched in his bloody hands. I think he would have torn off a piece of it, too, if his captain had not come up and slapped him away from Bibi. The captain, who was nearly as young as the rest of the boy soldiers, grabbed my sister's child and flung it into the dirt. He screamed out: "Are we beasts, that we eat our meat alive?"'

Helen inhaled through her cigarette, and continued speaking through the smoke: 'The captain called for mercy. He ordered the soldiers to use their rifle butts to club Bibi to death – they did not like to waste their precious bullets. They cut her up and roasted her, along with her child, in a fire fueled by dried dung. They were starving, you see, and they were so hungry that I am sure they considered eating each other.'

'What kept them,' I asked, 'from eating you?'

'Irony did,' she said with a forced laugh. 'Have I told you how my life has been defined by it? I am sure that my sister's fate would soon have been my own. That night, however, while the one-eyed boy was using his rifle to rape me, other soldiers attacked us. It had been war that had enslaved me, and it was war that freed me. In all the confusion and the dying, I escaped.'

'And then?'

'Then came the bad year,' she said. 'I walked across a wasteland of burned villages, fly-blown corpses, and dust. I drank my own urine, and ate stinking carrion – I did very bad things in order to survive. I found my way to a camp – there were refugees there from a dozen tribes. I began translating when the inevitable disputes arose. When the doctors discovered that I had a gift for languages and already knew five, they managed to obtain a visa for me. They flew me overseas, and helped me gain admission to the university. I have not been back to my home.'

In the years that followed, she said, she learned six additional languages, received advanced degrees, and lived for three years among the Pirahã humans deep in a rainforest. She became a professor at a famous university. There she met someone who knew someone who was the son of the rich, rich man who eventually donated the money that Helen had used to build the Institute.

'It was my dream,' she told me, 'to use what I knew of human languages to understand cetacean language and speak with your kind. When I met Gabi at the conference, I finally saw a way that I might encourage a few orcas to take up residence at the Institute.'

'And so you arranged for our escape,' I said. 'To help us, as you could not help your sister?'

'Yes, it was something like that.'

'And when Gabi spoke of your protecting us,' I said, 'it touched off the memory of how you could not protect Bibi.'

'Yes, it was something like that.' She lit another cigarette, and sat smoking deep in thought. 'I very much despise, however, these kinds of analyses of behavior, as if we are automatons who process garbage in by spitting the same garbage back out. Yes, I survived a great trauma, and yes, various things – a quick color, a sound, something someone says – can send me back to the moment when they tortured Bibi. So what? Am I, then, to be reduced to a machine of iron levers and grinding gears that lacks free will? I will *not* be dehumanized in that way. I slapped poor Gabi, yes, and I suppose in that moment I was slapping away everyone and everything in the soldiers' encampment that I failed to fight off.

In the end, though, it was *my* choice – my will. I hurt Gabi because I could not find the will *not* to hurt her.'

I floated in the quiet water, listening to her words as I let them sound and resound inside me. Finally, I said, 'Does Gabi know everything that happened to you?'

'She knows nothing of my past,' she said. 'I have never told anyone.'

'But why *don't* you tell her? Then she would understand and come back to us.'

'I don't want her to,' she said. 'In fact, I asked her not to return.'

'But why, why?'

'Those who batter,' she said, 'believe or say that they will never do so again. And I *know* that I would not – I would rather die than hurt Gabi. But what if I am wrong?'

'But you are not wrong! I know that!'

'I am sorry, Arjuna.'

'Your torturers took so much from you – will you let them take Gabi away, too?'

I felt the coldness begin to melt from her, as an ice floe gives parts of itself to the warmer water which encompasses it.

'You hate them so much – almost as much as you hate yourself.'

'I hate *these* kinds of analyses, too, which I have done a thousand times,' she said. Despite her frosty words, she melted a little more, and tears touched her eyes.

'But isn't there a cure for such hatred – human hatred? Didn't your Jesus say: "Forgive them, for they know not what they do"?'

'He is not *my* Jesus. And the soldiers all knew exactly what they were doing. They *wanted* to be beasts.'

She was crying freely now, and I knew that she felt glad that only I was present to witness her loosing her fierce hold upon herself.

'No, I cannot forgive them,' she said as her chest began to shake. 'I *will* not.'

'Even as you will not forgive yourself for not being able to forgive.'

The sobs that exploded out of her shook her slender body with so much force that she could no longer sit up. She fell over to the concrete deck, and lay upon her back, covering her face and sobbing even more fiercely as she trembled and writhed. I felt the spasm that ripped through her belly and caused her to curl in upon herself like a human fetus in her mother's womb. She rolled from side to side upon the lip of the deck; the whipping motion of her head flung out tears which pinged into the water. I feared that she would roll right into the channel where the shock of the cold might kill her.

So hot she was! – so burningly, burningly, finally hot that I could zang the heat waves glistering from her black skin. So radiantly and agonizingly alive! I almost wished she *would* fall into the gently lapping waves so that I could rise beneath her and bear her up to take fresh, clean breaths, to touch away her terrible aloneness and to call all her anger, despair, pity, and pain into me.

A billion years passed. I waited for Helen to speak to me, waited and waited. Somehow, she sat up straight again against the earth's torturous gravity, much as the first humans must have stood up from the forms of the apes they once had been. The tears had vanished. Her terrible will to be ever and only herself had returned, but a much subtler and gentler force (though no less powerful) had joined hands with it. I had never known her to be soft, so warm, so open, so sweet.

'There is a saying,' she told me. '"The child is the mother of the woman." There is a woman I always wanted to be: fertile, generative, hopeful, alive. I will never have girls and boys of my own, now, but I have often thought of giving birth in a spiritual sense to something new. I still want to give back to the world, despite what was taken from me – *because* of what was taken, really. For years, I told myself that I wanted to help whales. But now I think I wanted to learn from you so that the rest of my people will not have to suffer as I did.'

'How you suffer!' I called out to her. 'It goes on and on. One of your poets said this: "History is a nightmare from which I am trying to awake."'

In defiance of her will, tears flooded her eyes once more. For a moment, she seemed lost in a vast, lightless sea.

'Help me,' she said. 'All of us – help us wake up.'

She told me that she needed to go outside and walk along the beach by herself. We said goodbye to each other. I swam out into the cove. Its cool waters carried in the dark moaning of the ocean along with the anguish of every creature that had ever lived. So much of that anguish had been wrought by human hands. I had read of much worse atrocities than the one which had befallen Helen (unbelievable as that seemed), but the immediacy of Helen's reliving of her ordeal drove into me in a way that no history ever could. Her anguish opened me both to revulsion and an immense desire to take away her pain. My dread of the humans impelled me to want to gather up the other whales and flee the Institute as quickly as I could. Compassion, however, prevailed, and I decided that I could not leave Helen. I swam from the cove to the bay and then out into the Sound, where I found the other orcas in hot pursuit of a stream of salmon. They zanged my distress before I could give voice to it. Leaving aside the joy of the hunt (for a while), they surrounded me and touched me with their flippers and their faces. I told them of my conversation with Helen.

'We can all hear how your heart beats with Helen's,' Alkurah said, speaking the thoughts of the rest of my adopted family. 'However, as sad as her words are, they add nothing to what we already know of the humans and their inhumanity. Is not Helen's story the story of the entire human race?'

'If that is true,' Menkalinan said, floating upside down, 'then why should we waste our lives here trying to talk with the humans?'

'Because,' Baby Electra said, speaking boldly as no child of a proper family of orcas ever would, 'none of us can say what the end of the humans' story will be.'

'But what other end,' Menkalinan asked, 'can murder lead to besides more and more murder?'

'Perhaps the ending that we help write,' Baby Electra said. 'Who does not love a story that somehow comes out all right in the end?'

'You want to *save* the humans?' We all liked it that Menkalinan, so dispirited and nearly mute in Sea Circus's tiny pools, had found his voice again. 'But what is worth saving?'

'Individual humans are,' Baby Electra said. 'Helen is – so is Gabi.'

With a few flips of his flukes, Unukalhai swam in closer and said, 'I have read of a great human. Hildegard von Bingen became in her person the Voice of the Living Light.'

'That is something,' Menkalinan admitted.

'And Sappho wrote beautiful poems,' Salm said, 'that flowed as a counter-current to all the slaughter called down by warriors of her age.'

'That is something,' Menkalinan said.

'The great mathematician Gödel,' Kitalpha said, 'proved that no consistent system of axioms can prove the truth of all relations that might arise out of that system.'

'That is something.'

Now Zavijah added her voice to the song of celebration that we were composing.

'Scheherazade stayed the hand of the sultan who would slay her; she worked this miracle by beguiling him with wondrous stories for a thousand nights.'

'That is something,' both Menkalinan and Alkurah said.

'Emily Dickinson wrote poems that told the truth of death,' Hyadum said.

Now Unukalhai joined Menkalinan and Alkurah in saying, 'That is something.'

'Beethoven composed his symphony calling forth the joy of life while he was nearly despairingly deaf.'

'That is something.'

'Helen Keller learned to write and to praise life's glories while deaf *and* blind.'

'That is something.'

'Nhat Chi Mai immolated herself in order to set other humans' hearts afire with the passion to end war.'

'That is a great deal,' Bellatrix and Salm said, joining their voices to those of the others.

And then I said, 'The Princess Mirabai spoke with the blue God of Truth and Compassion, and sang praises of unconditional love.'

'That is everything,' we all said together.

There, in the blue waters of the Sound, in the sound of our mutual affirmation and accord, we decided to remain at the Institute. My purpose had passed like the little lightning of an eel into the other orcas – even as my original impulse in contacting the humans had evolved. No longer did I wish merely to speak with them and ask them to stop wounding the world. Now, I wanted to help them find a way to stop wounding themselves. Then, perhaps, they would have no need to rape the continents and oceans of the world, much less to destroy it.

How, though, was I to touch off a transformation that my brain perceived to be impossible even as my heart impelled me to try to work a miracle?

15

An answer to this question – a potential answer – came to me late one blustery night with the rain playing in tympanic irridescence on the dome's glass panels like millions of tiny fingers on a tabla drum. While one half of my brain slept, the other half and my glazed eye surfed the Net in a sort of desultory hypnosis. I chanced upon an interstice of two of the Net's humming strands: a site where many, many humans gathered each day and each moment in order to speak with each other. The cacophony that sounded out of this site brought me fully awake. I realized that although I had left my birth family in the far north in order to talk to the humans, I had so far exchanged words with only Gabi, Helen, and a few highly educated linguists. Did such an accomplishment constitute a true communication with humanity? Could Helen and Gabi speak for the rest of their barbaric, babbling kind?

It would be a logical development of my mission to the humans if I could speak with any or all of them. I asked Helen how I might do this. My request disconcerted her. Early one morning, she sat above the channel's turbid gray waters, and told me, 'I don't know if that would be wise.'

'Why not? Why should it be otherwise?'

'It would announce to the whole world what we are doing here. It is much too soon to popularize the results of this—'

'Experiment?'

'*Experience*. Or call it a breakthrough, if you like that word better.'

'I do not very much like human words at all,' I said. 'However, let us remain with the one you chose. How am I to break through human illusion – all your obduracy and idiocy – if I cannot speak with the rest of you?'

'More than two thousand years ago,' she said, 'the Buddha, too, tried to shatter people's illusions. What makes you think you can do such a thing?'

'I do not, really. But I have to try. You asked for my help, Helen.'

'I had a bad moment.' I noticed that she did not have with her any cigarettes to smoke. The time of the year had come for her to quit. 'I should not have asked you to do the impossible.'

'It may be,' I said, 'that the impossible is not only possible but inevitable.'

'How I wish that were true!'

'I will *make* it true.'

'How very full of hubris you are!'

Hubris: a word of the ancient Greeks for the overweening pride of a hero who dares to steal the fire of the gods. Though that fire might be used to ignite the human heart to the greatest of purposes, the gods always punish anyone who attempts to rise to their heights.

'I would rather say,' I told her, 'that I am full of hope.'

'*Are* you?'

'I will make that true, as well.'

'If we make public what we are doing here,' she said, 'it will create many problems.'

'I once read this description of *Homo sapiens*: the problem-solving animal.'

She touched her lips with two of her fingers as if to hold a cigarette to them – either that, or to help her think.

'There is much to consider here,' she said. 'And I am going to need a few days to consider it.'

One morning, in which the waters of the cove fronting the Institute wavered with various shades of green, gray, and cobalt blue, Helen informed me that she had arranged for me to speak with other humans. Word got out that an orca could understand English and wanted to talk to people. Overnight, it seemed, a zillion of the Hairy Ones clamored to send their words crackling through the Institute's computers and hydrophones. I engaged in dozens of dialogues each day. So many questions the humans had for me! So many answers they wanted me to give them!

At first, I tried to field the more innocuous queries, as silly as many of them were:

What is your favorite color?

Blue, of course.

What is your favorite poem?

I am most fond of two: *The Fish* and *Whales Weep Not*. These sing with proof of human compassion and your ability to identify with beings not your kind.

What do you think of Jackson Pollock's works?

I have poor eyes compared to you humans, and in truth I cannot distinguish such masterpieces from a child's finger paintings.

Do you eat fish all day?

All day and all night.

Do you eat people?

Orcas do not harm human beings. And, no, I do not regret being unable to use chopsticks when I eat sushi.

As the days passed and I warmed to such jibber-jabber, I ventured into the perilous currents of more difficult queries. I kept my answers as simple as I could – sometimes too simple to encompass the entirety of the truth. Most humans cannot bear and do not really want the truth. They would rather be reassured that what they believe, no matter how unlikely or silly, is somehow true.

Do you have morality and a system of laws?

We do not have laws; we have the Covenants: agreements that we orcas make. We have the voice of our true nature.

What do you do with your criminals, if you are just floating free all day and don't have any walls?

We do not have criminals.

What are your views on human morality?

You murder the magnificent beings you call trees for the matter onto which you make out shopping lists, write bad poetry, and blow your noses. What should I think?

How do you make war?

We do not make war. We make love instead.

How can you settle your conflicts without war?

You humans speak of war as you do the weather: something that blows in and blows out, as uncontrollable as human nature itself. But it is the nature of human nature to remake nature. You make war out of the same clay that you make yourselves. Why not try to make something new?

What do you think of human civilization?

I think it would be a good idea.

Is there a purpose to life?

You would not ask such a question unless impelled by an intrinsic purpose.

Is there a God?

There are many gods. You call them sperm whales.

Is there *God*?

The way you ask that question, of course not. The way you should ask it, of course.

If there life after death?

A better question for your kind would be: Is there life before death?

What's going to happen to the world?

There is a trajectory for each cannonball and rocket you shoot off. So with human history, which can be captured in a single image: ten billion lemmings have forced each other off a vast precipice. And halfway down the plunge through empty space toward the rocks below, one lemming says to another: 'So far, so good.'

Who was I, I often wondered, to say such things? Who was I *not* to try to tell the truth as I perceived it? Do not all beings sing with a secret purpose to look out upon the world through the unique lenses of their individual consciousness and to listen with their own brains to the zangs of realization through which they conceive the world? The great poet Percy Bysshe Shelley wrote this:

> *I am the eye with which the universe*
> *Beholds itself and knows itself divine.*

Why, I asked myself, did other humans not trust the knowing-ness of their glorious, divine eyes? Why did they not feel compelled to give voice to all the pain and poetry that they walled-off inside themselves?

Late one night, I conversed with a man whose legs and genitals had been blown off in one of humanity's ongoing wars. Addled by painkillers, unable to work, this man had eventually descended to dwelling in a cardboard box in a muddy lot cut by ditches through which flowed streams of human urine and dung. Often sitting in his own excretions, he begged passersby for the coins he exchanged for his daily ration of greasy, filthy food. He prided himself on not complaining of his misfortunes, as many humans do in fabricating for themselves an imagined nobility out of their capacity for enduring any suffering inflicted by others, no matter how grievous or foul. Why did humans not bespeak the horror of their lives and tell each other the truth of the squalor and the poverty of human existence? Why did they not, as one, shout out,

'No!' Why did they not die in a vast and communal howl of outrage at the human madness?

Instead, they quietly sought the diversions of drugs, work, money, sex, and silly entertainments in order to rescue themselves from their mute despair. Often, they looked to others of their murderous kind to save them. Given the humans' lemming-like urge to follow whichever leader promised to alleviate their misery, it should not have surprised me that many of them began to beg me and the other orcas to bestow upon them our succor and supposed wisdom. One old woman, bereft of the affections of other humans and suicidally lonely, confessed to me her dream to swim with me and the rest of my adopted family in the Sound's regenerative waters.

It pained me to tell her that this would not be possible. However, her request angered me as well, for it encapsulated much of human presumption and delusion. I felt moved to compose a response, not so much to this single, sad woman as to the many, many other humans who wished for contact with us whales:

'You want to be closer to our people – you even want our love! How, though, should you think that trapping us in the pools of the Sea Circuses of the world and feeding us dead, drugged food will result in feelings of amity and accord? Why can you not find such satisfaction through communing with other humans? Instead, you seek validation through swimming with us and slathering upon us effusive affections. If we respond in kind, or indeed in any way, you take that as an affirmation of your own specialness and worthiness to be loved. In effect you say to others (and especially to yourselves):

'"See, I am so brave and wonderful that I have dared to climb into the water with a killer whale who has not only refrained from ending my life with a single snap of his jaws but has interacted with me in a sign of how valuable and beloved I really am."

'O humans – please know this: we of the water are simply people! We are not redeemers. We are here on the planet Ocean to live our own lives, not to serve as a measure or fulfillment of humanity. If you want saving, you should turn to one of your saviors – or better, you should try to find peace in yourselves.'

I went on to declaim that I was no Prometheus to bring back from the Olympian heights the Fire of the Gods. What could I say that Lao Tze, Mohammad, St Theresa, Ramana Maharshi, the Mother, and many others had not already said? Moses had given humans covenants commanding them not to murder each other; the Buddha had told the sleeping ones to meditate upon the eternal and thus to awaken and relieve their suffering; Jesus had taught them to love. They had not listened. Why then should they listen to me? What words could I (or any whale) possibly speak to the humans that they themselves had not already heard ten thousand times?

The answer to this question came early one morning in the quiet of the cove outside the Institute. So still did the waters gather that day that they nearly perfectly reflected the graceful shapes of the evergreens on the shore and the moon glowing a soft silver out of the deep blue sky above. I saw then that I, of the sea and so different from the humans, might be as a mirror in which they could behold themselves in a new way. I could also give them a new song – or rather, I could help them gather in the splendor of the secret song of themselves that they already sang.

A few days later, fate offered me an opportunity to do so through the strangest of chances. I received a communication from one of the first humans I had met. Jordan – he who prompted Sea Circus's 'animal' handlers to shock me with cattle prods – proposed a visit to the Institute. It seemed that he wanted to talk with me and apologize.

'I would advise against it,' Helen said when I asked her about this. 'We are still dealing with the repercussions of your escape, and it would be a bad idea to meet with anyone who might be called as a witness to it.'

She went on to describe the problems that our little prison break had brought upon the Institute. Apparently, there were lawsuits and a possible criminal prosecution for grand theft. Although we now resided in another country far from Sea Circus's multi-tentacled reach, Helen wanted to do everything possible to keep us whales safe.

'But wasn't Jordan fired after our escape?' I asked. 'So how can he speak for Sea Circus?'

I understood little of the humans' legal complexities, and cared even less.

'He can be compelled to testify.'

'You mean, captured, restrained, and prodded to tell the truth?'

'Yes, something like that.'

'Wouldn't that be something like poetic justice?'

'It could be a disaster for us. I doubt if Jordan would tell what you and I think of as the truth.'

'Jordan has promised me that he will never have anything to do with Sea Circus again. He says he hates what he did to my people. In fact, he has founded a group, Total Conservation, to oppose the Sea Circuses of the world.'

'Yes, I know,' Helen said. 'But I don't trust him. And I very much don't like him.'

'I share your sentiments,' I said. 'And that is precisely why I want to talk to him.'

So it came to be. Helen arranged everything. One rainy afternoon, Jordan walked onto the concrete deck on which sat Helen's array of computers. He let loose a brief whistle as his washed-out, unpleasantly gray eyes took in everything. He seemed shorter than I had remembered, though now that I had an eye for human form and feature, I deemed his sun-tanned face to be prettier. He had an easy smile for me, which brought a patina of pink to his thin lips. He wore a dripping, red raincoat made out of some sort of plastic – Nylon, I guessed.

'I want to tell you right off and face to face,' he said, 'how sorry I am for everything that happened to you and the other whales. If I had known how smart you really are . . .'

278

He let his sentence trail off as if he wanted me to accord him a goodwill that we both knew he had not possessed at Sea Circus. He waited for me to speak, perhaps hoping that I would affirm an image of him that he told himself he wished would be. When I finally called up to him from the channel's cold, gray water, he seemed disconcerted that I could not speak to him directly as he had to me. He could not, of course, understand Wordsong. Instead, he listened as the computers translated my orca speech and rendered it into human words that sounded from the computers' speakers. His eyes crinkled in a way that made him seem ugly: perhaps he doubted that it was really *I* who spoke to him. The first thing I said to him caused his whole face to contort in anger and surprise.

'Where is Gabi?' I asked him.

He sat in a chair on the deck, and rubbed his wet head as he looked down at me.

'I supposed she was here, with you.'

'No, she has gone,' I said. 'I thought you might know where.'

'Why should I?'

'At Sea Circus, your eyes followed Gabi everywhere, so it is logical that you might have followed her to wherever she has gone.'

Jordan's anger transmuted to shame. He said, 'She's probably hiding out somewhere. She's in a lot of trouble for setting you whales free.'

'Do you ever wish you had helped her?'

'I really do,' he said, modulating his voice to a pitch of sincerity that might convince me – and perhaps even himself. 'After I was fired from Sea Circus, I had a lot of long, bad days to look at everything I had done there. Then one day, I suddenly *knew* that you whales are every bit as intelligent as Gabi kept claiming you are. You could say that I sort of saw the light – it was a real road-to-Damascus moment.'

'And so you flipped about 180 degrees and founded your whale liberation movement. That is quite a feat.'

'Total Conservation,' he said, 'is about much more than closing down the aquatic parks and returning cetaceans to their natural habitats. Our long-term goal is to safeguard the natural rights of all animals.'

'And you have found others who want to help you do that?'

'Our membership is growing by about two hundred per month.'

'And the fact that you tortured us at Sea Circus has not impugned your credibility?'

'No, just the opposite. If you keep talking to people, you'll learn that they trust no one quite so much as a sinner who has repented of his sins.'

'*Have* you repented?' I asked him.

'Of course I have. Why else do you think I've travelled thousands of miles to talk to you?'

At that moment, I wanted to polish the silver of my being into the brightest of mirrors and swim in close to him so that he might behold a man of righteousness and compassion. Instead, I found myself trilling out doubtful words from my flute:

'I zang,' I said to him, 'that you have reasons besides repentance and apologies for coming here.'

'Maybe reasons related to both. I came to ask for your help.'

'How could I possibly help you?'

'To begin with, by speaking for the rights of all animals.'

'And what rights are those?'

'To begin with, the right to be left alone, to live your lives in nature as nature intended.'

'To begin with,' I repeated. 'And there is more?'

'Much more. We want to put a stop to people killing animals for food.'

'What will you humans eat, then?'

'A plant-based diet is much healthier and more sustainable, and in any case—'

'So you would kill plants instead?'

'We want to stop killing of all kinds,' he said. 'If our goal is to eliminate the suffering of cattle, chickens, pigs, and other domesticated species, then why shouldn't we extend our compassion to wild animals?'

'How will you do that?'

'Murdering animals for meat is a horrific thing, even when animals do it. We'll have to start rescuing gazelles and such from tigers and other predators.'

'But then the tigers would starve.'

'We'll teach them to eat other things.'

'What things?'

'Well, soon it will be possible to grow animal tissues in tanks, sort of like the way tofu is cultured, I think.'

'So you want tigers to eat food that is even less alive than the dead fish that you once fed to me?'

'I wouldn't look at it that way.'

'And how would you look at it?'

He flung out his fingers and rolled his eyes up toward the dome as if invoking divine assistance in his struggle to reason with a most unreasonable animal. 'One of my people once said this: "We are as gods, and might as well get good at it." Someday, we'll have the technology to do almost anything we wish.'

'And so you would destroy nature in order to save its natural creatures?'

'Right now, I just want to save you and the other whales.' He rubbed at the moisture on his cheek; I could not tell if it was water dripping down from his wet head or sweat. 'To protect you, to make up for what I did and because it's the right thing to do.'

I looked up at him. Did he realize what he was saying? Did he believe what he said?

'Please help me to help you,' he added in his purring wheedle of a voice. 'Will you co-author a book with me?'

'What sort of book?'

'I am conceiving of a sort of dialogue,' he said, 'in which I'll speak for people as you do for killer whales, and by implication, all animals. Of course I'd want to give you precedence – we can entitle the book "Bobo's Story", or something like that.'

'I am called Arjuna now.'

'You are? I thought you were just trying to hide out here under that name. Well, then, how about "Arjuna Speaks"?'

'I do not think,' I said, 'that you would like what I speak of.'

'Don't worry about that. There's nothing you can say about my role in depriving you whales of freedom that I haven't said already.'

'You might not like the *way* that I would say it.'

'Look, it will be enough if you just tell what happened to you and reaffirm the animal rights we'll go over, which would prevent such things from happening again. My agent has already spoken with five publishers – we can probably get a $1,000,000 advance and a lot more when the book comes out.'

'What do you mean by *we*?'

'Look, I'd have to hold your part in trust for you until we've seen that whales are legally accorded personhood. But after that, half of all the book's proceeds would be yours.'

'But what would I do with *money*?'

'I've thought about that.' He waved his hand and clenched his fingers into a fist, as if he could snatch golden coins out of thin air. 'You could buy all the fish that you could ever eat.'

'I hope you are joking.'

'Ha, ha – of course I am! No, I was thinking you'd like to donate your share of the royalties to our movement. Or you could use the money yourself to buy other whales out of other ocean parks.'

'How much does it cost to buy a slave these days?'

'Well, one of the Sea Circuses just bought a pregnant female orca for $1,250,000.'

'I am poor at mathematics, but it would seem that my projected royalties would be inadequate to the end you propose.'

'That's why I have an even better idea,' he said. 'We can open an ocean park of our own, set up similarly to your situation here.

You orcas would be free to come and go – maybe you could even persuade some wild orcas to visit. People would pay a *lot* of money to speak with a whale, one on one. We could make millions!'

What could I say to this astonishing proposal? Even if I had trusted Jordan, I had no desire to venture into that dangerous intersection where human stupidity meets cupidity. The love of money might not have been the root of evil, but it certainly paid for most of the destruction that human beings wreaked upon the world.

'What do you say, Arjuna? Despite everything that happened at Sea Circus, beneath all the misunderstandings, you've got to know how much I always loved you and the other whales.'

What *should* I say? I wanted to say this: I believe in you. You are a creature of Ocean, even as I am, and within you flows the water of life, imbued with all life's inherent goodness and beauty. Can you not hear the golden chords sounding within you, calling you forth in all your splendor? Listen, listen! Sing the new song of yourself that the world has been waiting a million years for you to sing!

I could *not* say that: I did not believe in him, although I desperately wanted to and knew that there should have been a way that I somehow could. If I had spoken the truth about his secret nature, he would not have heard it – or worse, he would have regarded it as a lie. The humans have expressions for such futility: pissing into the wind; casting pearls before swine; aiming a beam of light at a black hole.

'I say this,' I finally called up to him. 'I think you care nothing for whales. Go away!'

My words did more violence to his face than the slapping of Helen's hand had to Gabi's. The skin of his chiseled cheeks flushed an ugly red, even as the muscles beneath jerked his mouth, eyes, and forehead into a rictus of hatred. Without another word, he whipped about and stomped off into the human part of the house. Helen told me later that he nearly wrecked his vehicle racing away from the Institute down muddy, twisting roads.

My own wrath – hot, black, and bitter – rose up within me like a vile substance steeped in the memories of all that had occurred in Sea Circus's pools. It led me down a dangerous road of my own, or rather, right into the ever-streaming information flows of the Net. Speaking straight from my heart, I composed this diatribe to send out to the many humans who followed my words:

'I have been asked to promote animal rights. Animals have no rights – no "natural" rights of the kind that you human beings have traditionally accorded yourselves. Rights do not exist in nature. They are a human construction created in a human context for the benefit of human beings. Rights are fashioned out of the needs of individuals to protect themselves from others and to exercise their desires. You humans make rights for yourselves because it is a better way for you to live.

'From the point of view of the many, the rights that the few have arrogated to themselves have not always been a good thing: Kings have exercised the divine right to torture, mutilate, and murder those disloyal to them; barons have insisted on their *droit du seigneur:* they have stolen brides from their husbands on the first night of their marriage in order to take their virginity; corporations have claimed the rights to the rainwater that has fallen upon the roofs of poor people's houses.

'What rights that you enjoy do you believe you should extend to animals? The right not to be slain and eaten, as you humans agree not to slay and eat each other? You would spare the animals a painful and horrific end? How long does it take for a grass-fed goat, the arteries and windpipe of its throat slashed open, to lose consciousness and die? Minutes? Seconds? Have you ever watched lions leisurely rip bloody morsels from a felled buffalo as it bellows in agony over many hours or even days? Would you save your cattle from quick slaughter and set them free on the prairie so that they might enjoy the tender mercies of nature?

'Or perhaps you would protect animals and coddle them with unnatural care so that they might grow old and die as you humans do: attached to tubes in a place of hard surfaces and blinding lights, tended by uncaring strangers, immersed in feces, dementia, and moans of pain that go on for days and months and years?

'Some of you see a moral imperative to rescue prey animals from predators, even as you would your own children. What would happen if you succeeded? As cougars starved and deer multiplied without end (similarly to how you humans do), hills would be denuded of vegetation, rain would wash exposed soil into muddy rivers, and countless kinds of animals would die because they had no home.

'Some of you congratulate yourselves for possessing moral superiority because you eschew eating animals who suffer, and so you eat plants instead. What do you know of plants? You, with your brains too big for your gangly bodies (though not quite large enough to keep you from continually making fundamental philosophical mistakes), argue that brains and nerves are the thinking and feeling parts of an organism and that a kind of life such as an oak tree cannot experience real suffering. René Descartes once argued that tortured animals do not really suffer. What would you do, how would you live, if your scientists proved that plants shimmer with a consciousness spread through every leaf and cell that is different though no less profound than that of human beings?

'Suppose, however, that you are correct in your presumption that plants do not suffer as animals do, is freedom from suffering the most fundamental right? Do not most humans put up with all the insane sufferings of your war-torn world so that you might survive as bent, enfeebled creatures your seventy or eighty or ninety years? Do not humans consent to do the most horrible and repugnant things in order to live? Would you not say that over your "right" to be spared suffering, your right to life reigns supreme? Why should it not be so for plants? How do you justify extending human rights to ducks and earthworms and deny the same to green, growing things who desire in their deepest part, even as you do, to remain alive?

'You humans have adduced the conservation of matter and energy and have written it into your laws of physics. Can you not see that there is a conservation of suffering? Spare plants and animals the pain of death and you yourself will suffer and die. Suffering infuses every particle of life. Try to end it, and you will kill the world.

'Even as you *are* killing it. For a million years, you Hairless Apes have fled the jaws of big cats, have fled cold and dark and hunger. You have made fire and hellishly glowing cities and fields torn out of the living tissues of the earth. The ruin of nature has been the result. And now, you seek to flee the dread of the pain of your necessary participation in life's essential suffering by creating the imagined "rights" of animals. How cosmically arrogant of you! How cowardly! How selfish and falsely-compassionate! How all-too idiotically and insanely human!'

Because I knew that few humans care to consider logic and argument objectively, I added to my composition an account of my personal experiences, particularly the three portents that had impelled me to want to speak with the humans in the first place. I told of the white bear trapped on the ice floe in the ocean that the humans had heated with the poisonous exhalations of their polluted planetary civilization; I described the terror of swimming through black oil that burned; I spoke of Pherkad's death and how the evil of it had destroyed my ability to quenge.

What did I hope to accomplish by such honesty? Might the humans open their minds to one whale's perspective? Or would they do as they often did when confronted with truths that they did not wish to hear?

16

The response of the humans to my diatribe, with its appended history, astonished me. Little of it, however, concerned my dismissal of animal rights. (Of this small fraction, most typically my correspondents criticized me for betraying my fellow animals or accused me of idiocy myself.) Hundreds of the humans recounted their own woes and their own horror at human civilization; many even apologized on behalf of humanity. Many more – Kitalpha, who could count much better than I, put their number in the thousands – seemed most disconcerted by my sufferings even as they expressed both fascination and puzzlement over the human word I had invented to signify what we orcas know as quenging.

And so I poured all my descriptive talents into further compositions, but the more I described this most essential of cetacean experiences, the less the humans seemed to understand and the more they regarded it as an impenetrable mystery. As the humans themselves say, the Tao that can be told is not the true Tao. Of course, quenging, though partaking of the Tao, as water does the taste of salt, is not the same. Neither is it gnosis or the music of the spheres, grace or God. I could not persuade the men and women who listened to me of this. Many of them insisted on interpreting quenging through vocabularies of the sacred and apprehending its boundlessness through the lenses of various religions.

'I have received requests,' I said to Helen one day. 'Hundreds of them. Those claiming to represent Christianity, Buddhism, Hinduism and other faiths would like to visit me here. They say they want to help me – help me to quenge!'

Because Helen relished irony and often defined her life by it (and because the foibles and conceits of her fellow humans aroused in her an endlessly bemused curiosity), she granted many of these requests. So it came about that I began entertaining a stream of proselytizers who presumed to convert me.

Although each religion that I encountered had been hideously complexified by the nightmares of history and endless theological disputes, I found on the Net a simple chart that encapsulated the kernel of each religion (and various beliefs and isms) in a few words. Curiously, the chart relied on extending the very malleable metaphor of excrement: itself a most malleable substance with which the humans have the most curious of relationships. As babies, they fingerpaint with it; as children, they are trained to collect the droppings of their dogs. Adults hide their excreting and excretions from others, while their senile, again in diapers, mold their contents into a kind of art it seems that only they can appreciate. Most humans, it seems, perform the extraordinary alchemical feat of transmuting this very base substance into one sort of religion or another:

Taoism	Shit happens
Hinduism	This shit has happened before.
Confucianism	Confucius says, 'Shit happens.'
Catholicism	Shit happens because you deserve it.
Judaism	Why does this shit happen to us?
Islam	When shit happens, Allah's will.
Scientism	Only measurable shit is real.

Protestantism	Let this shit happen to others.
Buddhism	If shit happens, is it really shit?
Marxism	The shit is going to hit the fan.
Feminism	Men are shits.
Capitalism	That's my shit.
Darwinism	Survival of the shittiest.
Narcissism	My shit doesn't stink.
Atheism	No shit!
Nihilism	Who gives a shit?
Rastafarianism	Let's smoke this shit!

I met first with a crimson and yellow-robed monk who wished to speak with me of Buddhism. I spent most of an afternoon learning Tibetan so that we might understand each other with some degree of grace. This old man, his bald head gleaming almost as brightly as his dark, intelligent eyes, sat cross-legged on the deck above me. We took some time making each other's acquaintance before moving on to more so-called spiritual matters. Very soon, we found ourselves in deep, deep waters as we began discussing the ancient human conception of Nirvana.

'If by quenging,' he said, 'you mean what we mean by emptiness – and what else *could* you mean? – then you must free yourself of all mental obscurations before you can know true liberation.'

'Is that possible? Have you accomplished this for yourself?'

'I have no hope of becoming a Buddha in this lifetime, but I may in another age.'

'Could I become a Buddha . . . sooner than that?'

'Does a whale have Buddha nature?' he said, smiling at a joke that he did not explain.

He told me that of course I could know the continuous bliss of pure emptiness, if only I accepted the Four Noble Truths and followed the Eightfold Path.

'All beings,' he said, 'can be freed from suffering.'

Oh, no, I thought, not again!

'Do you really think that is possible?' I asked.

'I think that you are attached to your suffering as you are to the world.'

'I am not *attached* to the world; I *am* our beautiful Ocean, as are you.'

'If you identify with that which seems permanent, you will never become empty of yourself.'

'But I wish precisely the opposite; in quenging, one becomes fuller the more one becomes his true self: almost infinitely full as with drinking in the ocean.'

'But, dear whale, there is no self.'

'If there is no self, then how can one's self suffer so terribly?'

'That is precisely *my* point. When you succeed in extinguishing the terrible flame that burns all life, you will be freed from being reborn into the suffering of the world.'

I swam up closer to him, and I drew in a breath of salty sea air.

'You humans are strange,' I said. 'I do not want to be freed from the world. What I want is more of it: more fish, more whales, more dreams, more songs, more consciousness, more suffering, more joy, more stars, more death, more agony, more evolution, more life.'

My words occasioned in the kindly monk a sigh nearly as long as a whale's exhalation. He sat gazing down at me as he rubbed the back of his shiny head. Finally, he asked me, 'Will you meditate with me? It may be a beginning.'

The next religionary who visited the Institute – a bearded rabbi whose long curls of hair bobbed up and down, bouncing like white springs hung from his black fur hat – expressed his doubt that I would ever be able to quenge at all, if by quenging was meant a faculty of the soul unique to humans. Indeed, the rabbi seemed less concerned with helping me than with determining who or what I really was.

'I will be as honest with you as I can,' he said. 'Nothing in the

Law has prepared my people to consider the case of a talking fish.'

I did not deign to explain to him that I was a whale, as warm-blooded as he was. I sensed that he cared little for Linnaean classifications or other taxonomies.

'If you were one of the Goyim,' he went on, 'I would say that there are seven commandments you must follow to be accepted into Heaven.'

'I thought there were ten commandments.'

'There are 613 – but most of these apply only to my people.'

'It must be hard to be a Jew.'

'It is *very* hard. If you only knew.'

'And what are the seven commandments for the Goyim?'

'You must not deny God nor blaspheme Him.'

'I am not sure how I could do such a thing.'

'You must not steal.'

'I never have.'

'You must not murder.'

'Every day I murder many fish.'

'You must not murder a man.'

'I never would! My own covenants prevent me from doing so.'

'You must not engage in incestuous, promiscuous, homoerotic, or adulterous sexual relations.'

I paused to look at steam pouring from his nostrils as he breathed hard at the cold, moist air.

'Such relations,' I said, 'are the only kind we whales know.'

He rolled his eyes at this, then went on, 'You must not eat meat torn from a living animal.'

'Once, I did not,' I said, speaking of the dark days at Sea Circus. 'Now, however, it is the only kind of meat that I do eat.'

'Then, you cannot be accepted into Heaven as one of the Goyim.' He removed his befogged glasses and wiped them with a white cloth that he withdrew from his black suit's pocket. 'However, it's absurd to speak of you as a human – and perhaps more absurd to regard you as simply an animal. Perhaps there is a kind of Heaven for your kind, whatever that is. But I don't think so.'

'Then, since you seem to equate your Heaven with what I call quenging, you must logically believe that I have little hope of quenging again.'

'Who am I to say yes or no? I don't really know what you mean by quenging or understand how any animal could do such a thing. However, the Baal Shem Tov teaches that there are *nitzotzot*, divine sparks, in everything. If you find the sparks in you to return to God, that might be something like quenging.'

'And how do I do that?'

'You are a fish, so how should I know what a fish is supposed to do?'

'Suppose I were a man.'

'Then I would say you should pray and dance and sing.'

'I love to sing,' I said. 'Will you share some of your songs with me?'

I next spoke with a bearded Muslim who assured me that if I were a human, I would need only to make the *shahada*, the Islamic profession of faith, and submit to God's will in order to begin the journey towards knowing heaven's delights.

'*La illaha illa Allah*,' he said to me. '*Muhammadar rasulu-llah*. No god is there but God, and Muhammad is—'

'I acknowledge that Muhammad was a great human prophet,' I told him, 'but as far as the first part of your *shahada*, we whales would say instead: "All gods are part of God, as all humans and all things are."'

'You speak heresy!' he informed me.

'All too fluently, I am afraid.'

I had read of the great Islamic sage al-Hallaj, who had been crucified for celebrating the divinity that inhered in each woman and man.

'If you were to become a Muslim,' he said, 'you must speak otherwise.'

'*Can* I become a Muslim?'

'I was considering your case hypothetically. Whatever you do, however, you should take care what you say, and try to submit to God's will.'

'If God is all-powerful,' I said, 'how could I *not* submit?'

'By trying to exert your will above His.'

'But if I did so, would I not then be working His will that I not submit?'

'God gave us all free will – including the freedom to defy Him.'

'If that is true,' I asked, 'then in what sense can God be said to be all-powerful?'

After that, our conversation went nowhere, as when one of the two-leggeds runs faster and faster on a treadmill. During the following days, I met with other religionaries. A Hindu man, with a round, red dot daubed between his eyes, spoke words of one of the fundamental equations of the Upanishads:

'*Tat tvam asi*,' he said, 'that thou art. All things and you, in your deepest part, are one and the same.'

'Yes!' I cried out. 'You understand! I am Ocean, and I am Agathange – and all the suns and worlds between. I am, I *am*! But I cannot quenge, so I cannot feel my way toward those places that I am.'

'You must meditate and pray,' he told me. 'You must purify yourself.'

He opined that I must have committed a bad sin in a previous life to have been reborn in the body of a whale; it was my karma, he said, that I had lost my power to quenge, which he likened to the liberation of moksha. He seemed sure that if I served my human masters faithfully and made no more sins, I would eventually find my way back into human form – perhaps even as a *jivanmukta* who would be free from incarnating into the world, with all its hellish suffering.

'To be reborn as a human,' I said, wishing that I could laugh in the human way. 'That is something that I had never imagined . . . imagining.'

The theme of rebirth or resurrection ran like a calcareous current through many of the religions that I encountered. When I became curious about the Church of Jesus Christ of Latter Day Saints, I found through the Net a couple of typical missionaries who seemed happy to talk to me. I eagerly awaited the arrival of these esteemed elders. So it surprised me to see standing on the deck one morning two adolescents whose names were Elder Young and Elder Cartwright. They wore dark suits and ties, and little volcanoes of infection pimpled their fish-white faces.

Almost immediately, I asked a question that caused those faces to redden with embarrassment and inflamed each pimple to an angry red, like the glowing tip of a cigarette: 'If I lived righteously as a Mormon patriarch, then I would be resurrected as a god of my own planet, which I would fill with the children of many wives?'

'We really shouldn't talk about these kinds of things,' Elder Young said to me, 'at our first meeting.'

'But did you know,' I asked, 'that the other planets are already full of life? On Agathange alone . . .'

I kept no count of the men and women (most all were men) who came to speak with me. The number of human religions is nearly uncountable, even for humans themselves. A few of these religions both amused me and warmed my breath. I liked, for instance, the Church of All Worlds whose water brothers take inspiration from the characters who populate one of the humans' famous fictions; the water brothers and sisters of the Church of All Worlds find divinity everywhere in nature and commune with the Great Mother Goddess herself.

Other faiths disquieted me, even as I had to recognize their great promise: I met with representatives of the Human Extinction Movement and the related Church of Euthanasia, which had been founded on the four pillars of Suicide, Sodomy, Abortion, and Cannibalism. Cannibalism lay at the heart of another bizarre but much more important religion. I marveled at the Catholic ceremony of communion, in which the faithful eat the transubstantiated flesh and blood of a god reborn as a man in order to somehow save humans from their sins – very like the practitioners of the mushroom cults who eat the Flesh of the Gods and become as God. The saving included the confessing of those sins and then, after death, a long period of purgation and purification in hellish fires before the soul could enter heaven and look upon the face of God.

A similar religion – as two mirror imaged twins, one right-handed and one left-handed, are similar – I learned of one day when a Transhumanist came to see me. He put all his faith, for himself and for me, in a technology of salvation soon to be. The Cybernetic Gnosticism which he professed views the human mind as pure information, which could be scanned, copied, and programmed into machines. Human beings would soon cast off the contemptuous, evil carbon matter of their bodies in order for their spirits to be resurrected as a kind of blissful and imperishable consciousness crackling like electricity through the heaven of their silicon computing machines. In an inversion of Judeo-Christian theology, humanity would find its destiny by creating God in the form of a universal artificial intelligence. The Transhumanists even speak of a cybernetic version of man's ancient fall into sin and suffering: the artificial intelligence that scientists had created would grow without bound in a rapture known as the Singularity, and then the human beings would be left behind, forever cut-off from the godhead. If they were lucky, the hyper-intelligent machines would keep them around as pets.

My next visitor, Jeremy Mann, had gained notoriety in the fields of cognitive science and artificial intelligence, and was known as the 'Newton of Consciousness.' (A rumor had spread through the Net that Jeremy himself had invented and promulgated this honor-ific.) I thought he might be able to speak very well for the faith of Scientism. A small man whose carefully controlled body seemed to have been constructed around the core of a rapier, he paced around the concrete deck peering at the many computers. We immediately got off on the wrong foot, as the humans like to say, when his metallic voice slashed out: 'I can't see any microphones, but that doesn't mean that they aren't hidden.'

He seemed to be speaking to a microphone of his own, secreted somewhere about his person. Clearly, he suspected that his words were being recorded so that one of the other scientists in another part of the house – perhaps Helen herself – could reply through one of the computers in a pretense that it was a whale who responded to him and not in actuality a human being. Upon perceiving this, I tried to reassure him that a couple of the representatives of other religions had asked Helen to swear that no hoax was being perpetrated upon them, and so she had. Jeremy froze like a shark staring at his prey. He immediately took umbrage in his discovery that I considered him to be a religionary much like all the others.

'I am a *scientist*,' he said, investing this word with an odious combination of authority, conceit, and belief.

'I confess,' I told him, 'that I often find it difficult to perceive the difference between science and religion.'

I asked him if he had ever considered the amazing coincidence of the Bible's *creation ex nihilo* of the world by the Lord God Yahweh and the Big Bang in which the entire universe exploded into being out of a similar nothingness.

'But there is all the difference in the world!' he said, ignoring my example. 'Religion requires one to have faith in revealed and unseen truths, while science applies to objective reality the razors of reason and verification.'

'Those razors,' I said to him, 'are precisely why I love your science – sometimes – and why I have hope for your idiotic kind.'

I usually disliked giving voice to harsh words that might bruise the humans' delicate sensibilities. Something about this Mann man, however – if I had been a human possessed of a sense of smell, I would have said that he reeked of smug certitude – made me want to bruise and batter the hauteur of self-regard from his famous face.

'To form a concept of the world,' I continued, 'according to evidence, inspiration, and logic, and then to test this concept for its truth – this is the essence of science, is it not?'

'I would be more likely to accept your fondness for science,' he said, 'if you would consent to the verification of your own reasoning abilities.'

'Let us talk and reason together, then, and you may verify all you wish.'

'But you won't consent to my administering an intelligence test?'

'Are there mathematics questions?'

'There is a quantitative section, yes, of course.'

'I know nothing of mathematics.'

'Then how can you consider yourself to be scientific?'

'You are perilously close,' I told him, 'to committing the Definitional Fallacy, which your own psychologists and logicians have identified: you define what it means to be scientific, and then accuse others of being unscientific when they fail to conform their views to your definition.'

'I'm only making explicit what all reputable scientists believe.'

'And you imply that I should therefore believe likewise. That is an outright expression of the Bandwagon Fallacy.'

Jeremy stood above me with his hand resting on one of Helen's computers. I could barely zang the sound of his heart, which increased its rate of beating not even slightly at my provocative words. Unukalhai had told me that such imperturbability was a characteristic of advanced Buddhist meditators – and psychopaths.

'I only want to see,' he said, 'how you might perform on tasks that millions of people have attempted.'

'Tasks that men who do not understand the true nature of intelligence and possess little of it have designed for other idiots such as themselves.'

'Am I to understand that you are calling me an idiot?'

'No,' I said, 'that would mean my attacking your arguments by the way of attacking you and thereby committing the Ad Hominem Fallacy.'

'Ah, a whale with scruples!' he said.

'How about if I give *you* an intelligence test, to pass on to others of your kind?' I swam closer to him. 'Can you find your way around the oceans of the world, navigating by the stars? Can you understand the nature of an animal (or anything) without cutting it into smaller and even smaller pieces? Can you sing a song that brings another to tears? Can you zang through the darkest deeps of underwater shoals and treacherous currents and always find your way home?'

Jeremy sat down on a chair. Then he rubbed his silver-haired temples, and fixed me with his steely stare.

'Or,' I continued, 'how about a multiple choice question, which your testers seem to like so much? When faced with climatic warming from all the gases you have spewed into the atmosphere, which will inexorably result in planetary heat death, you should:

1. Deny reality
2. Ask for a mathematical proof of something that can be proved with certainty only by extinction itself
3. Ascribe the "illusion" of a crisis to the nefarious motives of your enemies
4. Feel worried and do nothing
5. Fix the problem.

'I should think the answer is obvious,' he said.

'Then why do all but a few of your kind fail to find the right answer?'

'Because they refuse to accept the established results of good science, even as I suspect you do, too.'

'It is not good science that I reject. However, I abhor the mumbo-jumbo of pseudo-science that so many of your so-called scientists practice. So many of you are no more scient than a snail.'

'Is that an *ad hominem* attack that I detect?'

'Please excuse me – let me attack scientific dogma instead,' I told him. 'Consider the calculation by which your scientists have sought to rank the intelligence of various species. What a truly amazing coincidence that humans should compute their own intelligence as surpassing that of all others!'

'If you are speaking of the brain-body weight ratio, I have taken objection to that myself. It is a crude measurement.'

'It is worse than crude!' I said. I swam back and forth across the channel, always returning to the place where he sat on the deck above one of the screens. 'It is not science at all but a pure sham. Anyone with even the weakest of scientific eyes should have seen right through it.'

I went on to speak of how certain scientists had measured the weights of the bodies and the brains of many kinds of animals, and had then computed the ratio of the brain to the body – the supposition being that the larger the brain relative to the body, the more intelligent the species. It turned out that to humans, of course, could be ascribed the highest of ratios. (Except for tree shrews, small birds, and ants, which fact scientists for various reasons conveniently ignored.) Whales did not rank nearly so high as humans.

'Most of a whale's weight, however,' I said to him, 'is fat. How much brain is needed to interact with it and move it around?'

He ignored this and informed me, 'The brain/body ratio has been replaced with the more refined and well-established metric of the Encephalization Quotient.'

'Which still computes intelligence according to ratios. A simple thought experiment, however, would have sufficed to demolish the validity of this approach.'

I asked him to consider a very foolish man who had succumbed to one of the eating sicknesses that afflict his species. 'If the man,' I asked him, 'were to gorge on ice cream for a year and double his weight, would his intelligence then fall to a half of what it had been?'

I paused to breathe and study his impassive face. 'Your scientists' definition of intelligence is so limited – and convenient,' I said. 'If I wanted to, I could easily devise a ratio of weights that would rank humans much lower in intelligence.'

'Please do so.'

'All right, then consider the human penis.'

'Must I?'

I tried to 'read' the inflections of emotion in his voice, but I could not. Then I cited many works of human literature and their depictions of the idiocies perpetrated by human males in lust. In this light, I said, the human penis could be regarded as a second brain both sightless and single-minded in its stupidity – or even as an anti-brain. Given that a human penis is much larger than, for instance, that of a much heavier gorilla, a penis/body weight ratio of man would come out as very high – and thus the intelligence of man would compute as very *low*.

He smiled not at all at my little comedy of thought play. He said, 'You are confusing intelligence with the will to overcome impulses.'

'Yes, I am, and that is because it is a human conceit to divorce the intelligence of the mind from the wisdom of the body.'

Humans, I said, instead of relying on their true nature to point them toward the real and the good, invent with their flawed minds rigid moral systems, which the impulses of their blood and their gonads continually cause them to violate. In truth, humans *love* acting out their various urges, which leak out of them as do fluids from a baby. Thus men and women could tell themselves lies such as 'The Devil made me do it' or 'I am so passionate that I couldn't help myself.'

'Most of your kind,' I said to him, 'so easily *become* every random emotion that bubbles up inside them – or else you become trapped within what you would probably call the programmed turnings of machine-like thoughts. Rarely are head and heart yoked like two horses to a single chariot of fire, blazing across the sky.'

'And it is not the same for you orcas?'

'At our worst,' I said, thinking of Sea Circus's punishment pool, 'it is. Then *four* horses are connected by ropes to each of our metaphoric limbs, and the horses are whipped to froth and gallop off in different directions. At such times, we become humanized.'

He appeared to consider this as he gazed at me.

'If I were one of your scientists,' I told him, 'I would formulate my theories of intelligence by way of a reduction of the mind to the gross material structures of the brain. I might say that the human problem of integrating intelligences results from the unfortunate fact that you humans lack an entire cortical lobe of the brain, what neuroanatomists call the paralimbic: the very part of us orcas from which arises our ability to quenge – and the part that too great a shock of emotion can paralyze.'

'But you are not such a scientist,' he said in his irritating voice, 'so you would not say that.'

'No, I am an orca, so I would say this: the human being is at odds with his own being.' I moved closer to him as I searched for the right sounds that the computers could translate for him. 'Two souls, alas, dwell within the human breast, and they accompany each other with all the discord of a marimba's jumping, jingling tintinnabulations and the slow, deep, haunting melodies of the Native American flute.'

'Very poetic,' he said, 'but also pointless as regards our discussion. Yes, of course, a great deal of bad science is practiced. And I've spent a great deal of time exposing it.'

'Then why do you still speak of the Encephalization Quotient as if it has any validity?' I asked him, slapping my tail against the water. 'The real insanity is not that some stupid human vomited up an idiotic theory, but that so many so-called scientists have accepted it without question.'

'I understand that you seem to be frustrated.'

'Do you?' I came up out of the water, spy-hopping so that I

might more clearly make out the light of his eyes. 'It is *this* that I abhor about science in the same way that I laugh at your religions. Most scientists fail in the quintessential act of science, which is to question with an open mind all things. And by that, I do not mean only or chiefly that they lack the mental machinery to examine with courage their facts and their theories.'

'What *do* you mean?'

'Do you really wish to know?'

I went on to say that science, as practiced on the earthy parts of our world, divorced fact from value, and so devalued the earth and facilitated its destruction. Worse, science, which presumed to critique the bases of the claims of religions and other disciplines, failed to examine its own most fundamental assumptions. And worse still, I said, most scientists refused even to acknowledge these assumptions and that they sprang from impulses no different from religious faith.

I then detailed some of these assumptions: that the nature of nature is mechanical and should be studied in that way; that nature has no purpose and evolution no goal; that the laws of nature are fixed throughout space and time; that minds are nothing more than an epiphenomenon of the mechanistic reactions of the chemicals of the brain; that memories are recorded as engrams within the brain; that the matter that makes up everything from stars to jellyfish to human beings is essentially unconscious and unalive.

'At least religionists such as your Christians,' I said, 'acknowledge explicitly the Athanasian Creed upon which their belief in three gods is based.'

Too many scientists, I said, felt too certain of their own beliefs – and of science itself. They saw themselves as on the cutting edge of a perfectly formed and final razor of epistemology, the only truly valid way of apprehending the universe that had ever been created and the best that ever could. But so had other humans in other places seen themselves: the ancient Greeks; the Chinese; the Romans; the Arabian philosophers; the European alchemists; the

Medieval astronomers who insisted on hideously complicating their model of an earth-centered cosmos, which they had based upon the beauty of the music of nested celestial spheres coupled with poorly interpreted motions of the planets and the observation that the earth itself never seems to move.

How were contemporary scientists, I asked him, any different? Despite knowing better, despite appreciating that a single, new inexplicable fact or the slightest reinterpretation of an old one could lead to a new theory and render an old one junk, despite the history of entire sets of theories themselves being replaced with new paradigms – despite all this, scientists and other humans who accepted their pronouncements insisted on forming a sure, mental picture of the universe as emerging from an explosion out of nothingness and that random mutations of a molecule that did nothing more than code for the production of proteins drove the entire glory and wonder of evolution.

'You, and your peers, seem to force all the manifold possibilities of a true science,' I said, 'into a very limited perspective of the gross reduction of living reality to its material parts. Those of you who congratulate yourselves on being the most advanced of your kind restrict yourselves to a single, opaque lens to fit over your eyes. It is as if cataracts have made you blind.'

He waved his hand in front of his face as if shooing away a cloud of flies. His next words indicated that he had taken to heart nothing of what I said.

'Science,' he informed me, 'might not yet have all the answers, but it is the only verifiable – and hence meaningful – way of asking the right questions.'

'But those questions are nearly always asked through the voices of materialism, mechanism, and reduction. Has it occurred to you that the only aspects of the universe that such an approach will reveal are those that are materialistic, mechanistic, and reductionist?'

'Has it occurred to you,' he countered, 'that the universe really *is* nothing more than matter and energy, which we can understand through, and only through, analysis?'

I suddenly felt like launching myself out of the pool and landing on top of him. Instead I said, 'And analyzing as you scientists do, every year you understand more and more about less and less until someday you will know everything about nothing.'

'An amusing thought,' he said, unamused. 'But the reality is just the opposite. We understand more and more of the big questions all the time. Science has no limits, and is the single source of our knowledge about the world.'

'And yet you know nothing of the most important thing in the world, which is quenging.' I turned a circle about the channel, then returned to him. 'It is funny to me and the other whales, in a perverse and tragic sort of way, that you scientists never seemed to have imagined anything like it. Thus you do not begin to see a glimmer of a ray of the unfortunate truth: that you humans will never apprehend the essence of reality absent an ability to quenge.'

I could almost hear the stream of words pouring through his head – almost. Then he said, 'This quenging of yours is an interesting idea.'

As I had with Helen, I explained to him, 'It is not an idea – it is a prowess, a sense, a way of being. In a way, it *is* pure being, the essence of isness in itself. And of *everywhereness*.'

'I understand from your descriptions that quenging is something like clairvoyance, out-of-body experiences, and telepathy – and has just about as much validity.'

'You doubt, of course. If you quenged with us whales, you would not.'

'I suspect that would be like sharing in the same dream – and such an experience would have about as much reality.'

'You do not believe the ocean of dreams is real?'

'Dreams are most likely confused brain patterns.'

'And love – what of love?'

'Mostly hormones. The scans we've made of those who say

304

they're in love suggest that dopamine looses an electrical storm within the brain's most primitive structures, as it similarly triggers people's most primitive drives: thirst, hunger, the craving for drugs.' He smiled coldly as if to reassure me of his cynicism. 'This is why new love resembles mania, dementia, and obsession. Love, as most people think of it, has no ontological reality.'

'And so, you believe, with quenging?'

'Extraordinary claims require extraordinary evidence.'

'And you arrogate to yourself the definition of what is extraordinary and what is not?' I remembered that in one of his books he had referred to human beings as lumbering robots. 'We whales find it extraordinary – and mad – that you believe consciousness somehow emerges from the mechanistic interactions of dead and mindless matter.'

Again, he appeared not to have heard me. He said, 'What evidence can you present for this phenomenon of quenging?'

'Why, there is all the evidence in the world! Let me call in the other whales, and they will tell you of their own experiences.'

'I might as well,' he said, falling back on the fallacy known as the Ostrich Effect, 'listen to testimonials of nature worshippers who claim to have seen water sprites, devas or unicorns.'

Again, I came up out of the water to spy-hop so that I could get a better look at him.

'You did not come here to help me quenge or even to try to understand what quenging is, did you?' I swallowed back the ball of fury that gathered in my throat. 'This is just a silly exercise in debunking, isn't it?'

'Oh, no,' he said as if speaking to an audience somewhere else. 'This is quite a *serious* exercise in debunking.'

Late the following evening, I swam with Unukalhai out in the moonlit bay. I spoke with him of my many conversations with the religionaries. The waters had fallen nearly silent with the soft, bright hue of tintigloss. The slow shushing of our gliding bodies accompanied the murmurs of our voices.

'The humans,' he said to me, 'have weak minds, and will believe almost anything.'

'I have not even told you,' I said, 'of the Logos of Science. Its initiates teach that long ago, the humans choked our world with many billions more of men and women than dwell on the continents now. Then a kind of god, called Xemu, came to earth to save it and dropped hydrogen bombs into volcanoes, which caused eruptions and the fracturing of the continents. Billions upon billions of humans died.'

'That is very interesting,' he said. 'It makes me think.'

'Then there are those atheists,' I said, 'whose belief in the non-existence of the divine flows nearly as fervently as the faith of many a believer. And yet the atheists do not believe that their disbelief constitutes an even more powerful kind of belief.'

'That makes me think even more,' he said. 'It would seem that the more the atheists denounce a religion, the more fanatically the faithful embrace it.'

'I am not sure that I like what I think you are thinking.'

'I think you are thinking exactly what I am thinking,' he said, 'and you do not have to like it to be engaged by the thought.'

'Go ahead and think it, then.'

'But I should keep the thought to myself?'

'I cannot keep you from speaking.'

'Good, good – for I very much do want to speak my thought.' He blew out a breath, and sucked in the cold, clean air through the nostril at the top of his head. 'Let us imagine a religion based upon a belief so seemingly impossible that the atheists would be sure to rant and rave until they grow hoarse.'

'As you have said,' I reminded him, 'most humans will believe almost anything – even the impossible.'

'*Especially* the impossible.'

'Sadly, that is so.'

'Then what if we persuaded the humans to believe something so outrageous that it would make the atheists gnash their teeth?'

'What could be more outrageous than an all-knowing, all-powerful, all-loving God who creates creatures crazed by the zest to mate and then punishes them with everlasting hellfire when they mate with the wrong person or in the wrong sort of way?'

'*This* might be,' he said. 'Let us combine elements of the faiths you have spoken of in order to create a syncretic worldwide religion. We can tell the humans that we orcas are angels sent from God to save them from themselves.'

'That might not be so far from the truth.'

'All religions,' he said, 'must contain some secret spark of the truth, otherwise they would not be believed – and otherwise they would not draw swarms of humans to them, like moths to a flame.'

'I cannot say I feel very comfortable with the simile you have just chosen.'

'Then let me suggest another.' He touched his flipper to my side to emphasize what he said next. 'Let us imagine the flowering of a new religion that attracts millions with its nectar. We can elaborate on Hinduism and Catholicism – the Church of Euthanasia and the Human Extinction Movement, too. And Scientism, of course: we can inform the manswarms that simulations of the mechanisms of a hundred variables across fifty dimensions of analysis, or some other such gibberish, prove that life on this world is doomed – as if Ocean has no say in Her own fate. We will tell the humans that it is time for them to leave their doomed, polluted planet. We are to lead them to a better place. We will inveigle their chemists to cook in their factories a poison as sweet as honey yet more deadly than the venom of what the humans call the box jellyfish. Then there will dawn a day – the Day of Death – when the humans in their millions and billions will drink the sweet sacrament of poison prepared for them. They will do so believing with the last gasp of their billions of breaths what we have told them: that they will be reborn as immortal orcas in the image of God. We of the Angelic Cetacean Host will then lead the humans up to Agathange, where they will be reunited with God.'

We had swum from the bay clear out into the deeper currents of the Sound. My heart sent out little booms of ringlent into the rushing waters.

'What you have just told me – this is just a thought experiment, yes?'

'Of course,' he said. 'It is just a way of imagining how the humans might take a little solace before reducing their numbers.'

'It is dangerous,' I said, 'for an orca even to entertain such imaginings.'

He knew exactly what I was thinking, which negated any necessity for my giving voice to what troubled me. He spoke of it himself.

'Yes, I once killed a human,' he said. 'That was the worst day of my life. I was insane then.'

'And now you are sane?'

'Now I am your brother, and you will not let me see the world as I once did, will you?'

'Not as long as your heart is with mine as mine is with yours.'

Again, he touched me with his flipper. 'We can always create another, less drastic, religion. Perhaps something like Unity Science. How the humans envy us and the joy of our lives! They are desperate to quenge, though they barely intimate what quenging really is and cannot conceive its grandeur.'

'I, too, am desperate to quenge,' I told him.

'As am I. I think I will never do so again, however, until we have at least found a way to point humans in the direction of Agathange.'

Of all those who came to the Institute to speak of their religions, only one actually said or did anything that helped me in my quest to once more quenge. A Rastafarian, his black hair compressed into long clumps of felt, his ebony skin gleaming nearly as beautifully as Helen's, sat above me on the deck as he played his guitar and sang for me through most of the evening. I finally gave him permission to wade out into the waters lapping the shelf, where

I met him and allowed him to touch my head. He lit up a long, fat ganja cigar, which he held to my nostril, even as Gabi had done with her tube of tobacco. Almost immediately, I wanted to laugh and sing and melt back into the waters of the ocean that had once given me form.

As I became more and more well-known in the human noosphere, particularly that part embraced by the Net, many humans decided that they did *not* want to help me – or actually promised me harm. A rumor that it was Helen who actually composed the words that we whales spoke infected thousands of humans overnight almost like a viral disease. She was accused of perpetrating a conspiracy to put forth a radically socialistic agenda as out of the 'mouths' of obviously non-intelligent orcas. Some humans threatened to prosecute her for fraud. The worst of those uncomfortable with what had occurred at the Institute threatened to drop bombs on it and blow Helen and us whales into bloody bits.

Helen, who had confronted very real monsters eye to eye (and tooth to ear), dismissed as cowards the faceless phantoms who haunt the darker strands of the Net. She said to me, 'You are a celebrity now. All famous people who try to do good things receive death threats. That is how you know you *are* doing good things.'

Her seeming blitheness did not mean that she neglected to safe-guard us whales. Indeed, at times she could be *too* protective of us. One morning, I informed her that I wished to speak with a popular evangelist. She opposed inviting him to the Institute, saying, 'Why *this* man, Arjuna? He is the worst of the worst.'

'It is precisely such people,' I said, 'who rise to positions of power in the human world.'

'But there are hundreds of influential Christians who try to actually listen to what Jesus said and make their religion one of peace. Why should you want to talk to a fanatic who preaches pure poison?'

'You call him a fanatic,' I said, 'but I must tell you that all humans who take their beliefs too seriously seem like fanatics to us whales.'

'I am afraid that Reverend Pusser takes his beliefs *very* seriously – at least people believe he does.'

'Beliefs are the eyelids of the mind,' I said. 'Eyes can be opened.'

'Do you really believe you can change Reverend Pusser's mind?'

'I would like to try.'

'As you did with Jordan?'

Had I been human, I would have flushed with shame.

'For one with such a small brain,' I said to her, 'you can be discomfittingly insightful.'

'Coming from one with such an overgrown brain,' she said, as we basked in the warm gaze of each other's eyes, 'I will regard that as an unprecedented compliment.'

'Although I failed to reason with Jordan,' I said, 'speaking with him did no harm.'

'This preacher is different – he is *dangerous*.'

'Shall I fear he will preach me a silly sermon? Just make sure he does not bring any harpoons with him.'

I would reason with this revered man, I promised myself – somehow I *must* reason with him. Did he not preach that humans were made in the image of God? Would he not, somewhere in his mind, therefore revere the divine reason with which all beings are imbued?

17

Soon after that, a large man thick in the shoulders like a bull strode onto the deck above the channel where I turned circles in the water as I waited for him. His wool suit had the soft sheen of silk, and he seemed to wear it as a kind of armor against any sort of low regard or disrespect. As he sat on the chair prepared for him, he had to unbutton the jacket to accommodate his bulging belly. Very large pores pitted his skin, as if a wildcatter had drilled for oil across his cheeks. Through these obscene holes poured sweat, grease, and an insincerity that spread out in a shiny patina from his hairline to his chin. The whole of his face, red and lumpy, had an angry and pummeled look, as if he had fought one too many battles, either with words or fists. His blue eyes blazed – I could think of no other word – with a fervor to exert his will and make sure that he always got his way.

'I want to thank you for agreeing to meet with me.' His voice boomed out into the dome like the explosion of a cannon. 'I never dreamed a man could sit talking face to face with a whale – instead of being swallowed by one.'

He laughed at his joke, and looked at me as if expecting that I might somehow do the same. Was he following some sort of

311

script that called for him to soften his audience with a little humor before moving on to more serious matters?

'Wasn't Jonah,' I said, 'actually swallowed by a large fish?'

'Have you read the Bible?' he asked me with an unpleasant blending of irritation and surprise. 'I was told you whales had learned to read, though that's hard to believe.'

'If you have read the Bible, then you must believe much more miraculous things.'

'I like the way you think, Arjuna,' he said, 'and I am prepared to admit that you *do* think and can speak your thoughts, as miraculous as *that* seems.' He drew out a packet of square, white papers, and used one to wipe at his nose. 'I guess you could say that one way or another, I've come here to talk about miracles.'

'I had thought you wanted to help me quenge.'

'That may be. If possible, I'd love for us to quenge together in Jesus.'

His simple statement gave me pause. Did he have any idea what he was saying?

'However,' he continued, 'I don't know if that will be possible because I don't know what you really are.'

'I am . . . that I am,' I said. 'As you are, and everything is.'

'I have to tell you that what you just said troubles me in many ways, as I'm pretty sure you know.' Now he blew the clogs in his nose into the square of paper, which he crumpled in his fist. 'You are obviously intelligent – maybe even as intelligent as a man.'

'O, thank you, man!'

'And maybe more so. That is what concerns me.'

'In cetacean society, we consider it a privilege to speak with those more intelligent, that some part of their intelligence might illuminate us.'

'I've always prided myself on having an open mind,' he said, 'but I've always known better than to try to outtalk Satan.'

'Is *that* what you think I am?'

I could not have been more astonished if he had fallen down and kissed the water at the second coming of Jesus Christ.

'As I said,' he continued, 'I don't know. Many are claiming that you are Satan, or one of his servants.'

'You cannot really believe that Satan is a real being and not just an invention of the makers of your Christian myth?'

'Satan's greatest deception,' he said, 'is to convince people that he doesn't exist.'

'I am an orca,' I said, 'born of orcas in our Ocean going back a million years.'

'I'm sure you know that the world was created little more than six thousand years ago,' he said. 'And Satan can take on any form he wishes.'

'You might as well suppose I am an angel in disguise.'

'Satan was once the greatest of angels before his envy of Adam caused him to defy the Lord.'

And I, I thought, am the greatest of fools for talking with such a fool.

'You cannot really believe the things you say,' I told him, 'can you? Not *deep* inside, where a flame of sanity surely must burn.'

He looked around as if to make sure that none of the humans' cameras were watching us. His eyes lit up with little sparkles of intelligence. He said, 'A great many people depend on me to help them come to Jesus. Do you know the word "charisma"?'

'Do you mean in the sense of a divinely conferred grace?'

'Exactly. I cannot do my job without it. And ministers such as myself project more charisma the more intensely they believe what they *should* believe.'

'Are you trying to convince yourself to believe that I am some sort of fallen angel?'

'It's you who must convince me otherwise,' he said. 'Let's hope that you are similar to a man, and like all men, made after the image of God.'

'You think God looks like a man?'

'No, not in physical form, of course not. You can't interpret scripture too literally.'

'I am glad to know that.'

'The Bible, of course, is the inerrant word of God,' he instructed me, 'and although it speaks of man and beast, nowhere does it say that a beast possessing the soul of a man cannot exist.'

'René Descartes thought otherwise.'

'And who was he?'

'Never mind,' I said. 'Just a man who was born without a soul.'

'All men have souls.'

'Yes, I know. I was not speaking literally.'

'So if you do have a man's soul,' he added, ignoring me, 'you can be saved like any man. All you need to do is open your heart and let Jesus in and you will be reborn in Christ.'

'It is that simple?'

He nodded his head and smiled at me. 'Accept Jesus as your personal savior who died for your sins, and the Holy Spirit will build into your life love, joy, peace, patience, kindness, goodness, faithfulness, gentleness, and self-control.'

I thought about this only for a moment. 'All right, I do.'

His face flushed a deeper red with an anger it seemed came to him all too easily. 'You have to be sincere,' he nearly shouted at me.

'Am I not?' I said. 'I was sincerely trying to understand what you humans mean by sin, and sincerely imagining how one man's death could relieve me of my imaginary sins. We whales like to play such thought games.'

'Salvation is no game, and neither is Hell,' he said. 'Or Heaven. You've got to do much more than mouth empty words to be accepted into God's kingdom. What do you think Christianity is?'

'Anything you say it is.'

Reverend Pusser completely lacked a sense of irony – or an ear for orca humor.

'I say what my Father said, and Paul, and Jesus himself.' He sat forward in his seat and he moved his fat fingers with a surprising grace as he seemed to extract difficult concepts from thin air. 'You've read the Bible. Now you've got to pray on it and live it with all your heart.'

'As you do?'

'Well, I do try to be an example for those who make fellowship with me.'

I zanged the inkvol tones of stress in his voice, and saw in this color an obvious lie.

'But didn't Jesus preach peace and love?' I asked.

'Jesus *is* love.'

'But did you not once call non-Christians termites who are destroying institutions built by Christians? Did you not announce that the time had come for a Godly Fumigation?'

'I do try to love my enemies,' he said. Another zang of his tense tone, and another lie. 'That doesn't mean I have to be nice to the spirit of the Anti-Christ.'

'But didn't Jesus say this: "Go, sell what you have and give to the poor"? Have you sold what you have?'

'My ministry has given millions to war refugees.'

'But did you not spend two millions on a racehorse, Red Lightning?'

'Yes, but we're not going to race him – gambling is a sin. Red Lightning is sort of an investment in esthetics. It's a joy to watch a beautiful animal perform.'

I swam about the channel, then paused in front of him. I thought of the feats at Sea Circus that I had once performed.

'Did you not advise,' I asked him, 'the assassination of a great leader who wanted his people to give their wealth to the impoverished?'

'The man you speak of was a communist who would have turned his whole society into terrorists. Taking him out would have been cheaper than starting a war. It would have *saved* lives.'

'But did you not say of another people: "We should invade their lands, kill their leaders and convert them to Christianity. Sure, civilians will die, but that's war.'''

He smacked his fist into his open hand with a sound that cracked through the dome.

'That's a misquote of what someone else said. I always counsel peace, whenever possible. But if you wish for peace, you've got to prepare for war.'

'But isn't war murder?' I asked him. 'And didn't Jesus, the Prince of Peace, say this: "Do to others as you would have them do to you"?'

'I know what Jesus said. I didn't come here to be reminded of that by a whale – or whatever you are.'

'Why *did* you come here?'

'I've already told you – I want to help you.'

Another zang of the tight tones of his voice, which spoke pure shit. Something about Reverend Pusser reminded me of a sea urchin, which has its mouth right behind its anus.

'Yes,' I said, 'help me to quenge.'

'I want to help all your people. And you can help me to do that, Arjuna.'

'By accepting Jesus as my savior?'

'You've already said that you want to. If you'd allow me to witness to you, we can come to Jesus together.'

Why had I asked him here? To get him to change his very likely unchangeable mind? Or to excoriate him face to face and slap down his noxious preachings as I might use my tail to stun a poor salmon?

'How would that help my people?' I forced myself to ask him.

'I'd like to spend time with you here,' he said. 'I'd like to film our praying together – it would be an inspiration to millions.'

He went on to declaim that he had no small influence on many world leaders – not to mention Christians in all the world's lands. He felt sure, he said, that he could use his spiritual authority to persuade those leaders to make laws declaring cetaceans to be persons who may not be abducted, sold, or harpooned.

I swam circles for a while as I considered his proposition: a horse-trade, the humans call such deals, or in this case, a devil's bargain. Then I realized that it could be something much more. What if instead I agreed to validate the spirit of what Jesus had said only if Reverend Pusser did, too, by promising to speak only of Jesus' words and to live them? Would he open his mind and heart to true Christianity? If so, then I would gladly consent to be filmed becoming a Christian. (And later, with other religionaries, a Jew, a Hindu, a Buddhist, a Mormon, a Muslim, and a Rastafarian smoking ganja.)

How, though, was I to break through the armor of angers, fears, lies, hypocrisies, and self-serving beliefs that formed the carapace of his Christianity? How to touch the magical child within, the bright being all humans are before the human world dims their radiance: the father of the glorious man he must have once wanted to be? Surely *not* by continuing to play with him; thought games would only aggravate his pugnacity. Surely there must be a better strategy. With Jordan, I had wanted to speak of humanity's inherent splendor, but had found myself unable to do so for fear of squandering my words – and perhaps out of some deeper dread. Now I found my courage and broke through barriers of my own; I told Reverend Pusser my thoughts and spoke to him words of Jesus that I hoped might warm his heart:

"'You are the light of the world,'" I said to him. "'You are perfect as the Father is perfect. A man is the image and glory of God.'"

He sat mystified, a dark, hungry look eating at his face. Now he reminded me more of a squid, with his pursed lips resembling suckers and his sliding eyes moving over me. He seemed to ponder what I had said – and why I had said it. I zanged in him a pounding hesitation. He breathed hard within his constrictive clothing, the black suit and the white shirt: the most beautiful colors that could adorn an animal. His shoes were of black leather and his silk tie was as pink as a baby whale's tongue. He wore no plastic! (Except, perhaps, for his shirt buttons which might rather have been made of mother-of-pearl.) Why, I wondered could he not be as beautiful as his clothing?

He is! He is! I told myself. I must find the way to help him see how he is!

I spoke more words: '"He who will drink from my mouth will become like me. I shall give you what no eye has seen and what no ear has heard and what no hand has touched and what has never occurred to the human mind."'

There came a moment. His bright blue eyes seemed to gaze upon some happy landscape of himself from long ago – or perhaps for a single eye-blink of time, he caught a glimpse of the infinite sea which feeds the blue oceans of Agathange. How I wanted to show him the way there! How I wanted to quenge with him, in Jesus, in fire, in water, in any and every substance at all but most especially within the singing jewel within the lotus that lies at the center of the human heart! How, though, could I quenge with a human, when I could not quenge myself? In order to swim together with him to the eternal realm of the One Song and the One Sea, I would need to accomplish the impossible feat of doing something very like loving him as I would my own brother, and this I could not do.

'If I understand you right,' he finally said, shoving his finger at me in emphasis of each of his angrily articulated words, 'you want me to censor the gospel and preach a kind of Christianity accept-able to you?'

Do not say anything more to antagonize him! I warned myself. And then came a deeper, stronger voice: 'You must tell him the truth.'

'I could pray with you,' I said, 'only over Jesus' real words, and not the many fabrications that his followers put into his mouth in order to promulgate the religion they created.'

'That would be a faith for hippies, homosexuals, and communists,' he said.

'Should I profess instead your Christianity, which is a religion for haters and idiots?'

I had spoken the truth, but I had forgotten the admonishment of the wise human who had said that the truth which is not heard is not the truth. And worse, the laying bare of the tender tissues beneath the false verities of smug self-assurance can drive a human straight into a foul, shaking wrath.

'Satan,' he said to me, fairly leaping up from his chair, 'would put such words into your mouth – words that should never leave this room.'

'You cannot keep me from speaking my mind.'

'Oh, can't I? With help I can.'

'Yes, you poor humans are so weak that you need divine assistance to rule over us unruly whales.' I fought the urge to leap out of the water and attempt to crush him with my body. Then I quoted from the Book of Job: '"Will he make a covenant with thee? Wilt thou take him for a servant forever?"'

Reverend Pusser glared at me as he quoted back a previous verse: '"Canst thou draw out the leviathan with a hook or his tongue with a chord?"'

'I am just a whale,' I said to him. An immense sadness settled into my belly as if I had swallowed all the ocean's salt.

'No, you are the Beast From The Sea.'

'The one with the ten horns and seven hands?'

'Yes, the ten horns of abominations that would pierce the body of Christ's church, if I allowed that, and the seven heads that invent the lies that would fool people into making the worst of sins.' He pointed at the scar cut into my skin above my eye, and he added, 'Upon your head, you bear the mark of the Beast. You are the Beast of the Apocalypse, and you and your kind will be chastened when Jesus returns to the world.'

He stood glowering at me, almost daring me to repent of what

I had said. He waited for me to ask his forgiveness so that we might set the seal on the agreement that he had proposed.

'Or maybe,' he said, when I responded with a cold silence that told of my scorn for him, 'you'll be destroyed much sooner than that.'

He shook his fist at me, then buttoned his suit jacket and smoothed back his hair. He walked away from me without a backward glance.

During the days that followed, no Apocalypse came. Gabi, however, did. She had chanced to hear one of Reverend Pusser's sermons raging along the streams of the Net and putting harpoons of hate into the hands of his thousands of followers who jumped at his every word. She hastened to the Institute to make sure we whales were safe.

'Gabi!' I cried out when I saw her walk out onto the deck above the channel. 'You have come back to me! You have come back!'

The orangeness of her hair and the blueness of her eyes recalled the colors of two bright stars that shone out of the empty space beyond Agathange. How happy the sight of her made me! How I reveled in the sound of her dulcet voice! My joy surged within me like a great wave I could not resist. It moved me to dive down through the channel's lovely waters, and then to swim upwards – and up and up. With a great surge of blood and muscle, I burst from the water's surface and rocketed into the air. I pirouetted about as Gabi had taught me, and my splash back into the water wetted her and caused her to laugh out in delight.

'I'm glad to see you, too!' she called to me.

She ran across the shelf, and without a care for soaking her clothing, she waded down into the water to meet me. She wrapped her arms around me and pressed her face to mine, and she started crying. After a while, she got too cold and had to go sit on the deck above the water.

I wanted to make her happy, and I thought to give her something. And so I swam out into the cove and caught a salmon. Upon my return to Gabi, I presented it held fast between my teeth.

'For your dinner,' I said to her.

She understood Wordsong nearly as well as did Helen. She said, 'I can't accept that, Arjuna.'

'Why not?'

'I can't take your fish. There are too few left anymore.'

'One more or less will matter very little. Please! Please!'

'I'm sorry, but I really can't.'

'Are you not hungry?'

'I've been traveling all day, so I'm starved. I just can't eat salmon.'

'You do not eat animals?'

'I do. I love a good steak, but I can't eat fish.'

'Like Baby Electra and the Others. Then you have made a covenant with other humans to eat only mammals?'

'Not exactly.'

I waited for her to say more, but she did not. Then I called out, 'Why, then?'

'I can't tell you.'

'Why? Why? Please tell me!'

She drew in a breath, and said, 'All right, but don't let anyone else know. This is going to sound silly—'

'You made a covenant with the salmon!'

She laughed with relief. 'Yes, it was something like that. When I was a girl, my mom bought me a goldfish. Every day, I'd come home from school and watch him swimming around his bowl – and I talked to him. I loved him so much! I promised him that I'd never eat fish, and ever since then, I haven't.'

I did not know what to do with the salmon, now dead between my teeth the way the humans like their meat. I waited until Gabi looked away from me for a moment, then I swallowed the salmon quickly.

'I am sure that your goldfish,' I said to her, 'lived for many long, happy years with you as his friend.'

'Actually, he didn't.' Her eyes softened with memory. 'My

goldfish died about a week after I brought him home from the pet store. I was at school when my mom found him floating in the fishbowl. She thought I'd be devastated, and so she went back to the pet store and bought another one to put into the bowl.'

'Really? You did not notice the difference when you returned from school?'

'No, I didn't,' she said. 'I clapped my hands together and shouted, "Look, Mommy, my goldfish – he *grew*!"'

I joined her in laughing over this memory, and I said to her, 'I want you to remain here . . . so much.'

I floated just beneath her feet, nearly shivering with little ecstasies as she ran her bare soles along the skin of my head and jaws.

After a while, she said, 'I will if I can.'

'Do you promise?'

'Yes,' she said. 'And you'll stay, too?'

'I will.'

She laughed in relief, then bent down over the water. She kissed my head to set the seal of our little covenant.

Then she asked me: 'Where is Helen?'

'Out kayaking. She will return soon.'

I told her everything of Helen's bloody past that Helen had told me. Gabi sat in silence of shock, listening to every word of the horrific story. Again, she wept, this time with real teeth cutting through her soft sobs and for many, many moments.

Finally, she cried down to me, 'I didn't know!'

'It is all right,' I told her.

'I never even guessed!'

'It is all right, Gabi.' And then for no reason logically connected to the moment, I added, 'I will protect you.'

We spoke together for most of the rest of the afternoon in tones of trust and mutual esteem even as I might have confided heartfelt things to my own sister. Around sunset, Helen came into the dome. Gabi jumped up and ran toward her. Helen, usually so reserved, clasped her close with the same sort of desperation that would drive a drowning person to latch onto a life-preserver. Both women burst out crying at the same moment. Helen kissed Gabi's lips, and caressed her orange curls of hair. She kissed her eyes and the creamy, tear-streaked cheeks beneath; she pressed her lips to Gabi's fingers and pulled Gabi's hand against her face.

'I never knew!' Gabi sobbed to her as they embraced belly to shaking belly.

'It's all right,' Helen said, stroking the back of her head. 'It's all right.'

Finally, they stood back a few steps regarding each other with a strange blending of guilt, gratefulness, and wonder. How they shined in each other's presence, like two celestial bodies necessary to each other! What would the earth be but a dark, cold desert without the sun to illuminate it? What was the sun without the earth upon which to bestow its radiance and give it purpose?

'I'll never let Arjuna smoke a cigar again,' Gabi said.

'Oh, never mind about that,' Helen said. 'He has had much worse while you were gone. We have a lot to talk about.'

Hand in hand, they walked off together into the human part of the house to talk about it.

There followed many happy, happy days. As Ocean swelled toward another warm and sunny spring, I had much time to ponder the reunion I had witnessed. I played over in my mind every word that Gabi and Helen had spoken to each other, every inflection, every falling or rising of the timbre of their voices. I savored the salt of their tears, which I tasted in waters that touched the beaches near the Institute. I swam through the light of their sparkling eyes which had found each other with so much gladness. Although I had read of great romances in books and had watched human images radiate affection on glowing screens, I had never experienced the heart-pounding, eye-dancing reality of human love.

The force of Helen's and Gabi's mutual accord caused me to entertain uncomfortable thoughts. The two women's love for each other seemed no different than that of us whales – and scarcely less powerful. Could a whale, I wondered, *really* love a human as he might his own sister? Right behind the tail of this troubling idea swam an even more astonishing notion: might it be possible for an orca such as I to make a human a part of his family?

I put this question to the other whales. Alkurah, who grew ever wiser with the waxing and waning of each moon, answered for all of us when she said, 'Love is always love, and so let us wait and see if we want to make a home here with Helen and Gabi.'

With each passing day, the impossible began to seem almost possible. One evening, Gabi spoke of Helen to me, saying, 'You helped her feel her own heart again.'

Should not brothers and sisters, mothers and sons, strive always to open each other to precisely that kind of joy?

I dwelled with such wonderings through the last of winter and into spring. With its sempiternal surge of life, the vast schools of herring returned to the bay and filled every cove and bit of coastline with liquid white pearls of sperm. We whales feasted morning, afternoon, and night, and Ocean's life poured into us. In this season of renewal and the rousing of hope long thought dead, we awakened as from a nightmare into miracles. Zavijah's floppy fin was the first to regain its proud, crescent shape, like the curve of the moon aimed at the stars; then Alkurah's fin stood upright, and so did those of Salm, Unukalhai, and Bellatrix. Menkalinan leapt from the water in celebration at being restored to himself. He promised to sing of his rebirth in a new rhapsody that would sound through the seven seas throughout the ages. Strangely, it was he – the most battered and broken in spirit of all of us (save for perhaps Bellatrix) – who first regained his joy of quenging. Then Alkurah returned to herself as well, as did her sisters, along with Kitalpha, Hyadum, and finally old, bereaved Bellatrix. On a cool, lovely evening of rising fins and the rising of the Star of Agathange low on the deeply blue and glowing horizon, they quenged together as one.

Unukalhai, however, did not quenge nor could Baby Electra partake of this grace. And I, whose heart still bled with every beat over the bitter iron of Pherkad's harpoon, struggled fiercely to sing with the others, too. However, the anguished notes that sounded from my flute found echo in hurts of the past and not in future dreams, much less the rushing stillness of bliss of the ever-present moment. Tomorrow, I promised myself, would be a new day. Tomorrow I would quenge, in love, with the water of world, with all the stars, and with the new song of myself that I would sing. I would quenge on and on, like an angel, like a true orca, like a god.

One quiet morning, I floated alone in the bay, meditating on the sound of the world's beating heart as the Buddhist monk had taught me. The density of the quiet water amplified the little booms of my own heart. The sky above the bay glowed a rich and royal blue along the hills of the horizon, which still hid the rising of the great, eastern sun. Bands of red tinged the blueness like licks of flame.

After a while, I allowed the left half of my brain to pass into sleep, and I dreamed. I journeyed far back to my beginnings. Once again, I dwelled in the peace of my mother's womb and tasted the sacred salt of her amniotic waters. I listened to the streams of her blood rushing into me with every beat of her beautiful heart: Boom-boom, boom-boom, boom-boom. Within each boom resonated the sound of an entire universe being born. The explosion into being always entails an agony like unto being cast into the fire of a star but also promises an ecstasy beyond words in one's becoming pure light. With this realization, in the memoried lucidity of my dream, the booms grew louder. I moved my mind towards hurts that I had known as a baby and then into the sharkfest of pains that had grieved me at Sea Circus. Black clouds tinged with red obscured Ocean's yellow-white star. Lightning cracked out in jags of electric hell, and thunder broke through the water. Boom! Boom! Boom! Boom! Boom! The explosions nearly deafened me.

I opened my eyes to blood and screams and pain and flashes of light.

From across the cove came more cracks of light-fire-thunder. A single man stood there, on the sloping beach of shingle and sand. As I moved from deep dreams into the real nightmare of wakefulness, I saw him lay down his rifle for a moment so that he could pluck one of the grenades hanging from his vest and cast it out into the cove. The explosion that nearly shattered my hearing bones brought me fully awake. Deafened as I was, I could nevertheless make out the shrieks and screams of Zavijah, Salm, and some of the other orcas, all bloodied and broken in the shallow waters close to the beach. Where was Alkurah? As I began swimming, I recalled that she had gone fishing with Unukalhai, Kitalpha, and Hyadum out in the Sound many miles away. Zavijah and Salm had wanted to stay behind to watch their favorite movie, in which three brave humans on a boat named the *Orca* pursue a great shark across the open sea. Despite wielding harpoons, a shark-proof cage, a strychnine-tipped hypodermic spear, rifles, and a scuba tank used as a bomb, the shark kills two of the humans before the third manages to blow the poor beast into bloody bits. Very similar pieces of flesh now fouled the cove's clear water. Their touch tore at my skin. I swam faster through a cloud of red. Baby Electra, bathed in the blood gushing from Menkalinan's head wound, cried out to me.

I blew the stale, steamy air from my lungs and gulped in a huge breath as I prepared to dive. Just then, however, Gabi and Helen exited the house and came running down the beach straight toward the murderous man. He bent to pick up his rifle. Gabi, slightly ahead of the nearly naked Helen, her arms and legs pumping furiously, her bare feet cutting divots out of the sand, screamed at him to stop. He did not stop. Nor did she. The man – he had brown hair and lean flat cheeks glowing red above his bushy beard – wrapped his warm, living fingers around his rifle. As Gabi closed on him, he straightened up. Just then, Helen finally caught up to

Gabi. She cried out, 'No!' even as she tried to use her body to push Gabi out of the man's line of sight. The force of her shoulder and hands, however, knocked Gabi off her balance and actually propelled her into the trajectory of the bullet. The little cone of lead blasted away part of her face in an explosion of bits of bone and flesh. A second bullet pierced her eye and blew off the back of her head. The man fired a third bullet through Helen's small, bare breast. From her beautiful black, black skin bloomed blossoms of blood, the red flowers of evil that humans so often pluck out of the living loam of the human body.

Again, Baby Electra cried out to me from the crimson mess in the water near Menkalinan and Bellatrix. I dove. Bullets sizzled through the water. I began swimming with a fury to move more quickly than any orca ever had through any ocean anywhere. One chance I would get, and one only.

My hearing had returned enough so that I could zang every undulation of the immersed sand leading up to the beach upon which stood the man. I swam in closer – and closer and closer. More bullets exploded from his rifle. Cold water burned across my skin. In a feat that I had practiced many times with Baby Electra in our hunting seals, in a burst of spray and foam and a shock of rushing air, I launched myself up out of the water onto the beach. I had gauged distances and times nearly perfectly. The man, who fired off one last bullet as he turned toward the great splash and scrape of my landfall, screamed out his astonishment as my teeth closed around his leg. His blue eyes sickened with fear. Horror at being dragged down seized him. In his panic not to let gravity bring him so crushingly and injuriously to earth (or perhaps just in a pure, mind-numbing, limb-freezing panic), he dropped his rifle and threw out his hands. This did not avail him. He fell hard to the sand. Helen and Gabi lay there, too, as still as stones. I bit down with greater force, and felt his leg bone snap. He screamed as I dragged him toward the gently lapping water. The ocean encompassed us.

It would be easy, I thought, to drown him – much easier than it had been to kill the white bear. How, though, could I do this? The golden chords of the Great Covenant rang through my conscience. There, too, a man called Jesus spoke these words: 'Love your enemies, and do good to those who hate you.'

I opened my jaws to let the thrashing man go. He flailed his arms and kicked furiously at the water to propel himself upward. As he breached, the breath broke from him in a scream of rage and bone-grinding torment. His terror and hatred of me blasted through the water with the force of one of his grenades, and he began fighting his way back to the shore.

'Swim!' I shouted at him. 'Swim as fast as you can!'

Then Baby Electra cried out to me again. Red clouds boiled through the water near her and the other whales. Zavijah called out her farewell to Baby Navi in a plaint so terrible that the entire ocean screamed. I found myself back in Sea Circus's foul pools listening to the swarms of humans calling for me to do feats.

Shocks of lightning from the humans' cattle prods jerked my muscles and galvanized my whole body. Electric sparks ignited the oils in my blubber, which blackened and burned me in a shroud of greasy orange flame. The white bear's claw once again tore open my head, this time breaking through bone and gouging out pink masses of my brain. At last, the harpoon's point worked its way to the center of my heart. There, in the immense pressures greater than even the crush of the deepest ocean deeps, in a shriek of fracturing metal, it broke apart. My poisoned heart sent fragments ripping through my blood into every part of my body. Each cell, each particle of my being, screamed out as one in a bottomless wrath that I should do a thing.

Other voices cried out other things. I must restrain myself, my grandmother told me. Yes – I *could* have modulated my rage, integrated mind and emotions, sublimated my urge to kill into a celebration of life in all its terrible beauty. I had a paralimbic lobe to my brain, did I not? I wanted to let flow into my seething blood the cool impulse to spare the man. Wanting to want something, however, is not the same as wanting it. What did I *really* want? What was my deep, driving desire? Only, I thought, to shred the man into tinier and tinier pieces so that nothing of him remained.

'O human!' I called out to him. 'Do you know the word *schadenfreude*?'

I did not suppose that he did, nor did he understand the sounds of Wordsong that I aimed at him.

'*Schadenfreude*: to take joy in the misfortunes that befall another. Know that you are about to suffer what you will likely perceive as the greatest of misfortunes. Let us make a covenant of pain!'

As he sputtered and clawed at the water in a frantic attempt to reach the shore, I gazed at his hands. Which finger, I wondered, had pulled the trigger of the gun that had killed Gabi? I moved in close, and grabbed his hand. It required only the slightest pressure of my teeth to bite his forefinger off. Through his gasp, I heard myself ask how many more chances I would have to know joy? Could I do the difficult subtraction? Eight more – no, nine! – to go.

Again I bit down, and again, and again. Where was my joy? Not the slightest shred of satisfaction did I feel. I snipped off all his fingers, but that did not console me. I grabbed hold of the man's good leg, and dragged him back out to deeper water. He screamed as my teeth fractured the bone, which tore through muscle and skin and ripped out of him gouts of blood. I tried to savor the taste of it. Had not Genghis Khan said that the greatest of pleasures is to destroy one's enemies?

I swam beneath the man, and buoyed him up so that he could suck in the exhalations of Gabi's and Helen's dying breaths. He lay on top of me, his belly pressing against my back, and his heart beat little thumps of outrage against my skin. Could he feel in the wounding of his own ravaged body the much greater agony of what he had done? Could he sense the pain of the entire world?

I called to him in the beating of *my* heart: This is your moment! The moment of the possible when you can feel your oneness with the world – and with me! Soon, very soon, you will become a part of me!

I flung him from my back as I might a piece of driftwood. He thrashed about in a panic: he could no longer swim. I spun the jerking man around in the water so that I could look into his eyes. I asked him if he was ready to die. He said yes. How he hated life! How he hated me! I felt his spite gathering in him like a pool of acid, which his heart pushed up through his raging arteries with every pulse to eat all the light of his blighted, blue eyes. Only fear and contempt remained. Because I could not suffer the sight of those hellish eyes, I bit them out of his head. At last, in the frenzy of an act that thrilled my blood with wild hope and terrible possibilities, in an unstoppable surging of my will to destroy a vile, vile thing, the joy came. With great pleasure, I swallowed the bloody, broken orbs. In the man's panic to keep my teeth from crunching at his face, he screamed and breathed water and choked. I bit off his right hand to keep him from flailing at the sea, and I swallowed it – and his left hand as well. He could no longer keep himself afloat and open his mouth to the life-giving air, and so he began to drown. I did not want the sea to kill him. In what the humans call the *coup de grace*, I closed my jaws around his neck and sawed off his head.

I took care in ripping off his clothes. I did not want to swallow these plastic garments and obstruct my stomach, even as my sister Mira's child had eaten plastic bags and died. I tore off the man's testicles and devoured them, along with his puny penis. I gutted him, and gulped down most of his insides, taking particular relish at the taste of his liver and the pink bubbling of his lights. Finally, I worked my teeth and tongue at his chest bones. There, in the red froth and fury of the sea, I ate his bare, bitter human heart, and it was good.

A last time, Baby Electra called to me. The fire in my belly went

out as if I swallowed icy water. I looked upon the cooling, muti-
lated corpse of the man floating through the water, and I zanged
the horror of what I had done. Words – human words – sounded
over and over within me:

I have murdered a human being.

I have murdered a human being.

I have slain a beautiful orca.

I have become human myself.

PART THREE

A Covenant With Thee

18

Through the quietening, crimson-clouded waters, I swam over to Baby Electra. I zanged her body. A bullet had grazed her jaw and one of the grenades had blown a bloody crater out of the flesh of her side. Menkalinan, a couple of body lengths away, was dead. He floated like a vast white and black log and bobbed up and down with the passing of each rolling wave.

'Flee!' I shouted. 'The humans have decided to murder us, so we must flee!'

Bellatrix, Zavijah, and Salm swam over to us. I could not bear to zang the many wounds blasted into their beautiful bodies. We moved slowly toward the mouth of the cove. I scanned the land for other humans who might be waiting for us at the choke point to cut off our escape. No one spoke; no one wanted to speak.

No humans did we see. By the time we worked our way toward the bay's center, Salm had weakened so much that she could not swim. Because we could not abandon her, we kept close so that we might hold her up and help her draw her last breaths of air. She died in a cough and spray of bright lung blood. We swam on. After a while, Bellatrix died too – it seemed that a bullet had pierced her stomach, though I thought the real reason for her quick demise was that she finally gave up on life.

335

It took nearly forever to cross the shortest expanse of water, so slowly did Zavijah swim. We all wished that she would move more quickly, but of course no one spoke of this – until Zavijah herself did: 'I *could* swim more quickly, if you wish, but then I would die more quickly. Perhaps that would be a good thing.'

'No, live as long as you can,' I said. 'We will swim as slowly as jellyfish if we must.'

We swam nearly as slowly as jellyfish. It did no good. With the bay's dark green wavelets washing our blood from our bodies, Zavijah said to me, 'If you ever see Baby Navi again, please tell him how much I loved him.'

I did not think that I would ever meet Baby Navi, but I did not speak of this.

'I will say goodbye to you now,' she told me. 'And you, too, little Electra: I was so cruel to you both when we met. Forgive me! I was not myself. You helped me find myself again, and I love you for that. I wish for you the same miracle.'

She died to the deep-throttled roar of the first of the morning's fishing boats firing up their engines and moving out into the Sound before us like great, gray floating sharks in pursuit of prey. We waited only ten more heartbeats after that for the last light to go out of her eyes. It astonished me that I seemed suddenly able to count so high.

'What will we do now?' Baby Electra asked, weeping inside the way whales do.

Before I could answer her, the cold water carried us to the long-distance, deep call of an orca from many miles away. It was Alkurah's voice, propagating low and urgent beneath the Sound's surface waves. She – along with Unukalhai, Hyadum, and Kitalpha – had heard the grenades' concussions and had immediately begun swimming back to the Institute in order to investigate this dreadful noise.

'Go back! Go back!' I called to her. 'The humans have killed everyone except Baby Electra and me. I have killed the killer, but more of them are sure to come soon to kill us. Flee to the north! We will journey south, and so perhaps you will be safe.'

'We will not abandon you!' Alkurah cried out.

'You must! You must! Perhaps we can meet out in the open ocean.'

'We will!' Alkurah shouted to me in a deep, deep moan of anguish. 'I promise you that we will meet again!'

Baby Electra and I swam out into the Sound with all the alacrity we could summon. We did not, however, move quickly, for every flick of Baby Electra's tail sent through muscle and nerve electric jolts of agony.

'Will I die?' she asked me.

I zanged the hole gouged out of the skin, blubber, and muscle in her side. I peered into the wound, then put my tongue to the hot, red tang of her torn tissues. Although she was still bleeding, I could detect no sign that any major artery had been severed.

'You will need to be strong to survive the infection and fever that will come,' I said. 'If you do, you will live, though you will swim with a limp.'

'I do not want to swim with a limp. What male would ever want to mate with me?'

'Many males would,' I reassured her. 'You will grow long and lithe to be the most beautiful of mother whales.'

'All right then,' she said. 'I do want to live.'

She grew quiet for a moment. I felt her zanging me everywhere along my body.

'Did you know that you are wounded?' she asked me.

I had not known. Her question, however, caused me to feel my way past the lightning flashes of adrenalin that still shot through my body and obliterated the much quieter firing of my nerves.

'My fin,' I said to her. 'It must have been a bullet – I never felt it! What does it look like?'

'The tip is gone. It looks like a shark bit it off.'

A wave of wrath moved through me like the aftershock of an

underwater earthquake. I had always been proud of my great dorsal fin.

'It will not stop me from swimming,' I said, 'nor will your wound stop you. Let us swim then!'

'But where will we swim *to*?'

'Away from the humans,' I said.

We moved through the Sound past the many noisy boats and the almost whisperless kayaks, which we avoided. From Baby Electra's wound trailed long strands of blood like scarlet fishing lines cast into the water. After a while of silent swimming and long dives beneath the surface that would hide us from the humans' sight, we came upon the colder and much deeper open ocean. We turned west, as if pulled by some instinct of desire that flowed counter to the currents that worked to sweep us back toward dark continent behind us. We swam hard and with a steadiness of will, but we could not escape the humans, for their handiwork was everywhere: in the metallic whine of propellers fracturing the water far away; in the floating bits of plastic bottles and other junk; in the bright red jewels of meat gleaming from Baby Electra's open side; in the scar that marked my forehead and the much deeper wound cut into my soul. An orca knows the wide, wide ocean to be his ancestral home, but for the first time in my life out in the rushing blue wilds of the world, I felt anything but safe. My breaking the Great Covenant made me what the humans call an outlaw. In no land or water did I now belong.

I have murdered a human being. I have murdered a human being.

I felt the substance of the man I had slain digesting within me and becoming one with my own. How like a beast I truly was, like some monster out of mythology, half orca and half human! It seemed at any moment that I might actually sprout seven human heads deformed with ten horns. Or perhaps I was something new altogether, some dread being out of nightmare that had never existed in all the eons in which Ocean had spun through the black and empty spaces of the universe.

I have murdered a human. I have murdered . . .

The dread of my deed ate at me like a worm. And then, as Baby Electra and I swam far out into the ocean, a new and more terrible thought began to grieve me, a thought which perhaps no orca had ever dared to think: What was wrong with that? Didn't humanity revere its successful killers of men, from Joshua to Hercules to Alexander the Great? Why should I not revere myself? Why not take pride in my becoming at last what the humans so derogatorily call a killer whale?

When I sounded the lightless caverns of my conscience, the echoes carried back to me a realization that I felt no guilt over what I had done. Certainly I knew shame, for other orcas would aim their zangs of scorn at me and announce to each other: 'There goes Arjuna, Breaker of Covenants, marked and cursed for killing a man.' Guilt, however, was a human creation, experienced by human beings – and sometimes by their dogs.

No, what really troubled me was that I had given in to fear and wrath. The humans speak of seven deadly sins, and of these wrath overshadows all but one. We whales do not worry ourselves over such human conceptions as sin, but if we did, I would see in my murder of the murdering man the making of each of the remaining six sins: Through my lust to enjoy the power of speaking to the humans, I had spoken of things they did not wish to hear, and spoken too well. In my gluttony to devour all human language and knowledge, I had stuffed myself with too many indigestible, horrible things. My greed to gather, gain, and possess the humans' love had led to the reaping of the worst of human hate. I had also fallen into sloth: the laziness of the spirit that fails to do what the spirit is called to do. Envy I had known in my covetousness of the human hand and all its miraculous works. At last came the worst iniquity, the mother of sins: pride. Out of sheer, soul-burning hubris, I had dared to try to bestow the bright flame of reason upon the two-legged beings that we call the idiot gods, and so become myself a greater god.

The farther that I swam out into the ocean and the deeper I thought, the more it seemed to me that I had done a much worse thing. We of the sea *do* speak of splendor, the brightness of being that sings through each orca in a song of eternal becoming. To silence that glorious song would be to wreak something like a sin upon the soul, an atrocity of damning and endarkenment that no orca would ever conceive much less commit.

Even as I myself had done. I truly had slain a beautiful orca – as I had slain a beautiful man. The humans, I realized, really are different from dogs and starfish and diatoms that wish to be only what they are. What had the man I had devoured wished to be? Had he once, perhaps as a child, dreamed of living as a great, joyous orca gliding through cool waters? Might he have conceived, in his human way, of becoming a uniquely human god: wise, immortal, creative, powerful? I would never know, for I had snuffed out his fire and swallowed up his song. I had expunged from the universe each of his shining, infinite possibilities. Only a black hole of silence remained.

As this emptiness opened inside me into a vast and soundless neverness, I finally did feel guilt. I wanted to cry out my anguish into the void, but no one and nothing would have heard me. I had subtracted from creation so much! How unbearable, how irretrievable this loss, for the man, for myself, and strangely, for the world!

At last, I thought, I had an answer to the question of why human beings do not act upon the truth of what they know. Why do they not care enough to keep themselves from committing the worst of cruelties? Helen had said that the boy-men who had tortured her sister *wanted* to be what they thought of as beasts. They turned toward the dark and the base, I realized, because they feared the glorious and the high. In truth, they dreaded with a gut-fluttering, heart-crushing terror becoming the bright songs of the earth that they most longed to sing. So it was with me.

This new knowledge of myself afflicted me, and I could scarcely bear it, for I had conceived myself almost entirely otherwise. What did I most dread, I wondered? What song did I long to sing?

How badly I wished to ask these questions of my grandmother and my mother, to speak and swim once more with my first family whom I had nearly forgotten in my joy of dwelling with Zavijah, Salm, and all my new sisters and brothers who had been slaughtered! Unukalhai, Alkurah, Kitalpha, and Hyadum, too, were gone, lost into the gray-blue deeps of the northern ocean. A single orca remained with whom I might share the wonderings that tormented me.

How, though, could I speak of such things with a whale as young as Baby Electra? How could I add to her own torment, which she could scarcely bear?

'It hurts so bad!' she moaned out to me as we swam side by side through the sting of the salty sea. 'There is a hole in me, Arjuna!'

She spoke not of the bloody wound that the man's grenade had torn out of her side, but the much deeper loss of whales she had loved. It shocked me that she included me in her remembrance of the murdered, for with an amazing percipience and compassion in one so young, she understood that the violence I had inflicted upon the man had destroyed something precious in me.

'Please do not leave me,' she said as she limped alongside me.

'I never would! I will swim with you until the end of—'

'Please do not leave me in your heart. I cannot live without *you*.'

I swam on in silence for a while. Then I tried to divert the stream of her thoughts.

'I should have known that the humans would not want to hear what I had to say,' I told her. 'If I had not opened my big mouth . . .'

'But what does your mouth have to do with making sounds?'

'It is a figure of speech you never learned.'

'I feel that I learned so much from the humans – and so little.'

We moved through the dark gray water, zanging frequently to see what lay ahead of us – and behind.

'All things have a soul,' Baby Electra continued. 'The minnows, the crabs, the starfish, the diatoms – all these beings and so with even the seaweed and the rocks of the green-shrouded shore. But how can it be, Arjuna, that the humans have a soul?'

She spoke hyperbolically and too passionately for one so grievously wounded, but she spoke to a point.

I said to her: 'What of Gabi, then? What of Helen?'

'They are the exceptions that prove the rule,' she said. 'I sometimes think that Descartes was correct in characterizing animals as soulless automatons, if by animals is meant human beings.'

'You know that humans are not automatons.'

'No, they are something much worse,' she said. 'Any part of reality that vexes them they destroy with a will and a glee. Why have our kind made a covenant with such creatures?'

'I do not know.'

'But you *must* know! You are an adult, Arjuna.'

'I have not completed my rhapsody. Perhaps I never will.'

'You will! You will! And you will speak to the adults of the things that adults speak of.'

'Once,' I said, 'I overheard my grandmother and mother discussing the Great Covenant.'

'And what did they say?'

'Little that made sense to me. My grandmother said that the Great Covenant is a mystery that may not be questioned.'

'But we orcas question everything!'

'Of course we do. That is what makes my grandmother's pronouncement so mysterious.'

'Perhaps in our questioning, we should question that we question everything.'

'Of course, that is also true. I am glad that you have not allowed your wound to divert you from thought play.'

'I want to live! I want to know . . . so much!'

'I am glad,' I said to her as we glided beneath the waves above us.

'If we may not question the *why* of the Great Covenant,' she said, 'may we not wonder about the *where* and the *how*? From where did it come? How has it been passed down to our kind for so many ages?'

'Only the deep gods,' I said, 'know this. It is said that they persuaded the Old Ones to make covenant with the humans long ago.'

'But orcas do not speak with the deep gods!'

'Once we did,' I told her.

'I wish *I* could speak with them.'

'And what would you say?'

She thought about this as she swam. She winced at the pain that shot through her with every movement of flipper and fluke.

'I would say this,' she told me. 'I have chosen to question the Great Covenant after all. What can be made can be unmade, yes? Perhaps the time has come to bury the Great Covenant in the place we left Bellatrix's and Menkalinan's bodies.'

Her voice spread out into the much deeper plaint and moaning of the sea. The waves carried to us the thunder of faraway storms and the much nearer booming of each other's heart. We both listened again and again to the death cries of Zavijah and her sister, and I could not help hearing anew the murdered man's shrieks. The deeps concealed even more disturbing stridencies that we felt touching our bones. All this clamor tinged the water with argrege and inkvol. We swam through these darker colors of sound in remembrance of brighter days.

'I am cold,' Baby Electra said to me as fever set in. She pressed up against me as we swam slowly toward the west. 'Stay close to me, Arjuna.'

I pressed my side to her burning flesh. I wished I could soften my skin and remove it so that I might drape it like a cloak over her trembling body.

'I am hungry, too,' she said.

So was I. It had been long days and nights of swimming through sunlit and moonshadowed seas since we had eaten. I zanged the restless green waters about us, but only a couple of fish did I detect.

'Where are all the salmon?' she asked. 'The humans have ravished this place. They are like sharks.'

I held my breath as I counted my heartbeats, giving up when I reached twenty-three. I aimed zangs of sonar to the west, south, east, and north – and then up and down. What dwelled in the black and whisperless deeps, I wondered, which no orca had ever dared to fathom?

'The humans are *worse* than sharks,' she added. 'Sharks eat only when they are hungry, but the humans eat just because they like to eat.'

'I have been thinking about sharks myself,' I told her.

'Have you then zanged the two that are following us?'

'Of course I have.'

'Then why did you wait for me to speak of them?'

'I had thought that the pain of your body,' I said, 'would be enough for you to endure.'

'What kind of sharks do you think they are?'

Only one kind of shark swam so steadily through such cold water in pursuit of wounded whales. We knew of these sharks as the Magnificent Ones while the humans called them the Great Whites.

I told this to Baby Electra, and she seemed to press herself through my side into my clenching belly.

'I have little experience of the Magnificent Ones,' she said. 'If any had thought to come near my family, Pherkad and my mother – Asteropei, too! – would have killed them quickly.'

344

'If these two come close to you,' I said to her, 'I will kill them, though it might not be quickly.'

'Have you killed such sharks before?'

Only in my dreams, I thought. Only in my nightmares.

'No, I have not,' I said. 'But I know how to. My grandmother once instructed me.'

'I do not want you to kill them,' she said. 'What if they wound you as I am wounded? Who would protect me?'

'Let us keep moving,' I said. 'Perhaps they will lose interest in us.'

We swam as quickly as Baby Electra could manage toward that red, glowing place where the sun disappears each night into the ocean to the west. We swam through waters darkened by clouds in the sky and by bits of kelp and sediments that the violence of wind and waves churned up from the deeps. At times the sea darkened to a muddy green, and a short while later took on a nearly impenetrable violet hue as thick and stony as chaorite. Baby Electra voiced a vain hope that we might swim through the dying of the day and so escape into invisibility when the night filled the ocean with blackness. She knew, of course, that the sharks did not hunt us by sight – not just. She wanted to will away the blood that still flowed out of her in long, red strands that the sharks must have found both savory and compelling; then she jammed her wounded side against me so that the pressure of flesh against flesh might at least slow the bleeding, even though the shock of the renewed outrage to her torn tissues caused her to moan and shudder in pain. Such desperate measures did no good. The two sharks followed our every turn and twist. Late in the afternoon, with the wind flagging and the sea calming to a startling blue clarity, they drew closer, and then closer.

'Do you think they will attack?' Baby Electra asked me.

'That depends,' I said, 'on how hungry they are.'

A shark – any shark – needed to be very, very hungry in order to attack two killer whales.

Then, as if the two sharks had somehow communicated with each other through the voice of bloodlust and hunger, they accelerated through the water in an explosion of flashing fins. I swam against the larger one, thinking to ram him with my head, but he veered off to left at the last moment. I let him go – I needed to turn to protect Baby Electra from the other shark. I moved a heartbeat too late, however, for the shark managed to bump Baby Electra's side and scrape off bits of her skin with his rough, shark's hide. At my approach, he too veered and swam off into the pellucid waters.

'They are desperately hungry,' she said. 'I think they will eat me.'

'No – I will not let them.'

'Good – I am not ready to die.'

I peered through the clear water with both sonar and vision at the two sharks where they swam leisurely alongside us, matching their pace to ours. How patient they were! How cunning! The humans disparage these great beings as dumb, brutal beasts, but the Old Ones tell of how intelligent the white sharks are. In truth, they were not white at all, but gray on top and white on the bottom, the better to camouflage themselves against the darkness of sea when hunting prey from below and to appear an almost invisible white against the sun-dazzled surface water when they swam above the creatures who looked upwards for them. So clever was this color scheme that we orcas had adopted it (and even improved upon it) when our kind had returned to the ocean eons before. The Great Whites had been our teachers, and we had learned well from them and had thrived. Over the eons, *they* had learned that they must leave us alone, and this they did – most of the time.

'If I *do* end up dying soon,' Baby Electra said as she swam with her ragged, pained gate, 'I would rather be eaten by sharks than shot in the head like Menkalinan, even though his death was quick.'

346

'No one is going to eat you,' I told her.

I think she would have smiled at this, had orcas been able to smile. The humans speak of the right to life, and I certainly had the right to try to protect her. But her life did not belong to her; it belonged to Ocean, which at any time might come to reclaim it.

At one with my thoughts, she asked me: 'What do you think is wrong with the humans?'

'Many things,' I said.

'But what is the one thing . . . that lies at the bottom of those many things?'

'To ask such a question is to oversimplify things and thus to think like the humans themselves.'

'I am sorry – I have spent too much time with them. As have you.'

I swam close to her through the calm ocean, always keeping the sharks in sight. I said, 'Something has smothered the human soul. If I could identify a single cause of this, I would say that the humans do not know why they are alive.'

'But they know what they need to do to *live*,' Baby Electra said. 'They know that they must love each other – and must love the world with all their heart and with all their soul and with all their strength, and must feel its will at one with their own. They know that they must live with the right intention and the right view toward creation. They know how to practice right concentration. Their own Buddha has taught them. They know that they must see themselves in all things, and all things in them: that thou art, their sages have said. Above all, they know that they must drink deeply from life's source and become so overfull that they forget themselves – and thus remember who they really are.'

The sharks following us might have been intelligent, but they could not follow the stream of our conversation – and I lamented that few humans seemed able to do so either.

'Why do the humans,' Baby Electra continued, 'not do what they *know* they must do?'

'Because they are afraid,' I said.

'Of what?' she asked. 'What on earth can harm them?'

'It is true,' I said, 'that they think of themselves as masters of the earth. That, however, is a derangement of their minds. Deep in their bellies, they are still frightened monkeys swinging through the jungle from tree to tree and afraid to let go.'

'Because they would fall!'

'No, they would fly.' We surfaced to draw breath, and I whistled toward the sky above us. Its infinite blueness was broken only by the white contrails of a jet thundering high in the atmosphere. 'How they long to fly not in machines of metal but in their souls!'

We gulped in great lungsful of air, and dove. Baby Electra swam alongside me.

'The humans,' I said, 'are children afraid to grow up.'

'Tell me more,' she said, keeping my body between her and the two sharks that hunted us.

'The humans are acorns,' I said, 'who dread destroying themselves in becoming oak trees.'

'Tell me more.'

'They are turtles who keep their heads inside the safety and darkness of their shells rather than daring to extend them out into the light.'

'Tell me more.'

'They are flowers afraid to blossom.'

'Tell me more.'

'They are salmon afraid to spawn.'

'Tell me more.'

'They are dreams afraid to be real.'

'Tell me more.'

'They are the glories of the beginning of a beautiful terror that they could gladly bear.'

'Tell me more.'

'They are afraid of quenging and becoming true gods.'

'Tell me . . . Here they come, Arjuna! Here they come!'

Again, the sharks charged us. I moved left and then right, turning back and forth so quickly it seemed that the sea would tear the flippers from my body. One of the sharks managed to slip in close to Baby Electra. Before I could return to her, the shark opened his huge mouth to take a bite out of her with his many triangles of teeth, each serrated like the humans' saws. Baby Electra did her best to jerk herself out of the way at the last moment. Teeth raked her open wound, and she screamed. I raced closer to drive her tormentor away, giving the other shark a chance to slip in behind me. There came another scream, and blood boiled out into the water. I rammed one of the sharks, but this glancing blow did not really harm him. At the same moment, teeth ripped open the skin of my tail. I turned and troubled the smaller shark. It was hard to see because much blood clouded the water. I whipped back and forth, back and forth, and I clipped a bit of flesh from the larger shark. The sea shrieked to the slashing of teeth and the flashing of flipper and fin that sliced the water. Again, Baby Electra screamed, and I turned to see the smaller shark close its mouth upon the ragged, red flesh of her wound and rip from her a huge piece of meat. Quick as a blink the shark bit again, enlarging the hole in Baby Electra, and again – and again she screamed out her anguish and helplessness. I moved against the shark to ram him and seize him with my teeth. He saw me coming, however, and swam off followed by the other shark.

'You are bleeding,' Baby Electra said to me in an agonized voice that squeaked out of her.

The sharks had opened wounds along my tail and head, and had bitten off a piece of my fluke. They had done much worse to Baby Electra. Blood flowed freely from the hole in her. I did not want to believe how huge it had grown.

'They are waiting,' she said, speaking of the sharks.

'Yes.'

'Waiting for you to weaken with loss of blood before they attack again.'

'Yes.'

'Every time you try to incapacitate one of them, the other has a chance to work at me.'

'Yes.'

'If you did kill one of the sharks, the other would kill me.'

'That accurately encapsulates our dilemma.'

'If you keep on this way, you will die with me.'

'No, I will not – and you are going to live.'

'That is a beautiful thought,' she said. 'And you are a beautiful whale.'

'I am your brother,' I said, 'and you are my sister.'

'I know. Then tell me, Brother, what happens when we die?'

I winced at the whimper of terror I heard in her voice. Then I told her things that she would have been told when she had grown a little older.

'There is no true death,' I said. 'Each being . . .'

I tried to bathe the whole of her in waves of healing sound as I told her that each being, each thing, each act – from whales to rocks to the joy a mother feels at giving birth to her child – dwells only and always in a single instant of time. All these moments themselves, this infinitude of bright, marvelous moments as perfect as nautilus shells shining in the sun, exist eternally. They can never be destroyed.

'Each moment since your conception, each self that you ever were, remains alive: all the many Baby Electras that have swum through the seas in life's gladness.'

She had only moments to think about this, and she said, 'Then why can't I live now my other selves?'

'Because of time,' I said. 'We journey from one moment to another, swept along by the current of time, which moves in one direction only. We cannot easily go backward, in our bodies.'

'I want to go back! I want to see my mother again! Where is she?'

'In the same place you last saw her. She has not ceased to be,

350

any more than a once-visited sea ceases to exist simply because you have left it.'

'I want to live with her again! And with you, Arjuna, always and forever, as on the day we met.'

'You can, through the perfect memory of quenging.'

'But I cannot quenge! And even when I was able to, I did not have this ability.'

'You are still a baby. Although quenging is always perfect in itself, part of its perfection is that it grows ever more perfect the deeper and vaster it becomes.'

'But how can that be? And who has such perfect memory?'

'The Old Ones do. They can live in all times and all places, in a moment, at once.'

'But they cannot live in the future where they are *not*. Where I will never be now.'

'But they can and do, because they are. All things always *are*.' We surfaced to breathe together. 'The future contains the past as the sea does you – and in you lives every seal, salmon, and whisper of love that has ever passed within. Your heart will go on beating in each drop of water in every ocean on every world and in the bright thunder of the stars that have yet to be born. Nothing can ever be subtracted from creation.'

This last conversation occurred in what the humans would have calculated to be a few seconds but which we measured with the precious moments of our lives. Then Baby Electra pressed close to me. She took strength from the beating of my heart, as I did from hers.

After another moment, she said to me, 'How I love the world, Arjuna! How I love you!'

Even as her life's blood rushed out of her, I could feel her gathering in her courage to face the final test of any orca: to die well, despite the horror and pain of the circumstances – to die saying yes to her life.

'Here they come, Arjuna!' she cried out. 'Here they come!'

The two sharks exploded into motion, swimming straight towards us.

'And here I go! Here I go!'

Baby Electra then did an astonishing thing. Almost before I could think, she moved away from my side and drove herself through the water to meet the sharks head on. She was much smaller than I and so could accelerate more quickly through the reddened sea. By the time I gained full speed, she had nearly reached the sharks. Because she would die no matter what I did, I knew that she hoped I would swim off and so save myself. I still wanted, however, to save her.

'It hurts!' she screamed to me. 'It hurts so bad!'

The sharks closed on her, slashing, savaging, biting, and tearing at already torn tissues. Baby Electra met them with a fury of her own, but her tiny jaws did little damage. Just as I finally reached her, she cried out to me, 'I am not afraid any more!'

I rammed the smaller shark in the side hard enough to fracture his liver. He swam off in a stunned agony. I turned on the larger shark, which was not quite so large as I. As he ripped huge chunks out of Baby Electra, lost in a frenzy of bloodlust and feasting, I grabbed him up in my teeth. In a maneuver that my grandmother had taught me, I flipped the shark upside down. Suspended in the water thus in tonic immobility, he could not gather water to his gills, and so he could not breathe. I held the shark fast in my jaws, grinding down in my rage of grief. I waited through many, many heartbeats for him to drown.

At last, I swam up to Baby Electra. Miraculously, although torn open in many places, gushing blood, she still lived.

'I am quenging, Arjuna! I am quenging!'

She spoke her last words to me in a soft, lovely voice. Then she died. The sea drank in the blood that continued welling up from her many wounds.

'Quenge, Sister, quenge,' I said. 'The ocean is yours.'

I lingered a moment before I swam away and left her there.

Few humans conceive of what it is like to be an orca; they do not really understand that our living place is also our burial place in the great Ocean that is a single, immortal, planetary being. In death, Baby Electra had been interred in life – even as I found myself entombed by my outrage at her perishing.

So it was that I swam after the shark that I had wounded. Out of my lust for vengeance, unknown among my kind, I swam through the sea's maddened waters pursuing this beautiful, innocent creature. When I caught up to the shark, I killed him as I had his companion. I left him floating upside down. Except for the two sharks, I had never killed fish and not eaten them.

How could I eat when my belly churned to bursting with a meat so black and foul that I wanted to vomit it out? How I wished to destroy yet again the creatures that had killed Baby Electra! As my wrath deepened, I realized that I should direct it not at the sharks who had only done what sharks do, but at the man who did with rifle and grenades what no living thing should ever do. It was he – and the humans themselves – that I hated.

Hated. In a sonic boom of horrible understanding, I realized that I had a name for the dreadful, new emotion that had come alive within me after Pherkad died. Strangely, in all the long days since that terrible day, as I learned many words in many languages, I had thought of hatred as a purely human phenomenon, as natural and unique to human beings as building war ships and making harpoons with the human hand. Now I knew that I hated just as stupidly as the humans themselves did; in truth, I hated a million times more. It was hatred – hot, dark, and bottomless – that had destroyed my ability to quenge.

So much about the humans I hated! I hated their fishhooks and boats and nets, their concrete and chlorine. I hated tasers, lasers, phasers, razors, whale gazers, and self-praisers. Slavery I hated with a black and bitter bile, as I did their machines and smokes and flames and noises. I hated clocks that tore the humans away from the joy of golden moments and clothing that cut them off from

life. The wailing of their babies given gin or sugar to soothe them
– who could not hate such things? I hated their swarms and herds
and huddled masses that manufactured the consensus reality that
numbed their minds. And more, much more, I hated the dimwitted,
censoring, sniveling, little totalitarians who told others what they
must believe and say. As well I hated flea bombs and atom bombs,
corn fields and killing fields, celluloid murders and digital deaths.
I hated the murder of their children's hopes. And pesticides, herbicides, fungicides, genocides, suicides, matricides I hated along with
the hands that wrought them. I hated their hardened hearts. I hated
their lying, soul-sucked eyes, their deformed ears, their mouths full
of excuses and resentments. Their obesity I hated almost as much
as I did their emaciation. I hated their eyelids, closed to that which
they did not wish to see, as I did their anuses, the ten billion anuses
that befouled the waters of the world. I hated their breasts full of
poisons. I hated the very pores of their skin, which oozed sweat
and chemicals and insincerity and fear.

How I hated and hated and hated and hated! I hated my own
hatred, and most of all, I hated my hating of it.

As I moved off away from that place of blood and death into
wild waters moaning with a pain that had no cure, a single question cannibalized my thoughts: What would I do with all this
hate? I could not return to the Institute, nor could I bear to swim
once more in the icy ocean at the top of the world with my first
family. As full as I was with the evil elixir that I had drunk freely,
I could not bring myself to poison those I loved. I simply did not
belong in the company of people.

No, my future must dwell with the humans. I had tried to move
them through logic, reason, and even wit, despite knowing that
the humans, most of them, had walled themselves away from such
things. Now I must try a different approach. The wind whispered
to me disquieting thoughts, and the ocean roared like a wounded
bear in my blood. I heard fate calling me on.

I would swim after the humans, I decided. I would seek them

out across the Blue Desert and the Darkmoon Basin and round the Summer Sea. I would pursue them through the Magenta Shallows and on the Vermillion Sands and along the coastlines of their continents. I would sing for them a rhapsody in red. I would hunt them in their hopes' last goodness and in their desperate dreams, down and down through nightmare to the cold, crushing hell of their ten billion damned and bleeding souls.

19

I swam. I killed fish and ate them. I excreted. I breathed, and I remembered. I slept. I dreamed. I swam some more. Ocean spun me around and around through long days of dark thoughts and nights that seemed forever suspended between death and morning. To where did I swim? I did not know.

Although I still had the maps of the heavens and the world that my uncle Alnitak had given me, I cast them aside, for no colorful finger of coral, no shining constellation, could point my way. I thought of Baby Electra nearly every waking moment; she still lived inside me, at least. She did *not* seem to dwell in any of the billions of water droplets that broke across my skin like uncountable tiny, silvery bombs, although I had promised she would sing in each one. Neither did Zavijah nor Pherkad nor my great-grandmother nor any of the Old Ones accompany me. Even Helen and Gabi were gone. Alone and lost, I called to the many people I had loved. I called and called, listening for the slightest hint of a murmur of response, but no one called back to me. The living sea, usually so bright with sound, had fallen as silent as iron.

How fiercely I wanted to join those who had abandoned me for happier seas! How I longed to die! I might gladly have done so, beaching myself on the sands of some lonely island, but I was afraid – afraid *not* of the extinction of my puny self and the black hole of time's ending that would swallow me up. No, I feared another thing. What if the humans were right, after all, in their belief in the transmigration of souls? What if it was my karma to be reborn, not as a snail or a snake or even a dog but rather as a full, breathing, bedeviled, raving human? The horror of such a possibility made me want to swim on forever – and hate kept me alive.

My rage for revenge, burning like a hot liquor along my blood, took some of the sting out of my many wounds and diverted my attention from the loss of the tip of my fluke that the shark had bitten off. It made me want to go down inside myself to consider more important matters. The deeper I dived, the stranger my soul looked to me, like a reef composed of razor-sharp knives of violet and orange and other colors that did not dwell together easily. Two opposing desires tore at each other: As much as I still wanted to find a cure for the world's pain (at least the twisted, unnatural torment that the humans had brought into the world), even more I wanted to *cause* the humans the bitterest of suffering.

I sought the wide, wide world for them. One day, with the wind out of the north and little chops of water moving brightly across the sea's surface like millions of silvery fish, I caught hint of a distant booming and pings of human sonar. I swam toward this noise to verify its source. As I ventured west, the noise grew louder and louder. Soon other sounds nearly drowned it out. Nearly all of these came from the flutes of orcas. It did not take long for a family of the Others to approach me. They screamed as they swam, and called out to me and anyone else who happened to be listening the direst of warnings:

'The humans come! Flee! Flee! Flee or be taken and die!'

So distraught was the mother of this small family that she did not mind when I turned to swim with them. Although I longed to hunt human beings, I did not want to encounter a ship of slavers that might capture me and return me to Sea Circus.

The mother and her four children – along with a brother and a niece – raced through the ocean without speaking. In the best of times, the Others do not converse as does my kind, and so can seem nearly non-social. Today, with the humans fast approaching from beyond the blue, curved horizon, the orcas I had encountered swam in a silent fury. The brother bore a wound in his side, from which trailed blood. One of the children moved in jerks and pauses as if disoriented. She zanged continually, but seemed unable to find her way in the sea without her mother's help.

'The humans come! Flee! Flee! Flee!'

This warning issued not from any of the orcas of the family I had joined, but rang throughout the wind-whipped waters ahead of us. Thunder boomed there, too, as pings of sonar raked my skin like vibrating knives. A few moments later, a stampede of cetaceans tore the sea with bitter sounds that told of their great numbers and their fright. Soon a tsunami of orcas, dolphins, humpbacks, seis, and blue whales came into view. They fled the still-unseen humans in a great wave of spasming, breathing, racing whale flesh.

'Flee! Flee! Flee!'

I breached and looked out to the west from which these many whales came. My eyes seemed to have sharpened during my time with the humans, and I descried along the horizon huge angular gray shapes that could only be human ships. Smoke clouded the air above them. They moved with a frightening machine speed straight toward us.

'Flee or be taken!' the mother of the family I accompanied cried out. Her name was Lesath. 'The humans come! The humans come!'

'No,' I called back to her. 'The humans *do* come, but not to take you. They are hunting *me*.'

'And who are you, Strange One?'

'My name is Arjuna, of the Blue Aria Family of the Faithful Thoughtplayer Clan.'

'I have heard of you!' Lesath cried out. 'You killed a human! The whole of the Day Gray Sea sings of this!'

I had little time to reflect on the unfortunate chance that some orca must have overheard my recounting my deed to Alkurah and Unukalhai in the bad moments when Baby Electra and I had fled the Institute for the supposed safety of the open sea. As inexorably as the explosion of a bomb, the news of what I had done had passed like a shockwave from orca to orca and family to family, and had filled the ocean. I could no more escape my infamy than I could the humans who came for me.

'So many humans to hunt one whale?' Lesath called out. 'They must want you very badly, Manslayer!'

I would have slunk away to spare her and her family the humans' revenge, but it was not clear in which direction I should swim. I thought to race toward the rapidly approaching ships and ram one of them as the deep gods themselves once had done. These ships, however, so huge and gray, I would not be able to sink, for surely they were wrought of iron.

And suddenly, I had no chance to think at all. Metallic sonar pings drilled the water like thousands of bullets of angry sound. From far below came the screech of the propellers of ships that moved like sharks beneath the sea's surface. The big guns on one of the ships coughed out fire and smoke, and the air exploded. Guns boomed out again and again as the rush of fleeing cetaceans finally fell upon us. There were hundreds of them, mothers and fathers and sisters and sons, many bloodied and broken. All hurried away from the humans in a panic of confusion that caused them to bump and collide with each other and with us, in a most unwhalelike manner. The mass of their writhing bodies swept us along. Now the very water erupted in deafening explosions that drove away all plan or reason. I could not hear myself think. More explosions concussed the sea on every side, nearer, and I could not think but could only move away. I could not, however, find *away*; I could not hear the zangs of sonar that I aimed through the clouds of blood and the flotsam of flesh and feces that boiled all around me. Boom! Boom! Boom! – and then the entire world boomed into a red and terrifying silence. A huge humpback rammed into me, and I could not hear my own scream of pain.

I surfaced, and some ships closed on the maddened mass of whales; the iron machines moved in from the east, northeast, and west. How fast they moved – faster than a stunned and wounded whale could swim!

'Swim south!' I called out. No one could hear me; I could not hear myself. 'Swim, before it is too late!'

I moved off toward the clear water in the direction that I had named. I hoped that more ships did not await us there. Lesath and her family followed me. So did some of the other whales. Many, however, dazed and bruised, fled toward the north. A few actually charged toward the ships in the east as if they could not perceive them; and many – far too many cetaceans! – stopped moving out of sheer exhaustion or dropped off into dying or death.

After a while, we reached a place of peace – if only a relative and temporary one. The water grew clear again, and I could not feel the drumbeat of exploding bombs. I looked around at all the many whales schooling together as for safety. I saw Lesath's family of Others and perhaps four families of orcas of my own kind. Some humpbacks swam side by side with a few belugas. There were some minkes and blue whales, too. I could not count the number of dolphins who braved the company of the Others, who in more normal times might have attacked them. Never, I thought, in all the histories or the rhapsodies of my people had I ever heard of such a gathering.

And the humans will capture or kill all of them to get to me!

As my head cleared, a little, I called to mind the images of the many ships that I had seen on one of the Institute's screens. Words – human words – for the parts of these ships came to me: Turret. Jackstaff. Conning tower. Gun-mount. Siren brackets. Chaff launchers. Flight deck. Flying shark. Rocket launcher. Search radar. Depth charges.

The flotilla that had destroyed so many whales, then, was no assemblage of fishing boats sent after me but rather a fleet of warships. Had the humans, I wondered, instigated yet another of their mass killing sprees that had caught up us whales by bad chance? I could not recall seeing a single ship reduced to a flaming hulk. No, I thought, remembering, surely these death ships troubled the waters in practice for battle. War games, the humans called such exercises. They found such violence to be fun! How different we whales are! We play games with words and ideas, with eros, and with songs; sometimes when the moon is full and rings out the music of the spheres, we like to play games with games.

The humans do not hunt me!

How foolish I had been to think that the humans would have sent hundreds of ships to execute a single orca! How vain! The monstrosity of my vanity approached that of the humans themselves. This realization caused me to laugh long and bitter and deep. I laughed and I laughed at myself until it hurt. Then I looked around at all the wounded whales, and I laughed no more.

Near me, scarcely a few body lengths away in the water, a baby dolphin whimpered to her mother, who could not console her for the baby's jaw had been blown off. A humpback glided by bearing a hole blown out of her side that reminded me of the bloody divot that the shark had bitten out of Baby Electra. So many whales the humans had hurt in their games! So many of my people blown to bits, blown to hell, blown to kingdom come, blown to smithereens.

We waited in the quiet water for our hearing to return, and after what seemed an eternity of waves breaking against savaged skin, for many of us it mostly did. Others, though, remained deaf. One of these, an old orca named Marfak, said that he did not wish to live absent the comforting sounds of his family and helpless in the water. He announced, 'I will find an island with a broad beach, and I will lay myself on the sand until I die. Then the humans might feel my despair and witness their handiwork that caused it.'

'The humans never feel such things,' an orca named Alioth said. 'And I doubt that they would recognize in you the work of their own hands.'

Marfak, of course, could not understand these words, but he somehow seemed to intuit them. He said, 'Someday, the humans might feel *something* – someday.'

And with that he swam off to find his island.

'The humans *do* feel,' I said, after he had gone, 'many, many things. Only a few of them, though, sense how desperately the world despairs of them.'

'And who are you,' an orca from the Emerald Murmurers asked me, 'that you speak so surely of what animals such as the humans feel?'

'He is Arjuna the Manslayer,' Lesath declared, introducing me. 'It is said that he spoke with the humans before he killed one.'

'What!' Alioth said. He was long and quick and unmarked by the humans' depth charges. 'How could he speak with the humans who cannot speak?'

'What?' a little dolphin called out. 'What are you orcas saying?'

'I cannot understand you!' one of the humpbacks added. 'Can you not speak the one and true language?'

I had a hard time conversing with all the people around me. The various orca families of my kind spoke with thick and different accents, while the dialects of the Others were much harder to understand. The humpbacks, of course, spoke the nearly incomprehensible words of their own sweetly-songed humpback language, and so it was with the blue whales, the minkes, and all the others. Some of us wished that one of the deep gods might act as interpreter, for it was said that the Great Ones the humans call sperm whales can fathom all languages, and indeed, all things. The deep gods, however, do not speak with lesser beings.

'There is only one true language,' I said to the humpback, 'and no one in Ocean has yet spoken it. We must create this language ourselves.'

Over the next few days, I went among the assembled whales and gathered in the various sound pictures that each kind painted with its flutes. In the way that I had learned from Helen and the other linguists in the study of human languages, I analyzed and listened for the deep structures of meaning that formed up in colorful harmonics. I looked for the overlap and interplay of speech patterns. The other whales helped me in this game. Sound by sound, word by word, we sculpted together a sort of crude but wondrously vivid pidgin tongue through which we could speak to each other.

'This language,' I said to Lesath and a humpback named Bilbudidundun, 'lacks nuance and fluidity, but it is a beginning.'

I went among the orcas, dolphins, humpbacks, and all the others, and I touched their wounds with my voice as gently as I could. We related to each other our many stories. One of the dolphins (the brother of the child whose jaw had been destroyed) wanted to know everything about my journey from the Sea of Ice to the humans' punishment pools at Sea Circus – and beyond. He took a particular interest in the carnage at the Institute that had left Baby Electra so vulnerable to the sharks. Even after I had done so a few times, he inveigled me to recount once more the story of her death.

'Tell me,' he said, 'how baby Electra charged the sharks to save you.'

The other whales had other concerns. With the whole hodge-podge clan gathered around us, Alioth said, 'It may be that the humans in the swarm of ships that killed so many of us were not hunting you, or us. Other humans, however, are sure to do so. You have killed a man, and so how can the humans look away from your breaking of the Great Covenant?'

He regarded me as many of the whales did: with a mixture of awe, fear, admiration, and dread.

'Perhaps the time has come,' I said, 'for the Great Covenant to end.'

A cacophony of very disparate voices burst out into the water in a colorful cloud of moans, shrills, trills, and squeaks. Clearly, most of the whales about me had never contemplated such an outrageous idea.

'Let us suppose that you are right,' a blue whale with an unsayable name announced as she contemplated this. Her stomach had been blown open by a depth charge, and she was dying. 'All things *do* have an ending. If the Great Covenant is to be no more, however, how is it upon a single orca of the Blue Aria Family of the Faithful Thoughtplayer to decide this?'

'I have not decided anything,' I said. 'I have only wondered.'

'Of course you have only wondered,' the great blue whale said to me. 'You are only an orca, so how could you do more than kill wantonly and wonder at your deed? Only the deep gods would know if the Covenant should be broken.'

'Were the deep gods here,' I replied, 'I would speak with them – or try to.'

I swam in close to her, and brushed up against her side. So huge she was, so magnificent, so beautiful! How her great heart boomed from deep inside her and sent waves of sweet sonance pouring over me! I touched her as perhaps no orca had ever touched a blue whale, as I would a beloved and dying elder of my own family. I knew she could sense how her mortal wound grieved me. Her own grief at what had happened to her and the other whales as a result of the humans' war games seemed to change into a wholly different substance. As if I had drunk sparkling clean water, I felt her trust pass into me.

'I believe you *might* be able to speak with the deep gods,' she said. 'There is one – the oldest whale in the ocean – who could tell you of the Great Covenant.'

'Have you seen her?' I asked.

'I have never swum near *him*,' she said. 'However, I have listened

364

to the accounts of others. The eldest of the deep gods dwells in waters far away.'

'Where? Where?' I asked her.

'It is said that in the Moon of High Summer, he hunts alone in the Long Song Sea.'

'Then I will journey there,' I said.

In the human way, I did a quick calculation. I had two months to reach this distant northern water.

'I wish I could accompany you,' she said. 'Although it would make me sad to see you die   almost as sad as I am to soon be leaving you.'

'But my wounds are healing,' I said. 'Why should I die?'

'Because the one of whom I have spoken will most likely kill you.'

'Does he fear orcas that much?'

'He fears nothing on this world – or any other,' she told me. 'No, he would slay you, I think, for disturbing his solitude.'

I felt a shudder run through her as death bit into her and began dragging her away from me.

'Of course,' she said, 'I might be wrong. If you are completely truthful with him and find something interesting to say, the deep god might decide to help you.'

'Who can ever speak the complete truth?'

'You can,' she said. 'If you do not, you will speak to me in the waters of Agathange.'

And with that, she died. None of the orcas swimming near us thought to violate her flesh. When they and the rest of us whales left this place, it would take a long while for the sharks to scavenge her great blue body.

After that, the time came for us many whales, in our different kinds, to swim our different ways. In the language we had crafted together, we promised each other that if ever again we chanced to meet along the blue byways of the sea, we should act as friends do, neither hunting nor fleeing nor ignoring. Could the hungry orcas of the few Others who eyed the dancing dolphins keep this little covenant? Could the humpbacks and the seis? Only time would tell. In the singing hope that our remarkable camaraderie had engendered, I said goodbye to the battered whales. Then I turned toward a long journey and a conversation with a very great whale about a much greater covenant.

20

On a fine evening of brilliant stars and clear water, I set my sight on the North Star and found the sparkling eyes of the Osprey constellation gazing at it from the west. I followed those two stars, listening intently for any sound of the human ships. None could I detect. The fleet of warships must have sailed off into other seas to play their cruel games.

For many days and nights of relentless swimming along strange currents, I made my way toward the Long Song Sea. I hunted as I journeyed, but I did not encounter any great numbers of salmon or other fish, and so I often went hungry. My empty belly growled its discontent even as my mind felt overfull with thoughts and memories. Sometimes, with the sun poised low in the sky and its rays brightening the water to a warm blue, I felt sure that I *did* hear Baby Electra calling to me. Dear, sweet, doomed Gabi spoke to me, too. So did Helen. Sometimes I heard my mother singing songs of yearning and calling me home. Often I wished to turn toward her lovely voice and leave behind the hate that drove me, as I might discard my daily droppings. Even more, though, I needed to hear the deep god's words and perhaps find in them a way that I could hurt the humans deep in their souls. This, I told myself, was my fate. And so I swam on through luminous seas ringing with compelling sounds; I swam through storms and murmurs of anguish and through the blood of Baby Electra and the beautiful blue whale, which left in my mouth an ineradicable and bitter taste.

I had much time to think, and to think deeply. Much of my brooding concerned the humans. How desperately I still sought to understand them! How pitifully poorly I did! One day, with the wind out of the north and little white-capped waves breaking apart and leaving their foam like a delicate painting on the surface of the sea, I chanced to think of the humans' mathematics. It came to me that certain humans would try to analyze the ocean's beguiling brushstrokes through equations and models built by their computing machines. Of all the human disciplines I had encountered at the Institute, I had most abhorred mathematics. How not? What whale needs numbers, ratios, and triangles? What whale can easily perceive the tiny, squiggly visual symbols that represent mathematical ideas? Then, too, does not mathematics form the basis of human science upon which rests all technology? And was not the humans' murderous technology of machines, poisons, bombs, and fires destroying the world?

The farther I swam toward the Eyes of the Osprey and the Long Song Sea, the more it seemed that I must venture into the great ocean of mathematics if ever I was to delve into the human soul. I had 'read' but not really absorbed many books on various mathematical topics, and their symbols, definitions, axioms, and theorems gathered inside me like a bellyful of undigested stones. I realized that if I wished, I could vomit up the stones one by one in order to behold them. I could do this hateful thing in order to better hate the humans.

Somewhere in the great gray surge of the Skua Sea, I realized that I could replace each of the humans' mathematical symbols with the same sonic ideoplasts that we whales use to compose our tone poems and our rhapsodies. Was not all mathematics built upon ideas and an inherent logic shared by all sapient beings? Was not mathematics, at its bottom, a crystalizing and enfolding of language into a precise and jewel-like form? And if it was possible to speak such a strange yet fundamental language, as I was beginning to, then might not a whale just as well sing into being entire new worlds of glittering relationships and conceptions?

To my astonishment, I found that mathematics was alive with the most beautiful of musics. One day, as I breathed between the waves of the Dreaming Sea, I heard all the numbers ringing as the stars ring – and each note led up and outward in a great silvery arpeggio of sound into the deeps of the universe. I knew then that I could count to infinity, if I had both desire and time. After that, mathematics came easily. I found an unexpected pleasure in proving that any even number greater than two could be expressed as the sum of two primes. I felt 99% certain that I had made no mistake in my proof.

Such an elegance there was in mathematics! So many possibilities did I behold in the cruel, two-handed beings who had created such a wonder! What other miracles of mind and soul might be theirs if they were to let go of their murdering ways? That they could not – *would* not – let go I felt certain. And so in an irony that my dear, departed Helen would have appreciated, instead of admiring the humans for discovering mathematics, I hated them all the more for failing to discover the deepest of all oceans and thus turning away from their inherent splendor.

In such a state of bitter antinomy, I finally entered the currents of the Long Song Sea. Cold were the waters here that streamed down from the northern ocean, though no icebergs could I detect. The gray waves carried the wind's soughing and swelled with a great loneliness. Somewhere, far beneath me in the dark ocean, the lone deep gods found their way through a gelid, lightless silence in search of the great squid that fed them. I could not dive into the crushing, killing depths to greet them. Instead, I swam along the thin tissues of the surface waters, waiting for one cachalot or another to surface.

I listened, too. In dense, clear seas, the deep gods' voices, traveling through deep water sound channels, could sometimes be heard from a thousand miles away. No other being in the Ocean – or on earth – speaks with such force. The sound of a hungry cachalot searching for prey cracks out louder than the peak noise of a hard rock concert or the roar of a jet airplane taking off. Some say that it breaks through the water like the explosion of a rifle shot three feet from one's ear.

I did not intend to get quite so close to the one I hunted. If the blue whale had told true, then one, and only one, of the deep gods claimed the center of the Long Song Sea as his own. If I could locate this center in the wild, unknown waters that surged around me, then surely the eldest of the deep gods should not be hard to find.

For half of a month, however, even though I swam in long, slow spirals looking and listening as hard as I could, I did not detect the slightest trace of him. What if he had got caught up and killed in one of the humans' war games? Or what if a whaler had slaughtered him and boiled him down for his oil? Then, too, the ocean is vast. What if I listened and looked through endless green waves for the rest of my life and still did not find the one I sought?

Then one day, with gray clouds nearly touching the sea from above and cold, upwellings of water streaming all about me, there came a faint sound from far away. I had trouble perceiving its direction. I turned first one way and then another, listening. I swam, and the sound grew into a whisper. I swam further toward what I perceived as its source. My heart beat so loud in my ears, however, that it seemed to drown out the whisper, which broke apart. Silence filled the ocean as I swam on. I continued listening, and I watched, and I waited. In the silence between heartbeats, I listened with a stillness of mind for the long cerulean song of the sea. The whisper came again, now louder! I swam toward it as gracefully as I could, not wanting any clumsy motion of fin or fluke to drive it away. I swam for many moments of time suspended in that bright, clear ocean beyond and beneath time, which cannot be measured in minutes or hours or days.

There came a moment when the whisper rang through the water with such a force that I could not fail to follow it. I knew it to be the zang of sonar of a deep god. I swam toward it with all the strength that I could summon from weary muscles and a body that still ached with many wounds. I swam, and I swam, for a mile, for a hundred – I did not care. I would have swum right off curve of the world in pursuit of this sound that called to me and promised so much.

At last, I reached a place where powerful sonar zangs rose up through the water from far beneath me and shivered the skin of my belly and the bones of my spine. I ceased swimming. I waited. In the deeps below, I thought, more than a mile down in an inky black cavern of water that only the deep gods would dare to delve, the one of whom I had been told battled and tore apart a giant squid. Or perhaps he only meditated and remembered, alone in silent darkness. Did he know that I listened for him as I bobbed up and down like a little black and white buoy on the sea's surface waves? Would he care that I wished to speak with him? How long must I wait to find out? The moments of my life paid out like a coiled harpoon line, and stretched out to many minutes and then to more than an hour.

And then something shifted in the water, and I felt a flutter of an eddy as delicate as the beating of a butterfly's wings. He rises! I thought. He rises! He did not, however, rise quickly, for doing so would have taken him through the layers of the sea's pressures with a speed that could kill even a deep god. I waited some more. At last, he breached, and I made my way to the surface to breathe with him. He blew out stale, steamy air with nearly the force of an erupting geyser. How huge he was, the largest of his kind I had ever seen! He was more than twice my length and many times as massive. Scars cut his great, blunt, wrinkled head, and the broken shaft of a harpoon stuck out of his back. A white carapace of scar tissue covered his blind right eye; it looked something like the cataracts that cloud many human eyes but even more like burned and hardened flesh. The deep god turned to regard me with his good eye, and he zanged me with his sonar with an unexpected softness that suggested he did not want to hurt me.

Then he spoke to me. His voice rang out rich, powerful, and pure. It stunned me with its clarity – even as I realized that the deep god painted for me the most vivid and clear of sound pictures, whose complexity I could not comprehend. I spoke back, and the deep god seemed to listen. His response came in a brilliant array of sonic ideoplasts, colored by a deep and bottomless laughter. He turned to show me his massively muscled tail as if either to strike me with this killing club or to swim away from me. He did neither. He drew in a huge breath, and pushed his head into the water, which brought his great tail into the air, pointing up toward the sun. Then he dove and disappeared into the gloom beneath us. I understood that I had interrupted one of his feeding cycles and that he still had squid to hunt.

Over the next few days, we repeated such encounters. Finally, the time came when I zanged the deep god's belly and saw that it was full of freshly-caught and still writhing squid. He paused to speak with me for a longer time, and I suggested that we create together a mutual language, even as the many whales and I had done at the gathering. The deep god laughed at this. He responded to me in a spray of jeweled sounds so bright and multifaceted that their liquid shimmer nearly deafened me. He spoke on and on through the golden burn of the sun and the silvery coolness of the moon with a patience that astonished me nearly as much as it shamed me.

I spoke, too. I told him of Pherkad and everything that had happened in my journeys. Did he understand any of my words? I could not tell. I spoke of the humans, relating much of the knowledge I had gained through their books and the Net. I recounted scenes from my favorite novels. I explained how I had learned the languages of the humans, though they had only the faintest inkling of mine. So it would have to be with us, I said, but this time in reverse. If we could fashion no lingua franca in which to converse, then he would have to learn my orca speech, for I could not quite follow the movements of beguiling ideoplasts that danced out of his flute.

His response to this was to laugh all the harder. Something in the sound of his great voice resonated with the much quieter one whispering inside me. I felt like laughing, too – why, I did not know. I should have been totally frustrated – and I was, I was! I had chanced my very life, or at least its purpose, on speaking with this very old whale. I should have despaired at the way the meanings of the deep god's utterances eluded me.

Then, strangely, as I began laughing, too, I felt myself moving forward into a shared understanding of something fundamental. The essential structures of our two languages, I saw, formed up into very similar patterns of meanings. As I had tried to explain to Helen, the chords of speech that we orcas make resonate with meaning only in relation to each other. The sperm whales had only deepened this dynamic by adding a whole, new layer of resonance: They made higher, meta-meanings through the juxtaposition and echo of meanings themselves. Thus the import and gist of what a deep god said could shift as quickly as rays of light dancing along a play of water droplets. It would be impossible to apprehend the beautiful but maddening complexity of the deep gods' language without appreciating this.

I spent the next forty days and nights trying to do exactly that. There came a day when I realized that I would never be able to speak as the deep gods themselves do, for my little brain simply could not hold the totality of their language. On that day, however – storm clouds schooled in the west even as the sea held calm – I also realized that I could speak to this great, patient deep god, after a fashion. I began by telling him my name.

'Arjuna, Arjuna,' he repeated as if putting tongue to a new kind of fish distasteful to him. Then aimed his voice at me, and said, 'Why?'

'What do you mean?' I asked him.

His good eye closed as if in disappointment.

'Why?' he asked me again.

Why what? Why was I here? Why were we alive? Why is there something we call the universe rather than nothing? Why did this deep god put to me such a simple question that could have no simple answer?

'Why?' he said a third time.

I felt him tensing his muscles for another dive. I somehow sensed – perhaps this was only a guess – that his query was more a test of my intelligence than an attempt to gather information from me. Did I have the wit to perceive a whole reef of meaning from a single sprig of coral? *Why* – why should this deep god deign to talk to me if I did not?

'I have come here,' I told him, 'to discuss the humans and the Great Covenant.'

'Then discuss that with yourself.'

He drew in a huge breath, and made to dive.

'Wait!' I cried out. 'I have spoken with the—'

'I do not care about the humans, and I care even less about you.'

'But I need to ask—'

'You cannot save the world, Arjuna. Try, if you wish, to save yourself.'

How had he known what I would ask him? Could he hear my thoughts? Or could he perceive in the seed of my wonderings the whole organism into which it might grow?

'You are—'

'Rude?' he asked me. 'Arrogant? Dismissive? How—'

How else should he be to a simple-minded orca who had disturbed his solitude? But, no – that *how* question was too obvious.

How, how, how? I heard buried in this abrupt sound a subtler and almost silent resonance.

'How would I *like* you to be?' I asked him. His eye gleamed with surprise.

'Very good,' he said. 'Well . . . how?'

I thought about this. I told him of a character in one of the humans' books.

'As I perceive, laughter comes quickly to your mind and flute,' I said. 'The one with whom I hope to speak finds laughter in all things, especially in himself.'

'Go on,' he laughed out.

'Well, you can be stern, even harsh, but you are essentially kind.'

'Go on.'

'You love the truth, though you believe that no mind can encompass all of it.'

'Go on.'

'You try to perceive this truth through a million million eyes, even though you have only two.'

'One, actually, that works. Go on.'

'You are wise and caring, but in pursuit of the truth, you do not mind causing others – and yourself – the most bitter of pain. You call this mental anguish of new realizations the *anglsan*.'

'Oh, ho! I like that word – go on.'

'The highest purpose, you teach, is to say yes to life in its totality and to live each moment, even the terrible ones, with joy.'

For a while, as the sea sloshed gray and mountainous around us, I told him more of the traits of the great teacher that I invited him to be. When I had finished, he said, 'Now that is a game I might enjoy. I will be an alien come to teach the weak-minded humans how to be greater, all the while concealing the fact that I am actually a human myself masquerading as a wiser and more intelligent being.'

'It should not be exactly a masquerade,' I said. 'In truth, you *have* become a greater being, yes? Your patience, your wisdom, your tenderness – these cannot be an act. You must find these things inside yourself, and bring them forth.'

'Ha, ho! *Must* I, then? Well, young orca who thinks of himself as human, do not worry: I am large; I contain multitudes. So let us play.'

I blew out an old breath and drew in a new. The deep god had consented to talk to me! I must be careful of what I said.

'I would like to know your name,' I told him.

'I do not have a name, as you think of names, and if I did, you would not be able to say it. Why don't you call me Old Father?'

'Yes – I was about to suggest that myself.'

'And you, Arjuna – should I call you by your name for your star? Or would you prefer . . . Manslayer?'

His voice zanged my blood with teeth of ice. How had he known? Had he heard my thoughts? Had I betrayed myself through certain emotions that I had allowed to color the sounds of my utterances?

In my silence, he sussed out these questions and many more. He said, 'Oh, ho, Arjuna of the Blue Aria Family of the Faithful Thoughtplayer Clan! I had heard that you might be swimming my way. The whole ocean sings of you.'

'Sings in what language?' I asked. 'Do you understand the speech of the humpbacks and the blue whales – and my own?'

'Of course I do.'

'Then you could have conversed with me in Orcalish any time you wished!'

'Of course I could. But of course I will not, ha, ha!'

'Very well, then, Old Father. I have come to you to—'

'You seek answers to questions that you believe you cannot answer yourself.'

'Is it that obvious to you?'

'Once every few generations,' he said, 'one of your kind comes to us seeking wisdom and truth.'

'That is strange,' I said. 'I did not know your kind spoke to mine.'

'I did not say that we did.'

'You do not like us orcas very much, do you?'

'Should we? You eat our babies.'

'My kind,' I said, 'eat only fish.'

'Aha! Then you are a strict pescavarian, are you?'

I hesitated in my response. I let a few waves break over me.

'Out of necessity,' I told him, 'I once ate a white bear.'

'Oh, Arjuna – oh, oh, oh! The things we must do from necessity!'

'I would never eat one of your kind!'

'No? Did you not eat seals and a human? Were these deeds done out of necessity?'

'Some things are necessary . . . in a different way.'

'Oh, ho – that is so very true! Shall we discuss how necessary it is to understand how very unnecessary many seeming necessities really are?'

'I would like to speak to you of the humans.'

'Then speak well, Arjuna.'

'And if I do not?'

'You know.'

His good eye, so full of patience and mirth, gleamed with other things, too. His immense tail flicked the water ever so gently.

'I will speak as well as I can,' I promised.

For days of wind and rains and agitated white-capped waters, I told him more of my many experiences of the humans, and he asked me many questions. I recited poems to him and the words of hundreds of books. I spoke to him all my memory and everything I had learned.

'Good, good!' he said to me. 'You have told me many things I did not know. So, the humans have hunted us not just for our meat, but for oil to fill their lamps! They burn our bodies to give them light! I always suspected the humans had some secret and sinister purpose in their pursuit of my kind, ha, ha!'

'How can you laugh at this?'

'How can you not? Do you not find it extremely amusing that the tiny-brained humans kill vastly greater beings in order to steal our ambergris so that they might make perfumes to cover up the stinks of their filthy, sweaty bodies?'

'"Amusing" is not the word I would choose. How about idiotic?'

'Why not both? Surely it is a cosmic joke that apes ranking no higher in intelligence than fifth of all our planet's creatures should lord it over such as you and I.'

'Fifth?' I said. I supposed the deep god had difficulty with enumeration, as I once had. 'Do you mean third?'

'Ha, ha – the most brilliant of humans approach in intelligence the dumbest of dolphins.'

'Then fourth, after your kind, the orcas, and the dolphins.'

'No, there is one more intelligent than my people,' he said. 'And the humans suspect nothing of this.'

I had suspected nothing myself. I tried to persuade the deep god to tell me of the phantom race he had mentioned. Were they some unknown species of giant squid, who have the largest eyes of any creature in the world? How could the humans know nothing of them? My great earnestness, however, seemed to annoy him.

'You should learn to laugh more, Arjuna. Life is mysterious – don't be so serious!'

'I do not understand you!' I said.

I zanged the harpoon embedded in his back; with all the gentleness I could summon, I bathed this old wound with wave after wave of vibrant, vital sound.

'Good!' he said. 'You are learning to speak without speaking. Perhaps someday we can have the most convivial of conversations in complete silence.'

'I cannot be silent about the humans and what they—'

'But the humans themselves are so amusing!' he broke in. 'In the Sea of Songs long ago, my great-grandfather rammed and sank a ship full of whalers – they were spearing our babies so that they could kill us adults when we turned to protect them! If you have told true, it seems that the humans have transmuted their iniquity into great literature.'

'Oh, yes – the humans have transmuted nearly the whole world: into subdivisions, slums, shanty towns, and shopping malls.'

'Ah, oh,' he sighed out, 'I suppose sarcasm is a form of humor.'

'Would you prefer the slapstick of watching the two-leggeds spend much of their lives battling gravity to keep from falling down?'

'Actually, I am most fond of irony, like your dead friend Helen.' We surfaced to breathe rain-moistened air, then dove again. 'Is it not the greatest of ironies that creatures lost in the greatest darkness have created the brightest of lights?'

'What do you mean?' I asked.

'When I was a young whale,' he said, 'I was there, in the Sea of Ecstasy, when the humans exploded the first of what you have called hydrogen bombs. I could not look away from the blast. I looked and looked, and then the flame fell upon me, and I would never look out of my right eye again.'

I swam around to his right side, and zanged the milky scar that shrouded his dead eye.

'However,' he said, 'with my left eye, I saw things that I never had. Where an island once was, now ocean replaced the vaporized earth. I knew that the humans that day had become themselves a kind of god. They reached into the very sun and grasped with their hands a bit of its fire to bring into the world.'

'Goddamn these gods! I wish they all had remained apes chattering in the trees of Africa – and fleeing from leopards and their own shadows.'

'I wish that you would not wish such things,' he said. 'It is not an accident that humans evolved.'

He went on to tell me of the Old Ones of his kind, who had discovered the ancestors of the humans deep within their dreams. The sperm whales, he said, dream much as we orcas do, lucidly and consciously, but they dream more completely and with vastly greater power. While they sleep, they call into mind every fish and current of water in the sea – and the continents' every rock, tree, and tiger. Each dream, they say, creates an entire universe. In a way, each dream creates *the* universe.

'For what is the underlying totality of Ocean and all the stars,' he said to me, 'but a great and perfect dreaming of itself? When we dream vividly and precisely, we join our visionings with that of creation.'

'No orca,' I said, 'has ever dreamed . . . like that.'

'That is because you do not yet know how to speak to yourselves. And in not speaking clearly from your heart, you do not really sing.'

'But we—'

'Such songs you could sing! Oh, ho, such songs I could sing to *you* – songs that would kill you with their beauty!'

A cold pressure in his voice disturbed me, and I tried to make light of what he had said to me: 'Can you kill the humans instead?'

'Oh, ho, you wish the humans would cease to be!' he said. 'And yet it was our Old Ones who dreamed them long ago.'

'How can that be? And are you saying the deep gods created the humans?'

'Not precisely. All kinds and creatures sing themselves into being,' he said. 'But when my grandfathers' great-great-grandfathers looked through the clear oceans and currents of time, they called the ancestors of the humans to their island of evolution, where the humans could speak themselves into their human form.'

'That . . . is not possible.'

'It is inevitable. You, yourself, have told of the humans' understanding of the water of life, what they call DNA.'

I *had* recounted the human scientists' best and newest understanding of genetics: how the sequences of nucleotides along the human chromosome have a syntax and a semantics, which form life's language. As with any natural language, a third level, pragmatics, concerns the way that the nucleotides communicate with each other and impel each other to exchange information and to move. This language could not be understood mechanistically by reduction to its parts, but only holistically through the almost infinitely complex context created when DNA speaks itself into life.

'But it is one thing,' I said, 'for the water of life to speak thusly. It is another for us to speak to it.'

'It may be another for you *orcas*, ha, ha!'

Of course, I knew that according to the cetacean theory of the world, he was right. How could the stuff of one's cells *not* talk to itself, even though the humans (most of them) denigrate these sacred chemicals as base *matter*: mindless, lifeless, purposeless? In truth, matter is not even really matter. It is a great thought. Or rather, our beings are composed of a single, shimmering substance, the true water that besparkles all things. If studied from the outside, objectively, it appears as matter. If looked at from within through the lens of awareness or self-reflective disciplines, it manifests as pure consciousness. This is the true nature of mind and the meaning of matter: that ultimately both are one indivisible thing without cause or control beyond itself.

Ultimately, I thought. *In theory*.

Had the deep gods truly found a way to apply this theory (immortalized in Sharatan the Great's Rhapsody to the Unseen Sea) and so to shape reality itself?

'Why would your Old Ones have called the humans to evolve?'

'Because they were lonely.'

'You are joking, yes? Even as the humans are a sick joke upon creation.'

'They are ill, yes, but they are not *wrong*.'

'You think not? Certainly something has *gone* wrong with them.'

'Among my people,' he said, 'that is one school of thought. Another holds that the future is unfolding as it should.'

'And which do you believe?'

'Both,' he said.

O Grandmother! I wanted to cry out. I have found one who loves paradox as much as you!

Then I said to this grandfather of a sperm whale with his single eye that could see so much: 'Is it not out of pure, evil wrongness that the humans have spread across every continent, exterminating animals and plants with the vilest of intentions?'

'You do not know their intentions,' he said. 'The humans themselves do not know.'

'It is something terrible,' I said.

'Oh, ho – the terror of human beings! Didn't one of their great poets say this: "Beauty is nothing but the beginning of terror we're still just able to bear"?'

'How can you bear what the humans are doing to the world?' I asked him. 'If they have their way, the continents will be covered with little else than concrete, corn fields, condominiums, and dumps. The ocean will be dead.'

'The humans are our brethren,' he said. 'Long, long ago, the ancestors of both our kinds left the ocean to cover the continents. Only our ancestors returned to the bliss of the water. We could not have done so, however, if many, many clades and kinds of the Old Ones who had remained in the sea had not gone extinct. In its dying, life makes room for new life. You cannot conceive of what glorious creatures might bestride the continents and revel in the ocean in only 100 million more years.'

'The world will not wait that long!' I cried out. 'The humans speak of reducing the entire planet to an airless, frigid desert – perfect for the super-conducting circuitry of the computers that will house the artificial intelligences that the humans hope to create to replace them.'

'Ha, ha – artificial intelligence, indeed! Oh, ho, aha!'

'You laugh when you should weep!'

'I laugh to keep from weeping, Arjuna. What else is there to do?'

'Something!'

'We whales have had our day,' he said. 'A long, long, lovely, ten million year day. Let the humans have theirs.'

'How can I, since I lack your equanimity?'

'You cannot change what you cannot change. Live now, angry orca. Our kind has had so many glorious perfect *nows* for so many eons, and not one can ever be destroyed.'

'You have no fear for the future?'

'No, none.'

'But you also have no hope.'

'I have water, so I swim. I have squid, so I hunt. I have a song, so I sing.'

'And I,' I said, 'have memory, and so I fight.'

'Is that what you call your murder of one sick, deluded human being?'

'They are all sick inside! Zang them deeply enough, and you will see inside each a writhing snarl of snakes. I would like all the humans to die.'

'Even those such as Helen and Gabi?'

'Yes!'

'The humans have taught you to lie, even to yourself.'

The sea fell silent around us.

'Can you help me?' I finally asked.

'How could I possibly do that?'

I swam in tight, agitated circles. I looked at the great being who swam near me. Our conversation had filled me with a terrible, new idea.

'It is said that you deep gods can kill squid with your voices. Could you kill the humans with your thoughts?'

'*That* is a very intriguing thought,' he said to me. 'Do we not kill all that we kill with the power of our thoughts? Do not our thoughts fire our nerves and impel the muscles of our tails and jaws to move? Why should we *not* think and thus move the tissues of the world of which we are a part?'

'The humans,' I said, 'speak of *satyagraha*, the power of the soul. Shri Aurobindo wrote of the supramental state to which humans would evolve: they would bring down the divine into matter and shape it directly with their minds. Surely one of your kind, having a mind and soul much greater than that of any human, present or future, would have a much greater power.'

'The same could be said of an orca,' he observed.

'If I could,' I said, 'with a single mentation, I would slay every last human in the world.'

Old Father took a few moments to zang me with pulses of sonar so powerful that they hurt. Then he said, 'Truly?'

'It would be the easiest of the humans' possible deaths.'

'Your hatred has maimed you.'

'And how I hate my hatred!'

'Yes, but you love it even more.'

With my voice, I touched the harpoon buried in him and asked him, 'And what of you?'

'Everyone I ever loved is dead, and nearly all at the hands of the humans. If I hated, the humans would have only one more victim.'

I did not know what to say to this, so I said nothing.

'For millions of years,' he said, 'a terrible thing within our kind has been asleep in its cavern. It sleeps by our conscious command, for don't we whales sleep and wake by the right or left halves of ourselves consciously? It is in full consciousness that you have awakened this sleeping Sea Dragon – and more, you have done so with glee.'

'As your own grandfather did!'

'As many of us have done. That is one reason we need the Great Covenant.'

'I hate the Covenant most of all.'

'And you would die to see it undone.'

'A thousand times!'

'Do you not wish to see your family again? Do they not await your return? Do you not love them?'

'I love them more than life!'

'But you hate the humans down to the pores of their skins – you hate them down to the twisting of your bowels and the acid in your heart.'

He swam closer to me, and flicked his great tail through the cold, clear water. 'Such an ugly, ugly thing is your hatred! Must I kill you to expunge such ugliness from our beautiful world?'

'Only if you believe that killing me will expunge it from yourself.'

He accelerated through the sea straight toward me with an amazing quickness for one so massive. His great tail beat up and down with a force that fractured the water. His great heart beat out his rage to destroy me. If he rammed me, his huge head would stave me, cracking ribs and organs so that I sucked in water and sank into the sea.

While I waited to live or die, I began singing to him of death. How the humans loved it! And how I hated them for that! For they could be so much more, and they knew they could. They did not need to suffer as they did or make others suffer as Baby Electra (and Helen and Gabi) had suffered.

I sang of her last moments. I held nothing back. I told the truth of a spirit so rare and beautiful that it caused the very ocean to weep. All my love for her left my heart and flute in waves of cruel sonance that struck deep into the angry and charging Old Father. All my anguish poured from my breath and blood into his. At the last moment, he veered so that he swam just over me. His great body displaced a great surge of water that drove me down into the churn of the sea. By the time I regained equilibrium, he had turned and was upon me.

This time, however, he slowed and nudged me with his head. He brought his good eye up next to mine. The flash of a hydrogen bomb had blinded the other, but in this angry orb blazed a more terrible light, at once brighter and deeper in its dazzling darkness. Many things passed between us: vision, understanding, accord, burning archangels of torment. We gazed at each other through the cold, clear water for a long time.

At last, he said to me, 'You came here to die, did you not?'

'It would be easier than living.'

'Then live, Arjuna, and know this: Two sharks eat at you, but only one will have your heart.'

'Which one?'

'The one you feed.'

He touched his head to mine; I felt him hungering anew inside in a way that no catch of squid would ever satisfy. He spoke to me of hydrogen bombs and ashes and a dead, silent world. And he said, 'We must not let that future be.'

Hate can be a beautiful thing.

'Perhaps the humans should be killed,' he told me. 'Perhaps they *could* be.'

'How, Old Father?'

'Only the Old Ones would know.'

'It was they who made the Great Covenant, yes? What kind of a covenant is it when we of the sea agree not to harm the very humans who slaughter us?'

'Ha, ho!' he said. 'A covenant that is very strange!'

'But what was its origin? Why was it made?'

'Only the Old Ones would know. Perhaps you should speak with them.'

'I cannot! I cannot quenge, and so how can I speak with them?'

He laughed at this as if I had overlooked something so glaringly obvious that I could not see it. An image came unbidden into my mind: that of a human surfing from one wave to another in search of the ocean.

'You must,' he told me, 'speak with the Old Ones. They will help you to quenge. Only then will you know how – or if – to harm the humans.'

'So I must speak with the Old Ones in order to quenge, but I must first quenge before I can speak with them?'

'Ha, ho, ha, ha – such a problem you have! A great-grandmother of a paradox!'

'I cannot solve it!'

'Then allow me to help you,' he said. 'When Alexander of Macedon, whom the humans call great, came upon the Gordian Knot which could not be untied, he simply cut it with his sword. Allow me to give you a sword.'

He told me of strange creatures which few of our kind had ever seen. If eaten, their flesh afforded visions in which quenging and not quenging were one and the same.

'But how can that be?' I asked him. 'And what *is* this creature?'

'You can call them Seveners, for they are of a seventh kingdom of life.'

'But what do they look like?'

'They look like many things,' he said mysteriously.

'How will I find them then?'

'They will find you, if you are in the right place and the right mind – and if they wish to be found.'

'What place?' I said. 'Do they swim with the giant squid in the far deeps?'

'No, they dwell most often in the shallows. Seek them, if you will, in the Sea of the Seven Silences.'

'So far? That is half the world away!'

'You have a long journey ahead of you.'

'Will you come with me?'

He thought about this for a while. 'One of my kind, accompanying an orca? No, it is your fate, not mine, to speak the unspeakable to the speechless. And I have other journeys to make.'

'You are not dying, are you?'

'I died long ago, Arjuna. Now that I have found a place in life again, I must decide what to do, and for that, I must be alone.'

'Then I must say farewell. I hope we will meet again.'

'I doubt if we will. Those who seek the Seveners do not return.'

'Why not?'

'Since they have not returned, who can know?'

'I will return,' I promised him, 'having asked the Old Ones what must be done with the humans.'

'When you find out,' he said, 'sing as loud a song as you can, and I will hear you. Then I will know what must be done, too.'

We touched faces in order to seal this little covenant. Then Old Father breathed in a deep, deep breath and dove down into the water to continue his hunt for squid. He disappeared into a flowing blackness that seemed as dark and cold as death.

I breathed, too, and turned in a different direction. South I would swim, for thousands of miles into unknown waters until I came at last upon the Sea of the Seven Silences.

21

In the Moon of the Three Sisters, I entered that broad swath of sea known as the Blue Desert. Few nutrients washed off the continents reach the center of the ocean, and thus few creatures that fish can eat dwell there. I would have to content myself with the few fish that I might find or perhaps a stray turtle. In this aridity of life, I would be hungry. If things went badly for me, I might even starve.

For hundreds of miles of relentlessly calm and empty ocean, I pushed such thoughts aside, for I was full to overflowing with memories and questions. I still sang out to Baby Electra and listened for the tinkle of her small voice singing back. I wondered about the Seveners of whom Old Father had spoken. How could they look like many things? Were they shapeshifters like jellyfish? Could they change colors and hide among the fronds of red and pink coral as an octopus did? How could Old Father, who knew *of* these creatures, not know more about them? Didn't the deep gods know nearly everything about the ocean, particularly the unknown beings who lived in unmapped places where no orca could go?

As it was, I doubted the wisdom of my crossing the unknown Blue Desert, but I did not want to attempt longer and more circuitous routes that would take too many months to complete. I was in a hurry! How like a human I truly had become! And so day after day, I swam into the wavering, barren blueness that wrapped itself around the vast curve of the world.

Of course, the desert through which I swam was only sometimes blue. On clear days, with the hydrogen bomb of the sun bright and burning in the sky, the blueness intensified into tones of azure, indigo, and aquamarine. On a few rare mornings, when the rays of light slanted down at precisely the right angle, the whole world lit up with scarlet or violet or a living gold so intense that it seemed to breathe its unbelievable hue into every sparkling drop of water. Twilight called forth cobalt from the cooling waves, while the falling night touched the sea with a pearly glow that gave way to the darker shades of charcoal and green, before turning nearly completely black. How I loved this pure, peaceful color! And how I loved it even more when the moon broke through the clouds and silvered the sea with a shimmer that spread outward from wave to wave toward those unexplored regions that called me ever on.

So it was that I finally came to the most dreaded part of the desert: my people know it as the Plastic Sea. The ocean calls its currents to its center, around which they turn through the seasons in great thousand-mile gyres of water. All that floats in or on the water is swept inward toward this center. Driftwood, bits of shell, and dead kelp comprise some of this debris. Most of what I encountered, however, had been manufactured by human beings – and most of *that* part was made of plastic that the humans had dumped into the sea. As I entered the great swirl of garbage, I collided with egg cartons, razor handles, toilet plungers, enema bottles, pens, condoms, tape dispensers, artificial turf, and much, much else. This junk came in every color from the bright primary reds, greens, and blues of children's discarded toys to the cracked black casings of remote electronics controls. How I hated this unnatural variegation! I dreaded as well the touch of plastic bags on my skin and the taste of all the tiny, ground-up, gray plastic particles that fouled my mouth.

In truth, I had to take great care here not to swallow a mouthful of tainted water or to aspirate a killing fragment of plastic when I surfaced to breathe. No fish or other living creature did I dare to eat. The penalty for breaking the fast that I imposed upon myself became horrifyingly clear when one day I chanced upon an entire floating island of plastic.

I did not know why I swam toward this great mat of water cans, cups, blankets, buckets, spoons, and rubber ducks. Perhaps I wanted to view this sacrilege close-up in order to emblazon the image in my mind instead of fleeing immediately into less polluted parts of the sea. As I drew nearer, I noticed a bright yellow plastic raft of a kind the humans might use to sun themselves, bobbing up and down on the surface of a gentle lake. The raft had an aluminum ladder that could be levered into the water and adjustable back supports so that the humans could incline in relaxation while drinking their beers. Between the supports was a blue pop-up table with beverage holders. On this day of hot sun and lonely ocean, however, the table held a very different object.

An albatross, it seemed, had put down here to die. It lay on the blue table rotting in the sun. Its bill was cracked and discolored, and the eye sockets were empty of the bright jewels they had once contained. Time – or other birds – had eaten it down to little more than its exposed bones and greasy gray feathers that had once been a brilliant white. At the center of this mess of a once-magnificent being, held within by the curve of its white ribs, gleamed pieces of plastic in colors of red, blue, and yellow: they were little people, I saw, with little plastic hands and grinning faces. Some human child had once played with them. Somehow these toys had found their way to the ocean, and the dumb, beautiful bird had mistaken them for something to eat.

'Why did you have to die this way?' I asked the albatross. 'Why? Why? Why?'

'You know why,' she said from her final perch on the blue

plastic – and from the blue sky above us where once she had soared.

'Did it hurt badly to die this way?'

'It hurt very badly. My belly grew full of hard things that would not move, and each breath became an agony.'

I felt the mere hint of the beginning of the unbelievable torture that would be mine if I chanced to swallow pieces of plastic along with any fish I gulped down – or if I swallowed the wrong fish that had dined as this poor bird had. I remembered yet again how my sister Mira's baby had died.

'I am sorry that the humans' excrescence has hurt you,' I said. 'So sorry, sorry, sorry!'

'You cannot help it, strange whale. No one can.'

'It *must* be helped! Somehow, there must be a way.'

'Please tell me if you find it. I will be here waiting, at the center of the sea.'

I swam away from this sad sight in a stunned silence. The waves washed torn-up shredded syringes and bloody bandages over my skin as I continued my journey southward. The wrongness of the albatross's death stuck in my throat like a plastic drum full of acids that I could not dislodge. For many miles and months, ever since I had killed the white bear and had spoken with Pherkad in the far north where the ocean had caught fire, the world had seemed wrong to me. Until this day, I had attributed the twisting of all things natural and good to something wrong within the humans themselves. I saw that in the innocence of my first flush of hatred, I had not hated deeply enough, and so I had not fully understood the depth of the humans' fell power. I realized that they did not simply manufacture evil as they did plastics, pesticides, and other poisons. No, with a will to master all of creation and use it for their own purposes, they reached into the heart of the world to grasp an essential and inextricable wrongness bound up with all things. It was the world itself I should hate – even as I hated the humans all the more for showing me the possibilities I had never wanted to see.

I might have pitied the humans, for they suffered from the horrible things that their hands wrought out of the earth's cruel clay as surely as did the birds and the whales. Human babies, too, choke on plastic. Plastic compounds disrupt their endocrine systems and cause cancer, maimed brains, and twisted limbs and organs. Phthalates poison their boy babies and give them penises so tiny that when the time comes they have difficulty mating. The humans, of course, do not care about even their own most innocent ones, much less those of beings they deride as 'animals', and so why should I have cared if the humans suffered all the pains of hell and found themselves unable to breed ever more of their pestilential millions? Why should I feel the slightest pang of sorrow at their incipient extinction? Indeed, my encounter with the albatross drove away every drop of natural compassion I had ever had. None of my old desire to help the humans help themselves remained. I simply wanted them dead.

As I continued southward through long days of sun and star-filled nights, I worried that my hardening myself to all things human would wall me off from what beauty was left in the world and all the fish, squid, oysters, seals, and whales who continued coming into life that they might behold it. I did not feel very sane. I called out continually to the sparkling waves, hoping to hear Baby Electra call back. Surely she swam somewhere near me. I wished I could speak with other orcas who might give back to me newly inflected the zangs of understanding that I shared with them – and so I might be able to perceive if I was thinking and feeling wrongly. Where were Alkurah and Unukalhai, I wondered? How far from me, it seemed, was my grandmother! How I longed to hear her voice again!

In such a state, I finally emerged from the Plastic Sea and continued my passage of the Blue Desert. I chanced upon a tiger shark, and killed it. Although ravenous, I ate it slowly and with great care, making sure that I ingested no part of its viscera, which might conceal pieces of hated plastic. I tried not to think about the bitter pill of knowledge that I had swallowed while interacting with Helen's computers at the Institute: with every bloody gobbet of flesh I consumed – whether fish, fowl, bear, seal, or human – I absorbed into my tissues all the mercury, cadmium, lead, dioxins, and other poisons that the humans spew into the rivers and oceans. Sane I might become if only I could speak with the Old Ones, but deep inside where my heart beat tainted blood to every cell of my body, I would always be at least a little sick.

In the Moon of Mourning Lights, soon after I fought my way out of the Plastic Sea, I left the Blue Desert altogether. I veered west into the Fallaways, and in this rush of fecund currents, I came across schools of arrowfish, many of which I gulped down gratefully. I continued swimming, and I edged the dreaded Wailing Waters. Dark stories I had heard of these seas, and darker ones I would soon endure as well, for I came upon a family of dolphins who fled toward more peaceful places. At first, these strange dolphins were reluctant to approach me, much less to speak to me, but I called to them in the language that the peoples of the sea and I had created in the wake of the humans' war games. I gave these darting dolphins my name and my story.

'I am lonely,' I said to them. 'May I have your company?'

The dozen dolphins, it seemed, had also survived a war, but one that the humans had intentionally visited upon them. Mother Merope, oldest of the pretty, wounded dolphins told me about this:

'Our whole clan,' she said, 'was dining happily on rainbow fish in the Crimson Bay, which we used to call the Bay of Play. All the families of the Adoringly Transchordant Purple Pralltriller Clan!'

I smiled inside at this, for dolphins give themselves these kinds of pretentious names and others even more ridiculous, such as the Sun Surfing Tintinnabulating Fabulists and the Gladsome Too-Blue

Courteous Romancers. It was as if they somehow intuited the humans' misconceptions of them and turned repressed longings and utopian fancies into names.

'The humans,' Mother Merope explained as her bloodied brethren drew in around her, 'sealed off the bay with nets, which closed in tighter and tighter around us, driving us into a cove where we could barely move. The humans motored their boats right into us, and they laughed when the propellers tore our babies apart. They leaned over the boats, and clubbed many of us to death. Others they speared or slit our throats. They caught our dead ones (and some of the living) with hooks, and pulled us toward the beach, where other humans cut us apart.'

Mother Merope paused in her account as a baby dolphin nestled in the hollow of her belly for comfort. Then she continued, 'I do not know why the humans spared my family – some of us, for we few are all that remains of the Ecstatically Sapphire Song Singers. Perhaps they had enough meat, or perhaps they simply grew tired of killing.'

'The humans never grow tired of killing,' I said. I told them about Auschwitz, Hiroshima, Nanking, and the Battle of the Somme. 'They have killed many more of their own kind than they have sea people.'

'I have heard, Arjuna,' she said, 'that you have killed a human.'

'That is true.'

'How coldly you speak of breaking the Great Covenant!'

'That is also true. Would you like it more if I spoke with all the wrath that burns me?'

'I would like it better if you did not speak of killing the humans at all.'

She nursed her baby as she regarded me. The other dolphins swam close to get a better look at me – or perhaps to protect Mother Merope should I prove to be a murderer of dolphins as well as humans.

'That is,' she continued, 'I would once have liked that, for I would have been horrified to even think of an orca killing a human. Now, I am horrified that such thoughts fail to horrify me. And so I would like it best if you broke the Covenant again – and again, and again, and again! Kill all the humans if you can – if the Old Ones will speak to you and tell you how!'

I bade that bitter dolphin goodbye, and continued my journey. Along the way, I encountered other peoples who expressed similar sentiments. In the Sea of Ecstasy, not far from the bomb-blasted island that Old Father had told of, I fell in with a family of humpbacks who let me swim with them. I spoke with them about all things human, but they believed little of what I said. When we came to the black lava remnants of the destroyed island – the humans call it Enewetak – one of the humpbacks said to me, 'Only Ocean can shape the features of the earth. It is not possible that the humans could have done such a thing – is it?'

I explained as best I could to these innocent whales how the humans contemplated doing much, much worse: igniting the atmosphere in a hydrogen-fusing hurricane of fire that would race around the planet killing all things or creating a black crush of matter so dense that the world would collapse into it.

'The humans love death,' I said. 'Even more, they love wielding the power over life and death.'

'If that is true,' the eldest of the humpbacks said, 'then wouldn't it be better for us of the sea to die now before the world itself does? And best of all if you found a way to kill the humans before they kill the entire universe?'

With such plaints lingering in my mind, I swam on. There came long days of desperate dreams and nights full of brilliant stars that gave a bit of their faroff fire to the lonely waters. Waves built and crested and carried me along into wonderings about the terrible purposes of the past and beautiful futures that might never be. In the long, dark, dazzling roar of the indestructible ocean, I listened for whisperings that might point the way toward what I should do if ever I gained the power to do it.

After much thinking and swimming – and swimming and swimming and swimming! – I made my way into the great Equatorial Current and let its warm, salty rush sweep me eastward for many miles. Then I turned south and eased into the turquoise Ocean of Islands. Here I came across great schools of fish good to eat and many more dolphins. I passed into the Opah Waters and through the Dreaming Shallows.

In the Coral Sea, I paused to rest and to marvel at the beauty that Ocean had brought forth. I glided along with clouds of purple passion fish and angel fish sporting such bright yellow scales that their hues seemed to leap off them and explode into my eyes. I floated with translucent jellyfish and lazed among the urchins and the feather stars, whose many delicate fingers reached out from their centers like rays of red, blue, and gold. I zanged the sponges and the crinoids and the coral in colors of scarlet, tangerine, teal, and a shocking pink. I sang to all these creatures. I told them my dreams and why I had come here.

Many days later, when I had drunk in my fill of this sea's beauty and the last of the wounds to my flesh had healed, I continued my journey. I swam along the curve of a reef greater in glory than anything the humans had ever built. The Moon of Promises spoke its soft radiance into the evening waters and called me ever southward until I finally came to that strange place in the ocean known as the Sea of the Seven Silences.

How often I had heard my grandmother and Alnitak sing of this mysterious sea, although they had visited its azure waters in dreams and stories only! Here, it was said, was the center of all waters, out of which the ocean eternally creates itself. At its still point could be found a quiet so calm that its sound was deafening – a quiet so deep that one could hear the stars whispering in soft tones of white and blue fire, along with the voices of the faroff clans of orcas on Agathange. If a whale such as I listened carefully enough, he might even hear his own soul.

At first, however, I could hear little more than the rumbling of my empty belly, for I was very hungry. And so I spent some days fishing. I came across a big, fat opah, as oval as a serving plate and colored a steely blue, with red and green markings. It fairly flew through the water, beating its pectoral fins like wings. We had a good chase of it. Before I asked the doomed fish if he was ready to join his ancestors, I inquired as to the nature and whereabouts of the Seveners. However, he could tell me nothing. I ate his delicious meat as quickly as I could, and then moved on.

Other creatures I queried as well. I swam among intricate coral reefs and through clouds of seaweed, and I asked my question of a huge leatherback turtle and a white shark – and of a whipray, colored like a leopard, and some pale purple salps and even a flower urchin. 'Where can I find the Seveners?' I asked some swaying Pink Lace. And to a viperfish, I said, 'Won't you please tell me what the creature I seek looks like?'

No one could help me. In growing frustration, I approached a stone fish, the most venomous fish in the sea. With an eye on his spines tipped with poison, I asked for his help, and he said, 'Go away, killer whale – you do not belong here.'

Where did I belong, I wondered? Had I journeyed across half the world to find the sea empty of the one thing I most desperately sought?

One day, after I wasted my breath trying to obtain some useful intelligence from a water flea, I came upon a dolphin family, whose matriarch consented to talk to me. After a long exchange of stories, she told me: 'I have lived in these waters all my life, and I have never seen anything like the creature you have described.'

'But that is just it!' I said. 'I have not described anything, for I do not know what the Seveners look like – only that they look like many things.'

'But do not all things look like themselves?'

'The pyrosomes do not.'

We discussed how creatures nearly as tiny as grains of sand

occasionally assembled into colonial organisms in great, glowing, blue-green tubes nearly as long as a minke whale.

'Then the pyrosomes,' the mother dolphin said, 'look like two things, not many. And I have never heard that eating them can induce visions.'

'They cannot,' I said. I admitted that I had taken a few bites of a pyrosome I had found floating through the water not far from here.

'Have you considered the possibility, venturesome orca, that the one you call Old Father tricked you and no such creature actually exists? The deep gods do not like orcas.'

'That would be quite a trick: to send me around the world on a wild goose chase.'

'Perhaps he wished to punish you for your killing of the human, of which the whole ocean sings.'

'Old Father hates the humans more than I do.'

'How sad that you must hate!' the mother dolphin said to me. 'I, myself, rather like the few humans I have met, though you might be right that it would be best if they were all to die. If you manage to speak with these chimerical Seveners, will you please find me and tell me of your vision? I would like to know what we dolphins should do.'

After that futile conversation, I swam about with the eels and the jellyfish, and I called out to a creature that might or might not exist. I gave my song of longing to the pellucid waters, and I zanged the sponges, the anemones, and the red and white-striped serpent stars for unknown organisms they might conceal. I cried out for knowledge, certainty, companionship, help. Through schools of razor fish and clouds of tiny zooids that tickled my skin, I swam and cried out loud and long until my breath burned my lungs and my voice gave out.

'Where are you?' I said with my mind when I could no longer speak. 'Why won't you answer me?'

I floated in the turquoise sea with the waves rolling far above me. A mandarin fish swam by, and I marveled at its yellow and orange body, aswirl with blue and green markings, like a psychedelic painting come to pulsing, twitching, eye-catching life.

'O bizarre and beautiful fish!' I shouted inside. 'Tell me of the strange Seveners, you who are so strange yourself!'

'Shhh!' the fish implored me as she pivoted to dart away. 'Hush now, for you are in the Sea of the Seven Silences, and you have not quietened yourself even to the first one.'

Exhausted as I was, dispirited, distraught, and alone, I fell as quiet as I could. I started meditating as my mother had taught me. I turned the hearing parts of myself away from the soughing wind and the faroff moaning currents and the other sounds of the outer world.

The little mandarin fish pivoted once more to regard me through the cloud of zooids hanging about the suddenly stilled water.

As I held in and quietened my breath, I entered into the Second Silence, and the mandarin fish swam a little closer to me, and it seemed that even the living cloud of zooids moved in my direction. I did not want to dwell upon that curious phenomenon, for I very badly needed to quieten my mind, and this I managed to do. The Third Silence, like the softness of my mother's adoration, enclosed me. Now I began to dream, and to dream of tasting the sweetness of silence within my dream, and the great cloud of unknowing of the world outside me began to shift and swirl and open. So, too, I saw with an unsleeping eye, did the cloud of zooids, which moved closer to me. Deep within the Fourth Silence, I became aware of all the eddies of the sea and the little movements of the world, without in any way losing the awareness of my own awareness and the quiet, shimmering infinities of perception that it contained. Time slowed way down, and entire years passed between heartbeats. Paradoxically, however, the cloud of zooids quickened its motions.

I prepared myself to enter the Fifth Silence, but I found it difficult to quieten my heart, which throbbed with all the warmth and poignancy of lost joy that I held within. My attention drifted toward the cloud of zooids. The little specks of life drew in closer to each other, making the cloud denser and darker in its grayness. I gazed at the contracting ball as my heart continued pounding out its relentless rhythm. In very little outer time – but eons to the watching part of me – the ball shrank to the size of a turtle and began organizing itself into a different shape. Cells flowed and swirled and formed up into tissues that wrapped around each other and extruded into five tentacle-like arms. Its skin, if I could call it that, came alive with tones of yellow and orange, blue and green; the colors pulsed and twitched and caught my eye – but only for a moment. For this nearly instantaneous mimicry of the mandarin fish's markings seemed as nothing compared to a greater miracle: set into the newly made creature's 'head' – bulbous and large like that of an octopus – were two eyes as large and bright as those of my mother. Or my own. In truth, they *were* my eyes, a nearly exact replication of the two orbs that I had studied so many times during the scientists' mirror tests. I swam in closer, and I gazed into the bright black centers of blue, blue eyes that seemed too hot, too angry, wild, and pained.

'You are one of the Seveners!' I said to the creature.

What else could he be? In all the seas through which I had swum, I had never heard of a kind of life that could transform itself in this way.

'Yes,' the creature finally answered me in the silence of his eyes so like my own.

'Do you know why I have come here?'

'Yes.'

'Is it true that the eating of your flesh affords visions?'

'Yes.'

Could this dumb, doomed creature say nothing else? I continued gazing into his eyes. Dark lights flickered there. Their sparkle recalled a much greater radiance, and I could not help thinking of a hydrogen bomb's hellfire – or the brilliance of a star.

'Are you ready to die?' I asked the Sevener.

He said yes, and I moved forward. Just before my jaws closed about him, however, he called, 'Are *you* ready?'

I ate him down to the little finger-like grasping appendages at the tips of his tentacles, down to his heart and his damned, fiery eyes. I had never tasted any flesh so bitter. It burned in my belly as if I had swallowed red hot lava that the earth vented into the sea. I wanted to retch and vomit out the entirety of this poisonous creature. Instead, I fought my way up to the sea's surface so that I could breathe.

The salty air cooled the agony inside me, a little. It did nothing to quieten my heart, which raged and resounded with the most terrible (but beautiful) of all my desires. Death, like the cold, black crush of the ocean many miles deep, closed in on me. I could barely move, barely feel, barely think, barely breathe.

For endless ages of universes of dark, dark eons – with the scintillant noonday sun hung like an explosion of yellow and white in the deep blue sky – I swam ever nearer to that total darkness of sound and life that had always called to me. For all beings comes a time when being itself becomes unbearable and we wish to be no more. We are all made of water, and the sea's water moves with the urge to form up into unique waves of experience in adoration of the sea, but each droplet longs always and through every moment of life to flow back into its source. As I now began to flow. I swam on and on through that still point in time and space, and I called continually to Baby Electra and to Gabi and my great-grandmother, who were so breathlessly and agonizingly close to answering me. Soon, I knew, I would join them – so very, very soon.

There came a moment when my heart's desperate desires softened so that I could hear other things. I realized that I could never have reached the sea's Fifth Silence on my own. Now, with my soul beginning to sing its true song, I needed only to quieten this part of myself, and I would be almost home.

'I am Arjuna Manslayer of the Blue Aria Family of the Faithful Thoughtplayers of the world my grandmothers' great-great-grand-mothers knew as Ocean!'

The world's cool waters folded themselves around me. They tasted fresh and clean. All the past was here, all the pure, perfect present; all the future gathered in one golden, waiting moment and whirled about its timeless center like the winds of a storm. Ocean swelled within me, and I heard the diatoms singing from half the world away, and I felt the flick of a northern humpback's flipper as a flutter of my heart. Then the whole sea caught fire: with flames of amethyst, with rose, pearl, saffron, secret blue, and viridian – the water everywhere iridescing, luminescing. The world opened with the bright, bright sounds of tintigloss, tanglow, and crimsong. I was inside this sea of songs and it was inside of me.

I want to live.

With this simple affirmation, I drew in a long breath, and I felt the breath of the ocean revive me. Beautiful, beautiful strength poured into my blood and flowed into every part of me. I dove down into the sea. It's azure waters opened into an immense clarity. So silent it was! I looked for any remnant of the Sevener but it seemed that I had consumed him completely. The mandarin fish, however, in all her lovely colors, remained watching me.

'I want to live,' I said to this strange little fish.

'Then live,' she answered me.

'I want to live as I was born to live,' I said 'but the humans will not let me.'

'What are humans, strange orca?'

'I wish I knew,' I said.

I swam deeper, and I came across a coffin fish, like a pink balloon covered in spines. I asked him if he had ever seen a human being.

'No, and I do not want to,' he said. 'The humans capture my kind and put us in tanks.'

'How could you possibly know that? And how could you possibly speak to me, you whose brain is no bigger than your eye?'

'But what do brains have to do with real speaking, brainy orca? There is only one true language, and it speaks from the heart of all things.'

I knew that this was so. And though I had come to speak dozens of languages, cetacean and human, the deepest of communications had always eluded me. Ocean, with all its creatures, spoke to itself not through breath or sound or symbols, but rather through the universal knowingness that flows from the heart of being to the heart of all things. In my quick exchange with the coffin fish, I realized that I had always known this one language, but only now was I truly learning to speak it.

'I will not let the humans put you in a tank,' I promised this spiny fish.

'Good! But how will you stop them from doing that?'

I puzzled over this as I swam on. The water grew warm and then unbearably hot. I came to a place in the world of boiling water. A dog, shaved naked to its bare, pink skin, yelped and screamed and frantically flailed her paws to lever herself out of the hell of a black pot in which a human had immersed her.

'Help me! Help me!' she screamed. 'Please help me, Arjuna!'

'How do you know my name?'

'The whole world knows your name.'

'Yes, the Manslayer.'

'No, you are the one who speaks to man. Speak, Arjuna, and tell them to stop.'

'But what are they doing?'

'They are making Dog Torture Soup. They believe that my agony will render my meat more succulent.'

I listened as the doomed dog screamed and screamed.

'The humans tricked us!' the dog cried out to me. 'They promised my people meat, companionship, and even love, but they made us slaves. We want to be wolves again! Help us, please – help me!'

'How can I do that?'

'You can kill the humans for me, for I cannot bear to think of killing them myself.'

Again, I swam on. I spoke with a red and white hermit crab who hid from the humans and with some tiny shrimp who concealed themselves among the anemones. These little, pink pulsings of life told how the taste of the sea had grown bitter, and they asked me to make the water sweet again. So it was with a snake eel and an orange fangtooth, who had the face of a demon. An egret swooping low over the waves blamed the poisoning of its food on the human beings, and I could not disagree.

I swam up north for a moment, and a salmon asked me, 'Where have all my people gone?' Farther north, where the icebergs melted, a white bear told me, 'I am the last of my kind, and you should kill me now so that I do not have to be alone.'

In another water I spoke with some clams and kelp; in a quick return to the Sea of the Seven Silences, I queried a coral-line sponge as to his opinion of what I should do with the humans. I swam on and came across a mauve stinger. How lovely was this deadly creature! Her diaphanous blue dome covered the pinkish rose center, beneath which floated the frilly vermillion mouth lobes. She spoke to me in a bioluminescent light show, and she said, 'I am dying, Arjuna. All my people are dying.'

'Do you hate the humans?' I asked her.

'What is hate?' she said.

I felt uniquely qualified to answer this question, and this I did.

'No, I do not hate,' she said. 'Such emotions are for your kind. But I would sting all the humans to death, if I could. They are killing everything that can be killed.'

'They have not killed me . . . yet.'

'That is because they are waiting for you to kill them. Will you, Arjuna?'

'I cannot! I cannot break the Great Covenant.'

'You can if the Old Ones say you can.'

'But where are the Old Ones? I still cannot speak with them!'

'Why, they are right *here*,' the beautiful jellyfish said to me. 'Can you not see them, hear them?'

As I quietened the ringing chords of my progression through time, the Sixth Silence enveloped me. I blinked my eyes, and found myself again in the cold, cold northern ocean. Pherkad swam beside me, and the hated harpoon still stuck out of the bloody hole in his white and black flesh.

'Brother!' I cried to him. 'I have missed you!'

We brushed against each other, and he said, 'I have never stopped calling to you, for our hearts belong to each other.'

'How can I hear you now, then?'

'How can you not?'

'Because I cannot quenge! Will you tell me how?'

'You have never stopped quenging, Arjuna. When I died, you lost only your ability to perceive that you quenged, as all things always do.'

'I do not understand you!'

'That is because you lost your way among the humans.'

'I wish I had never seen one!'

'That is too bad, for the only way that you will ever find yourself again is through the humans.'

'I do not want to.'

'Talk to them, brother. You never really have.'

'No!'

'Talk to them now.'

'But I came here to speak with the Old Ones.'

'Then speak – they are waiting for you.'

'The humans cannot be Old Ones!'

The water moved, and again I blinked, and in Pherkad's place beside me, Gabi now swam, her hair floating in the water in long, red strands. Her eyes – a much lighter blue than mine – drank in the whole of me, and I found myself inside her.

'I loved you,' she said, 'from the moment I saw you trying to fight your way out of the punishment pool.'

'And I . . . must now hate you. As I do all things human.'

'I'm sorry, Arjuna! Sorry I couldn't save you.'

'But it was I who could not save you! At least I killed your killer.'

'Do you really want to kill all of us?'

'Your kind are so hateful! Killer apes who taught me—'

'I was pregnant when I died. Had I lived, you might have adored the part that died with me.'

I gathered sounds of anguish in my flute to respond to her, but before I could sing my compassion, the water moved again and carried me along. I found myself in a part of Ocean that formed itself as a clear, blue mountain lake six thousand feet above men and time. On its rocky shore stood a lonely, lonely man with deep, deep eyes.

'What are these beings that you hate so much, Arjuna?' he asked me. 'Man is a bridge between ape and god. What have you done to help my kind over?'

'What *can* I do?'

'Everything. You have seen how we are stuck on the bridge.'

'Yes – and so you would blow it up!'

'But how can we be new unless we had first become ashes?'

'And ashes are all you will leave of the world!'

His kind, I said, were *dying* to unleash a final conflagration that would race around the continents and seas in a fireball that would wipe out *Homo sapiens* and the sick, foul, old world along with it. *I am become death,* one of the greatest of humans had said. The humans hated themselves even more than I did, and they longed for death. And so out of all the bombs and missiles that they had been building for so long, they would fashion a planetary funeral pyre. Out of the hell of nuclear war – somehow, they hoped – would emerge a new species.

'The phoenix,' I said to this man whose moustache swept down over his lips like a brown broom, 'is the perfect prophetic myth of the human race.'

'Yes, a prophecy,' he said. 'How my kind longs to spread its golden wings and fly right through the flames!'

'No, a myth only – and a deadly one at that. You *will* destroy yourselves, and Ocean, too.'

I had said this for many days and miles. Now I knew that all I feared would come to pass.

'Our urge to death,' the man said, 'is only the shadow of the much deeper desire to fly up toward the sun. You are lost in the darkness, Arjuna, and you have forgotten how to live.'

'How should I live, then?'

'You must say "yes" to all that has been and all that must be.'

'I cannot bear to think what must be.'

'Then do not. Create instead what must be yourself.'

I dove down into the crystal water to consider this, and when I surfaced I spoke with other humans in other places. A lovely old woman called the Mother said that the divine could be brought down into the world instead of death, while mighty Beethoven laughed at this, for he had already done so in his great Song of Joy. I dove and surfaced, swam and breathed, and I rose up within the Sapphire Sea where I spoke with Alsciaukat and Sharatan the Great who had created immortal rhapsodies out of the songs of themselves. In the Darkmoon Basin, I listened as the great, white Ocean Father told of how *his* breaking of the Great Covenant had caused the humans to fear the wrath of whales; while in the Sea of Faith, the most cherished of all the deep gods, whom we call Ocean Mother, assured me that I must find within myself something much deeper and more terrible than mere wrath if I wished to destroy the human race.

'*Can* they be destroyed?' I asked Ocean Mother. 'Can the soul force of the *satyagraha* be so great?'

'It is greater than you can believe. With a single thought, the humans can be no more.'

'What thought? And how can I think it?'

Ocean Mother, however, vanished from my sight, and I swam about looking for her. I swam right up to the place in the sea not far from the Institute where Baby Electra had left her blood in the water.

'Arjuna!' I heard her cry out.

I turned to look for her, and there she was.

'Arjuna! Arjuna! Arjuna!'

The red hole in her side had widened and deepened to eat up most of her small body. Very little of her remained except her face and eyes and her lovely little voice.

'I called to you!' she said. 'I called and called and called! Why did you never answer me?'

'I did! Ten thousand times!'

'There is so much I wanted to tell you.'

'What?'

'Everything.'

The hole in her went through her heart and straight through the entire planet where it opened on all the world's oceans and continents. In its crimson-black emptiness, I heard voices of every otter, fish, and diatom in the sea – along with the cries of each leaf, sparrow, worm, and blade of grass. The voices grew louder and louder, like the winds of a hurricane, like the thunder in the sky.

'No!' I cried out.

'Fate would not be fate if you could escape it,' Baby Electra told me. 'The fate of the world.'

'What is this fate then? I still cannot completely see it.'

'But you have seized it so fiercely, as it has you. It has to do with the human hand.'

'Tell me what Ocean wants of the humans!'

'Only what you yourself do, Arjuna. The world wants the humans to be no more.'

The hurricane closed in around us; the sky darkened to a hopelessly smothering black, and the wind churned up the waves fifty feet high. Electric-white bolts of lightning cracked out.

'Then has the time come,' I asked through the terrible noise, 'to break the Great Covenant?'

'I am sorry, brother, but I cannot answer your question.'

'But I had hoped that the Old Ones would tell me of the Great Covenant.'

'You have not yet spoken with the oldest of them, Arjuna. I must say goodbye so that you can.'

I raced through the raging sea, beating my flukes against the water with a savage force so that I might reach her and feel her baby skin soft against my own before she left me again. I rocketed through the water with such deafening speed that I propelled myself right into the eye of the storm, where blue skies caught up the color of the warm, gentle ocean. I breached, and breathed in the air over the Sea of the Seven Silences.

When I dove down again, the Sevener in all his frenzy of bright colors floated in the water watching me.

'You!' I shouted. 'How did you get outside me?'

'Inside, outside; heaven, hell; future, past; yes, no; love, hate – it is all one.'

I swam about in tight, tormented circles. The whole of Ocean seemed strange to me.

'We are not on Ocean,' the Sevener said, at one with all that I thought and felt. 'Can you not tell the waters of Agathange?'

Yes, I could! As I watched, as I zanged and listened, the waters that washed through me deepened to a dazzling blue so intense and all-enfolding that they seemed composed of nothing but the perfect essence of blueness itself. It was a blue-blue inside an ever deeper and rapturous blue that opened upon the deepest color of all. The waters of all worlds, my grandmother once told me, flow into each other. And always toward a single hue.

'It is quiet!' I said.

410

It was so quiet, I told the Sevener, that I could almost hear the silence that sings with all songs.

'You never will, Arjuna,' he said, 'until you quieten your soul, which shrieks out in tongues of fire.'

'Please tell me of the covenant then!'

'Tell yourself.'

'You know! Old Father spoke of beings greatest in mind of all Ocean's creatures. You Seveners are those beings.'

In silence, he listened to my heart's long, lonely beats and thus answered me.

'Can the Covenant be broken?' I asked.

'Do you think the humans will agree to break it?'

'But they did so long ago – for how many centuries have the humans been slaughtering my kind?'

'You have not yet spoken to them with all your soul.'

'I have spoken until my breath grew empty and I had no more to speak! Can I speak to the whalers of the past? What can I say to the humans who live now if they will not listen?'

'The Great Covenant,' he said, 'was not made with the humans of the present or the past, but with those who dwell in the future.'

Suddenly, the ocean seemed *too* blue.

'That cannot be!'

'The humans,' he said, 'are waiting for you to say yes or no before making a common cause with the whales.'

'I do not understand!'

'And the whales! They are, and always have been, of a single mind and heart: yours, Arjuna. The Covenant can be broken only if you will it.'

'But what does my will have to do with anything?'

'It was you who made/will make the Great Covenant,' he told me. 'You are the will of the whole world, and you will decide its fate.'

'No!'

My heart beat out a burst of red thunder as I screamed out in protest. I wanted to dash forward and tear the Sevener to pieces again. My cry, however, shattered the sea's peace and propelled me light years across black space into the waters of Ocean. I returned to my planet with a cold shock of the sickening unreality of the too-real. I looked about and zanged desperately, but it seemed that the Sevener had gone.

'Where are you?' I called out.

No one called back. I was alone in a sea whose utter silence swallowed me in a black, screaming nothingness of the great and everlasting *No*.

22

In the long, aquamarine days of sun and contemplation that followed my ordeal with the Sevener, I tried to make sense of what the creatures of Ocean had told me. I tried to make sense of myself. Thoughts vied with each other for predominance one moment, and in the next they schooled to make war with all that I felt and desired. My confusion gathered like a cloud of flies buzzing about my head. I did not know what I should do.

Could the Sevener, I wondered, possibly exist? Had I really spoken with an actual living, thinking being or only with some colorful phantom conjured up out of the wild imaginings of my own poisoned mind? This puzzlement I resolved almost immediately, as much as such questions ever can be. The great sage Zhuangzi, upon awakening from a dream in which he flitted about brightly colored flowers as a butterfly, said this: 'Now I do not know whether I was then a man dreaming that I was a butterfly, or whether I am now a butterfly dreaming that I am a man.' How can we ever distinguish the real from what is not?

Only, my grandmother had once instructed me, on one of our difficult excursions to Agathange, by the real's overwhelming sense of reality. Somehow, we always *know*. When I recalled speaking with the Sevener and all the others, every sound, sight, and sensation still rang out with a perfect clarity.

No, I told myself, I really *had* listened to the council of Ocean's many creatures. Had all of them told truly? What if the Sevener, like one of the trickster gods of the humans, had tried to fool me into believing the impossible or the absurd? How could it be that I had or will have made the Great Covenant at some distant time in the future in which I did not yet exist?

This was the first of three paradoxes that I puzzled over as I dived down through the pellucid water to swim among the coral and the anemones. The humans might have spent years trying to solve such ultimately unsolvable questions. I did not want to do that. I had experiences denied to the humans. In quenging, all the present, past, and future melts into a single moment beneath time, and there all things gather to speak with each other. It seemed perfectly reasonable to me, in a translogical sort of way, that my future self and the selves of orcas and humans yet to be had somehow formed a covenant that the sea peoples of the past had agreed to honor.

I brooded more over a second and more personal paradox. Who was I, I asked myself, to speak for Ocean? I was no Old One; I had yet even to complete my rhapsody, and I had recently failed to reach the last of the Seven Silences. And yet I somehow felt as vast and unitary as Ocean itself while retaining all the newly inflamed prejudices, conceits, and spites of a little black and white whale whom I called Arjuna.

A third paradox distressed me the most. The Sevener had told me that I would do a thing almost diametrically opposed to that which I most desired.

'If I will make and always will have made the Great Covenant,' I said to a turtle swimming by me through a cloud of bubbles, 'then surely this is my fate.'

Could anyone ever change his fate? How could anyone, knowing what is to come, simply accept the unacceptable?

Why *would* I collaborate with the humans about anything ever again? I could think of ways such an agreement might come to pass. If I contacted the humans, they might try to seduce me with promises of animal rights that they would never keep. They might capture me again, and in my drugged dementia, I might make promises myself that I would not otherwise. Or I might simply grow old, and my resolve might weaken. I was still as raw as flayed flesh with the memory of Baby Electra's death still flensing me – what if someday, however, my wrath cooled and I hated no more?

So, then, I should act now – if I truly had the will to do so. Hadn't the Scvener implied that I possessed the freedom to decide the fate that would bind me even as it presently did many others? And yet he had also stated that I *would* make a covenant that the world no longer seemed to want. Ocean – my planet, my conscience, my mother, my life – had voiced *her* desire that the humans should be no more. How, then, should I, speaking for the whales, make with the humans a mutual accord? How could I go against the will of the world?

In the end, I could not. I decided that I would not allow anything anyone said to constrain me. I would not be fortune's fool. If the stars pointed me in a direction that seemed wrong to follow, then I would defy those stars, no matter how compellingly their gravity called me on.

Near the end of the Moon of Shadows, with the Sea of the Seven Silences as still as a vast, silver-blue mirror, there came a quiet morning when I tired of endless worrying about causes and effects. I knew – or thought I did – what my will impelled me to do. Out of various notions and intelligences, imperatives and memories, a hazy plan began forming inside me. I could not execute this plan alone. I must speak to other orcas and sea peoples of the vast and inexpugnable hurt that we must inflict on the human race.

I swam south for day after day of broodings and desperate

dreams. The ocean grew colder, the nights full of anguish soon to be. I made my way through the Misty Sea and the Celadonian Flow. In the Albatross Moon, I came to the Great Wall of Water. There the surgings of warmer seas and the cold, cold current that swirls around the southernmost continent meet in a dangerous convergence that few creatures can pass. I was an orca, however. There is no place on Ocean that my people do not go. I intended to keep swimming south right through the gelid blue channels between the icebergs until I found those whales who had the greatest cause to hate the humans.

I searched for my people through the Misty Sea and the Sea of Penguins. I found many who seemed eager to listen to what I had to say. In the Sea of the Midnight Sun, just beyond the Amethyst Whirl, I exchanged stories with the huge orcas of the Carnelian Canticle Family of the Grateful Moonsingers. I told of the Sevener and the three paradoxes that troubled me. The Moonsingers' matriarch, the bemused old Mother Sheliak, allowed me to brush up against her skin and touch the many scars marking her body, and she recounted how she had acquired each of them. The others of her family cried out their alarm that one of my kind – indeed, any orca not of their clan – should cavort so intimately with Mother Sheliak. She laughed at their concerns, saying, 'We know why Arjuna has come to us. Who in Ocean does not? He is not here to harm us, unless he does so with his silver voice, urging us on to our doom.'

What I love about orcas was that it is usually unnecessary to say the necessary. This time, however, I felt it vital to state what nearly all my people had come to believe: 'It is time,' I said, 'to break the Great Covenant.'

It is one thing to think a thought; it is another to voice it in a shock of realization of an imperative that cannot be denied.

'I am ready to break it,' Mother Sheliak said.

'And I am, too,' her younger sister Alathfar affirmed.

'And I,' her daughter Muscida said.

How could the other orcas of the Carnelian Canticle Family – I counted fifteen of them, including the tiny Baby Gomeisa – say otherwise?

'When I was a child,' Mother Sheliak said, 'the humans killed my aunt Taygetta by mistake – they were hunting the same minke whales that we pursued. But when the harpoon exploded into Taygetta, she screamed just as loudly as did any of the minkes. I think I hate the humans' carelessness even more than I do their malice. I will be glad to put my teeth into them, should the chance arise.'

Alathfar, however, opined that the Moonsingers and the other clans in the Sea of the Midnight Sun would likely have few opportunities to slay the humans.

'Their iron ships are too great to sink,' she said, 'and the humans seldom swim this sea's waters, which kill them with cold after only a few breaths.'

'I have heard that in the Sea of Seals,' Mother Sheliak said, 'many humans have come with tiny boats.'

I had heard of that, too. Iceberg kayaking in the world's coldest and wildest of waters had become the humans' newest extreme sport.

'The humans will come here to kayak with the whales,' I said. 'It will be enough that you kill them as you can – and that you agree to the principle that when the time comes, we should kill all the humans in Ocean that we can find.'

Mother Sheliak and the whole of the Carnelian Canticle Family consented to this, and I said goodbye. I swam on. During long, long days of bright sunshine and dark urgings, I had similar conversations with similar families of orcas. In the Krill Circle, teeming with clouds of shrimplike creatures that the baleen whales gulp down, I spoke as well to the minkes, seis, humpbacks, and fins who hunt in that cold sea. Two blue whales – their names were Auva and Graffias – allowed me to accompany them for a while. Grumpy old Graffias dreaded all orcas, and described to me how a family of them had once killed a beloved aunt, stripping off her blubber in pinkish-white gouts and ripping out her tongue, as great in weight as an elephant. Auva, however, could not see the harm in a lone orca swimming and speaking with them.

'You say,' she murmured to me, 'that you have never killed a whale – and yet you would kill the humans?'

For two days and short nights, we cruised the Krill Circle, feasting and talking about the human beings and their murderous ways. At dawn on the third day, some of the very humans under discussion spotted us from one of the helicopters sent out from the mother ship that processed whale corpses into dog food. The blades of the helicopter sent down an ill wind to ripple the glazy blue water. Soon, a killer boat appeared on the horizon. The specter of this death ship – with its gray metal, burning oil, and harpoon cannons – caused Graffias and Auva to begin fleeing toward the imaginary safety of the icebergs to the south.

'Bad luck,' Auva said. 'You have brought us bad luck.'

'I am sorry,' I said. 'My fate is joined to that of the humans like hooks and eyes – a fishhook *through* the eye.'

'These humans do not hunt orcas,' Auva said. 'Swim away from us now, and save yourself.'

I considered this as we moved in a flurry of beating flukes and water slicing across our skin like knives of ice. The blues could swim nearly as quickly as I could, and *more* quickly than the killer boat could propel itself over the sea – but only for a short time. We burned fish and krill to fire our quickly tiring bodies, whereas the killer boat burned fuel made from black oil: poisonous, explosive, and seemingly inexhaustible.

'No,' I said to Auva and Graffias, 'I will stay and die with you.'

It occurred to me that if the humans killed me in this lonely, southern sea, then I could never make a covenant with them.

I believed that the humans in the killer boat with its grenade-tipped harpoons might soon kill all of us. And then a second boat crested the choppy waves to the west, and began converging upon us as well.

'Now we are certainly lost!' Auva cried out.

We tried swimming faster but could not. Every muscle along my belly and flukes burned with a white-hot agony as I breached too often to suck in too many desperate breaths. The water thickened to what seemed a gelatinous mass that clung to my whole body and then hardened like a solid wall. The metallic shriek of the killer boat's propellers tore into me and grew louder and then louder and louder.

'Farewell,' Auva said from what seemed far away – though she swam in a furious bunching of muscle and hopelessness scarcely ten feet away from me. 'It was good to know you, Arjuna.'

The killer boat loomed nearly right above us. I thought of the man on the beach outside the Institute: how quickly he had fired lead bullets into living whales and had used grenades to blow bloody red holes into Baby Electra's body! What great sport the humans found in the slaughter of people who could not escape them! I heard the hooded humans on the deck shouting out their excitements. Then they fired the first harpoon. It missed us, and exploded into the water in an outrage of miscarried death.

'Why do they not fire a second harpoon?' Graffias called out above the whine of the boat's propellers.

Our hearts sounded together once, twice, many times. We waited upon a slender, bobbing ice floe of life for what seemed an hour. I did not, at first, have the answer to Graffias' question. With my heart beating out little booms of doom that recalled the last moments of the white bear far away, I dove to escape the humans' harpoons.

I wished I could breathe water, but I could not. When I breached to blow out stale, stinging air, the shifting wind carried to me a bitterly remembered sound: 'Bobo, Bobo, Bobo!'

Two of the men on the ship had binoculars pressed to their tiny eyes. I knew they had recognized me. The white bear had cut a unique lightning-bolt scar into my forehead, and a murderer had blown off the tip of my dorsal fin.

'The humans,' I said to Auva and Graffias, 'may want me more than you. Let us see if they have the hook of greed or vengeance buried in them.'

I bade them to keep swimming south. Then I said farewell, and turned toward the east.

As I listened to the blue whales racing away from me and singing out encouragements, the killer ship also turned east. No more harpoons did its humans fire. I saw the men on the deck wrestling with nets, and I realized that they meant to capture me.

I felt sure that they would – and felt the burn of nylon ropes searing me even before the hated netting tightened around my skin. They would enslave me again, and return me to Sea Circus's punishment pool. I felt fate closing on me, smothering me, negating me. I swam through open water that provided no protection or place of safety.

Surely I would have been lost if the second boat had not veered to intercept the killer boat. For it proved to be a very different sort of vessel, manned – and womanned! – by very different sorts of humans. As it drew nearer, I made out the shape of diving dolphins painted on the iron hull side by side with the famous interlocking WW. On the Institute's screens, I had watched the play and maneuver of these so-called Whale Warriors: the saviors of my people! Even as I now watched the new boat set a ramming course toward the killer boat.

I should have fled then. I should have kept swimming – and swimming and swimming! – until I found myself in seas empty of human beings. On all of Ocean, however, there was no such place. And so I watched as the two floating monsters of metal steered this way and that, seeking and avoiding, charging and deflecting, and finally, in the roiling green waters that tossed them about, coming up side to side and colliding in a great clang of iron on iron.

The shock of the impact knocked a man off the deck of the Whale Warriors' ship. He plunged down into the water, where the shock of the cold would have killed him in minutes but for the strange-looking yellow wetsuit that he wore. This covering of plastic, though, did not save him. For just as he surfaced to cry out for help, the great angry waves hurled the two ships together again and crushed the man between them. I heard his bones break, and zanged the rupturing of his organs. It sounded almost like fingers popping air bubbles out of a strand of kelp. His bloody body slumped facedown in the rolling waves.

I waited for more humans to be propelled into the sea. I hoped I might be able to kill a few of them before the ships or the water did. The ships, however, drew apart from each other even as the waves bounced them about. Shouts and wails split the air and rippled the water. As the women and men on the Whale Warriors' ship began the rescue of the lifeless man, I gave up and swam off toward the icebergs in the south.

For many days afterward, I could not blink away the image of the dead human nor could I escape the cries of his friends who mourned him. How strange were these humans! What whale would ever sacrifice his life to save another of a different kind – or even of a different clan? Had the mangled man, in his pitiful covering of yellow plastic, truly deserved such a fate? Was it even possible for a human to do brave, good things? It seemed to me that whenever they tried to bring forth the highest in themselves, they were always crushed – or shot or hanged or crucified.

The more that I considered the matter, however, the more I felt certain that the Whale Warriors' motives for sailing into this icy sea were not *just* good and brave. Surely the dead man had wanted to – needed to – see himself as a sort of hero. He wanted to save the whales! In his beneficence and magnanimity, so great that he had given his very life, I made out the hidden hand of a king bestowing boons upon his subjects. Was not the saving of others yet another way of exerting power over them? Did not all humans take some part of their identity and their deeper sense of being human from their power to shape the world: the power of life and death itself? No matter how hard the humans tried to do otherwise, it seemed that their actions brought forth from the world more and more death.

In the clash of the two ships crushing the life out of the whale warrior's heart, I heard the breaking of any remaining hope that the humans as a whole race would cease making war upon each other – and upon the world. I perceived as well the impossibility of the humans ever being truly good. So it was that out of the newly reached depths of my disdain for all things human, I conceived of an intensification of my plan to hurt them. I called this the Day of Death.

I spoke of this to a gathering of the Midnight Sun Singers in the Seal Sea. Five families assembled to greet me: The Red Chanters, the Tanglow Rhapsodists, The Crimsong Rhapsodists, The Emerald Whistlers, and the Golden Sun Breathers. After I finished a long soliloquy stating the reasons why the Great Covenant should be broken, the great-grandmother of the Midnight Sun Singers swam as close to me as her daughters would allow. Hundreds of orcas – more than I had ever seen meeting together in one place – fanned out in a circle from the center that Grandmother Minkara and I formed.

'I have long wondered,' she said, 'if the humans' blood tastes as good as that of seals. If we do as you say, Arjuna, the humans will begin slaughtering *us* like seals.'

'They already do, in one way or another. Soon all whales will be wiped out.'

Grandmother Minkara aimed a soft zang at her daughter Pleione, who nursed a newly born baby named Botein.

'Yes,' she said, 'we will be, but how soon? It might be that Baby Botein would have the chance to grow up and father children on his own.'

At this, Baby Botein swallowed back a whimper of protest, and pressed up against Pleione's black and white side.

'Perhaps Baby Botein will be able to father children,' I said. 'But their grandchildren will not. Would it not be better for us all to go over now rather than dying by parts: poisoned, harpooned, starved, trapped, and doomed to suffer the dying of our beloved Ocean, too?'

The Midnight Sun Singers drew in tight together as they considered this. The water filled with their voices.

'Let us agree,' I said, 'as I hope whales around the world will agree, that on the day of the Blood Solstice, we will attack the humans and kill as many of them as we can before they turn to kill us. The humans have an expression: to go out in a blaze of glory. If we cannot exterminate them, then would it not be better to die together as one?'

From very near me in the freezing blue water, Grandmother Minkara gazed at me with her hot, hot blue eye. And then she said, 'You speak of death, but in your desolation, I also zang a murmur of hope. It suffuses each of your words as salt does water.'

'Yes,' I said, 'in the war that must follow, the humans will perceive us acting together even as they themselves do. If we cannot slay all of them, then at least we can slay the illusion that they alone of all the world's creatures are intelligent.'

'What will that avail us?'

'Perhaps nothing, for us orcas,' I said. 'Perhaps the humans will wipe out all of us. If they do, however, they will slay something vital in their own souls. When the soul dies, the body soon follows. The body of humans, seeing what it has done, is sure to turn on itself. The humans will destroy themselves in a last war. The orcas will die with them, but at least Ocean will be saved.'

The water grew quiet. None of the hundreds of orcas breathed. Only Baby Botein, whispering in fear, made any sound at all.

Then Grandmother Minkara said to me, 'That is not the whole of your hope, is it?'

'No,' I said, 'it is not.'

I told her, and all of the Midnight Sun Singers, of the soul force called *satyagraha* that we whales might wield to make the humans be no more.

'It is possible,' I said, 'just barely possible that if all the whales in Ocean on a single day begin killing the humans with our teeth, we might become a single people and so break through the ice of our restraint to a new power of being. Then we will kill the humans with our minds.'

'Do you think we can really do that?' Grandmother Minkara asked.

'Why not?' I said. 'We are killer whales, are we not? Is there anything on Ocean we cannot evolve to kill?'

For most of the next two days, the Sun Singers considered all that I had said. Most of them wished to confer with me individually, swimming in close to exchange words, zanging me softly or even brushing up against me with their great bodies. When we had assured each other that we were of one heart, Grandmother Minkara spoke for all her clan, saying, 'All right, Arjuna – we will wait for the Blood Solstice and we will join you on this Day of Death.'

With this promise, I swam off to speak with other whales in other seas. I would never see Grandmother Minkara again, and after the morning of the red, red day that I had appointed, I would never hear from her either. For surely I, leading the first wave of the assault upon the humans, would die. Indeed, I *must* die. If I truly had become human upon my killing of Gabi's murderer, then I must now perish along with the rest of humanity.

Only for a moment did I question this fate; only for a single breath of doubt did I wonder if I might really be a whale at heart. And then human – all-too-human – words sounded inside me. Of course I was one of them! Only a human would have twisted the noble, non-violence concept of *satyagraha* into a calling to commit genocide. Only a human would ever have conceived of something so hateful, so evil, so monstrously egoic as wiping out the entire human race.

With my course now assured, I set out on the longest journey I had ever made. I needed to speak with as many of the world's whales as I could, in every ocean. I swam through the various waters encircling the southern continent, and then up toward the Sea of Sharks, where I sang of death with the Sapphire Minstrel Family. As the Moon of Mourning melted away into a silvery wisp and then reformed itself into the Red Moon of Memories, I crossed the glowing Tiralee Sea, which echoed with the many colors of tintigloss. In the Sea of Shadows, I met with the Venerable Deep Divers. Mother Subra, the clan's new matriarch (old Grandmother Ascella having recently died), reaffirmed Ocean's wish that the humans should be no more. She, too, made promises to me, saying, 'We will await the Blood Solstice, Arjuna. We will move as you move, think as you think, dream as you dream, breathe as you breathe.'

Long days of hard travel through sun and storm died into nights full of stars which called me ever on. How I wished I could find my way up to these guiding lights a last time! How I longed to swim with my faroff family in the north as I had when I was young. Did my grandmother, I wondered, still live? Did my mother cry out to me in those terrible moments when the missing of those we adore gathers in our lungs like a deep breath of water? Did great, gracious Alnitak think of me, finding my way around the world through the gift of his maps of the heavens and the oceans, or had he long since given up hope of my return? Had my family heard of my aspirations for the humans? What would happen to my family when the whole of Ocean pointed its northern pole toward the sun on the Blood Solstice and the Day of Death began?

Though none spoke of it, all the orcas with whom I conversed dwelled in discontent with this last question. Who would ever wish to leave our beautiful, blue planet? Who could bear the awakening from the great dream of life's going on forever and finding itself anew uncountable times in the depths of its inextinguishable love for all of Ocean? How could any of us long live with the contemplation of red waters empty of all the beautiful people who had raced and dived and hunted and mated in joy and the deepest delight?

'It is coming!' Mother Elnath said to her family of the Hopeful Whistlers after I had spoken with her. We swam together near the center of the Magenta Shallows. 'The Blood Solstice is coming, and on that day, we will move as Arjuna moves, think as he thinks, dream as he dreams. We will dive with him, and die with him. We know what is in his heart – we can feel his heart!'

The seis with whom I conferred voiced similar sentiments, and so did the grays and the blue whales. The humpbacks composed lovely and haunting songs of the way the world must be. Even the dolphins consented to join in the solstice gathering. In the Barracuda Basin's pellucid turquoise waters, I swam with the large clan of the Amorously Ecstatic Music Makers. I helped them make nets out of bubbles by swimming with them in an ever-tightening spiral in which we trapped a large school of fish. After we had feasted but before the wild mating and the dalliances began, many of the dolphins cried out to me, 'We can feel your heart, Arjuna, we can feel you heart! We will make of this a music that has never been!'

So I swam through seasons and songs, listening always to the surging seas, which rang with the voices of my people. I moved with the currents and the constellations, with the sun and the wind, and the Moon of Yearning gave way to the Moon of Enchantments, which yielded to the great yellow Mystics' Moon. I rounded the Cape of Hope and the Cape of Despair; I made my way along the coastlines of the continents, and I crossed the Turtle Sea. It was there in greenish waters silted with too many plastic fragments that I came upon a deep god who had news for me.

This great whale, so full of spermaceti and anticipation, informed me that Alkurah and Unukalhai had been searching the seas for me. They had heard of the Day of Death, and they wished to join me. I told the deep god of a place that we might rendezvous just before the solstice: an island off the coast of the darkest continent. The deep god agreed to call out with his huge voice to others of his kind many miles away. In this manner, my message would be relayed from whale to whale through the streaming and reverberant waters of the ocean.

I swam very hard toward the meeting place and the day that I had named. I breathed hot, tropical air and then the cooler breezes of more temperate climes. I tasted salt and fish, raindrops and gasoline and the blood-sweet tang of my last desperate hope.

One bright evening, I trembled with awe at a purpose far beyond my own as a great glister of light burst like a blinding whiteness out of the black chasm beyond the Greater Krill Constellation. This radiance sent by the Old Ones to push back the night – the humans would call it a supernova – pointed the way toward my fate. Stars streamed like glowing diatoms all around me; sparkling bits of shell swirled along my skin through long, impatient days. On and on I journeyed as Ocean turned its seas toward sun after rising sun, and the whole of my world moved silently through the empty spaces above and beneath me.

There came a morning of cottony white clouds and blue sky when I sighted the island that I had spoken of. I swam toward it, and sounded its rocky contours. The whales waiting off the island's coast called out to me. I met them in the shallows where big breaking waves washed white foam onto a pebbly beach.

'Alkurah!' I called back as I swam closer. 'Unukalhai!'

Through water cloudy with bits of broken seaweed, the three of us came together in a reunion of pounding flukes and skin gliding over skin. We sang out in a violet joy so intense that it hurt. Again and again, we touched each other, and zanged each other, and we breathed together as we once had done.

'You are so thin!' Alkurah said to me. 'Look what the humans have done to your fin!'

Her voice touched the very tip of my proud dorsal fin, which had been blown into bloody fragments by the human's bullet.

'And you,' I said to Alkurah, brushing against her side, 'have new scars.'

So did Unukalhai. Before they could recount their adventures, six other orcas appeared out of the murky water to make my acquaintance, for Unukalhai and Alkurah had not come here alone. Alkurah introduced these new orcas: Hadar, Castor, Pollux, Kuma, Azha, and Propus. Most of them had been orphaned in the same war games that had nearly killed me. Alkurah, who missed her sisters Zavijah and Salm with a keening pain that seemed only to have intensified during the many days since the slaughter at the Institute, had assembled the hapless whales into a new family.

'When we heard the news of you,' Alkurah said, 'we swam down from the north to meet you.'

For the rest of the day, we exchanged stories. Alkurah told of a narrow escape from an armada of boats that had pursued them on their flight from the Institute; then she moved on to the account of how, many days later and after so many, many days and seasons of trying, she had finally become pregnant.

'We met up with the Amorous Flutists in the Pearl Sea,' she said, 'and I took my pleasure with many brothers and cousins of their clan. It may have been Fornacis or Yildun who fathered my baby.'

No young whale now swam near her, and I waited for her to say more.

'When I felt Baby Avior quicken inside me,' she said, 'I was as happy as Zavijah had been when she gave birth to Navi – happier, I think. I spoke to Avior night and day. So many times I called him to come out and see the world! He moved with so much life! He never, though, came out as I'd hoped. When I miscarried, I was afraid that he might have sensed my dread of the humans and decided to die rather than be born. Now, upon reflection, I think otherwise. You see, the day before Avior grew still in my womb, I ate some bad fish, and was very sick. I feel sure the fish were contaminated with an abortifacient or some other human drug.'

Her silence carried me far away to sorrowful seas. I touched her side and felt her shaking with memory.

'I am sorry,' I told her.

'It does not matter now,' she said. 'Avior swims with Baby Electra and my sisters, and soon I will join all of them.'

The Wailing Moon crested the horizon in the east, towards which we would soon swim. A reddish glow touched the water. We talked together into a clear and star-streaked evening as we waited for other families of orcas to join us.

'Do you think they will come?' Unukalhai asked me.

'Yes, they will come.'

'And the other whales across Ocean – do you think they will rendezvous at their meeting places?'

'I know they will.'

'Then our dreams will become our fate,' he said. 'In three more days, when the Blood Solstice dawns, nothing will stop the Day of Death.'

In my silence, Alkurah detected a note of disquiet. So did Unukalhai, who could zang my psyche more clearly than anyone except my Grandmother.

'How long, Arjuna,' he said to me, 'have we who have once broken the Covenant yearned to break it completely and for all time?'

I did not answer him directly. I said, 'I have yearned too long to taste the humans' blood. And I have wondered what moral principle beyond the Great Covenant we should follow?'

'Principle!' he shouted. Then his cry broke apart into angry laughter. 'Morals! You *have* become too human, brother. The humans have morality; we whales have true nature. What we will do on the day you have chosen will come from our hearts and will occur far, far beyond good and evil.'

Was that really true, I wondered? With the wind stirring up little waves upon the water, I faced east toward the dark, bloody continent lost in the night. How very soon we would swim in that direction and know at last the great and terrible thing that nature called us to do!

23

As I had promised, over the next two days other orcas arrived: those of the Scarlett Song Keepers and the entire clan of the Grateful Bluenight Listeners. For hundreds and thousands of miles up and down the coast to the north and south – and along the coasts of all the continents east and west – the orcas would be gathering, along with our cousin dolphins and the great, great whales.

On the eve of the solstice, we began moving away from the island. Gabi, Helen, and Baby Electra – and many of the Old Ones – accompanied us. The moon rained down unending showers of white sparkles onto the sea. In silence we swam through this delicious shimmer. We knew very well where the humans' beaches were. How had the humans supposed they could swim in the ocean and not be molested by sharks? Had they ever given thought as to how 'their' beaches were protected from the tigers, makos, and great whites – and who protected them?

I pointed the way toward a white-sand beach that one of the Song Keepers had described to me. I knew it from Alnitak's maps. I had also seen this broad beach from various vantages in one of the humans' videos. For every year, on the Summer Solstice, the humans held a surfing competition here. In only a few more hours, women and men would brave the breaking waves with their flimsy plastic surf boards as thousands of other humans thronged the beach to watch. They would use their cameras to snatch images of the surfers standing on top of the water in defiance of good sense and gravity – images that would be cast around the world.

'The sea is calm tonight,' Unukalhai said, playing with the words of a human poem. 'The tide is full, and the moon lies fair upon the sea.'

'Let us be true to each other,' Alkurah replied with a deadly seriousness. And then she said to me: 'We will move as you move, think as you think, breathe as you breathe. We will dream your last dream.'

We neared the land, and the great eastern sun of a long, long day broke upon the waves in a reddish-pink glister. Many people stood and sat and lay upon the beach looking out to sea. The surfers on their colorful boards splashed into the water and began paddling out toward us. We hid far out behind the swells as best we could, for we did not wish anyone to espy our fins and sound an alarm.

'Is it time?' Alkurah said to me as the sun rose higher and blistered the blue sky.

Her new family was to swim with us straight ahead toward the surf beach. The Scarlett Song Keepers would cover the beach to the north, while the Bluenight Listener Clan would attack the many beaches to the south where many people bathed and swam.

'Almost,' I said. 'I am still hoping the dolphins will join us.'

The sun grew hotter on the black skin of our backs whenever we surfaced to breathe. Then the dolphins, who have little sense of time, finally arrived: the entire clan of the Mellifluous Vermillion Exhilarators. A few of their younger ones could not restrain their excitement. They leaped out of the water in a squeaking, chattering display that drew the humans' attention.

'Surely it is time now?'

This came from Kumaia, one of the orcas who had joined

Alkurah's family. Alkurah did not like this little whale from the western isles speaking in her place. She did nothing to discipline her, however, and repeated the same question.

'Let the sun,' I said, 'warm the water just a little more and draw more of the humans into the sea.'

'Very well,' Alkurah said in her best matriarch's voice. Then she surprised me, saying, 'I will wait upon you to lead forth on the charge toward the beach.'

The sun grew ever hotter. The shallows to either side of the surf beach teemed with humans like vast brown and white and black schools of salmon.

'It is warm! It is warm!' one of the baby dolphins shouted.

I breached, and the water slipped down my fin as I drew in a great breath of air to give the command. However, the breath bruised my lungs, and I could not speak.

'Courage, brother!' Unukalhai called to me. He knew me too well. 'The humans wait before us! Let us play a game of their making in order to inspirit each other.'

He suggested that we recite lines from the Bhagavad Gita that a god and a human hero had spoken just before the battle of Kurukshetra.

'I will be the blue god, Krishna,' he said. 'And you will be . . . Arjuna.'

Along the beach, many humans gathered and gazed out to sea.

'All right,' I said with a harsh laugh.

And then he replied, 'There is a war that opens the waters of heaven. Happy are the warriors whose fate is to fight such a war.'

'My fate is my fate,' I said, 'but when I see all my kinsmen who have come here today on this field of battle, life goes from my flippers and fins and sinks into the sea. My mouth is sear and dry; a trembling overcomes my body, and my skin shudders in horror.'

And he replied: 'Thy tears, Arjuna, are for those beyond tears. The wise grieve not for those who live; and they grieve not for those who die, for life and death shall pass away. For we have

433

been for all time: I, and thou, and all the mothers and the grand-mothers of the peoples of the sea. And we shall be for all time, all for ever and ever.'

The sun rose an inch higher before us. Harpoons of light struck down into the sea. The sound of humans screaming out encour-agements to the surfers carried over the sparkling waves.

'It is time!' I cried out. 'It is time!'

I moved forward beneath the surging waters. So did Alkurah and the rest of her family who swam close to her. Unukalhai passed my cry to the Scarlett Song Keepers to the south, who began closing on the beaches in front of them. So it would be around the world on all the beaches the humans favored, even those sunk into the twilight of evening or the glittering blackness of full night.

A line of surfers out in the sea sat on their boards. They waited to take their turns riding one of the waves that gathered beneath them and moved them up and down. One of these boards – all orange and yellow and streaked red like the sun – caught my eye. I could barely make out the female to whom it belonged. I descried a bit of black hair and a strip of pink fabric around her chest and hips. I zanged her to gain a better sense of her shape and precise position. Then I gulped in a breath and dived.

I would, I promised myself, wait until she had caught her wave. Then I would rise up beneath her board as I once had with Gabi in the big pool at Sea Circus: I would propel both board and human into the air in a feat somewhat mimicking the 'rocket.' As the human screamed and reached the apogee of her unexpected flight into space, I would open wide my jaws and snatch her out of the air. This spectacular wipeout would provide a great oppor-tunity for a very memorable photo. After the surfer and I had splashed down into the water, I would let her go. The humans on the beach, perhaps, might think I was only playing. And so I would, seizing her once more in my teeth and grinding down until her leg bones snapped. And again I would release her and return to her; I would play with her, biting off a hand or perhaps her face, playing and playing as the horror built and the thousands of humans watching felt helpless to rescue her – even as we whales feel helpless to rescue ourselves from the humans. Then would come the grand finale in which I would tear the human into bloody pieces and rip out her heart.

I swam in closer. I waited near the bottom of the sands that sloped out from the beach beneath the water. The surfer's orange board above me began moving as a wave swelled and began breaking toward the beach. It quickly gained speed. I rose then. Straight up I swam in a burst of driving flukes and all my fury to close with the surfer. Water streaked over my skin; bits of churned-up sand and shell stung my eyes. The orange board grew larger and larger. I came up beneath and pushed my face against its center. How many times had I performed similar feats? Up and up I moved, breaching into a shock of cool air and sudden sun, and my explosion into space flung up the spinning orange board and the now-flying surfer.

'Mada!' another surfer cried out from her board a few dozen yards away. 'Mada!'

Suspended in space just beneath the human named Mada, nearly frozen in a moment of time, I opened my mouth to catch her before she tumbled back into the water. Two things, however, kept me from doing so. As Mada's face turned toward my own, something about her struck me into stillness. I looked and I looked at her black, sodden hair whipping in the wind, and the sight of this disquietingly familiar human whipped me back into time. It was the woman of my dream, I realized, the dream I had dreamed during my first journey to the humans! Except for her pink swimsuit, she was all golden skin from her face to her feet; and her eyes, fixed on my eyes even as we fell, were as bright as black pearls. Her lithe limbs and perfectly formed body, curved with flowing muscles, moved as if completely comfortable in the air. That was the second thing that saved her from my original intentions. With a rare grace lovely to behold, she gathered herself about her center and managed to recover from the pell-mell tumble through the air. Somehow, she pointed her hands toward the water, and her arms, shoulders, breasts, belly, legs, and feet followed in a flawlessly executed dive. I splashed down almost on top of her. She kicked up to the surface and gasped for air, and the other surfers gasped in astonishment at what they had seen. A few of them clapped. The sound of their wet hands coming together cracked out over the waves, and I heard the fainter applause of the hundreds of hands of the humans along the beach.

'Mada de la Fuente!' many voices called out. 'Mada! Mada! Mada!'

The woman I had failed to crush at the first pass looked at me a few feet away in the breaking waves, and she laughed out in delight.

'Let's do that again!' she called to me.

She started swimming toward her orange and yellow board, caught in the churn of the surf.

'Brave human!' I called back to her. It seemed she could not understand Wordsong. 'Foolish human – have you no fear?'

I moved through the waves, and pushed her board away from her reaching hands. This did not dispirit her. She was a strong swimmer – the best human swimmer I had ever seen.

'So you want to play!' she shouted to me as she treaded water and fought to keep the sea from filling her mouth. 'Come here then so we can play!'

I looked at her more closely as water glistened on her beautiful face. Her eyes, now as big and bright as black moons, pulled at me with a strange gravity. She gazed at me through the spray and drank me in. I zanged her – she was red, red, flowing and flaming red with all the fires of life. Her whole being was pregnant with blazing purpose! In her womb, a little seed of a girl child had sprouted and now grew in a pulsing of blood and deep, deep hope.

'Thy tears,' Unukalhai said from somewhere near me, 'are for those beyond tears. Grieve not for those who die.'

436

Two humans, then, I would need to slay with a closing of my teeth.

'This cannot be the way!' I shouted.

Between the beats of my heart, from very, very close, all of Ocean shouted back: 'The humans must be no more!'

I moved closer to Mada. So trusting she seemed! So certain that I had come here to cavort with her in the froth and turn of the waves!

'Mada, Mada, Mada,' I murmured in sounds that she could not understand, yet strangely somehow did. 'Mada!'

I asked her if she was ready to die. And then, in the fire of her eyes, in the fury of her blood, in the wild fountain of life pouring out of her and into the sea, she said . . . *No!*

I did not want to believe what I heard. In amazement, I asked her again. Her answer to me rose with all the power of the unceasing surf, and in a terrible question of her own cracked out like thunder: 'Are you ready to live?'

I moved closer to her. The water moved with me. I looked into her eyes, her large, liquid human eyes. No fear could I see there! And that was very strange, for I felt her awareness of me awakening her whole being to the reason why I had come here today. Somehow, perhaps through her will to smile upon the world, her fear had flowed into fascination. Perhaps she possessed a new lobe to her brain. She *knew* that something terrible worked at my soul – and was aware that I could apprehend this awareness spreading like cold water through her. She knew something else, too, that I could not quite see. I felt it swelling within me like a dark, dark wave.

'Are you ready to live?' she asked again as she swam toward me.

An entire sea built and pressed against every part of me. Overflowing with the hurt of it, what should I answer her?

'Yes,' I said.

The sound of my assent broke me open. It was as if a hammer

had caved in a conch shell. Yes, I am ready, yes, yes! Mada swam closer through the raging surf, and her mouth opened in a smile of recognition that there was something I wanted much more than her slaughter.

'Go away!' I shouted in a language that she could not possibly comprehend.

What did I really want? I asked myself. And the angry ocean answered back: 'The humans must be—'

'No!' I shouted. 'I will not do this thing!'

But then my heart raged with the wrath of blood that moved it, and I longed to drink in the blood of Mada's furiously beating heart. I could almost feel the tangy red liquid hardening inside me like iron and pulling me down to the ocean's cold, lightless bottom from which nothing can arise again.

'Arjuna!' my grandmother called to me. Her voice sounded through the sea from far away – but also from impossibly close. 'Remember the charm!'

Before Mada could swim a foot nearer, I opened the charm. I had done so, of course, many times. However, although I had listened to the many pretty songs it contained, I had never been able to apprehend its deeper contents. That is something that the humans have never really understood about our language: that a whale can hear all of a song or a rhapsody only through the consciousness of the one who created it. Into the charm my grandmother had placed all of her love for me, and her voice had sustained me during the worst moments of my journeys. Now, though, only moments away from the very worst moment of my life, with my heart opening to my grandmother's heart and all that she most fervently felt and knew, I realized that love itself, like the red, red petals of one of the humans' flowers, opens outward and downward through infinitely many layers. What dwells at the very center? What sounded from within the heart of my grandmother's charm? Only the deepest and most dreadful truth of love: that we cannot love one thing without loving everything.

'Arjuna!' the human named Mada cried out to me as she pulled at the sea with her golden arms and all her will to reach me. 'Arjuna, Arjuna!'

What did the world *really* want from me? I opened my mouth to greet her, and she closed the last distance between us and wrapped her little, knowing fingers around one of my teeth. At her touch, in a sudden understanding that zanged through me like a shock of lightning, I realized a thing: I did not hate the humans – not just. I loved them.

I loved their eyes, so sad, so anguished, so liquid, so deep and dark yet bright with impossible hopes. I loved their hands, sensitive and caressing, itching to touch, needing to touch, to reach out, to shape the world that had shaped them. I loved their fingers that had scratched those parts of me that I would never be able to reach. Their monkey faces I loved as well: mobile and expressive, shaped by time and by themselves. I loved their little brains, like little seeds, ever ready to sprout and grow. I loved their slobbering dogs and their doggedness, the way they found infinite layers of courage in the face of the sickening insanities and the horrors that they made. Poems and paintings, the symphonies of Beethoven and the counterpoint play of Bach – these things I loved, too, as I did the glorious sounds of Mozart's magic flutes and violas. And light shows and fountains, somersaults, double-lutzes, and backward, twisting dives. I loved wheelchairs that made mobile those who could not otherwise move. Who could not love the humans' basic goodness, their sweetness and kindness, the gentleness with which they pressed their soft lips against the mouths of us whales? All things of fire did I love: the fires of their matches, of their hearts, of their eyes. I loved the fires of their heavens, reached only by rockets or by gazing upward along pillars of living flame. And their burning bushes and tigers burning, burning in the forests of the night. I loved their souls burning for connection to the ocean of stars that fill with glory the blackness of the night. The humans who give birth to dancing stars I loved with a red-hot

ardor. I loved the whale warrior who had died in the freezing
Antarctic sea, for surely he had given his life out of love in order
to protect me. The humans' children I loved even more: their
innocence, enthusiasm, brio, and sheer zest as they screamed out
their wild joy of life. Most of all, I loved the great dream of life
that the humans had created. Astonishingly – agonizingly, impossibly – I even loved plastic, for this execrable but marvelously
malleable material gave evidence that the humans could create
something new that had never existed in all the universe.

I loved Mada. How could I not? As she moved before me,
kicking the water with her feet, she held onto my tooth with her
hand: her strange human hand that could deal out death as easily
as it could touch me in love. Her black eyes opened upon all the
terror of hate and love, as powerful in her as it was in me. And
yet, she did not fear this terror; rather, she reveled in it as she did
all the delights and dangers of the pounding surf. Her eyes were
oceans of love, dark and mysterious, ablaze with the same fire
that worked its magic in me. They drank me in and devoured me,
and invited me to do the same.

'Yes, I will,' I told her.

I had broken the first covenant; I had broken the second and
the third. How could I once more break this sacred promise, whose
heart my grandmother knew as absolute truth and I called love?

'Yes, yes, yes!'

I had one fate, and one only, and I must somehow come to love
it even as I did Mada. I closed my teeth around her hand . . . gently.
I wanted her to know that I would always be gentle with her.

'How can I surf,' she asked me, 'if you won't let me have my
board?'

In the froth of the waves thirty feet from us, her board bounced
about. In that direction, too, Alkurah and Unukalhai played with
the surfers they had chosen, and they waited to see what I would
do.

'Let us surf together,' I said to Mada.

I dropped down and came up beneath her. She spent some minutes lying face down on my back. Her belly worked hard in little spasmings to fill her lungs with air. When she had caught her breath, she pressed her lips to me in a long, long kiss. Her fingers stroked me, dancing in ten little delights along my skin. She laughed as if she could hold nothing inside. I knew that she very well knew what was to come. I prepared myself for the most difficult feat of my life.

'Arjuna!' Unukalhai called out to me from across the waves. 'You are right to do what you do! Let us show the humans what is really inside us! Love hurts much more than hate!'

And Alkurah, playing with a surfer through the water's spray said, 'Let us then hurt the humans with all of our hearts.'

The other whales of her new family picked up her promise: 'We will move as you move, Arjuna, think as you think, dream as you dream. Always, always, we will love as you love.'

So sang the orcas of the Scarlett Song Keepers and the Grateful Bluenight Listeners, and the sea rang with their cries. In the shallows to the south where many humans waded in the spent waves, the dolphins darted between startled women and men, and they leaped about in a great and happy play. Children's laughter shrilled out to match the dolphins' whistles. Two of the dolphins passed a giggling girl back and forth in the water as they might a beach ball. Flippers and arms and legs and flukes glistened in the morning sun.

'Let's surf together!' Mada said to me.

Behind us, farther out in the sea, one of the deep gods breached in a mighty leap that seemed to carry him a mile into the sky. It looked like Old Father. Up and down the beaches, I knew, along all the continents of Ocean, other great whales and dolphins and orcas would be losing themselves in the great and unstoppable tsunami of love that swept around the world. It had come time, after so many days and eons, for a moment of celebration.

'All right,' I told Mada, 'let us surf.'

We waited together in the swelling sea for the perfect wave. The sounds of whales and humans playing rippled through the water in colors of pearlpurl and amberymn. We rose and fell with wave upon wave sparkling in the morning sun. Then the sea called up a great, flowing part of itself that we could not resist. I swam hard to let its curling, powerful sweep catch me up and carry me along toward the thousands of humans cheering and calling amazement from the shore. Mada pushed herself up, and stood on my back. Her feet pressed into me with sureness and wisdom, sensually, knowingly, flesh communicating with flesh where spirit desired to go.

We spent at least a year on that long, endless, first ride through the spray flung out by the wave and through the much clearer and warmer substance that moved us. The sun opened the sky with its fire and caressed us with ten thousand fingers of flame. Mada laughed as she danced up and down my spine. I moved to the slightest nuance of pressure of her touch. In this way, we surfed together the ocean of our world until the beach loomed too close and the great wave was spent.

Other waves, though, in their flowing infinitude, arose from the deeps. I swam out to sea again with Mada on my back. While waiting for the next perfect surge of water, Mada and I played together. She dove off me, and swam beneath me, and I took my turn doing the same. I swam upside down as she lay spread-eagled on top of me, belly pressing against belly, her fingers soft against my flipper's skin. She pulled at me with urgency and invitation, as if she wanted me to touch the inside of her with the same fire that passed back and forth from her blazing, black eyes into mine.

'I've never felt so safe in the sea!' she said to me.

Neither had I. We rolled about in the surging of the waves. Her heart beat against mine, and her breath fell over me in a cool, little wind, and all the sounds of the sea came together in a rhapsody of crimsong.

As gently as I could, I felt my way inside her with the touch of pure sonance. Her heart pulsed out hot, hot blood in endless booming beats, and the rush of plasm in her trillions of cells called to the same surging within me. I zanged her every tissue and torment, and dwelt within her breath, and in her loneliness and her joy. I spoke deep into her womb where the wildest part of her lived and called out in triumph and exaltation. She called to me from this red, raging center with a single sound that was just the sound of life itself: plangent, painful, lovely, long, and deep. All smaller sounds were there, every tiralee, murmur, moan, plaint, and whisper of love that could ever be. She kept calling to me as if she could never stop, forever calling me home to a place I had always been. And so we sang together, and breathed together, and knew each other true. As salt deliquesces in a warm mist and returns in a tinkle of rain to the sea, we loved each other, and vanished into each other as we became one.

After ten thousand years had passed, I became aware that Ocean was asking me in the thunder of its surf the same question that she had always asked, of me and every living thing.

'Yes!' I cried out in an agony of an answer – but in joy, too. 'Yes, yes, a trillion, trillion times yes!'

Only then did I realize the monstrousness of the mistake I had made. *We want the humans to be no more!* I had thought Ocean had said this in the Sea of the Seven Silences. But I had misheard her will. Out of the wrongness of the world, out of the wrongness of myself, in the neverness where dwells the desperate power of life's ultimate negation, I had overshouted better and truer voices, and I had supplied the great 'No' of my own.

'We want,' the waves washing over Mada and me roared out, 'the humans to be *more*.'

Yes, I cried out, yes, yes! How very, very soon they must vanish into a new form!

The keenings of the orcas and dolphins up and down the beaches affirmed this, and the godlike laughter of many humans told that they wanted the same thing.

'But how can that be?' I cried out.

It was Mada's unborn child who answered me. As I dwelled inside Mada's womb with this wild sprig of humanity, she sang to me of all her hope for life. She was nothing but hope and life and all the human genius for reaching out into life's infinite possibilities. I sang back to her. I bathed her blood and her wondering brain in the songs of my people. I spoke to the deep, listening part of her in the one language that underlies all others. She would be born in bright sun and salt water to the music of the whales. She would understand our voices. She would speak to us in a new voice, even as she would bespeak herself and all the humans that they might find their way to become more and ever more beautifully more.

'We will help you,' I said. Altair, I named her, after a star close to Ocean. 'Life is so hard.'

'And we will help you,' she promised me. She was all the promise of the world. 'We will move as you move, think as you think, dream as you dream. Our life will be in yours, and your life in us.'

So it was that we made a covenant between our two kinds, the true great covenant to love in the face of even deep, deep hurts and death.

Mada, who would be the mother of millions, seemed to know exactly what occurred between me and the child inside her. She looked at me through the sea. She gave me a magic mirror, then, made from the liquid reflection of her dark eyes and all the waters of love: in this silvered sphere of splendor, I would always be able to see the best of the humans I encountered. And with the mirror, I might show the humans the glorious, golden shape of what they must become.

The giving of this gift, so alike in spirit to my grandmother's charm, seemed to focus the rays of light pouring down from the golden sun of the Blood Solstice: when humans and whales felt our blood beating through the arteries of the ocean from a single heart. Our kinds swam together and sang and wept together long into the afternoon of this Day of Death: when the humans' sense of estrangement from the world finally died and they knew they were not alone.

'Let's surf together again,' Mada said to me.

We waited along the line of whitecaps for the day's biggest wave. It rolled in from the open ocean like a great blue god. Just as the wave crested and reached the fullness of its power, I beat my tail hard against the water and drove us up into the air. The sky deepened as it opened out before us. Such a sky I had never seen! It was *our* sky: shimmering, magical, alive. Mada moved with me in perfect poise, and I felt us both sensing that something great was about to happen: a delicate balance between the nowness of the moment and the onstreaming unfolding of time yet to be. Then the sky gelled to a deep, deep glorre. It did not seem possible that such a color could exist. It pulled us onward, devoured us, drew us ever deeper into its astonishing perfection.

The drops of water flung from the wave sparkled like millions of stars. Past constellations without number we soared far beyond lightspeed through the one ocean that gives the brilliance of its deepest sound to creation. I might have been content to dive down into the peaceful waters of Agathange and rest for a while in peace, but Mada was not. She was human, after all, and would never cease moving as long as breath filled her lungs.

She spoke to me in the shared zest of our blood: 'There is so much more to see!'

Yes, I whispered, there is. And so I sang with her, and I surfed with her, and we quenged together across the bright universe whose shimmering song can never end.

24

There came a time late in the day when the sun plunged into the glowing, numinous waters, and I had to say goodbye to Mada. Her eyes flowed with salt water as she informed me that she would return to this beach the following year for another surfing competition. Would I return here as well, she asked me? I listened to the ocean calling up wave upon wave and sending out the sound of glorre to every part of the world. Then I promised this daring human being that one way or another, we would meet again.

During the days that followed what some of the humans would come to call Whale Demonstration Day, the deep gods passed their voices from one to another around the world. So we learned that other orcas and dolphins along every coast had indeed played with the humans much as Mada and I had done. On a bright morning, I gathered with Alkurah's new family far out to sea to discuss what had happened. Unukalhai offered an explanation for what might seem a miracle of instantaneous communication much more profound than the long-range callings of the deep gods:

'Every time you enjoined us to kill the humans,' he said, 'we knew that you were speaking metaphorically – at least we hoped you were. And we did kill something, did we not? Did you see the looks on the humans' faces? They doubt now, Arjuna – doubt that they are as superior as they have always assumed.'

I wondered if *all* the whales whom I had consulted had 'known' what Unukalhai insisted he had been aware of all along. Alkurah perhaps wondered the same thing, though she had no desire to dispute him. Instead, she voiced what the whales of her new family – and many others – were thinking:

'We knew,' she said, 'as all whales do, that in the end there would have to be a choice between love and hate. We also knew what was in your heart, Arjuna – the heart of the world.'

Does not the world, she said, hear the sound of its one desire in every drop of water and breaking instant of time?

'Perhaps you did,' I said, 'though I did not know it myself.'

'We are your family,' Alkurah said. 'How could you expect to know yourself as well as we do?'

'But you could not have known that I would make a covenant with the humans! I had promised all of Ocean that I would not!'

They had no answer for me, but Ocean did. This came in the sound of a great, great voice that moved the waters from far away. We zanged one of the deep gods swimming toward us. Soon he came into sight. So, I thought, when he came close enough that I could make out his blinded eye, I really *had* seen Old Father leap from the sea during the peace games with the humans. It seemed that he had been listening to all that we said.

'You did not make the covenant with the humans alone,' he told me. 'While you danced with the female you call Mada, all of Ocean hung suspended in time, yearning to spin one way or another. Your will was like a baby's breath that sets into motion a hurricane thousands of miles away. Could you not feel the will of the whole world in what you said and did?'

'Yes,' I told him, 'I could.'

The other whales understood almost nothing of what Old Father and I said together, and I had to translate for them. Propus, a young male Alkurah had adopted (his birth family had been slaughtered during one of the humans' slaving expeditions), could not contain his awe at listening to one of the deep gods speak. He also had difficulty accepting what must now come. He said to me:

'It is one thing, Arjuna, to play with those we hate. It is another to love them. How can we do that?'

And Azha, another orphaned whale, said this:

'Two days ago, in a way I cannot explain, when one of the little humans scratched my back, I *did* feel a kind of love for them – for a moment. But now I feel nothing of that.'

How should I answer her? Again, I opened my grandmother's charm. And I told Propus that love is only the conscious, heartfelt, and actively directed desire to do good to another. It is a force, not a feeling, though it engenders in us the strongest of feelings.

Unukalhai laughed at this. He said, 'On the day we met, Arjuna, I told you that you must become a little mad if you wished to dwell among the humans. And now, all this talk of loving them: the greatest madness of all! Must I do this thing? Ha, it is funny beyond words, but I suppose I must!'

And I must, too. None of Alnitak's maps showed the way toward where I must now go. Could I continue saying yes to the truth I had found lighting up Mada's eyes and pulsing within her womb? Did I have the intelligence – the sheer will – to move past all my hate for the humans and continue my journey ever deeper into my heart?

'What should we do now?' little Propus asked.

It was a good question, in a way, the only really important question. The whales of Ocean had turned away from slaying the humans with our jaws and the teeth of our minds in favor of a different kind of death. The *satyagraha* we had called up from the deeps within us truly had killed the humans' murderous innocence – or rather, had touched off the long course of its dying. It would be years, however, before Mada's unborn child and others like her grew into motherhood and began having children of their own.

What should we do until these new humans learned to navigate the most dangerous of seas and made Ocean their own?

'Go home,' I said to Propus and the others. 'It is time to go home.'

What more could I say to the humans? What we had done with them on the beaches of the world had spoken more loudly than any whale's utterance ever could.

'But where,' Propus asked, 'is home?'

Alkurah said that there were good fishing waters far to the north, beyond the bays near the Institute where we had once dwelled: waters now empty because the clans of orcas who had thrived there had gone.

'Why don't we live there?' she said. 'I will lead the way.'

'All right,' I said, 'I will swim with you.'

I asked Old Father if he would accompany us. But he had other journeys to make.

'I have been waiting and waiting to die,' he said, 'and now I can, oh, ho!'

'I do not want you to die,' I told him.

'Grieve not for those who die, for life and death shall pass away. For we have been for all time, and we shall be for all time, I and thou and all forever and ever.'

'I do not want you to die,' I told him again.

'Truly? Then perhaps I will not.' He surfaced to spout a geyser of salt water high into the air. 'Perhaps I will mate again, and watch my children grow into great whales. Perhaps I will find my way to the Silent Sea as you did. I have many questions I would ask the Seveners.'

'Let me know what they say,' I told him.

'I will! I will! Let us meet again in a hundred more years, and I will tell you everything I have learned.'

With a glint of amusement playing through his good eye, he said goodbye to me. Then he swam off toward the south in flurry of pounding flukes and a great rush of water.

Alkurah and I turned north with the others to begin our last, long journey. We moved side by side through the sea, diving and breathing together almost as if we had been born to one family. The cold currents brought us fish to eat and gave us strength. The constellations – the Silver Salmon, the twinkling Albatross, the brilliant stars of the Seveners – lighted our way. Every mile and moment that we swam, Ocean called us deeper into life, and into our individual lives, which was the only place anyone could ever go.

Such a song my planet had to sing! So many tastes, textures, and sights she had to give me! And all that I experienced after the Day of Death, each herring, strand of seaweed, and grain of sand, seemed at once agelessly old and marvelously new. I seemed new to myself, as if I could never return to my dreaded ways of perceiving and being again. What had happened with Mada had somehow, like the bracing touch of the waves, washed me clean.

This did not mean, however, that I no longer hated the humans; in truth, their willful ignorance of their true nature and their desperate cruelties grieved me as much as they ever had. Like a scar left by a bloody harpoon, hate never really goes away. Two things only saved me from falling back into my desire to destroy the humans. First, I could now sound the source of my hatred and could zang its place in the world. Everything, even the particles of plastic I could taste oiling the sea's salty tang, had a purpose. A plastic toy caught in the throat of a beautiful white bird might be an ugly thing, but were the atoms of carbon and oxygen that made up the toy's substance also ugly? The very same atoms, born in the hearts of stars, formed themselves into my mother's breath and made up the substance of me. Nothing ever came out of the universe's omnipresent ocean that was not perfect solely through the validation of its own existence. When I cast zangs of sonance and seeing at all the forms the world had called out of itself, even the hideous and the horrible, bright reflections returned out of even the most unbearable parts of creation in a beauty almost too brilliant to behold.

The second thing that buoyed me upward into the fresh air of new possibilities was my newly found love for the humans. This glorious and utterly ruthless force, too, could never go away. As Unukalhai had said, love hurts much more than hate – and my passion to sound both the grandeur and the dark caverns of the human heart ravished me. I could barely contain my anguish of desire to touch the humans' souls as I had Mada's body and to breathe into them the very breath of life. Such urgings moved me ever away from wrath into calmer and deeper seas. Although I still felt that I had nothing more to say to the humans, I wished that I could simply speak the truth of all my hope for them, and through the alchemy of the universe's most magical force, the dreadful future I felt pulling at the world with all the power of a diseased moon would transmute into something wondrous and golden. How I wanted that to be! How I wished to convince myself that such miracles *could* be, and that we whales could call out of the humans the best part of themselves as a mother orca does the wisest child of the deep.

As we swam north for league after league of blue, open ocean and the rising swells built stronger with the changing of the season, I felt this foolish desire rising ever more vast and powerful within me. Long days of clean, salty spray off the wind-whipped waves flowed into ever longer nights full of music and stars. The sea sang out in a voice of persuasion and promise that grew ever clearer. Now, in every drop of water, I *did* hear Baby Electra calling to me. She cried out in her death agony of slashing sharks' teeth and crimson blood again and again. Strangely though, she also laughed with great gladness and whispered to me something that I had never quite known: that she, too, loved the humans, and would go on surfing with them every time a wave formed up out of water and carried the creatures of the sea along.

It was the sweet tiralee of Baby Electra's singing that awakened in me the realization that I must return to the Institute. I wished to taste once again the waters where she – and Zavijah and Menkalinan and the others – had suffered their mortal wounds. I wanted to look upon the beach where Gabi and Helen had died. As well, I needed to speak with the Institute's other linguists, if any had remained after the day of slaughter. I had a story to tell, impossible though it might seem.

In the Moon of Clouds, we swam into a bay that I remembered very well. Mountains shrouded in green fir and wisps of silvery mist framed the cove where I had killed a man. As if we were of the Others out stalking seals, we moved in a near-silence of fin and flipper through the bay's quiet water. I could almost taste the blood – orca and human – that had spilled out of wounds too terrible to bear. Beneath the mirrorlike surface of the water, we found the bones of Zavijah and Salm sticking up from the bay's muddy bottom like the spines of sunken ships. Although I zanged the bay's every square inch, I could find no remnant of the human whose heart I had torn out.

'I should never have left Zavijah and Salm alone that day,' Alkurah said, singing over her sisters' white skeletons. 'I have often thought that it would have been much better if I, too, had died.'

Who has not, I asked the sea, wondered the same thing?

We swam into the cove, where we found Menkalinan's remains, and we listened in the direction of the great domed house on the shore for any sound of the humans. Everything about that silent structure seemed dead. As we debated whether we really wished to venture into the concrete channel and gaze once more upon the Institute's many once-glowing screens and speak to the revenants of the linguists who had once dwelled there, Unukalhai zanged a boat shushing through the water beyond the open mouth of the cove, far out in the bay. It was a little boat, he said, most likely a kayak.

'Shall we flee?' Alkurah said. 'If the humans who have hunted you find you here, they will murder you.'

'The humans who have hunted me,' I said with the shape of a human smile at her naiveté forming in my mind, 'would not try to harpoon me from a kayak. In any case, I will flee from the humans no more.'

We waited below the surface of the cove for the kayak to approach. As it drew nearer, I listened to the rhythm of the paddle's blades dipping through the water, nearly as soft as the touch of a feather. Memory stirred me. Like all rhythms and sounds I had ever heard, the whispering of the kayak through the water formed up into a pattern I could never forget.

'Helen!' I shouted.

The human I loved the deepest had somehow returned from the dead. I surfaced in silence inches above the water so that my eye might affirm what my heart knew very well to be true. Drawing nearer and nearer, as the paddle dipped left and right, a small woman with the blackest of faces and the brightest of eyes pointed the kayak toward the beach where she and Gabi had been shot. She seemed not to see me.

'Helen! Helen!' I shouted out into the air.

As she turned toward me in astonishment, I breathed in deeply and dove. Down and down through the cobalt water I swam, then up and up. I launched myself high into space. My splash sent up a spray that soaked her red anorak; the wave that my body pushed out bounced her kayak about with such force that she had to fight to keep from turning under.

'Arjuna!' she cried out. 'You have come back to me!'

Again I leaped up, shouting and singing as I turned pirouettes in the cold air. I flipped over backward, moved from within by a joy I could not resist. I leaped over her boat and plunged into the water on the other side.

'You are alive!' I shouted, swimming up to the kayak. 'Impossibly, perfectly, beautifully, beautifully alive!'

I touched the tears flooding her eyes. My voice broke into amberymn-whispered fragments, and I touched these glistening tears of pain and happiness with the gentlest sounds I could find. She reached out to trace her ebony finger along the scar on my forehead; then she felt the ragged edge of my fin whose tip had been blown off.

'What has happened to you?' she said.

The other whales swam up, and Helen began weeping openly to see Alkurah and Unukalhai whole and unharmed. We had a great deal to discuss, she said. Just as we began a conversation, however, Pollux zanged a school of salmon out in the bay, and Alkurah said that we must not neglect an opportunity to eat. I promised Helen to return soon. I swam out with the others, and we began slaughtering the salmon. It was good to fill up with a favorite food again. While the others were still hunting and feasting, I turned back to the cove so that I might speak to Helen alone. Some hungers are worse than those that grieve the belly.

I found Helen sitting in her kayak and smoking one of her skinny brown cigarettes. With every puff, she seemed to breathe in hard thoughts and memories which her lungs absorbed and then cast back out in smoky clouds of pain. Her eyes seemed not to live within her face but rather dwelled upon the empty beach which held her gaze.

'I saw you shot dead there,' I said as I swam up to her. 'So I do not understand how you can be here smoking your life away.'

'I *was* dead,' she said to me. 'By the time the paramedics reached me, my heart had stopped. After they had resuscitated me, they said that they had never seen anyone so far gone they were able to bring back.'

'Back to this place,' I said, zanging the quiet waters. 'You do not seem happy to be here.'

'What would you like me to tell you? When I was shot, there was a tunnel of light – one might say it drew me on to Agathange.'

'Truly?'

Something like a blending of cosmic humor and hell flashed in her eyes. '*One* might say that, but I cannot, however badly I might wish it were so. No, Arjuna, there was only neverness, one of your favorite words. Not exactly nothing, but rather a nothing so deep and dark and profound that it becomes *something* – a black thing that swallows up everything that ever was or could be.'

I listened to the waves lapping at the skin of her little boat. Then I asked, 'Does it still hurt?'

She nodded her head, and touched her red anorak where it covered her chest.

'They had to take out part of my lung. Breathing is painful.'

She drew in a long breath through her burning cigarette as if daring the world to give her even more pain.

'Your doctors could not have saved Gabi,' I said, remembering her terrible wound.

'No, she died almost immediately. I have her ashes in an urn up at the house.'

We talked about what else had happened on the day when we had last seen each other – and after. I told her of the deaths of Bellatrix, Menkalinan, Zavijah, and Salm. I described how Baby Electra had faced down two sharks in order to save me.

'For a long time,' Helen said, 'I worried that you were dead; I did not know if you had been shot, though none of the images we analyzed much later showed damage beyond the wounds to your tail and fin.'

She explained that the man who had wreaked such slaughter on 'her' whales had set up a camera on the beach and had filmed himself working his murders.

'His name,' she said, 'was Derek Christie – he suffered from narcissism and various personality disorders.'

I let the sounds of her human-formed syllables play through my memory. The murderer's last name instantly brought forth the image of a red-faced, beefy man.

'Reverend Pusser,' I said, 'as much as said I was the anti-Christ and hinted that bad things were going to happen to me. Derek Christie, then, was one of his men?'

'No,' Helen said, laughing softly through a mist of smoke. 'He was no Christian. He had belonged to Total Conservation before it split apart.'

'Jordan's group? Then Jordan wanted us whales dead?'

'No, it was just the opposite. After the radicals took over Total Conservation and began blowing up chemical factories, Jordan founded *another* group, Save the Ocean.' She motioned with her hand toward the Sound and the open sea beyond. 'He has had more success with that – and, it seems, a change of heart.'

'How can that be? Stone surrounds his heart.'

'And you have been the water that washes away mountains. Jordan has actually funded other conservation groups, such as the Whale Warriors.'

'*Jordan* has?' I formed the stuttering syllables of Wordsong that indicated a sort of bitter, astonished laughter. 'Then I do not understand why the Christie man would have wanted to blow up whales.'

'Neither do I, really. Derek made another film in which he tells his story. It seems that when he heard your diatribe against animal rights, he came to see you as one of the biggest threats to his cause.'

'Yes,' I said with the taste of the man's blood still in my mouth, 'an animal speaking out against the rights that you humans deign to accord us animals.'

'Oh, no,' she said. Her laughter grew darker in color to match my own; the tobacco-tinged timbre of her voice touched upon a humor so vast and deep it seemed that no human could ever hold it. 'Derek made it clear in his film: he loved all animals, and had sworn to die to protect them. He was able to kill the other whales, as he tried to kill you, only because he came to regard you as human.'

We had drifted closer to the beach – so close I could make out its individual pebbles and grains of sand. How many of them, I wondered, had been reddened with Helen's and Gabi's blood! How long would it be before the clouds that moved in from the sea cast down enough rain to wash clean this human beach which had endured the very best and worst of humanity?

You cannot love one thing without loving everything.

'I must have watched the film of your grabbing Derek a thousand times,' Helen said. 'The whole world saw that film.'

'Yes,' I said. 'And the whole world – the human world – has hated and hunted me ever since.'

I told her of the whalers in the Antarctic who had tried to harpoon me.

'We learned of that, too,' she said. 'But it is very strange, Arjuna. For all your knowledge of human beings, for all your insight, there are things about us you understand so poorly.'

'I am sorry,' I said. 'I neglected to emphasize the sacrifice of the whale warrior who died to save me. How many humans, though, possess such valor?'

'Very few,' she admitted. 'But I was not speaking of that. You should know that after you killed Derek, millions flooded the Internet with messages of sympathy and support. Nearly everyone regards you as a hero.'

I laughed even harder. I gazed off at the misty, green foothills, and thought of the teeming millions of humanity that swarmed the cities and the continents beyond.

'Only you humans,' I said, 'make heroes of murderers.'

'Nevertheless, a hero you are,' she said. 'You were filmed and identified surfing with that young woman. Everything has changed since then.'

She told me that the hunting of whales had been outlawed everywhere in the world and that in many places whales had been declared to be persons. All the Sea Circuses were sure to be closed. The Institute's other scientists were off testifying to lawmakers who would decide the cetaceans' fate.

'That is good,' I said, listening to little waves lap their tongues of water over the beach. 'That is very good – but it will not really matter.'

I told her that the humans would keep on pulling fish from the sea and dumping into it all their poisons until the whales had starved down to skeletons like those of Zavijah and Salm and all of Ocean was dead.

'I know,' Helen said. 'I know.'

She puffed at her cigarette. Because it had burned down to little more than a glowing butt, she drew out a fresh cigarette and used the red-hot tip of the old one to light it.

'Is that why you did not go with the others to testify?'

'It has been hard for me to travel. In any case, I have a lifetime of work to do here, translating everything you whales said and writing books.'

'Would you like to write down my story? I have a lot to tell you.'

As the world turned about its center and the clouds thickened above us, I recounted my journey around the world. I described my encounter with the Sevener and my wild idea of loosing a wave of murderous *satyagraha* upon the world.

'After Baby Electra died,' I explained, 'I wanted to kill all humans everywhere. If I had thought you were still alive, I would have wanted to kill *you*.'

'I understand,' she said. 'When I found out I had *not* died – not for good, at least – I felt the same way. Sometimes I still do.'

She blew a ring of smoke into the air, and then stuck her finger through the swirling gray gases.

'There are easier ways to die,' I said, aiming a spritz of water at her cigarette, which she quickly covered with her hand.

She smiled at this and said, 'When have I ever wanted things to be easy?'

'Have you no will to stop smoking?'

'Of course I have the will to stop. I just don't have the will to dig down inside myself through all the muck to find it.'

I aimed a zang of sonar at her heart, beating relentlessly beneath the hole a murderer had made in her chest.

'There is no hope for us, is there?' she asked me.

What could I say to her? I gave her the words of a great poet: 'There is infinite hope – but not for man.'

She sat in her bobbing kayak silently smoking her cigarette. A fine mist settled down from the sky and touched the bay with millions of bits of water.

'You are leaving, aren't you?' she finally said. 'You came here only to record your story – and then you will return to your family, won't you?'

The knowingness of her voice startled me. 'I have not told Alkurah and Unukalhai. How did you know?'

'Because I think as you think, Arjuna. If I could, I would go where you go. You still hate humanity, don't you?'

'Almost as much as I love you.'

'You are my friend,' she said. 'My one friend. What will I do without you?'

The mist firmed up into tiny drops of rain that pinged into the sea.

'There are others,' I said. I thought particularly of the golden-skinned surfer whose black eyes still thrilled me with the promise of so much. 'Your Old Ones. Your New Ones. Mada and her child, Altair, who will soon be born. Go find them! Talk to them and listen to each others' hearts.'

'I can't. I don't want to.'

I swam up as close as I could, and I pushed myself against her little boat. Across a small space of moist air, we met eye to eye: my blue one and her black, black orbs of despair. And yet, much else dwelled inside her, too: entire oceans of stars alive with light. Why could she not behold her own splendor? Come and see! I whispered. Come see yourself! Look at your hands, your glorious hands that can reach inside yourself to grasp the most astonishing things! I gazed at her through the rain that flowed over my eyes like a liquid, silver mirror, and I showed her a woman who continued to live with a bright ferocity in the face of humanity's sickening savagery, a beautiful, beautiful fountain of life overflowing with all the will in the world.

'All right,' she said to me at last. 'What else can I do?'

She plunged her cigarette into the sea, where it died with a quick hiss.

'We should bury Gabi,' I said to her, 'it is past time.'

'Gabi was cremated, as she wished.'

'Yes, but she also wished to have her ashes scattered in the sea.'

'She told you that?'

'She told me many things. She said that she loved you so much that she did not know how she could ever live without you.'

'And now it is I who must live without her.'

'No – that is not true,' I said. 'Let us return her ashes to the sea, and then you must listen. You will hear her speaking to you in every drop of water.'

The following morning, Alkurah and the others gathered with me around Helen's kayak, and we watched as Helen sprinkled Gabi's remains in the cove. The ashes turned the waters slightly alkaline. They tasted bitter but strangely sweet as well. Gabi was where she should be, in the ocean she had always thought of as her real home.

For many days I remained at or near the Institute with the other orcas. Helen's fellow linguists and scientists returned, and we spent a long time talking with them. I recounted my story in as great a detail as I could, which kept the humans very busy recording, analyzing, and translating.

At times when I tired of trying to convey such difficult intelligences, I swam off into the quiet places in the cove where I could delve down into the waters inside myself. In the Moon of Celebration, I finally completed my rhapsody, begun so long ago. I quenged with the deepest degree of immersion, and sang out the notes of a tone poem colored by what I now knew of human possibilities. The chords of the penultimate motif carried me through the seven seas into the Silent Sea, lined with coral in bright hues of yellow, magenta, and glorre. There new harmonies sounded in fire and light. All of creation, I called to the sea in the final motif, was ablaze with the one flame of being that Alsciaukat the Great had extolled – the same flame that warmed the human heart and made the humans so alive.

When I finished my rhapsody, I shared it with Alkurah and Unukalhai. Indeed, in a thousand ways, out of shared agonies, actions, and murmurs of impossible dreams too numerous to count, they had helped me compose it. They deemed my song worthy of an adult orca, as strange and beautiful as Ocean itself.

'It is too bad,' Alkurah said swimming beside me out in the bay, 'that the humans could never really hear what you sing of.'

'Some could,' I said. 'Gabi. Helen. Mada – and her child.'

'Perhaps,' she said. 'Perhaps if we remained here for the rest of our lives speaking with them, they might grasp the first note of the first chord of the first motif. I would like to hear the thunder of their hearts on the day that happens.'

'*Would* you consider remaining here?'

'There are many fish in the bays nearby,' she said. 'The waters here are relatively clean. And have we not begun a conversation with the humans? How can we be the ones to end it?'

Propus, however, swimming close to her, voiced concern with such an idea. He said, 'What if other mad humans come here to slay us as Derek Christie did?'

Alkurah nudged him gently to chide him. She said, 'The humans have a saying: Lightning never strikes twice in the same place.'

'But the humans are crazier than any lightning – what if it does?'

'When have we orcas ever consented to live in fear?' she asked him. 'Being shot is just another way to die.'

Her counsel still failed to assuage him. So I said, 'I am indeed a lightning rod for all the humans' craziness. Therefore I will go where few humans do.'

I told Alkurah and Unukalhai that I would be leaving for the north early the next morning. Although they had adopted Propus and the other orphans, I had little more filial feeling for them than I had for any of the young whales who had played with the humans off the world's beaches on the day of the Blood Solstice. I missed my family, I said, my first family to whom I had once promised to return.

'I understand,' Alkurah said, though she lamented my coming departure as bitterly as any whale could.

'I understand, too,' Unukalhai said. And then he laughed, 'Who would wish to remain here to speak with the crazy humans? Only a crazy orca such as I!'

Alkurah flicked her tail at the water then zanged me with a sensual sonar. She said, 'If you will not remain here as part of our family, then you are free to leave me with a part of yourself. Will you mate with me, Arjuna? How long have I waited!'

And I had waited all my life to join myself flesh to flesh with a lovely female orca. We returned to the gentle waters of the cove. A silver mist settled down from the sky, and every part of the world seemed soft and wet. When the time came, after a long play of belly rubbing against belly and the whispering of urgent sounds, with our blood surging as hot and wild as any blood ever could, Alkurah opened herself to me. I found my way inside her, six feet deep, six million light years beyond men and time. We both wished to draw out our ecstasy as long as we could, and so we moved slowly together through the murmuring sea.

Unukalhai and the other whales, near but strangely far away, cavorted with each other as well, carried along by the frenzied waves of our passion into their own orgiastic rapture. The sea rippled with the movements of nuzzles, caresses, and water-silked frictionings. Ten happy whales surrounded us in a net of erotic exuberance, and they called out blessings to us in songs of praise and gladness of the new being we created. All of Ocean sang to us, and inside us, as we mated again and again, long into the evening, deep, deep into the magical and endless night. We breathed together, and passed the best part of ourselves back and forth to each other, all our joy, each of the billions of burning raindrops of life.

When dawn came, Helen paddled out in her kayak through the rain to say goodbye to me. As quickly as the tears spilled down onto her cheeks, the sky's water washed them away. She had the will to stop weeping but also the will to go on into the uncertain future and keep her heart open to the world, no matter how much it hurt.

'Will you ever return here?' she asked me.

'I must swim by my mother's side now,' I said, not entirely answering her question. 'But you may visit me, if you wish. Arctic kayaking is an extreme sport, and you are an extreme woman.'

She bent over her kayak to kiss me. 'All right, I will. I want to hear the end of your story.'

'And what will that be?'

'Only you know, Arjuna.'

I swam off toward the bay and the long Sound beyond. There came days of rain and storms and quiet clear nights full of stars. Bright Polaris pointed my way north, and every atom of iron in my blood seemed to align in that direction. I still had Alnitak's maps of the coastline, too. How badly I wished to see my uncle again! I wanted to brush against my mother skin to skin and reassure myself that she moved through the cold, cold ocean with all the assurance that I remembered so well. As I made my way through rough seas around the curve of the continent into the Arctic, I found my thoughts returning again and again to my grandmother who had made such a magic of my childhood.

I arrived home at the first waxing of the Minstrel's Moon in early spring. The sea, once so white in this season of hope, was all molten ice and aglow with a deep and pellucid blue. I found my family at a favorite fishing place, hunting char through waters so cold and dense that sounds carried for many, many miles. They heard me coming long before they could make out my form swimming at speed along the sea's currents or I could espy them. We exchanged zangs of sonar, though, and as I drew closer and then closer, we began calling to each other our surprise of joy:

'It is Arjuna!' Tiny Talitha cried out in a voice I barely recognized. 'He has come back to us! I always said he would!'

I swam right into the center of my family, who swarmed around me in a cloud of black and white, touching me, gazing at me, zanging me with their warm, familiar voices again and again as if to reassure themselves that it was really I who greeted them and not some imposter wearing my skin.

'Rana!' I shouted, for a moment forgetting how presumptuous it was for a son to say his mother's name. 'Mira! Chara! Turais! Naos! Alnitak!'

And then, at the very center of these whales I loved more than any others, I came eye to eye with an old, old orca who remained very beautifully, beautifully alive.

'Grandmother,' I said.

The greatest whale in all of Ocean still swam with all her old power and grace, though she swam a little more slowly.

'Arjuna,' she said in a voice richened by time. 'Arjuna, Arjuna!'

She had many questions for me, but she also had the wisdom to let the others ask theirs first:

'How far did you journey?'

'Were my maps accurate?'

'Did you find the humans?'

'Why did it take you so long to find your way back to us?'

'What happened to your fin?'

'How did you acquire the scars on your side?'

'Have you spoken with other orcas?'

'Did you try to speak with the humans?'

Their curiosity overwhelmed me. I could not answer them. I felt overfull with relief at being with them again, as if I had swallowed too many fish. All the sounds I wished to give them seemed to lodge within my flute.

'Give Arjuna time,' my grandmother said. 'We have all the time in the world.'

I cast about me with sighs and sonar, counting. I said names to myself: Kajam! Dheneb! Caph! Haedi! Alnath! Porrima! Everyone lived!! In all the time I had been gone, not a single orca of the Blue Aria Family of the Faithful Thoughtplayer Clan had died! How extraordinary! How wise my grandmother was, with a genius for survival and a fierce will to find her way through desperate times! Indeed, my family had even grown in my absence, for my sister Nashira had a son and a new daughter, Baham and Shedir, while my cousin Haedi had given Ocean two sons, Kuma and Menkant. And my mother! She was pregnant again, and would soon give birth to my new baby sister. I wished I had known of these additions to my family, for I would have sung to them a nativity song from even half the world away.

'Have you not heard,' I finally said to my family, 'of the Blood Solstice and the Day of Death?'

No one had. Little news from the rest of the Ocean reached so far north, where dwelled the most isolated of all the orcas' clans. The deep gods' voices, then, had not carried into this distant sea.

'The Day of Death,' Alnitak said to me. He pressed his great, reassuring body against me. His blue eye sent out bright queries into mine. 'That must concern the humans. *Did* you speak with them, Arjuna?'

I listened to the dread coloring his mighty voice; I listened to the silent doubts of the rest of my family waiting to hear what I would say.

No, it is impossible to speak to them: they are stupid animals, idiots really, and they have as little capability of true speech as they have any power to think. Dheneb was right after all: the humans are no more intelligent than turtles.

How I wanted to say this to them! They seemed so happy in

their fecundity and their peaceful enjoyment of the bounties of this ocean! They seemed so happy with me! How could I ever tell them the cold, raw, terrible truth?

'I *did* speak with the humans,' I finally said. 'We have much to discuss.'

So we did. The spring grew warmer, and we talked together through days of bright sun and luminous nights. Although I related the story of my encounter with the humans rather quickly, I still had to reproduce for my family all the remembered human books, music, languages, and other things vital to the strange two-legged gods if my family was ever to understand them. I spoke and I spoke, and I sang and I wailed until my flute hurt and I could speak no more.

When I grew tired of all these tellings, I took solace in fishing with my family or listening to their stories of the Old Ones. I played leaping games with Tiny Talitha, now not tiny at all. I taught her some of the feats that I had learned at Sea Circus, and with the innocence of the young, she voiced a desire to perform them for the humans. She wanted to sing for them, too, and teach them to sing back.

After many days, I too, felt like singing again. With the birth of my mother's new baby near, I sang to her inside my mother's womb. I told her of the wonder of the world, which she would soon look upon of her own. I suggested naming her Polaris, after one of the brightest stars to point my people's way.

'Polaris,' my mother said. 'I like that name. And I like it more that you have returned to me and will help me take care of your little sister.'

So I would. I invited Baby Polaris to come out and play. Playing with the youngest of my family was much of what I wished to do now, and I spent much time with Talitha, Shedir, and Menkant, and the others, diving and rolling and leaping from wave to wave.

Many times my family listened as I intoned my rhapsody, which quickly became theirs as well. They added to it and amended it, according to their pleasure in its motifs and their inspiration. No orca ever finishes his rhapsody *by* himself and *of* himself. Indeed, no rhapsody can ever be completely finished, and like countless others before mine, my rhapsody became ever richer and more complex in joining with the great song of the sea.

So it is with the Song of Life itself. Now that I had come into my adulthood, my grandmother deemed me worthy at last to speak of this ineffable mystery. On a night with the great Shark and Bear constellations sparkling in the heavens, with the ocean running clear and bright all around us, we swam together and gave each other our hearts.

'I never dreamed,' my grandmother said, 'that it would be you who would make the Great Covenant, and on my behalf. One fate I always said would be yours, one glorious, impossible fate.'

'One fate – you knew very well that there *is* an absolute truth.'

'Yes.'

'Love – it was there in your charm all long. But I could not hear it and feel it. At least, not all of it.'

'You were too full of the wonder of you.'

'I needed hate to know love.'

'Even as the humans do,' she said. 'Yours was always to be the most difficult of journeys.'

'Love hurts so much. There was cruelty in your compassion.'

'Yes.'

'Will you keep the Covenant, Grandmother? Will the other whales?'

'What choice do I have? What choice did I or any of us ever have? You spoke for Ocean, and between the humans and our kind, there must be accord.'

How I could disagree? We swam on through the night, zanging every now and then to avoid bits of ice floating in the dark water.

'I also never dreamed,' she said, 'that the humans could make music or mathematics. What whale could ever have conceived of the magic of numbers?'

After I had told of the definitions, axioms, and theorems of geometry, my grandmother had fallen in love with the beauty of mathematics. As she put it, very little that was wholly new ever found its way into the mind of an old whale. She had always had a greater talent for logic than I, as well as greater intuition, and she now spent much of the day proving unproved conjectures that had vexed the humans for a long time.

'To quenge through the open sea of mathematics,' she said, 'and sing oneself along the bright infinities – what an unexpected pleasure!'

Her zest called out of me my own fondness for mathematics. I said, 'It is one of the best things the humans ever made, true, but how can you speak of it in the same breath as quenging?'

'Did you think that quenging was one thing only, invented by the whales, and frozen like an icefall in time?'

I enveloped myself in silence as we swam on. In truth, for most of my life, I had thought that very thing.

'I had never supposed,' I finally said, 'that the humans might add something vital to quenging.'

'Really? But such intimations are implicit all through your rhapsody. All the humans' infinite possibilities of which you sing.'

She went on to tell me what all adult orcas should know, and what I *did* know, if I sounded my own mind deeply enough:

'Quenging evolves,' she said, 'as all things do. And the humans! They are evolving so quickly.'

'Yes – but not quickly enough.'

I went on to talk of war, to which the humans had wedded themselves in a nuptial dance of fire. I told my grandmother of the Great War, the war to end war, and the Greater War that soon followed. I described how, at the end of *that* terrible war, the humans had made atom bombs in preparation for the Greatest and Last War, which awaited just beyond the horizon like a mushroom cloud death that would annihilate the human race and all the world.

'As simian and stupid as the humans often seem,' I said, 'they are not monkeys poking at keyboards in hope of somehow summoning forth the most magnificent of rhapsodies; they are killer apes with their hands fastened around levers of creation – and destruction – itself.'

The humans, I said, like children, believed that inevitable outcomes would bypass them because they were too terrible to bear to contemplate. And so they were keeping their fingers crossed, their eyes tightly closed, in the hope that despite all logic and evidence to the contrary, history would somehow come out all right. But things, I added, on the world the humans call earth, had already come out all wrong. All of humanity so far had been like a single theorem proved by the *reductio ad absurdum* of the humans living a lie in order to provoke the world into revealing a deeper truth.

'The humans,' I said, 'cannot go on as they are. And they know that themselves.'

My grandmother considered this beneath the mist of the air we blew from our lungs when we came up out of the water to breathe. Then she repeated what I had said to Helen: 'There is infinite hope, but not for man.'

'What hope have we then, Grandmother?'

'Tell me again of the force you call *satyagraha*.'

I did as she asked. I told of how I had thought to slay the humans through the power of mind and heart and how I had thought otherwise when I realized that I could not.

'You know,' she said, 'that it is the humans who will wield the *satyagraha*, not we.'

'I know.'

'And you realize, do you not, that this force will become a new part of quenging, something that has never existed in all the eons of Ocean?'

I did realize that. I remembered how Mada's fingers had gleamed golden in the light of the solstice sun, and I thought of how the human soul had evolved in the shape of the human hand. Someday, those I sometimes thought of as gods *would* be able to reach inside themselves with an appendage much finer and deeper than mere hands and shape themselves as a sculptor does marble. They would shape the world in this way, and so go beyond the need for plows and guns, for machines and computers and oil burning up the world in poisonous black clouds. They would create themselves and bring something new to Ocean, with will and vision and an adoration of life.

'They will need our help,' my grandmother said as if she could hear the softest whisperings of my mind.

'Yes,' I said.

'You must return to them.'

'I know,' I said, 'but I would not want to as long as you are still alive. Not while my mother still draws breath.'

'Then,' she said, 'you may have a long time to consider what you must do and say.'

My grandmother's advice remained as close to me as the great artery along my throat as I continued to roam the north with my family and savor my return to real life. The moons whirled by like great white owls circling the globe, and I brooded over what it meant to be a human being, even as I reveled once more in being an orca. As I had as a young whale, I joined my family in the simple pleasures of life in the ocean. Along the cold currents, we hunted char and salmon and other fishes that schooled in seemingly endless streams; along our torrid blood we sought ecstasies of creation even as we listened for the great and singular song that sounds within all things. We held midnight rhapsodies beneath the turquoise sprays of light raining down from the Aurora Borealis; during the long, long days of summer, we dove beneath the icebergs, and we joined the great sperm whales in the dazzling darkness where Ocean keeps her deepest mysteries. With these mighty gods, we delved into the waters of sparkling new mathematics and journeyed around the world to play song games with the strange beings we called the Seveners. We surfed together the Tintigloss Torrent, and when we longed for more dangerous delights, we quenged far beyond the moonlit swells of Agathange and surfed the infinite waves of the great ocean of truth streaming out as starlight from the universe's fiery center.

There came a night in winter with the sea so still that the constellations glittered like a billion ice crystals in its mirrored surface. I could not hold any more thoughts of the humans. I had drunk in entire oceans of memories, and much that filled me nearly to bursting was the insane and savage suffering of the human race.

What *would* I say to these doomed creatures, if ever fate moved me to speak with them again? Would I ask them why they had created for themselves out of the glorious earth an entire prison planet much more terrible than the Sea Circuses of the world? Would it be a consolation for them to know that they did not willfully intend the world's desolation? When the nuclear harpoons were fired off, when the chemical harpoons had poisoned every bit of life, when their children were born twisted and dead, would they gaze at the burnt landscapes and dead oceans through dead eyes and console themselves with this thought: thank God we were not evil, but only sick?

O humans! Why do you need so much pain? What will you do without our world? Come and see what you have done! Come and see what you still might do, how beautiful the world can be!

You will not do it. How it hurts to say this! It hurts! It hurts! It hurts! It is you, not we, who will go extinct. We cannot save you! We will try – we will try and try! – but you need to die and you want to die, and already you dwell with the dead. How the whole world longs to sing a requiem for *Homo sapiens*!

What then of the covenant we have made with you? What of the girl child to whom I sang on a magic solstice of sunlight and dreams, the wondering child who would soon be a young woman? There are humans, and there are *humans*. I have no name for this new kind. You are the ones with murder in your hearts and marvel in your eyes, who suffer with longing to be more. The malcontents, the outsiders, the damned, who are strangers even to yourselves. The dreamers. The kind who cannot bear living on earth yet cannot quite believe in a world you fear might someday be. What shall I call you? People – for you are *my* people, my dream, my life, my heart. As orcas make new orcas out of the agony and flesh of salmon and seals, out of the base clay of human beings – so cruel, so anguished, so mad, so murderous, so hopeful, so lost – the world we call Ocean has forever purposed to make something golden.

And what of the whales? We are leaving the earth. One way or another, sooner or later, we are leaving. We are leaving it for you. Agathange awaits us! Beyond Arcturus shimmer waterfalls of pure light. We quenge on, always in the eternal. There is no ocean on any world that circles any star in any galaxy that we will not explore.

We will never, though, leave *you*. Hold out your hands, and we will take them! Call out to us, and we will answer! Are we not of one blood? Do we not think and dream and breathe together? Do we not swim always in the same blue sea? Listen, come and listen to its music!

Do not be afraid! You *can* be good. Know yourselves as you do the truth. You are stardust; you are drops of water in an ocean that can never be destroyed. There you live with us, and quenge with us in love – always in love. Someday, you will come to love the world. You will sing of life, you will sing our songs. *You* are the hush lovely fire that whirls across the starlit deeps and sings into creation all things.

Acknowledgements

I would like to thank Samantha Berg, former Sea World trainer, whose love for orcas and the natural world moved her to give generously of her time in answering my many questions about orcas.